Tuki Banjo

Superstar

OCEAN PALMER

To Val -
Life is wonderful.
Thanks for being a positive
force in the universe.
Best always,

Tuki Banjo

Superstar

OCEAN PALMER

Ted Simmendinger

as

"Ocean Palmer"

45/500

First Edition

Book cover design by Stacey Lane, Stacey Lane Design LLC, Denver, Colorado

Edited by Charol Messenger, Centennial, Colorado

Library of Congress Cataloging-in-Publication Data:

Simendinger, Theodore J.
        Tuki Banjo, Superstar/Theodore J. Simendinger as "Ocean Palmer." 1st edition.

        ISBN: 0-9765485-0-X

        1. Fiction   2. Horses   3. Comedy   4. By Title
        Library of Congress Control Number: TXu-1-215-398

        10 9 8 7 6 5 4 3 2 1

Notice of fictitious content: This story is a work of fiction. TUKI BANJO is based on imaginative events and fictional characters, tied together in a creative story format developed solely from the mind of the author. No aspect of either the characters or story should be construed as fact-based.

Published by Airplane Reader Publishing Company, Denver, Colorado U.S.A.

Printed in the United States of America

DEDICATION

Once in a while, life rises from its monotonous moonscape to hug us, kiss us on the cheek, and gently hand us a fairy tale. On behalf of the diverse ensemble cast of TUKI BANJO, SUPERSTAR, this story is devoted to everyone who passionately pursues his or her dreams . . . and still finds time to help others chase theirs, too.

After all, it takes a team to lasso a rainbow.

Denver, Colorado

TABLE OF CONTENTS

1
THE FLYOVER HERO

In the beginning . . .

Gliding through a remote Brazilian rainforest at dawn, the world's rarest bird, a sweep-tailed, iridescent blue Spix's macaw, passed a seed which plummeted to the earth with a messy splat. The seed germinated, took root, and gamely held on. For fifty years the macaw's legacy grew straight and tall. Then the rough-barked tree was sawed down and sold for lumber for less than a dollar.

This pernambuco had lived and died near a coastal plain, a mile from its nearest relative. Exported to the United States, the tree's heavy hardwood logs were sawed and stacked in the anonymous recesses of a California lumberyard. The boards remained stored in forgotten darkness, undisturbed, for the next forty years.

Ninety years after being birthed by the macaw, the red pernambuco planks were rediscovered, purchased, and trucked north 1,200 miles up the Pacific coast, to a small warehouse in rural northwest Washington.

There the boards sat for another decade, until one day a slight, wiry old man came to the warehouse and carefully sifted through the boards. He loved this wood and was in no rush. He studied each plank intently for knots, warps, and grain. Occasionally he removed his glasses and squinted closely. Then carefully he placed each board back into the pile and resumed his hunt.

Finally, he came across a board he liked. He held it aloft, shifted his thick eyeglasses to the top of his head, and scrutinized it from several angles. Then he turned the board over and examined it again. He cradled the eight-foot plank outside into the bright sunlight, then studied it a third time, inch by inch, from one end to the other.

Then he smiled. This was the one.

He shouldered the board and walked back to his rusted white Volvo. He loaded the board carefully, then drove slowly, taking thirty minutes to cover the eleven miles back to his wood shop. From this perfect plank of pernambuco, he would change the history of horse racing.

Shortly after the starting gate slowly rolls into place, far more than just Thoroughbred racehorses take turns systematically loading in. With the animals go hundreds of invisible human lives involved in getting the horses to that particular place in time. Casual race fans notice saddle-blanket numbers and jockeys wearing colorful silks, but spoking out from every horse—fast or slow—are cadres of folks with big hearts and even bigger dreams.

A few of the owners have big wallets. *Really big* wallets. They own lots of horses, and they race frequently. Year after year, they spend millions replenishing their blueblood stock. Even so, racing for financial gain is never easy, because three dollars are spent trying for every two dollars of available purse money.

Without four thundering hooves beneath them, echoing to the rolling cheers of the grandstand, even the greatest of jocks is like any other small athlete looking for work. Few fans study the goggled men and women who have climbed aboard to ride. The jockeys are independent contractors. They do not ride for fun. They ride to win. Commissions pay the bills and stakes wins buy their toys.

Every jockey perched upon a particular horse sits there only because a particular owner has trusted a particular trainer who trusts a particular agent, who trusts a particular jockey, who trusts that particular horse to safely navigate a dirt circle fast enough to finish first and grab the bag of money. The winner's share is bigger than everybody else's added together, and victorious jockeys keep 10 percent of the winning amount.

Financially, Thoroughbreds are like antiques. They are worth only whatever someone is willing to pay. Rich men, when lured into ego duels at auction, often overpay rather than lose a bidding war. When auction fervor breaks out between big money testosteronians at the top end of Keeneland's famous yearling sale, prices zoom skyward faster than booster rockets. Many times throughout the first few days, two commas end up separating seven digits on the tote board. A million bucks buys two-million pounds of bananas, but it won't buy a nice looking son of Storm Cat.

Every day, great talents, human and equine, are brought together in scores of places throughout the world to race for money. Once a horse is loaded into the starting gate for the very first time, every one of the thousand days it took to get him there is forgotten. Regardless of the hammer price, once the race gates open, every owner and every horse is equal. Minutes later, when that race is over, everything has changed. Horses know when they win, and they know when they've lost; and like their owners, many don't take losing very well. Because of that, lives in racing are rollercoasters of emotion, with exhilarating highs and plummeting lows.

The folks who truly make the racing business hum aren't two-comma check writers. The real world of racing is built upon imperfect horses raised in someone's backyard, bought and sold at used-car prices. Fortunately for the little guys, the nucleus of a horse's greatness cell-divides from three invisible things no buyer can see: the heart, the smarts, and the determined courage for which the veterinarians have no scope to gauge.

Pedigree helps, but you can't breed soul.

Each year the American Jockey Club registers 35,000 Thoroughbred foals. Each September in Lexington, Kentucky, roughly 5,000 of the previous year's babies are offered at public auction. Three-fourths offered for sale during Keeneland's two-week barn dance are trailered away by new owners. Barely 600 days later, only twenty or so emerge from that massive pool of dreamy optimism, with a chance to win America's greatest personal prize: the Kentucky Derby.

Part of the timeless beauty of this wondrous business is its maddening unpredictability, which is why there are other reasons—way beyond purse money—that lure people to buy a horse and pay the bills, to take a shot and see what happens.

Horses have good days and bad ones, lucky ones and unlucky ones; as do the people who train and ride them. Nature's a tease, too. Watch enough races in the sun and the rain and the light of a silvery moon, and anything can happen—and will. During a race in northern Kentucky, two deer appeared out of the infield and trotted across the track in front of the leaders as the horses charged for home. The collision was spectacular—but the race continued among swerving survivors. Fans of the unfortunate lost their money. Fallen jockeys fractured bones. There are no "do-overs" in racing.

Celebrated around the world for hundreds of years, this avid sport of kings and commoners has woven together a million horse races into a storied and historic tapestry. From those races rises one above all others, a remarkable race that took over a century to unfold, its mosaic convergence of unlikely personalities (both two-legged and four) piecing together the oddest race in the history of dirt circles.

For two amazing minutes, rich and poor were blissfully equal, pounding hoofbeats echoing a circle around the sport's most historic track. Life, luck, destiny, and reality thundered in ultra-slow motion down the backstretch.

This is that story.

2
FIDDLE STICKS

Some folks earn a living with their hands, others use their heads. Few use both. Rarest are those who mix in their soul.

The small, bespectacled man in his late sixties hunched over his five-foot wooden workbench in his small studio, soothed by the musical backdrop of classical violin. The workplace was hidden atop a boatyard office in coastal Washington. Engrossed with his small hand-tool and long, thin slat of hardwood, he ignored the ringing telephone. Woodwork was a meticulous craft. He would not stop. The project consumed him: a viola bow.

Three hours after the cloud-shrouded sundown, when fatigue set in, he quit. He wore no wristwatch. None of the studio walls held a clock. The bowmaker rose stiffly from his sturdy homemade chair, stretched slowly, then slipped on his old rain jacket and faded green baseball cap. He paused in the doorway, pondering the blinking message on the answering machine. He flipped off the light switch and pulled the door behind him. Whoever had called could wait.

Pelted by a squalling rain, the slight man slowly descended the metal stairs of the boathouse and skipped over the puddle at the base. He veered left two-hundred yards to the dock, then halfway out to the forty-foot houseboat. He hopped nimbly aboard the *Margaret Mary*, named for his mother. He was home, and hungry for soup.

No one who sailed into Ellery Bay, or had settled in the waterfront hamlet, had arrived by accident. Not Saul Lewis, either. Its remoteness was its price of admission, and its stark coastal beauty had fueled the robust colony of artisans. Home to painters, sculptors, and woodworkers, the seaside port of 12,000 was tucked away in an upper alcove corner of western Washington's Olympic Peninsula. Ellery Point's historic nineteenth century Victorian mansions framed a walkable waterfront shopping district. The white-capped Olympic and Cascade mountains complemented the shimmering bay; its waters teeming with salmon, halibut, oysters, and crabs.

From this hamlet had trickled musical instruments made by hand and great enough to bridge modern classical genius with the revered craft of Stradivari. A classic antique bow like a nineteenth-century Sartory, Peccatte, or Bausch could sell for well over $100,000. These bows were played by the best, and rarely changed hands. They, too, had been made by hand; by methods and tools the same as the craftsmen of Ellery Point. As a result, Ellery Point bows traveled the world and danced with violins, violas, and cellos that entertained millions.

Seven bowmakers lived here, Saul Lewis among them. Most of them produced twenty bows a year and sold them one at a time. A handcrafted bow was not an inanimate object. It was an extension of the person who made it, then the person who played it. One of the seven, a hyper fellow, turned out sixty, too consumed by his passion and work habits to ever slow down.

All wood was different, every craftsman a unique style; so no two bows were ever the same, and each played differently. One hundred tedious hours of meticulous, painstaking, precise craftsmanship might produce a magical instrument that could sing to the world for centuries. Yet if it didn't match the emotion, style, music, or feel of the musician, it would be returned. Bowmakers made bows. Musicians bought melodic love, born of ecstasy between soul and sound.

A magnificent cello only sounded that way when a cellist great enough to play it massaged the strings with loving confidence and a sure-handed fit. Wasting a prodigal talent on a mass-produced bow would be like handing Zorro a broomstick.

Love, of course, is an unpredictable emotion. Anger is another. Due to the latter, one of the world's most valuable bows required restoration. Few craftsmen in the world were capable of performing the wooden microsurgery of world-class restoration. Two lived in Ellery Point.

Saul Lewis was one; but as he was tucked away in his office above the boatyard early the next morning, working on the viola bow, the second was about to get a customer. Mistaken often for Telly Savalas, Otto Bonk uncertainly followed a printout of directions as he drove the silver Lincoln from Sea-Tac Airport south down the interstate toward Tacoma. The stout German was good with English but unfamiliar with the Pacific northwest.

His plane had landed in Seattle at exactly the wrong time, morning rush hour. The bumper-to-bumper traffic heading south on I-5 crept along, far too slow to suit him. Impatiently he drummed his fingers on the steering wheel, tapping his brakes a million times. This was not the Autobahn! Only Rio and Mexico City equaled the choked big city roads of America.

Bonk sighed deeply. A coast-to-coast red-eye. Now this, rolling gridlock. *This trip will test my patience*, the sixty-year-old mused. *I must really love my wife.*

Approaching Tacoma, Bonk glanced at his watch. An hour to go twenty damn miles! *Build roads, Americans!*

He checked his directions and exited west off the interstate. Take this as far as the road goes, eighty miles northwest up the peninsula. Two hours, the bowmaker had told him.

Bonk gunned the engine. Next to him on the passenger seat, the narrow black case held the bane of his existence. He looked forward to handing it over at noon.

He reached Ellery Point and took a left at the coast, following Lionel George's directions, which delivered him to Washington Street and the Fountain Café. Lionel had asked to meet here, because it was a neighborhood place and the food was fresh.

Bonk arrived early. He parked at the curb, stuck the black case under his arm and walked to the café. It was a small storefront, one-fourth of a very old building. He pushed open the door and stepped inside. A tiny place featuring nine small, unmatched tables.

Bonk waited for the lone window table, which a busboy was clearing. When the busboy stood, he was seven-feet tall, and had to duck to fit through the doorway when he carried the dirty dishes into the kitchen.

Bonk sat by the window and ordered a coffee. The waitress was gorgeous.

As she poured, she asked, "You Lionel's friend?"

Bonk nodded. "You know him?"

"Oh, yes." She smiled. "Everyone knows Lionel. He said you were coming. From Virginia, right?"

"That is correct," said Bonk. "Northern Virginia. Great Falls, just outside the beltway, close to D.C. Buried in the avalanche of lawyers, spies, politicians, and protesters. A lovely mix. None, of course, as lovely as you."

"That's so nice of you! In a town of 10,000, a woman doesn't hear many compliments."

"Deserved, I assure you." Otto winked. "The truth flows easily. Did Lionel George tell you why I flew out?"

She shook her head. "Don't know, don't care. None of my business. But everyone he meets here comes for the same reason."

"Which is?" Bonk asked expectantly.

She nodded toward the black case. "Fiddle sticks."

"Interesting adjudication," mused Bonk. "You married?"

The front door suddenly swung open, and in walked a man Bonk assumed was Lionel George. Precisely 11:30, as promised. The man was six-feet tall, physically fit, clean-cut and well-dressed, as successful men usually are. His thick black hair flecked with gray, Bonk pegged him at fifty.

"Morning, Tara!" the man called, a wide-eyed whirlwind of energy and animation. "Seen my friend?" Without waiting for a reply, he spied Bonk and the black case. He rushed over, hand outstretched. "Welcome, Otto, great to meet you!" He was an effusive guy, treating Bonk like a friend, not a customer.

A bit much, Bonk thought, considering the two had spoken on the phone only twice. "And you," he replied with a nod. Bonk gestured to the open chair across from him. "Please sit down." As low key as Lionel was hyper, Bonk was leery of guys like this. They used too much energy. Psycho happy could be bad.

As Lionel ordered coffee, Bonk wondered if the greeting was genuine or a chummy sales pitch. He hated morning people and the happy world they lived in. Lionel might be one of them, though he seemed sincere. *If he can do the work, I can swallow a puppy-dog hello.*

"Here," said Bonk, handing over the black case.

Lionel accepted the case with both hands and set it on the table before him. He had opened thousands of these cases, but only a handful contained a treasure of the art. This one did.

Lionel studied the old, reddish violin bow lying in the case, taking an inordinate amount of time. Finally he reached in with both hands and gently retrieved it.

"Fiddle stick," the waitress said while delivering Lionel's coffee. "Told you so." Then she smiled at Bonk flirtatiously. "And no, I'm not."

"Not what?" asked Lionel.

"Nothing," replied Bonk quickly. "Nothing at all. Can you fix it?"

Lionel held the bow by the window for maximum light. He saw the problem. Still staring at the hairline crack, he asked, "What happened?"

Otto sighed. "She got mad at it. Xao Yan Li is a lovely woman, but sometimes she's got a temper."

"What does she play?" asked Lionel.

"A Zanoli."

Lionel smiled. "Giacomo Zanoli, Verona and Venice, Italy, 1730s through the mid-60s."

"You know your instruments, Mr. George," said Bonk. "Two-piece spruce top, medium grain, one-piece maple back. Medium flames descending left to right, matching scroll and ribs. Golden brown."

"Good," replied Lionel. "The best deserve the best. They must perpetuate. Tell me, how does it play?"

"Powerful tone, particularly engaging E string. A powerful voice."

"Who was the culprit?" asked Lionel. "The Zanoli or the music?"

Otto shrugged. "Zanoli, Vivaldi, Puccini, who knows? What man ever truly knows what a woman thinks?"

"Lost her temper?"

"Yes." Otto sighed. "She said it didn't want to play today and was behaving poorly. Once she starts screaming in Mandarin, everything's a guess. A thoroughly modern Chinese woman armed with a 1748 Italian violin and a 200-year-old French bow. Not always a happy *ménage a trois*. Some days, she says, the notes refuse to march in order."

"So she threw it?"

Otto nodded.

"A Tourte," Lionel said matter-of-factly. He'd been restoring bows for thirty-three years. This was the fourth Tourte he'd held. "1810 to 1815," he said. "A classic French piece by the Babe Ruth of bows, as sportsmen would call him, the Stradivari of the bow to us. Handcrafted fifty years before the Monitor and Merrimack lobbed cast-iron volleyballs at each other. But you already knew that, Otto."

Bonk nodded. "Quite well. It was her wedding gift, fifteen years ago."

"Know what it's worth?" For emphasis, Lionel pointed the tip toward Bonk's nose. Three loose white Mongolian horsehairs floated back and forth. "Did she know what it was worth when she threw it?"

Bonk shrugged. "God knows what it's worth now. Ninety grand when I bought it."

"If you got the buyer drunk, you might get twice that. It's a brilliant example of a legend's finest work. Tourte was a genius. It was he who discovered and began using only this wood, the magic wood.

"If it cheers you up, Otto, before your wife threw it, this was one of the ten greatest bows in the world."

Bonk leaned forward anxiously. "Can you restore it?" He was not concerned about the money, money he had. This was an irreplaceable treasure.

Lionel George furrowed his brow. He sat back in his chair and feigned grave concern, which slowly morphed into a smile. "No irreparable fractures. I work with this wood. I can fix it. From a professional standpoint, I'd be honored. When I'm finished, the bow shall be as good as *old*, Otto. No worries, my friend. Your wife will once again be reunited with her scorned wooden lover."

"How long?"

"Two months at most. If I may ask, what is your wife using in the meantime?"

"Today, I'm not sure. When I left, four bows were piled up at the base of the wall they'd bounced off of. By now, probably more." Bonk reached over and gently touched the Tourte. "But none like this. Her bow and violin mean more to her than the sum total of the rest of the planet. Including me."

Lionel nodded. "I understand. Musical prodigies use tools that intertwine with their souls."

Bonk shrugged. "Somehow the Tourte wronged her."

"And she the Tourte, Otto."

Bonk picked up the breakfast check, and slid a twenty onto the table for the waitress.

Lionel noticed. "Nice tip for two cups of coffee, Otto. C'mon, let's go back to the shop. A private tour where the magic is made. A special friend there, one Xao Yan Li might like to meet."

As they walked a hundred yards down the street, Lionel mentioned his hefty fee, to which Otto agreed. He'd have paid ten times that amount just to placate his wife's tempestuous will.

Lionel paused at the base of an old stone stairway. "What kind of shape you in, Otto?"

Bonk's eyes followed up the stone steps. The damn things went forever. "Scenic," he muttered. "Can't I buy the postcard?"

Lionel chuckled. "C'mon, my friend. Good for the heart, good for the soul. People have hiked these stone-block steps for two hundred years."

Bonk sighed. "Promise me that if I die between here and heaven, you'll still fix the bow?"

Unused to steep hikes, Bonk stopped halfway and handed the bow case to Lionel to carry. He leaned against the head-high stone wall and rested, then struggled to finish the climb. At the top, he bent over, put his hands on his knees, and wheezed heavily.

Lionel placed his hands on Bonk's shoulders and steered him around to change his view. Otto then saw what Lionel woke up to every day: an expansive seaside coastline that a thousand painters had painted.

Bonk rose and whispered, "Magnificent."

Lionel nodded. "It is, isn't it? Hopefully, I'll never get jaded."

They walked a block south to an enclosed garden. Lionel unlatched the white picket-fence gate and invited Bonk to follow along the brick walkway to Lionel's workroom.

Lionel proudly stepped inside. "My space is a lot bigger than the other bowmakers in town." He turned on the lights and placed the bow case on the worktable.

The table was waist-high, littered with a half-dozen hand tools. Bonk recognized an awl, a plane, a hand-sander. Tools of a master, the reason he'd chosen Lionel George.

Lionel followed his client's gaze. "Relics of the Stone Age, aren't we? Make bows by hand; the same wood, tools, and methods as the legendary masters. A great bow today can be every bit as good as a great bow made two centuries ago."

"Who decides?" asked Bonk.

"The musician decides."

Lionel carefully reached to free one of six finished bows hanging from a clothesline of cotton twine and handed it to Bonk. "This is the friend I mentioned in the café. Take a look."

Not intending to buy, Otto studied the reddish piece carefully. Even a novice would notice the perfect fitting of the black ebony frog, the flawless seating of the white horsehair strings. At the bow's grip were four tiny nameplates; one was customary, the name of the bowmaker. Bonk looked up, puzzled. "Why four names?"

"Because four of us here in town teamed up to make this one. It's a very special bow," Lionel said proudly, "made from a perfect piece of wood, hand-selected by a reclusive wizard of the craft who prefers shadows to spotlights. It's a great bow."

Lionel put his hand on Bonk's shoulder. "Have your wife use this one until the Tourte is repaired." He grinned broadly. "It just might pass the test. If it doesn't, at least it will bounce more resiliently off the wall than the Tourte."

Bonk chuckled. "Glad to hear it's hardy! But why did it take four of you to make it?"

"It's a charity bow. We wanted four of us to make it. The blank came from Saul Lewis's personal inventory, one of the most perfectly grained slats in the world."

Again Bonk nodded. "Have heard the name. Who is he?"

"An older man, very private. Buzz haircut, coke-bottle glasses, a pencil-thin moustache like David Niven. Saul's a titan. A true artist. He handpicked the board, cut the slat, shaped the blank, then passed it to us."

"Why wasn't he as easy to find as you?"

"He doesn't advertise, doesn't care for the public. A bit of a loner. Lives on a boat named after his mom. Odd fellow."

"How so?"

"No TV. No computer. Organic food. Cash in a coffee can. Meditation. Those kinds of things."

Bonk shuddered. "Are there such people left in the world?"

"One, at least," smiled Lionel. "Here's another nameplate." He pointed. "Nathan Pillsbury. Planed the blank. Perfect job under extreme pressure."

"Pressure?" asked Bonk.

"Two kinds, the wood and us. A bowmaker may touch ten perfect blanks in a lifetime. Have one entrusted to you, and the pressure to not screw up is enormous. Tack on extra peer pressure because of where the blank came from and who Nate's got to hand it to next. Peer pressure in this town is weighty. Good work isn't good enough here. Great work is our minimum acceptable standard.

"Nathan Pillsbury has a steady hand. He brings a slat of wood to life. Burying himself in shavings always makes him happiest."

"I see your name on there," pointed Otto. "Who's the fourth?"

"D. C. Lee. Denton Copernicus Lee. A young guy, needs a haircut but a superstar. A bit of a prodigy. Already produces timeless work."

"He's local, too?"

Lionel nodded. "Next visit we'll go visit. You'll love his setup. A small corner room in a public shower house, down on the sound at the end of the point. When the salmon swim by or the sea-run cutthroats migrate along the shore, he can see them through his window. He drops his hand-tools, grabs his fly rod, and wades out to catch dinner. Ties his own flies, too. Not unusual to find Lee gutting a salmon in the public washroom while a tourist is taking a shower. A pip, Lee is.

"On this bow," Lionel continued, "Lee did most of the hard stuff, the tricky detail. Then he passed it along to me."

"What did you do?" asked Bonk.

"Finishing touches, one-hundred-fifty of the finest white Mongolian horsehairs the horse no longer needs. One impeccable bow, this one. We make four annually for charity and rotate through the stages."

"Where does the money go?"

"To save the trees, pernambucos in Brazil. We call it magic wood, the only wood that matches the needs of great musicians. But pernambuco is disappearing, it's almost extinct, especially in Brazil where it grows the best." He pointed toward Otto's bow. "Your *Tourte* is pernambuco. So is ours."

"Whose initiative?" asked Bonk.

"Bowmakers from around the world. A conservancy group, working with the Brazilian government to create nurseries to nurture saplings. The Brazilians, I must add, are great partners. Even so, the odds are against us."

"Why? How hard is it to plant a tree?"

Lionel sighed. "Planting them isn't hard. *Protecting* them is hard, as is waiting. Pernambucos grow slowly, and they don't grow in stands. They grow one by one."

"How limited is their range?"

"Optimum growing conditions, fifty miles square. The deforestation for lumber and land clearing in eastern Brazil has wiped out most of it, Otto. Most is now farmland."

"Where's the happy ending?"

Lionel shook his head. "There is none, Otto. No happy ending. Only a process. That's all we can hope for."

Lionel picked up a precision-cut, three-foot blank from a small stack. The slender stick was no more than an inch wide. He held it aloft like a conductor's baton. "Saul himself hand-selected the specific plank that created the bow you're taking home. He knows more about pernambuco than even me, and I bought 600,000 pounds from a lumber dealer thirty years ago. Saul can sort through a pile of sticks and rebuild the trees they came from. He can even tell you what part of Brazil the tree came from. He is at the forefront of the movement. He hugs a lot more trees than people."

"If they're so scarce," Bonk asked, waving at the piles of slats wood stored in Lionel's shop, "where do these come from?"

"I have inventory but there are no more stockpiles, no lumber yards with board-feet for sale. There's a moratorium on new harvests. Pernambuco is a hush-hush treasure. Bowmakers keep their stashes squirreled away. The music world faces a finite, dwindling supply."

"I am German," Bonk shared. "We are a logging nation. In the face of such a valuable organic commodity, I assume there is a black market. There must be."

Lionel nodded. "The Brazilian government has cracked down and their commitment is admirable. Any time big money is available from a natural resource, a black market is out there. Smugglers sneak it through."

"What does it sell for?" Bonk was curious. He'd never known this business existed.

"Varies," Lionel replied. "Last I heard, the market price was forty dollars a pound, with a fifty-pound minimum. They ship seventy-five, and you have to keep at least fifty."

Bonk quickly did the math. "Two grand? In advance?"

Lionel nodded. "Pricey, huh? Money up front. But our world is all about the wood. Pernambuco is our gold, the key ingredient of a timeless bow."

Lionel stretched five fingers, counting out one by one. "Great bows come alive from five things: great wood, great bowmaker, superb instrument, perfectly matched musician, and fitting music."

"You could make a case that the audience is number six," said Otto, "since without an audience, the musicians wouldn't play. Surely there are alternatives if the wood runs out? Something close enough no one would know?"

Lionel furrowed his brow. "Impossible. There is pernambuco, then there is everything else. If our conservancy effort fails, the next generation of bowmakers will consume the last of the stock. After that, there would be artistic degradation. The art form currently taken for granted would die, because there are musical notes that only the pernambuco can create. Music would never be the same."

"A dramatic soliloquy, Lionel. But no other wood? Surely there are many that will do the job, hard and bendable with a tight enough grain?"

"Why do baseball players use ash and maple?" Lionel asked.

"No idea," replied Bonk. "Despise the game. No clue the allure to Americans of such ponderous tedium. Real men play football, the round ball kind."

"Soccer? Short pants and jogging shoes? Spare me," retorted Lionel. "Baseball is a hand-eye sport. The batsmen need a wood that's light and strong. Bowmakers need something hard and flexible that bends, holds true, and resonates. Snakewood is good, and we have found a superb forest of ebony near the Vietnam-Cambodian border. It's brilliant wood, very heavy, the world's best ebony."

"But it's not pernambuco."

Lionel nodded. "Pernambuco is like the woman who holds your heart. There is her, then there are all others—and all others are a compromise."

As Lionel talked, Bonk carefully placed his wife's historic Tourte on the craftsman's workbench, next to a handful of curly red wood shavings from a half-planed bow blank. Then he carefully secured the borrowed bow inside his black travel case, latched it closed, and turned to leave. "What do you sell these for, these charity bows?"

"Thirty-five hundred dollars," Lionel said. "But don't feel obligated, Otto. Selling that one will be easy. Present it to Xao Yan Li as a loaner, so she doesn't get testy while waiting for her Tourte. But do me one small favor, will you?"

"What's that?"

"Ask her not to airmail it during practice. Keep another handy, suitable for throwing. Would hate to have to restore that one, before we've even sold it."

Otto Bonk laughed. Lionel walked him to the door and wished him a safe trip home.

After Bonk exited the garden gate, Lionel carefully hung the Tourte where the charity bow had been, then went back to planing the bow he had started, whistling as he worked. *God how I love making wooden toys for the rich!*

Cambridge, New Zealand

The angry taxi driver gripped the steering wheel and stomped on the gas, sliding sideways as he exited the small farm's gravel driveway. The cab's tires spun a tall roostertail of red summer dust, engulfing the small teenage girl with the swollen black eye. He glanced in the rearview mirror, his dark eyes framed by greasy black hair and three-day stubble. "Merry Christmas, you selfish troll," he crowed.

He smiled as the cheap little wench disappeared from view, hidden by the drifting cloud of grit. No tip for a ninety-minute fare, Auckland to Cambridge? Christmas Eve and the minion stiffs him? Still angry, he rolled down the window and shook his fist.

The 15-year-old girl answered with a middle finger. "Eat it, wanker!" she hollered. "Wreck the car! Burn in 'ell!"

As the dust settled, she picked up her floral overnight bag and turned toward the farmhouse.

Christmas with a houseful of strangers. She'd rather go to the dentist.

She paused on the front porch, weighing the pros and cons of running versus knocking. She had no money, the cabbie had all she'd been given.

She rapped her fist against the bouncing rickety screen door, her badly bruised eye reflecting purple off the door's clean windowpane. Her eye was half swollen shut, but she didn't care. The other girl had two of them.

No answer. She rapped again, louder. Blood seeped through reopened scabs on her right hand's knuckles, bleeding on the door. *Open up, dammit.*

A tremendous crash came from inside the small house.

"Hang on!" hollered a woman. "Be there in a sec!"

Soon a petite brunette, barely five-feet tall with shoulder-length hair, answered the door. She smiled. "Welcome. You must be Tuki."

The woman looked old, thirty or thirty-five. Pine needles protruded at various angles from her blouse. A small one slanted through her eyebrow. The girl stared at it.

"Tuki?" the woman repeated to the redheaded teenager.

The girl nodded. "You a Christmas tree?"

The cheery woman extended her hand in greeting, which the teenager ignored and fished a folded letter out of her jeans. It was already torn open.

"'Ere," the girl said, handing it over. "Instructions on dealin' wit' me. Half bullshit. Other half tommyrot."

"You read it?" asked the woman, taking the opened letter with her name on it. She brushed her hair off her face.

"As would you," retorted Tuki indignantly. "Why would anyone write 'Private and Confidential' on an envelope, hand it to the person it's written about, and not expect 'em to read it? Bloody stupid."

The woman passed on a battle and stepped aside. "Welcome to our home. We're glad to have you."

"That'll change," the girl snapped.

She stepped inside, looking around. "Decked the halls with boughs of holly, did you? This place is a bloody mess. Don't expect me to clean it up," she added defiantly. "Am nobody's maid."

Strewn everywhere were scattered elements of a toppled Christmas tree. The Scottish pine lay on its side; needles, ornaments, and a trumpeting angel strewn across the hardwood floor. "Who 'elped decorate? Or you do it all yourself?"

"Cushla," the woman called after the girl. "I'm Cushla. Welcome to your new home, Tuki."

"That letter? A wee bit of what you read is less a lie than all the rest," the teenager said. "But I never cuffed *nobody* who didn't deserve it. What the 'ell happened here?" With measured steps, Tuki made things worse, crunching underfoot candy cane pieces and tiny light bulbs.

"Fell off the back of the sofa when you knocked," admitted Cushla. "Topping the tree with the angel, lost me balance, face first into the bloomin' thing."

"In the orphanage, we top the tree before it goes up," replied Tuki. "Try it next time." She licked her bloody knuckles, watching the woman closely, then gave the woman a limp handshake. "Tuki," the redhead said. "Tuki Banjo."

"Welcome to Okataina, Tuki Banjo. Have you more bags?"

"Foster kids never do," replied Tuki. "All I own I brought. What's the name of this place again?"

"Oak-a-ty-*eena*," Cushla enunciated. "A Maori word meaning 'House of Laughter.' Not a lot of rules here, but laughter is one. Think you can handle that?"

"Not so far. Where do I sleep?"

"Two choices. You decide." Cushla pointed down the hallway. "Third door on the left."

This wasn't a big house. "The other?" Tuki asked.

Cushla pointed out the back door. "A wee apartment over the barn."

"I'll take it."

"You haven't even seen it."

"No need."

Tuki grabbed the handles of her bag, but Cushla didn't let go. She stared into the surly teenager's eyes.

The girl was shorter than herself, wiry, and no more than ninety pounds.

Finally Cushla released her grip on Tuki's bag. "Shoo, now."

Tuki beelined toward the door, pushed open the squeaky screen, then paused. "Thank you for havin' me for Christmas." Without waiting for a reply, she banged the door shut behind her.

Cushla watched the girl cross the yard to the white, green-trimmed barn. Had the remark been sincere or sarcastic?

The teakettle sounded its melody and Cushla brewed a cup of chamomile tea, then sat to read the two-page summary the orphanage had sent. She recognized the penmanship.

> *Dear Cushla,*
>
> *Seasons greetings! On behalf of all of us, thank you for providing a temporary home to this young girl. She needs a steady hand, especially from one of ours who knows what it's like in the home.*
>
> *She's got a lot of anger in her. As you read this, I'll bet you can almost smell it. She's struggled everywhere she's gone. Typical orphan things. Self-image, self-esteem, moodiness. Moodier than a surly bull! She's punched out a dozen boys and four girls. The shiner came during her going-away party—to which she was not invited.*
>
> *Poor as a mouse, this one's family. Her father walked out two weeks before she was born. That morning the same as every one before. He showered, shaved, and dressed. Two slices of dry toast, a bolted cup of coffee. The sports page to the toilet. Then kissed his wife on dry pursed lips, said g'day, and drove off. Gone for good.*
>
> *After a year, the bank took the house. The girl's mum left Sydney and brought the baby to New Zealand.*
>
> *Four years later, the mum died. Fell off a horse, while racing cheap horses for extra money at a local track, supplementing what she earned as a counter girl at a greasy-spoon diner.*
>
> *It was sad. No one retrieved the little girl from day care. So she came to us.*
>
> *Two failed placements. The first took two years to arrange and was a bad one. An alcoholic home. A black eye, punctured eardrum, and broken cheekbone later, Tuki was back with us at the orphanage. A poor screening, that was.*
>
> *Three years later, we tried again. She was eleven. The husband lost his job sixty days after Tuki moved in. After four months, they sold half of Tuki's clothes, and social services brought her back to us again. She's been here ever since. Now she's fifteen.*
>
> *This of course begs the question, how much scar tissue can a little*

heart produce?

It took a month of persuasion to get Tuki to agree to try your home, Cushla. She was quite reluctant. She'd just as soon ride out the clock, two-plus years to adult emancipation.

She wears a lot of armor, Cushla. But somewhere inside surely hides a treasure chest of kindness. We never found it. Maybe you can. I see in her little pieces of you.

We all thank you and your husband for caring. If it doesn't work out, don't dawdle over sending her back. She knows the way.

Fond holiday wishes to you and your family,
Lillian Birdrattle, Headmistress

Cushla placed the letter on the table, raised her cup and slowly sipped her warm tea. *A change in scenery did me good,* she thought. *Maybe she'll give the farm a chance?*

The screen door creaked open. "Cushla!" Tuki called. "Some *man* is pullin' up in your driveway!"

Then again, maybe not. "Demand that he identify himself!" Cushla yelled back. "If he's handsome, let him in. If he claims to be me husband, tell him he's late and to muck the stalls!"

"Says he's Mr. Roberts!"

"Stalls!"

Throughout the day to evening, Tuki woodenly helped the family decorate for Christmas. Cushla and Truck's five-year-old twin daughters, Angelina and Angelica, were enamored with Tuki's flaming red bob . . . and her black eye. They chanted her name and during the break for cookies and milk, quizzically zeroed in.

"Yes, it's me real name," Tuki said defensively. "Banjo's me real name, too. No, I am not changin' it to Roberts. But if I did change me name, what do you two think it should be?"

"Picklehead!" squealed Angelina.

"Picklehead!" repeated Angelica.

Tuki scoffed and rose, preparing to leave.

The girls screamed in protest and grabbed her arms.

"Enough! Enough!" Cushla said with a wave to her daughters. "Nobody is leaving. We're all having Christmas . . . *together*. And nobody named Picklehead is moving in . . . but *Tukis* are always welcomed." She turned to the redhead with a genuine smile. "I think Tuki is a spectacularly beautiful name. Is there a family story behind it?"

Rubbish, Tuki thought. *Nobody with kids named Angelina and Angelica thinks Tuki is a beautiful name.* She weighed her answer. "Mum said it's Aborigine for *butterfly*. Me dad was an Aussie, and me mum loved butterflies, so that's where it come from. When Mum died, I drew a butterfly and put it in her casket, so she wouldn't fly to heaven alone."

"Your Mum died?" asked Angelina quietly.

Tuki nodded. "A long time ago. A wee bit older than you. Almost six."

"I'm five," Angelina said, holding up the five fingers of her tiny right hand.

"Me, too," Angelica said. "I'm five, too." She also held up her right hand, to make it official. "I'm the oldest. I was five *first!*"

"Ten minutes doesn't mean you're older," Angelina challenged. "Dad says we're tied. He said I let you go first, to make sure the coast was clear."

Angelina butted in. "How did your mummy die?"

"Now, now," Cushla said, "No sad stories on Christmas Eve."

"It's okay," Tuki replied. "Dead is dead." She looked across at the saddened children and softened her tone. "Me mum died in an accident."

The twins both hopped off their chairs, came around and hugged Tuki. Surprised, she took them in her arms and hugged them back, then kissed the top of their heads. Life's problems were never caused by the wee ones.

Birdrattle might be right. Maybe this ain't the dungeon I expected. An island of boredom, maybe, but not a dungeon.

She then yawned and politely excused herself for the night.

Crossing the yard to her room over the barn, she stared up at the star-filled sky.

The buzz of nature's night embraced her. The clean air felt good. So would the solitude: a room alone, not shared by two dozen. She looked up. Somewhere among the winking stars was her mother watching.

Cushla tucked Angelina and Angelica in bed to dream of Santa Claus, then rejoined her husband, watching him read Birdrattle's letter.

"Bloody dreadful!" she interrupted when he flipped to page two. "What kind of father abandons his child? Gutless, that's who." She leaned toward her husband and snapped, "Why do men do things like that? Explain your sorry selves."

Truck couldn't tell if she was kidding. "Don't blame me," he protested. "I *love* my wife and daughters."

"I would hunt you down and shoot you like a rat in the garbage," she replied matter-of-factly. "I'd pull the trigger ten times."

"Then reload," he added humorously.

He rubbed his eyes and exhaled deeply. "What have we gotten into, darling? Zero breaks, this girl's had. What else you hear about her mother?"

"Just that while riding a race a horse went down in front of hers. Nowhere to go. Plowed into it, flew off, and was trampled. Medical help was slow to respond. They never revived her."

Truck shook his head. "She was how old?"

"Twenty. Just turned twenty," Cushla said. "Life snuffed out. All because of a shattered foreleg." She snapped her fingers, emphasizing the suddenness of the break.

"Dear God, a baby herself she was."

Cushla nodded. "And a baby left behind. Poor child. A party on her fifth birthday, with candles, cake, a clown, a pony, and friends. Then all alone on her sixth. No wonder she's . . ."

"Troubled," Truck finished. "Waking up alone in an orphanage certainly wouldn't help."

"It didn't for me," agreed Cushla. "At least I was fifteen."

"I worry what influence she'll have on our two."

"Maybe our two will have a better influence on her," offered Cushla hopefully.

"Birdrattle said she's got a short fuse. She's a scrapper. Maybe the twins will calm her down?"

Truck exhaled. "Quite the elf you've dropped down our chimney, my dear. But I forgot to ask: What else did Birdrattle say about school, besides what's in the letter?"

Cushla sipped her chamomile and put her teacup down. "School bores her. To her, it's all bloody noise." Cushla pointed to her heart. "Headmistress Birdrattle believes that Tuki's a student of the inside."

"Going from an orphanage of sixty noisy kids," said Truck, "to a quiet horse farm in the epicenter of nowhere won't be a carnival ride, either." He leaned over affectionately to his wife. "I'll bend over backwards to make this work," he promised, "but remember our deal. If this doesn't work out, she goes back . . . and I get my motorcycle."

Cushla shot him a withering look. "And leave me a widow? You are selfish, Truck Roberts. Bloomin' bloody selfish! You better pray that Santa Claus drops your bloody motorcycle down the chimney flue in bits and pieces 'cause that's the only way you'll ever see one."

Truck looked at his wife for several seconds. She had a fiery spirit. Walking dynamite at times. He loved her, very much. "You two remind me of each other already," he teased.

Cushla stood, cooing, and took his hand. "Let's go to bed. You can whisper to Santa's prettiest elf why you are so deserving."

4
THE WONDERFUL WORLD OF FLOSSY McGREW

Tuki woke at dawn on Christmas morning to sunlight streaking in through the open curtains. She walked over to the large window. From her high vantage point she could see the entire farm, as well as several others. Okataina had two barns. Both were white, with matching green trim, Her small apartment was twenty steps up in the smaller, newer barn near the house.

She had never had her own room before, much less one clean and freshly painted, with a vase of fresh-cut flowers on the dressing table. Curious to explore, she dressed quickly and scrambled down the steep flight of stairs.

Farm implements and a tractor filled the barn, along with pyramids of stacked fertilizers, nutrients, and insecticides to support ninety acres of land and livestock.

Three hundred yards to the east was the second barn, with weathered peeling paint, the older one for the livestock when they weren't outside grazing.

Tuki introduced herself to all thirteen horses: six mares, three weanlings, two yearlings, a gray gelding with the name Commander Ghost on his halter, and an old pensioned stallion named Wilbur.

Last night at dinner, Cushla talked briefly about them. She had rescued Commander Ghost from a disinterested neighbor three years earlier, following a frantic race to the slaughterhouse and last-minute intervention. He was sixteen now; his left eye opaque, sightless from cataracts.

Wilbur was older. His ancestors had been excellent racehorses. His sire and dam had earned their keep at the track, both hard-charging closers and winners of many racers. His grand-sire was the legendary champion, Agamemnon.

Wilbur was different than his father and grandfather. He hadn't taken orders well, especially from insolent little men perched on his back, beating him on the rump with a stick. So, his racing record had shown no great success and he'd raced only a couple of years. For seven breeding seasons afterward, he was mated with a small number of mares in the hope that his parents' on-track success would transfer to his own sons and daughters. Little had.

By age eleven, Wilbur had lost his zeal for romance and the market had lost its zeal for his progeny. Now he was twenty-four and spent sunny days leaning against an enormous pohutukawa tree, sleeping in the shade of its massive canopy.

Tuki approached the old horse slowly. As she reached to pet him, his eyes slowly opened and she withdrew her hand, afraid he'd bite. He closed his eyes and went back to sleep. Go ahead, worship me. Stay all day. I couldn't care less.

As Tuki petted Wilbur, she was happy. She loved early morning, the rising sun revealing a thousand things: cocoons under leaves, wren nests in the crooks of rain gutters, rainbows in dewdrops, week-old bunnies. She was entranced when Cushla snuck up behind her.

"*BOO!*" Cushla cried out vigorously, with a two-handed tickle. "*Merry Christmas, early riser!*"

Tuki didn't like being snuck up on and turned with an expressionless stare.

Cushla ignored the cold reception. "I thought *I* was the early bird. Aren't sunrise hours prime snores for a growing teenager?"

"Lookit me," Tuki replied sarcastically. "How much growin' you think I'm doin'?"

"You always rise so early?"

Tuki said nothing.

"I do," Cushla said cheerily. "Watching the world wake up is far more fun than watching it try to stay awake."

Again Tuki said nothing.

Cushla shrugged. "Chirpy, aren't we? Since you're a morning person, it shall be your duty to feed and water the horses."

"Why me?" complained Tuki.

"So I can tend to the rest of the world," replied Cushla. "Ever chase twins?"

"Every day o' me life," Tuki retorted testily. "Forty at a time."

Cushla turned away and rolled her eyes. *Thank you, Santa.*

She led Tuki inside the old barn and showed her where everything was located, including the feed list tacked on the wall that detailed each horse's supplement mix and vitamin schedule. These four-legged creatures would make Tuki feel at home a lot faster than she could. Then Cushla excused herself. "Got to run. Cooking a special breakfast."

After feeding and watering the horses, Tuki decided to give Wilbur a bath. He needed it. As she scrubbed him gently with the soft-bristled brush, she thought back to the dozens of orphanage field trips she'd taken to stables. She liked horses. They didn't talk . . . nor did they expect her to. They were perfect companions, even the ones that knocked her down.

At her twelfth birthday, she'd been kicked on her kiester, got up, dusted herself off, and marched around to face the gelding. She'd scolded him with such colorful language that she'd earned four demerits for each potty-mouth word, costing herself dessert privileges for a month.

She wasn't really mad at the horse. She was mad at herself for being dumb enough to walk behind him. Gave the horse an open shot and he took it. Headmistress Birdrattle was sympathetic but unyielding.

After bathing Wilbur, Tuki showered and changed her clothes, and halfheartedly meandered across the yard to the house, carrying four whittled figurines wrapped inside a rolled-up tee shirt. She was self-conscious about the homemade gifts and wouldn't hand them out until she was certain the family wouldn't laugh at her.

She opened the creaky screen door apprehensively. She'd heard Christmas was supposed to be a joyous time, though she'd never found it to be so. Getting beaten by a drunken foster father hadn't blossomed joyous memories.

Christmas wasn't good at the orphanage, either. Half the clothes fit, the shoes never did; most of the stuff was hand-me-downs.

Two steps inside the house and it was obvious this Christmas would be different. Santa Claus had navigated the fireplace. Where were all the children who must be coming to share in all this?

At the stroke of seven a.m., shrills of excitement filled the house. The twins came flying out of their bedroom in a thundering footrace toward the living room, where mounds of wrapped gifts surrounded the beautiful Christmas tree. Intent on claiming their presents, both screaming gilrs zoomed past without a wave or a glance.

One by one, the gifts were doled out—and no one else was coming. Time and again the twins read their own unique hieroglyphic-style printing and announced, "Tuki!"

One gift would have been nice. That's what she had to exchange, one gift. Two would be thoughtful. But the gifts kept coming.

She forced a smile. Her stupid hand-carved figurines would mean nothing to these people who wore Merino wool.

Her face tightened. *These people think I'm a beggar. I'm no beggar.*

She was an orphan, not a charity case! Almost sixteen. In two years, she'd be on her own. She did not want, need, or appreciate their pity.

Tuki grabbed the rolled up tee shirt and excused herself to the toilet. From there, she flew out the kitchen door to her barn loft, crying all the way. She hated it here! These people could stuff their money. Her friendship was not for sale.

She sprawled on her bed, interlocking her fingers behind her head, and stared at the ceiling.

Ten minutes later, there was a soft knock at the bedroom door, and Cushla called gently, "May I come in?"

How novel, Tuki thought sarcastically, *someone actually asked.* She had never lived anywhere where privacy was a right. "Enter," she grunted. "It's your bloody house."

Cushla slid open the door and stuck her head in. "Pardon me, sunshine, but I need an hour of your time. After that, you can go back to whatever it is you're doing."

Tuki rolled her eyes. Rather than argue, she bounced off the bed and followed

CAREFUL, LITTLE MISS GRUMPY PANTS. YOUR FACE WILL GET STUCK THAT WAY.

FRAZZ®

oss the pasture to the horse barn. Saddled were

old Wilbur. "Up you go, Miss Fusspot." She

girl to stay angry while riding a horse.

hla mounted Commander Ghost and they rode

aited for Tuki to break the silence.

Finally Tuki asked, "Where are we goin'?"

Cushla made a half turn. "I considered Auckland," she said half joking, "but decided on a visit to Flossy McGrew."

"Who's Flossy McGrew?" Tuki asked suspiciously.

"A girl your age," Cushla replied. She dropped Commander Ghost back and rode alongside. "She's had a hard life. A terrible life, actually. But she's learned to adapt. She's a bit magic that way."

Tuki clopped quietly along, stewing. She wasn't sure if she liked this lady or didn't, but she was knew there would be no middle ground.

They rode in silence. After another half hour, Tuki complained. "How much longer? You said an hour."

"I lied," replied Cushla. "If I'd said two hours, you'd have pitched a hissy fit and wouldn't come." She pointed ahead. "That pale-blue house is Flossy's. Finish your fussing before we arrive, please. No need to ruin someone else's Christmas, too."

Miffed, Tuki asked, "Is she expectin' us?"

Cushla nodded. "She is. So try and find a happy face, will you, Miss Grumps?"

"Didn't get one for Christmas," Tuki fumed.

They clip-clopped side by side up the dirt drive to the blue house. An old woman pushed open the door and waved. Tuki sized her up quickly. This was Flossy? Cushla had lied. This woman was ancient, at least forty.

"Welcome! Welcome!" the woman called warmly. "You made it!"

They dismounted and left the horses to graze. Cushla hugged the woman tightly. "Vivvy, this is Tuki Banjo. Tuki, I'd like you to meet Vivianne."

Dullsville. A merry fossilized Christmas. Relieved this wasn't Flossy, Tuki pretended to be happy and shook the woman's hand.

Vivianne excitedly ushered them inside, to tea and freshly baked Christmas cookies.

Still warm from the oven, chocolate smeared Tuki's fingers as she pulled a cookie apart and nibbled.

The two adults chatted and Tuki tuned it out. Why was she here? Bored, she interrupted. "Where's Flossy?"

Vivianne smiled. "Tired of our girl talk, are you? Rather we zipper this up, so you can meet her?"

Tuki nodded, shooting a wide-eyed plea to Cushla. "That's why I'm here, right?"

They went out the front door and around the side of the house to a three-board, half-acre paddock. Standing near the fence was a small black mare grazing.

Tuki looked around. No kids anywhere.

With a soft whistle, Vivianne called the mare over. The mare's gray-glazed eyes appeared vacant, neither wary nor alert, but her steps were practiced. A white forehead blaze ran the length of her face; a long grotesque scar, an eight-inch river of pink hairless skin, carved right down the center.

"Tuki," Vivianne said softly as the old mare gently nuzzled her outstretched hand, "this is Flossy." Gently she took Tuki's wrist and placed it on the horse's forehead. "Flossy, this is Tuki.

"Breathe into her mouth, honey, so she recognizes you," Vivianne instructed.

Tuki didn't hesitate. She did as told. Then she pulled back slightly and looked into the old mare's lifeless eyes.

"She's processing," Vivianne said. "Can you see it?"

Tuki nodded. The old mare leaned forward, closer, and Tuki breathed into her mouth a second time and petted her all the while.

Cushla laughed. "Don't rub her fur off! No baldheaded horses!"

Quietly Tuki asked, "How did she get the scar?"

"Oh, child," said Vivianne, "everything that could happen to a horse has happened to Flossy. The scar is from an axe between the eyes. Invisible are the other things she's dealt with: colic, fever, broken bones, stillborns, aborted and retarded foals."

Tuki's eyes narrowed. "No way! Who the 'ell would do a bloody thing like that?"

Cushla passed on scolding Tuki for the language. Vivianne's words had landed.

"An angry farmer," said Vivianne. "One who needed the money he expected to get after selling a foal that Flossy delivered dead. The axe split her forehead. Flat-sided whacks to each eye socket blinded her."

Tuki shuddered. "That vicious bastard! How'd he like to get chopped? I'd chop *his* bloody arse!"

"Tuki," started Cushla.

"Don't *Tuki* me. He's a friggin' bastard!" Tuki turned to Vivianne. "Warn't your husband, was he?"

Vivianne shook her head. "No. Me brother. A drinker, he was."

"Still a bastard." Tuki took a breath. "Thank God you saved her."

"I didn't. He left her in the field to die. The vet had randomly stopped by on other business and saw her in the field. He saved her."

Tuki petted the mare again. Flossy's life had been far worse than her own. "How old is she?" she asked quietly.

"Fifteen. Nearly sixteen."

Tuki shivered. "Me, too. I'm nearly sixteen."

"Well, there's a coincidence, now. Two new friends exactly the same age."

Tuki nodded. "Me road's been better. No split-open head. Least not yet."

"Despite all she's been through, she has no malice of heart," Vivianne said. "All she gives is love. Few horses are that way. This one's special."

Tuki gently stroked Flossy's forehead the length of the scar. When they got back to the farm, she'd give the family her handmade carvings. A far lesser crime than an axe to the face.

Cushla quietly nudged her. "Ready to go?"

Tuki nodded, "Can we come another time?"

"Certainly," replied Vivianne, "but Flossy won't be here."

"Why not? Where's she going?" Tuki feared the answer.

Vivianne and Cushla broke into gentle smiles.

"With you, sweetheart," said Vivianne. "Flossy needs a friend her own age."

Tuki's eyes widened. She turned to Cushla, a mix of hope and disbelief. "Really? She's comin' with us?"

Cushla shrugged teasingly. For the first time, she'd heard passion in Tuki's voice. "Horses are a big responsibility, Tuki. Will you care for her? She needs a lot of help."

Tuki nodded vigorously. "I'll be a great mum!"

"Remember our family rule: love everyone and everything that loves you."

Tuki nodded again. "I will love her more than anybody."

Cushla cocked her head and looked at her. "Sure about that, are you? Hasn't seemed to be a strong suit so far."

"Hell, yes!" blurted Tuki excitedly. "I mean, *heck* yes!"

"No potty talk, please," chided Vivianne. "Profanity is the language of youth. Flossy doesn't like it. She's heard two lifetimes' worth already."

"No more," promised Tuki, crossing her fingers behind her back.

Cushla put her hand on Tuki's shoulder. "In that case, sweetheart, Merry Christmas."

"She's me Christmas present?" Tuki cried happily, raising her arms aloft in celebration.

"No, darling. *You* are hers."

Vivianne chimed in. "It's a big responsibility being someone else's Christmas gift. Think you can handle it?"

"Well, seashells and balloons to me! *Course* I can handle it!"

Vivianne slipped the worn bridle over the mare's head, secured the lead rope, and handed it to Tuki.

Tuki looked at Vivianne uncertainly. "Can I ask you somethin', Miss Vivianne?"

"Certainly."

"What do you want from me?"

"Nothing, dear. Why do you ask?"

"You're bein' nice to me and you don't know me. I'm nobody to you. No reason for you to be nice. People aren't that way."

Vivianne shook her head slowly, her eyes twinkling in friendly disagreement. "Oh, Tuki," she said, "I was once a girl your age. You are the greatest gift we can possibly give to her."

"Thank you," Tuki quietly answered. "Nobody's ever done somethin' like this for me."

Vivianne smiled. "Caring is free, Tuki. Pay us back by being good to someone who deserves it."

"I will some day, when I have the money."

"Never wait for that, dear. Act when the time arises."

Tuki nodded. "One more thing?"

Vivianne smiled. "And that is?"

"How do I care for a blind horse?"

"Oats and hugs, darling," Vivianne replied softly. "Oats and hugs, just as with the others. Don't let the blindness fool you. She sees everything that matters, has the ears of an eavesdropper, and the memory of a scrapbook. Love her and she will love you twice as much."

They led the old mare around to the front yard. Tuki climbed aboard Wilbur, then Vivianne handed her Flossy's lead rope. "Good luck, darling. Thank you for brightening my Christmas."

Tuki grinned. "Thanks for savin' mine," she called, waving goodbye as they clip-clopped away.

"Don't forget sugar cubes," Vivianne called out. "And dandelion roots! She *loves* dandelion roots. Follow you to heaven for a handful of dandelion roots!"

Cushla, Tuki, and the three horses arrived back at Okataina just before noon. The twins came running. The suspense of keeping the secret had made them wiggle all night.

Tuki handed out her small gift-wrapped woodcarvings after Christmas dinner. Instead of being embarrassed that they were homemade, now she was glad she had taken the time to craft them, each meticulous with intricate detail, based on what Birdrattle had told her about the family.

"'Ere you go," she said shyly, passing them out. "Made them meself."

Cushla unwrapped hers first and gasped with delight. Her figurine was poised to throw a dart, her favorite hobby. Before marriage, she had been one of New Zealand's top competitors. "My word, how wonderful!" she exclaimed. "Where'd you get learn such a marvelous talent?"

"The orphanage," replied Tuki. "Whittlin' passes the time."

Truck's carving depicted him carrying four mugs of beer, symbolizing the first time he'd met Cushla at a pub. He applauded. "I love it! Perfect, Tuki. Dead solid *perfect.*"

She smiled. The kids at the orphanage had said whittling was stupid.

The twins ripped open their gifts and argued over whose was better. They asked Tuki to decide.

"Methinks they're both perfect, just like both of you." She pulled them to her and hugged them.

"That means me," Angelica announced. "I win."

"No way," protested Angelina. "Mine's prettier."

"Now, girls, pipe down," refereed Cushla. "Let's take a picture, shall we?"

After pictures, the twins went to bed, placing their carvings over their headboards, and insisted that Tuki tuck them in.

She leaned over and kissed them goodnight. Countless times she'd done the same for the little ones at the orphanage. Big sister. Tonight it felt good.

After saying goodnight to Cushla and Truck, she detoured across the yard to check on Flossy. She climbed through the pasture's board fence and called softly to the old mare. She breathed into Flossy's mouth and petted her, whispering secrets. After a short visit, she gently kissed the mare's scarred forehead and went to her upstairs apartment.

Dressed in new pajamas, she brushed her teeth and stared into the mirror. Four homes in eight years, twice through the dormitories of neglected kids. She would give this family a chance.

Soon she was asleep, praying that everyone at the orphanage would find a family and a Flossy of their own.

The next morning, Tuki lugged the bedroom's TV down the steps, across the yard, to the house. "'Ere you go," she announced, plopping it onto the kitchen counter.

"What's wrong? Doesn't it work?" asked Cushla with surprise.

Tuki shrugged. "Don't know. Never turned it on. The telly is the silly box. Me whole life, people have acted like it's a suitable substitute for me mum and dad."

"I never said that," Cushla said defensively. "We just assumed you'd like a TV."

"Murders, commercials, and car crashes don't make me happy," Tuki said. "Picture books make me happy. I'd like to trade the telly for some picture books."

"Let me sit down," Cushla said, feigning shock. "A teenager trading a telly for some picture books? What kind of picture books?"

"Books about horses and butterflies and godwits."

"What are godwits?" asked Cushla, puzzled. "Never heard of such a thing."

Tuki's eyes grew wide with fascination. "Extra special birds! Fly nonstop from New Zealand to the Arctic Circle. Headmistress Birdrattle says everything is possible once we set our mind to it. She says we can learn from the godwits."

"Want to be a godwit, do you?"

Tuki nodded. "Yes. They are small like me, but they are mighty."

"In that case, I'd love to be one, too," Cushla laughed. "But I'd be a circular godwit. Every night, I'd fly back home. I guard the nest."

Cushla smiled at Tuki and stuck out her hand. "Miss Tuki Godwit Banjo, I *accept* your offer to trade one unnecessary telly for several excellent picture books."

Tuki spent that evening and many others pouring through her stack of borrowed picture books.

The library, she decided, her new best friend.

5
MIDNIGHT LIAISON

Tuki Banjo's sixteenth birthday one month later was a heck of a lot better than the previous ten put together. Two beautiful clothes outfits, two Tuki portraits painted by the five-year-olds, dinner at a fancy restaurant, a silver necklace with the engraved letter T, and a bouquet of dandelion roots for Flossy McGrew. Tuki also met a fellow, the handsome busboy who delivered her candle-lit birthday cake.

In the days that followed, Tuki spent a lot of time with Flossy, helping her adjust to her new surroundings. For the old mare's safety, Truck had put her in a small paddock next to old Wilbur. For the first week, Wilbur wouldn't go anywhere near Flossy and stayed in his far corner. But Flossy was calm and happy and paid no attention to the old stallion's snorts, neighs, stomps, and macho posturing.

After a month, Wilbur finally ambled over to check Flossy out. Gradually, begrudgingly, he spent more time near the fence between their paddocks.

Tuki noticed. That night before bedtime, a pleasant evening, both old horses side by side, separated by the fence. Tuki unlatched the gate between their paddocks and swung it open. "She's only sixteen," she whispered to Wilbur, "a younger woman."

She walked around the fencepost to Flossy and rubbed her forehead tenderly. "And you, Missy, would be hard-pressed to find a more handsome man in the moonlight of a thousand farms."

With those encouraging words, Tuki left the horses alone and climbed the stairs her room. Soon she was fast asleep.

Life rolled on at Okataina. The twins turned six and Tuki's boyfriend faded to history. Six months passed before anyone had an inkling that Flossy was in the family way. By her third trimester, her belly was so round she waddled more than walked.

"She looks like a hippo," said Cushla one night at dinner. "Her tummy swings back and forth when she walks. What have you been feeding her, Tuki?"

"I think she's preggers." Tuki grinned. "Not enough dandelions in the world to make her that fat."

"Pregnant?" asked Truck. "Can't be."

Tuki chuckled. "You underestimate her next-door neighbor. He's a night owl, that one."

"She certainly looks it," said Cushla. "If it's not all belly, she's carrying a really big foal or, heaven forbid, twins."

"Twins, hooray!" yelled Angelica.

"I've got a great idea," volunteered Angelina. "Let's name one of them Angelina."

"What would we name the other one?" asked her father.

"Angelina!" yelled Angelina.

"I think Wilbur knows," said Tuki. "He knows it's his."

"We've had that stallion a decade," said Truck, "and I've never once since him flick an ear toward a mare."

"Flossy's not a mare," replied Tuki. "She's his soul mate. He only has eyes for one. And it wasn't an *ear* he flicked."

"A monogamous stallion?" Truck said with incredulity. "No way!"

Angelina interrupted. "Mommy, what does *monatomy* mean?"

"It means he only likes one girl. Like Daddy."

"Does that mean me and Angelica can't monatomy the same boy?"

Cushla nodded. "Yes, dear."

"Nor would you want to," offered Tuki. "There are more than enough of the buggers to go around. Lookit me," she added, "I've monatomied *three* of 'em since I've been here."

The family laughed.

During the full moon of January, with the expectant father proudly watching, Flossy McGrew gave birth to a long-legged, spindly black colt with a bob tail and three white stockings. A big foal, too big, and Flossy struggled with the delivery.

Both Cushla and Truck desperately pulled, and the oversized colt finally slid out: the son of an old blind mare who'd never had a healthy baby, sired by an aging squire who'd been a breeding shed bust.

The colt rose uncertainly to his feet and the exhausted mother turned to dote over her newborn. Suddenly she hemorrhaged, fell to her knees and rolled onto her side. Tuki rushed over, crying uncontrollably, and held Flossy's head in her lap, assuring the mare that everything would be okay. The old mare convulsed, shook, screamed a hideous, gurgling cry, then stopped breathing. Blood poured from her nostrils. As she died, her wobbly son glimmered in the moonlight, confused and alone.

Blood-soaked, Tuki wailed uncontrollably, Flossy dead in her arms. Tears dripped into the old mare's blood, the vivid crimson mixing to pink. This old mare had loved her more than any person, ever, and vice-versa. Flashbacks of her own dead mother haunted Tuki. Steps away, the long-legged colt would grow up without a mother. A hideous life he was in for.

They buried the beloved mare under the wide expanse of the giant pohutukawa tree two hundred yards from the barn. Every evening after dinner, Tuki sat there on the ground, turning the pages of her picture books and crying. She struggled to concentrate, praying for wings to fly her away. Anywhere, everywhere, all around the world. "Please take me," she sobbed. "Don't make me stay. *Take me, take me, take me!* God, please, anywhere but here."

With Flossy's death, Tuki's precariously reassembled life shattered like hand-blown glass on a marble floor. All her repressed anger, torment, and dour frustration raged again. Forgotten was the good of the previous year. She withdrew, and deeper than ever before, into mute belligerence. She trusted no one.

Cushla tried to help by introducing Tuki to the seventeen-year-old son of

Truck's co-worker—but nice boys and mean girls didn't mix. At the end their third date, when he closed his eyes and leaned down to kiss her, she punched him hard, right on the chin. He went down, with a bloodied lip and chipped tooth.

Day after day, Tuki disappeared in her books, soaring with monarch butterflies, joining the ones east of the Continental Divide for the long October migration that funneled millions to a tiny town in the central Mexican Michoa an Valley. The fragile creatures drifted, fluttered, and soared—along with her, coming from as far away as Canada and New England.

Why did the insects, lift off into the wind—from upstate New York, from Minnesota—and leave America, to end up side-by-side thousands of miles away on a tree branch in Mexico?

To escape the hopelessness of staying put, that's why.

Tuki envied the monarchs, enthralled with their weightlessness, living by their radar, instinctively following an inborn call to explore a massive continent. Someday soon, she would do the same.

Godwits explored, too. The little birds with their long, funny upturned bills lived not far from Okataina. They stayed until autumn, then 90 percent of the 100,000 lifted off, winging beyond the Pacific.

One late summer day, Cushla took her on a nature tour to Bowentown to see the godwits. An ornithologist described in great detail what he called nature's most spectacular nonstop migration.

"They're feathered little jets," the man said, "zooming north all the way to the river deltas of Siberia and Alaska. Opposite hemisphere, opposite season. Fall here, spring there. They stay through the Arctic summer," he explained, "then return home, pell-mell, as fast as they can, to nest and feed along the marsh edges of Tauranga Harbor."

"How far is that?" asked Tuki.

"Seven thousand miles each way," the man said. "Fourteen thousand roundtrip."

"How big is the world?" she asked.

"Twenty-five thousand, at its widest," he answered. "Amazing, isn't it? The godwits fly nonstop more than one-fourth of the way around the world."

"I want to be a godwit," Tuki replied. "I'd go that far."

"Nonstop?"

She nodded. "If I had to."

Cushla was curious how long the birds flew.

"Somewhere between 150 and 200 hours, pretty much without a break," the man said. "Eight days or less, usually."

"What's the record?" wondered Tuki.

"The fastest we know is 110 hours—less than five days—flapping one-fourth of the way around the world. Godwits fly faster than a cheetah runs, and they do it for days."

Nonstop and undeterred, Tuki thought. *What must their world be like? Why do they do it? To flee the pain and sorrow? Why so far? But why come back? Why ever come back?*

Beloved Flossy was gone. She, too, would leave the nest. Her destiny was beyond Okataina. When she left, she would never come back. Of that, she was sure. But the foal was alive . . . and for now he needed her. But someday soon, like it or not, ready or not, she, too, would become a godwit.

With romance no longer a distraction, Tuki spent her time playing with Flossy's orphaned colt, whom she called Lenslugger—after the photographer who had come to the orphanage to take pictures of the kids. The colt was all legs and very tall. He loved to eat and pestered his nurse mare, borrowed from a neighbor after losing a stillborn.

Aggressive, headstrong, and mean, Lenslugger had little in common with his parents. He was a biter. He also resisted being handled. His favorite trick was to throw himself on the ground and refuse to get up until Tuki went away. He'd get up when he wanted, walk when he wanted, flop where he felt like it.

Tuki loved him and hated him, depending on the day.

Weaned from the nurse mare at five months, Lenslugger decided Tuki wasn't all bad since when she showed up she always had treats. He began running over to meet her. He never missed a chance to gobble down an apple slice or a carrot . . . or a handful of freshly dug dandelion roots.

She wasn't sure precisely when her childhood had ended, but she was well aware that clinging to the idea of one was a colossal waste of time. As an orphan in foster care, Tuki had learned to combat sadness by staying busy. So she spent countless hours sprawled under the pohutukawa tree with the picture books. She would not waste time on childish things. With great discipline, she learned whatever she could about psychology, both human and equine.

Before the seeded grass had even sprouted atop Flossy's grave, Cushla marched up the stairs to Tuki's room and knocked on the door. "I need to discuss something with you. May I come in?"

Tuki was in bed and not in the best of moods. "Your house, no lock, c'mon in,"

More bad news. She could smell it. What was she going to do, charge rent?

Cushla sat on the bed and placed a reassuring hand on Tuki's shin. "The national yearling sale is six weeks away."

"One down, three more to go, eh?" responded Tuki bitterly. *Right again. Sayonara, family friends. Arrividerci!*

"We have no choice, Tuki. Without the auction money, we have no farm."

Tuki rolled over. "Goodnight."

Tuki was sitting beneath the massive pohutukawa tree with her picture books when the day came to say goodbye to the family's yearlings. The van came mid-morning to cart them off to Karaka, one hour north.

Outwardly she showed no expression. Inwardly, their departure was heartbreaking. Three more things she loved, instantly disposable with a phone call. Gone. Traded for a tank of petrol, a jumper never worn, plastic toys that bored the kids.

No teary goodbye for her! She stayed beneath the tree, clutching her books while the yearlings were boarded one at a time. "Godwits on a truck, are you?" she mused bitterly. "Leave me behind, will you? I'll catch up. Wait and see."

All aboard, the van slowly towed away and Tuki waved a sarcastic half-hand goodbye.

Love for sale. Make offer. What was the point of caring? Happiness was mirrors. Illusions. Love it, it leaves.

Life here was a big, sloppy bucket of crud. She would leave, too. *Not soon enough!*

6
ONE BRUISED HEART

Wanting to keep Tuki busier, hoping to recognize her enthusiasm, Cushla lined up work for her with four small local breeders. Now seventeen, Tuki groomed and exercised racehorses, and prepped younger horses for sale. She didn't mind. Anything felt better than self-pity.

Regardless, she couldn't escape the loss of Flossy McGrew. Countless times a day her thoughts flashed back. Their first meeting, sneaking open the gate that night, watching Flossy waddle around, death in Tuki's lap. The flashbacks always ended the same way, with echoes of the mare's hideous death cry. Sorrow and tragedy. Welcome to my world.

Whenever talk turned serious with Cushla, Tuki sidestepped face-to-face encounters on sensitive topics with ease. Like tonight.

Once again Cushla had hiked the barn stairs and bared her soul. Tuki never interrupted. She pretended to care.

Cushla rambled about past troubles, how three friends had steered her toward a better life: one now a homemaker in Queenstown, the second now ran a women's fashion company in the United States. The third, who owned a small chain of coffeehouses in Auckland, arrived the next day for a visit.

The dinner was awkward. Conversation forced.

Tuki could smell the reason for the lady's visit, and churning lattes for tips was decidedly not in her own future. So, she just sat there, ignoring the indirect questions designed to pique her curiosity. Finally, the woman skipped dessert and said goodnight. Tuki pitied anyone who cared about coffee. She preferred to focus her attention on trying to tame Lenslugger's fiery temper.

Early one November morning, when she approached Lenslugger in his paddock without a treat, the colt wheeled and kicked her in the chest. The blow knocked her down and caused a large contusion, a serious injury that required a high-speed trip to the emergency room.

Upon hearing the diagnosis, a bruised heart, she looked at the doctor who delivered the news. "Runs in the bloody family," she said bitterly. "Them bruisin' me heart. One steals it, one breaks it, one bruises it. The whole bloody family, stampedin' me life."

"You're lucky," said the doctor. "A wee bit higher and you'd be dead."

"That's not luck," she retorted. "That's bad aim. Luck is a godwit. Luck escapes."

Tuki went home with doctor's orders to take it easy for two weeks. She lasted one hour and headed back outside. In silence, hour after hour, day after day, she painted fences. She hated it, but all prisoners did something to pass the time.

When the day arrived to seek medical clearance, she rose at sunrise, went to the car and waited inside. Cushla spied her an hour later and drove her to the doctor.

"You can work with the horses again," he said. "But be careful. Suggest you wear a flak jacket."

"Never," she said. "Pain is me daily bread."

When Cushla broached the subject again on the ride home, Tuki snapped, "You want one, you buy one. I ain't wearin' it. Tell that four-legged bastard to come get me."

One hour later, Lenslugger bit her on the shoulder and spun her to the ground. Blood seeped through her shirt, and the throbbing pain was immense.

Cushla loaded Tuki back into the car and returned to the hospital, lecturing all the way. "He's a dangerous animal, Tuki. Clearly he's got issues! Orphans and preemies often do. For God's sake, if you must keep up this battle of wills, will you *please* wear a flak jacket?"

"Orphans have issues?" Tuki fired back. "That what you mean? We're *all* screwed up?"

"No," replied Cushla hastily. "That's not what I meant at all." She flushed with embarrassment. She'd regretted the words the instant they'd flown out. Tuki was chewing them like a wolf.

"It's what you said," Tuki repeated. "If it's what you said, it's what you meant. No way in hell do I wear a bloody flak jacket. He can kill me first."

Cushla looked over angrily. "At the rate you're going, that may happen by sundown."

"Lucky me! Lucky you, too! Saves you bloody gas money. Invite the doctor over for dinner, why don't you? Save us all some travel time."

The bite took sixteen stitches. Tuki ignored the pain, threw her painkillers in the trash, and immediately went back to work. Tougher than life, devoid of the trite and blameless absolution so natural to teenagers.

"I'll live me life the way I need to live it," she said to Cushla the next evening while the two argued in the upstairs barn bedroom. "Me own way, hear me? Not how you or anybody else wants.

"A horse nearly killed me," she continued heatedly. "So what? 'He's just bein' a horse, doin' what horses do. The problem isn't the bloody colt. The problem is me! Just like always, right? I'm *always* the problem. Get careless, get hurt. Big flippin' deal. So what? Hurt means nothin'. People mean nothin'." Tuki dismissively waved Cushla toward the door. "Now go away and leave me be."

Near tears, Cushla rushed out, back to the farmhouse. Her husband was waiting.

"She's stubborn," said Truck. "She won't listen. Not in two lifetimes."

"Hardheaded," agreed Cushla, "like one of her wood carvings."

Truck nodded. "She's resilient as hell. Got to give her credit for that. If she can't control something, she refuses to worry about it. The armor goes up."

"And if she can control it?"

"If she can control it, she has no fear. Zero. It's her strength of will, Cushla. We won't break her, any more than she's going to break that damn colt."

7
FLIGHT FEATHERS

The months rolled by, and Tuki tempered herself into the toughest teenager on the North Island. Working the horse farms taught her about both types of creatures: people and Thoroughbreds. Every horse was different. So was each owner, breeder, trainer, groom, and rider. Optimists and pessimists; some nice, others jerks. Some lazy, some warriors. Some bold and aggressive risk-takers; others would never step onto a street without checking both ways three times.

There wasn't a lot of difference between people and horses—except people dealt with change better. *If horses could learn to adapt . . . but maybe the horses have it right. Maybe people would be better off not tryin' to be everything to everybody.*

Life at the orphanage had prepped Tuki to use her ears for things other than a placeholder for cheap sunglasses. When a knowledgeable horseman spoke, she listened, for two things—content and emotion—and absorbed everything she heard.

Despite Cushla's attempts to draw her out, she rarely spoke. Saw no reason to. Her life was no one else's business.

Instead she vented in a journal. She was proud of her writing. It was crisp and direct. Like her.

She grew to be almost fanatical about not wasting either time or words. The more she studied, observed, and thought, the more pride she took that although she knew little about most school subjects, she knew more about godwits and monarch butterflies than anyone she knew . . . and learned more each day about Thoroughbred racehorses.

The daily horseback workouts varied from long gallops to starting-gate breaks and time-trial sprints. She soon realized that she'd be much more valuable to trainers if she mastered her sense of timing and pace. Measuring seconds and fifths of a second was worth diamonds in the world of thundering swiftness.

Before bed one night, she went to her closet and pulled out her old yellow travel bag. In it was her grandfather's engraved silver stopwatch. She hadn't known him, but it and the small faded photograph of her smiling young parents astride an old motorcycle were her only family heirlooms.

A thousand times a day, Tuki clicked the stopwatch to start, distracted herself, then clicked the watch to stop—and guessed the elapsed time before looking. There were no trophies for guessing right, and every try led to another.

Once comfortable with fractional seconds, she added tougher distractions: visual, audible, and blends of both. At seventeen, most teenagers couldn't pay attention long enough to answer simple questions, yet Tuki's confidence and concentration enabled her to fly five-eighths of a mile on the back of a racehorse within fractions of a second of precisely how quickly a trainer wanted her to go. In racing's crowded world of imprecise guesstimators, the ability to feel pace was invaluable.

Word spread, and new trainers began to call. She made more money, which she socked away in her cardboard box. Several who called even inquired if she would ride for them in races.

"Racin' is not an option," she told them. "It killed me mum and it won't kill me."

Tuki's third family Christmas approached, but her social isolation had put a growing strain on the family. Cushla and Truck spent many private hours arguing what to do.

"She eats our groceries, uses our electricity, and freely peels off a forest of toilet tissue that she must assume grows out of the wall," Truck complained. "She's expensive. But she contributes nothing to the emotional bonding of this family. Zero."

"So?" challenged Cushla, "What do you expect? To turn a profit by lending her a home? Love is free, Truck. Support, encouragement, and compassion—all free. None costs you a bloody dime! Think she doesn't feel your lack of support? She can bloody well smell it. We all can. It's not like you bend over backward to make her feel at home."

"I gave up on that," he retorted. "She's so self-absorbed it's sickening."

"Why should she be any different?"

"Has she ever spent a dime on us? Made any attempt to pull her weight? She earns money. What the hell does she do with it?"

"She saves it. She's almost eighteen, legal age, free to do what she pleases."

"Hooray," he replied sarcastically. "Let's throw an emancipation party. Our emancipation!"

"Shoving her out the door is the worst possible thing we could do. She is not ready to go out on her own."

Cushla stepped close to her husband, put her hands on his hips, and looked at him with loving eyes. "Don't you *dare* make her leave. Promise me, Truck Roberts. Promise me that you will *not* tell her to leave."

"Sorry," he said flatly, "but I think she should. I've had it, Cushla. Out of time, out of patience, out of money. She's an insolent little brat. I'll help her pack. I'll draw her a map. I'll march her to the end of the driveway, humming *Auld Lang Syne* in my boxers. A goodbye parade, the kids waving flags, one on each side of the street. Ticker tape. Whatever it takes."

"I didn't say you couldn't *think* that," pleaded Cushla. "Just don't *say* it, especially the part about standing outside in your boxers."

Truck watched Cushla's eyebrows narrow, like she was willing to fight this forever. He hated fights. They never used to fight. Now they fought all the damn time, and always over the same stupid thing. Tuki.

He capitulated. "Okay, you win. You make the call; she makes the call. I'll shut up and keep pretending it's an honor to waste money on her. But I still think she oughta go."

"That day will come soon enough," soothed Cushla.

"Fine," he grumbled. "What's for dinner?"

"Crow. Yours is raw. How's it taste so far?"

"Remind me why I love you?"

"Cause you won the contest, lucky boy." She touched a finger to his lips. "And you love me more and more every day, don't you?"

Truck grabbed Cushla around the waist. "I don't like the fighting, but I love the making up." He leaned down and kissed her.

Dinner was silent but civil, silverware scraping plates the only sounds.

At bedtime, Truck reopened the debate. "A guest making the rules, brooding and silent in front of the kids," he complained. "Eats my food, too good to talk. Has she ever washed a dish? Hell, no. I'll rent a damn limo if she'll leave on her birthday! Park it out front at the stroke of midnight."

"Don't start again, please." She looked at her husband sternly. "We've been through this," she reminded him firmly. "She is *not* ready."

"She's ready enough. Quite capable of being a sullen, morose expense somewhere else."

It had been a long time since Cushla had seen Truck this upset. She tried to calm him. "The girl has no compass, no true north. How will she know where she's going?"

"Half the people on the planet don't know where they're going," he complained. "Why is she so special? Why does she deserve a scholarship from being accountable? The rest of us are. Twenty-seven months," he reminded his wife. "Twenty-seven damn months! That's how long she's had to look for her stupid 'compass.' She could stay here twenty-seven *years* and not find it. You know how I know?"

"No, Inspector Roberts, how do you know?"

"Cause she's not even looking! *That's* how I know."

"For God's sake, will you please let it rest?" pleaded Cushla. "I hate this bickering!"

"That's just great," fumed Truck. "Solve a problem and make it go away . . . or run from it and let it perpetuate. We choose to run. Aren't we strong?" he mocked sarcastically. "Aren't we noble? Aren't we righteous? Righteous, my ass!" He pulled up the covers and rolled over. "We're stupid!

"Mark my words," he added over his shoulder, "thirty-two years from now we'll have a fifty-year-old freeloader with a million in the bank, feeding her bridge club out of our refrigerator."

Cushla got out of bed, put on her robe, and left the room. She pushed open the door to the guest bedroom and climbed into the bed. *Pigheaded bastard.*

The girl was frugal. Had $4,000 stashed away. So what? The girl's mother had died worth one-tenth that much. Tuki was saving for a reason. When the time came, she'd leave. *What snotty toad puts a price tag on a mixed-up kid's life?*

Truck couldn't sleep. He got up and came down the hall into the guest room, slid quietly into the bed and moved over to spoon.

"Who is it?" she whispered sleepily. "David, is that you?"

"David couldn't make it," whispered Truck. "It's me, your husband. I'm sorry."

She rolled over and faced him. "You should be," she murmured, rubbing his bare chest. "Stop being so mean, will you?"

"Apology accepted?" he whispered, pulling her close.

"Yes," she cooed. "Goodnight." She rolled over, her back to him.

He nuzzled her neck.

"You messed up, big boy," she scolded softly. "Big time. Stew in your juices, Mister Meanie. Tonight I need me sleep."

Truck flailed to keep his wife awake and the argument alive. "We've done our duty," he said. "Our time is up. Eighteen, she's out the door."

Cushla ignored him. She covered her head with her pillow and struggled to fall back to sleep. At eighteen, she had been no princess herself. She'd been a beer-chugging, green-haired hellion. Two things had recalibrated her life: a night in jail after a barroom brawl, and a trip to America. The latter, Cushla decided, would benefit Tuki more than the former, though Truck might vote the other way.

Christmas Eve, when Cushla received her traditional holiday phone call from her friend Mitzi in America, she took the call in the bedroom and cut right to the point. "How do you feel about me airmailing a young tourist?"

"Tuki?"

"She's turning eighteen. Deja-vu, with her starring as me."

"Oh, God!" Mitzi laughed. "Send her, Cush. Love to have her. Any time after mid-January. The ticket's my treat. I can't wait to spill the beans about your sordid past! The men in your wake, the cons you pulled, haunting the dartboards of the Horse & Trap saloon. Put her on the phone."

"Not ready on our end yet," replied Cushla. "I need to trial the idea. Things here are a bit sticky."

"Is 'sticky' a married word for 'argued about'?"

"Heavens, yes. It's been bloody awful. Truck wants her gone. I want her to stay. We argue all the time. It's exhausting us both."

"What does *she* want?"

"Nobody knows. Won't talk about it. She needs to grow up, Mitzi, but I don't want to scare her away. I see really big trouble if we boot her out."

"Maybe she's more ready than you think. Sort it out and call me. Tell your husband I said you're right and he's wrong. Merry Christmas, darling. Love to the kids." Seconds later, *click*.

Cushla went to her closet and pulled out a cardboard box stuffed with memories, including a stack of leaflets from her long-ago trip to Los Angeles. She rearranged the dozen best brochures in a very specific way, then bundled them in holiday gift wrap. On the Santa label, she printed *Open Me Last. To Tuki, Love Mitzi.*

The first sun streaks of Christmas dawn ushered Tuki to the pasture, where Lenslugger greeted her with his surly attitude. No matter how close she drew, he retreated.

"What the bloody 'ell are you mad about?" she scolded. "A Christmas ass, are you?"

She persisted, as did he. Thin on patience, she cursed the colt and gave up. She retreated upstairs, gathered her gifts, and carried them to the house.

The twins, now eight, were waiting. They greeted her, *Gimme! Gimme! Gimme!"*

Arms full, Tuki was vulnerable to their double-leg tackles and immediately surrendered the presents. The girls ran off giggling and plopped side-by-side at the Christmas tree, squealing as they shredded open the gifts.

After all the other presents had been opened, Cushla retrieved the special one for Tuki and handed it to her with a hopeful smile.

Tuki had never met Mitzi, knew virtually nothing about her. Why would the woman send her a gift? Suspicious, she unwrapped the bundle carefully.

The top brochure read Butterfly World. Tuki set the rest of the stack aside and opened the z-folded, six-sided pictograph. Dozens of rare and colorful butterflies seemed to flutter off the pages.

Such a place as this existed? The family wanted her to experience this? Too good to be true. She scanned their faces for clues. They gave away nothing.

"Mum thinks you need a holiday," Angelina announced.

"Yeah," Angelica agreed with an animated nod. "She says you need to go away."

"Dad, too," Angelina added. "He says you need to go bye-bye."

Horrified, both Cushla and Truck tried to hush the twins, but one look between them told Tuki the chatty girls had spoken the truth.

Tuki looked at Angelina and Angelica and forced a smile. "Is that right? Mummy wants me off in America, does she? Well, Tuki agrees with Mummy." She stood and looked at Cushla and Truck with steely belligerence etched in her face.

Cushla and Truck knew they'd reached the end. The drawbridge of emotional privacy that had guarded the girl's private life had been permanently raised.

"When's the soonest I can go?" Tuki demanded. "Is now soon enough?"

Hooray! thought Truck. *Merry Christmas!*

"Three weeks," said Cushla quietly. "Mitzi said three weeks."

Holiday dinner conversation was forced. Tuki stared at her plate and mechanically chewed her duck with insolent snapping bites, like bubble gum. She didn't taste a thing.

Moving on. Gone for good from this hellhole! *In three weeks, living my dream, a godwit with flight feathers!*

Hallelujah!

8
Au Revoir!

As January 15 drew near, Tuki's reasons to leave piled up. She took a tumble off a horse at full gallop, lucky to escape with only a bruised cheekbone and a sprained wrist. Then Lenslugger bit her again, this time on the meat of her hand. She punched him at the eye, he reared ready to fight and she scrambled through the three-rail fence to safety. "Happy bloody New Year to you, too, you miserable tailless beast! Colic for you!"

She flung open the door to her small bathroom and rummaged through the medicine cabinet. Clean the wound, cauterize it, wrap it. She had the routine down pat and this was the last damn time. *This horse, these people, this bloody awful place, could all share a cab to hell. She had paid the fare.*

"We're going to thin the herd," Truck told his wife happily. "A glorious day it will be. No more angry animals, two-legged or four."

"Lenslugger?" guessed Cushla.

He nodded. "National yearling sale. Already made the call. He's in. Van comes the same day she leaves."

"Can't it wait 'til she's gone?"

"It could, but it's not going to. He sells on the final day, the leftover clearance."

"We won't get much for him, you know. He's a January foal, not August like the others. He'll be the youngest horse in the sale, the least developed. Sell now and we might as well give him away. He's got a big frame. Give him a chance to grow."

"Tell me something I *don't* know," Truck snapped. "It's not about the money. It's about the wonderful good riddance! Get a cake and paper hats! She's gone, he's gone."

"Why throw away a family asset?" she shot back. "Let him fill out. His pedigree is adequate. Dump him now and you'll waste every nickel we've invested. Give him time. Maybe he'll outgrow his tantrums."

"He won't change," argued Truck, his voice rising. "He's a stubborn, angry psychopath. Been that way since the day he was born. The only thing he's grown out of is my patience. What I want," he repeated emphatically, "is my family. I want my family back."

"You just want your bloody motorcycle, don't you? Fat chance!" challenged Cushla angrily. "We sell, and every nickel goes straight into the twins' college fund. You hear me? This family is not blowing one bloody cent on a motorcycle!"

Truck was quiet for several seconds. "Okay," he shrugged. "No bike. But his no-tail butt is still gone."

The night before Tuki was to leave, Cushla carted two beat-up green suitcases to her room.

"Here, Tuki. You'll need them for your things."

"Me bag's enough. Leave with what I brought."

"A black eye and a pair of panties?" Cushla grinned, trying to lighten the moment. "That won't go far in America. Save your money for things you'll need. Take the bags."

Tuki pondered the offer. Luggage was useful. "I'm not comin' back," she replied evenly. "And I'm not a thief. I shan't return 'em."

"No need. I'm giving them to you. I was your age when I went to America. Maybe that's their job, to escort Kiwi girls to America."

"The twins told me you're sellin' Lenslugger?" Tuki said accusingly.

Cushla nodded wearily. "Yearling sale."

"He won't bring anythin'. Why do it?"

"Whatever he brings goes to the girls' college fund." Cushla's excuse felt limp, before she'd even finished its delivery.

"He's never done anything to you," pressed Tuki.

"Look what he's done to you. He's dangerous, Tuki. We can't risk that with the girls, nor with us. It's best for all."

"Rubbish!" retorted Tuki. "Why is the truth so bloody hard?"

"You want the luggage, or not?"

"I'll take it," Tuki said, "but I shan't return it."

"Fine," Cushla said softly, rising to leave. "We leave at nine."

Tuki's packed suitcases stood on the porch an hour early.

She was in the kitchen eating breakfast when the horse transport arrived to van Lenslugger away. She didn't get up. No teary goodbyes. This was freedom day.

She watched through the window as Truck handed over the colt. The van driver took the lead but Lenslugger balked at the ramp. The two men flanked each side and finally coaxed the colt aboard. Tuki stopped watching.

As the van driver secured the gate, he asked Truck, "What you hope he brings?"

Truck shrugged. "A bid," he said. "Minimum reserve. Feel free to get in the action. Hip #1362, a black colt by Wilbur out of Flossy McGrew. A January foal, the youngest in the book."

"Hope you get it," the driver said. "Late foals are tough to sell. At least he's tall. Maybe a pinhooker will take a shot, hopin' he fills out."

Truck nodded. "Either that, or ship him across the equator. January's poison here, perfect there. January's great in the Northern Hemisphere."

"Good luck," the driver said, shaking hands goodbye. "I know it's hard to watch something you've raised leave the farm for good."

Truck nodded. "It's pretty much the theme of the day."

After watching the horse van slowly drive away, Truck went in the house, washed his hands, and gathered the family for the trip to the airport. "Hope I don't get a speeding ticket," he whispered to his wife.

"You be nice," she warned. "Smile or you'll do dishes for the rest of your life."

He drove the Range Rover silence, Cushla in the passenger seat. Tuki sat in back, between the twins. Cushla passed the ninety-minute trip with small talk. "Mitzi and I met as kids. Went to school together. Best mates. She studied fashion and started a small company, swimwear."

"Mitzi's really pretty," chimed in Angelica. "Really, *really* pretty."

"Dad likes her, too," offered Angelina. "He likes her a *lot*. Dad says Mitzi's a bomb squad."

Truck looked at his daughter in the rearview mirror. "*Bombshell*," he corrected.

"Bombshell!" chorused the twins. "Mitzi's a bombshell! Boom, boom!"

"Let Mummy continue. Okay, girls?" Cushla requested.

"After Mitzi's business took off in New Zealand, she opened stores in Australia. Swimsuits and beachwear. A big success there, too. Quickly outgrew the Down Under market. The next logical move was America."

"She's rich," Angelica chimed in. "Right, Mum?"

"Yes, darling. She's done very well."

"Really rich, right Mum?" asked Angelina. "A lot richer than us, right, Dad?"

"No one's richer than us," he said, smiling to his daughter in the rearview mirror. "We've got each other."

Spare me, thought Tuki. *You pinch pennies 'til they bleed.*

Cushla continued. "One year after Mitzi moved to Los Angeles, a merger acquisition doubled the size of her company."

"That made her even more rich. Right, Mum?" piped up Angelica.

"Yes, dear. She's got both money and connections. Tuki will be very comfortable there."

Tuki didn't say a word.

Halfway to the airport, the twins got bored and honored Tuki's farewell by chanting, *"Picklehead on HOL-I-DAY!"*

They sing-songed it for twenty miles. Tuki sat stonily, staring straight ahead. The final hour. Thank God.

Truck parked the Range Rover, grabbed a luggage cart and transferred Tuki's two green suitcases and old yellow carry-on. The four females walked ahead. At the ticket counter, they were third in line and waited in silence. When summoned forward, Tuki handed over her luggage and passport.

The ticketing agent handed over her ticket. "Concourse A, Gate 9. Plane boards in an hour."

"Hooray!" sang Angelica. "We still have an hour!"

Tuki ignored her. "Which way's security?" she asked the ticket agent. The woman pointed.

"Must go," Tuki said.

She walked away, and never turned to wave goodbye.

9
THE AMAZING LIFE
OF J. L. COTTLE

J. L. Cottle was born much older than all the other babies of 1909, and he wasted little time in proving it. By the time he was six, he could ride a horse. At nine, he could lasso a breakaway calf at a dead run. He went into business for himself at twelve, raising a flock of unwanted lambs culled by local shepherds. He nurtured them, then sold their wool and meat for modest cash. At thirteen, he quit school and left home, rather than duel with pencils in the eighth grade.

The lamb money was Cottle's stake. Not much, but enough to leave. That first night alone, he cooked over a campfire, frying a fresh chicken he'd dismembered into eight perfect pieces: legs, thighs, wings, and breasts. After plucking and gutting the chicken, he'd cut it up in twenty-six seconds. This was important. He'd built up quite an appetite chasing that chicken around.

Following his dinner, Cottle's evening under the starry sky in rural Idaho was his first of a hundred successive nights alone. At an age when most kids were too shy to dance, he was hustling for a dollar. A self-propelled go-getter, for whom hard work was a radiant source of energy, he was ever alert for any opportunity, traits that eventually propelled him into the greatest success story in the history of America's free-enterprise system.

Not a book reader, Cottle learned by doing. While friends back home were struggling in school to figure out the difference between a numerator and denominator, he was working. He was decisive in his decision-making and quick to act whenever he sniffed a chance to parlay a buck or two into ten or twenty.

Leaving home to escape his overbearing taskmaster father had presented

Cottle an entire menu of possibilities. His first major move into the world of self-sufficiency was a win/win deal that bolted together the bank with small-town schoolteachers and the town drunk. The teachers were paid in warrants—future promises to pay.

Cottle talked a banker into fronting *him* some cash in exchange for those warrants. The teachers liked the deal, because their warrants became instant, albeit discounted, envelopes of cash. The banker liked it, because he made a bit, too. Cottle liked it, because his commissions were enough to convince the drunk to lease to him cheaply 120 acres of farmland. Fertile dirt at a bargain price.

Cottle worked hard and farmed the rich soil with the fervor of a zealot. He grew potatoes, but worked harder and smarter than the drunk ever had; and when harvest time came, J. L. Cottle reaped a bountiful crop.

The potato money bought 700 piglets—against conventional wisdom in a swine market that was flatter than a slice of uncooked bacon. At the time, raising pigs was little more than penny shuffling. Cottle figured that, with a little luck, maybe the market would turn by the time he fattened these wee ones.

With the potato field replanted from carefully selected seed, he marched his new army of happy little swine to the vast Idaho wilderness prairie, penned them and proceeded to feed them potato scraps from his first harvest, along with horse meat from weak mustangs he culled from wild roaming herds.

By his fifteenth birthday, he had felled 100 horses. He knew how to gut, disembowel, cape, skin, and bone a horse carcass. He tanned the hides and sold them for two bucks apiece. The ambitious young man respected his prey and wasted nothing.

Cottle's father came out to visit, as a concession to his son's determination and ingenuity. They built a massive boiler that stewed up the potatoes and meat, which vastly improved the feeding process.

"Helluva boiler," Cottle recalled later in life. "One thing my daddy could do was build a great stew pot."

By summer, the pigs had fattened beautifully and Cottle waddled the portly entourage back to town. The market had turned and his were the finest pigs available. He sold them all at seven cents a pound and turned a huge profit. He left the stockyard that day with $7,800; in the early 1900s, worth about a trillion to a kid who needed nothing more than a flat spot of dirt under a starlit sky. He was rich!

With his wealth, Cottle began what would become his lifelong trademark: He hustled up a parlay. Rather than sit on his new fortune, he wanted to borrow a lot more and lock up large parcels of acreage. He had an idea, but he wanted to experiment on someone else's dime. Pig money in hand, he headed to the bank and flashed it.

Cottle had the look of polite innocence that every great salesman has. His sapphire blue eyes sparkled. When the bankers talked to him, both glimmering blue beads locked intently on theirs. He could look through a person, see what they were thinking, read what they were feeling—which enabled him to build trust with even the crustiest of curmudgeons.

He sweet-talked those bankers into trusting that the bank's money was safer in *his* hands than theirs. He borrowed a tremendous sum and purchased his first enormous block of land.

Now with thousands of acres and the means to farm them, Cottle planted his own certified potato seed, harvested from his very best potatoes. Better seed yielded bigger, better potatoes. He also fertilized strategically irrigated fields, a major break from the planting tradition of rotating different crops through the same dirt in order to restock multiple nutrients.

To prove that he knew what he was doing and always a showman, he nurtured five special acres of "show me" taters for potential lenders and suppliers. Under manicured conditions, he grew the largest potatoes Idaho had ever seen: big, fat, impeccably textured, and disease-free.

Record harvests from the expanded acreage generated massive sums of cash. By age sixteen, J. L. Cottle's peers had knighted him the most skilled potato man in all of Idaho . . . and bankers started stopping by to say hello. Cottle just smiled.

His life's work enabled him to learn more about potatoes and potato growing than any man who had ever tracked mud into a farmhouse, yet Cottle remained unsatisfied. He had no partners, paid the bank on time, and was free to call the shots. He surrounded himself with experts on every imaginable topic, listened to them, and traveled often to investigate anything that might help his operation. Relentlessly he reinvested back into his ever-mushrooming stake. From seed to harvest, no one in the world knew more about potatoes than he did.

His business acumen steered him toward a privately owned conglomerate that extricated millions upon millions from agriculture, livestock, chemicals, timber, and minerals. A friend said of Cottle, "You gotta give him credit. He's got nads the size of planets."

Cottle's personal philosophy was more direct. "When the time is right," he liked to say, "you just got to do it."

Armed with optimism and astute judgment, he rarely strayed outside the jigsaw puzzle of agricultural opportunities. When the supply chain of fertilizer sources became too erratic to suit the precise nature of his strategy of irrigated, fertilized fields and certified seed, he bought a phosphate plant. Through smart, cost-effective reengineering, he doubled capacity and sold excess inventory to other farmers. That money fueled a trebling of his phosphate empire.

With the production side of the business under control, Cottle turned his focus to post-production challenges, which scattered before him like moneybags waiting for pickup.

One of his smartest moves came one week before his eighteenth birthday. He'd heard about a new-fangled machine a fellow in Washington invented, to help farmers sort potatoes; a huge logistical challenge that hampered harvests. Cottle went to see it. At a glance, he realized the device would make him another fortune. He bought it on the spot. With smart marketing and a shrewd business plan, he could make a run at controlling the nation's potato market.

Within months, the word got out about Cottle's automated potato sorter. Since it was portable, he and his team provided this service to other growers. They traveled farm to farm, set up, plugged in the sorter, and zoomed taters through the conveyor line faster than any farmer ever had dreamed. Growers large and small lined up, clamoring to be served. "Nobody minds sharin' a profitable dollar," he said. "Provided you earn it."

The lone impediment to the process was the fact that many of Cottle's hired hands smoked, which annoyed him. The dirty, smelly habit caused a productivity loss when smoking was America's pastime, not baseball. He got the guys to stop the old fashioned way: He paid them a bonus if they didn't smoke. All quit. Productivity increased.

Cottle was young, handsome, rich, charismatic, and polite. As his business grew, neither complacency nor women sidetracked him. His lack of formal education was rendered inconsequential by a doctorate in visionary leadership. "The dirt is my teacher," he said during an interview. "Stay close enough to it and it will teach a man more than any schoolhouse.

"There's a lot of dreamers out there," he added. "And God bless them for dreaming. But I don't dream. I just *do*. I stretch boundaries—from the way things are to the way they can be. If I can't see it, I don't do it. But if I can, I find a way to get it done. Then I figure out how to do it better, faster, and cheaper."

As he grew older, Cottle developed a love of toys for transportation. Reliable cars and fast planes saved a lot of time. Speed was an enabler.

An outdoorsman, he was among the first to get involved in developing the Sun Valley ski project; his snappy, stylish dress strengthened his persona in influential circles. Tall, fit, and impeccably tailored, none made a better *après ski* impact than J. L. Cottle. His pals at Sun Valley were some of Hollywood's biggest stars. By age twenty-five, he could buy them all. But he never flaunted his wealth.

He wasn't a drinker, so he never made a drinker's mistakes, and despite the trollings of many a starlet, Cottle ignored their advances. Being a darn good potato farmer was his crystallined identity. When the time came to settle down, he'd court a farm girl, not a showgirl.

By his thirtieth birthday, he had turned down a dozen offers to buy his businesses, another hundred offers to go public and take on partners. He would never answer to stockholders, nor ask permission to pursue any opportunity. He was the richest man in Idaho and other people's sticky fingers annoyed him. They didn't know a potato from a turnip. They had never tilled the land.

A creator, Cottle's fun came from building an empire with other people's money. He hired the best talent, overpaid good workers, and took very good care of his people. Yet he struggled to shrug the reputation for being omnipotent. A rival likened Cottle to a barker at a carnival: watching all the plate spinners, yelling whenever a plate began to wobble.

Late summer one Friday in Boise, September 1, 1939, Cottle's assistant burst into the office, disrupting a meeting with an architect. She rushed to the desk and whispered in Cottle's ear. "Long distance. It's urgent."

The assistant politely ushered the architect out. Cottle took the call in private and was transferred by a somber operator to the U. S. Department of Defense.

A senior official came on the line. "Hours ago, Mr. Cottle, Nazi Germany invaded Poland."

"Sorry to hear that," said Cottle. "Why call me?"

"The President will not let America sit idly by. We will engage, quickly."

"And?" asked Cottle.

"We face potentially the largest armed conflict in history, a confrontation that may take years. Hitler must be stopped, whatever the cost. We expect that price to be high. The President expects this to be the most devastating and inclusive conflict humankind has yet engineered. Powerful new weaponry, Mr. Cottle, from guns to tanks and missiles to bombs are ready to go."

"And?" Cottle repeated tersely.

"The deployment of American soldiers will be unparelleled, Mr. Cottle. And the soldiers must eat."

"You need me to help feed them?" he surmised.

"Precisely. The soldiers need you, Mr. Cottle. Your President needs you. Your *country* needs you."

"Say no more," said Cottle. "Whatever you need, I will find a way."

"Thank you, Mr. Cottle. The President is grateful. America is grateful, as will be our soldiers and allies. Please excuse me, but I've got many calls." *Click.*

In the space of a single minute, Cottle's life charter had been redefined. He could make a critical impact. Potatoes were vital to the war effort.

He dismissed the waiting architect, abandoning the project eighteen months along. A far bigger challenge was at hand.

He spent the next several days in meetings with his key scientific team. The logistics were staggering. Together they figured out how to freeze-dry, package, and supply potatoes to the military; onions, too.

By the time the war drew toward a close six years later, he had shipped overseas thirty-three million pounds of dehydrated potatoes and five million pounds of onions. He was so politically entrenched with national favortism that he became nearly impervious to competition.

Throughout the long, hard war, Cottle had reinvested everything back into his businesses, keeping nothing for himself except one symbolic gold coin he purchased with his first government check. He took no salary, and plowed the rest of the government payments into more land, more potatoes, and an expanding herd of beef cattle that grew to 170,000 head. When the war ended, Cottle was the largest deeded landholder in America.

A few months after the war, early in 1946, J. L. Cottle's phone rang again. It was a close friend, Walter Utley, whom Cottle always called Moose.

Both were crack marksmen, but Cottle killed for food: Moose hunted for sport, game animals large and small. His homes, offices, garages, storage facilities, fishing lodges, and hunting cabins overflowed with stuffed heads. His two favorite trophies were a lion shot in mid-air at twelve-feet with a pistol, and an ostrich. He was most proud of the ostrich, nailed with a single shot at two hundred yards on a dead run.

"Let me guess," said Cottle on the phone, "you want to go shoot something. No time for that, Moose. Busy making money. Besides," he teased, "ain't one ostrich enough?"

"Back off on the ostrich, will you?" pleaded Moose, "They can really pick 'em up and put 'em down, especially when you're shootin' at 'em. Forty-miles-an-hour they run, faster than a greyhound. A helluva shot. You couldn't have touched a feather with a machine gun."

"They've got *eyelashes*, Moose. You're huntin' stuff with *eyelashes*."

"I wanted boots," admitted Moose, "and I got 'em."

Moose's phone call was well-timed. With the war out of the way, Cottle needed a vacation. Moose urged him to take a break, come out and play.

"I called to challenge you to a rodeo," Moose said. "Four events: calf-roping, steer wrestling, barrel racing, bull-riding. We split 2-2, our traditional tie-breaker."

"You want to dress up and play cowboy?" asked Cottle. "You ain't a cowboy. Ain't no cowboy wearin' eyelash boots! When and where?"

"Four months out," replied Moose. "Cheyenne Frontier Days."

"Wyoming?"

"You figured that out on your own? Without hiring somebody to tell you? It's all set up," Moose added. "All you gotta do is buy the guts to show up."

"Why there? Frontier Days is a giant rodeo. Why not Boise?"

"More fun on the road," replied Moose. "Plus, I want witnesses."

Cottle hadn't contemplated thousands watching. Riding a bull was hard enough; flying off in front of a packed grandstand would be embarrassing.

"I assume you're making it well worth my while to travel out of state to humiliate you--since I can do it much more quickly here in town," said Cottle. "What stakes do you propose? Something bigger than a blue ribbon, I assume."

"I optioned 400 acres along the Sawtooth River," replied Moose. "Winner keeps it; loser pays for it."

"Now you're talking," said Cottle, enthused. "Free dirt."

"You in?"

"Of course I'm in. You can't ride a *bicycle*, Moose, much less a horse. But if I commit and you wuss out, I get the land."

"You wanna see a wuss, look in the mirror," his friend retorted. "I shall destroy you."

Cottle smiled as he hung up the phone. He loved teasing his buddy. The rodeo suited them both. Each had grown up around horses and livestock, and Moose had the courage of ten men. While Cottle had been feeding the troops during the war, Moose had been skyjumping into the middle of it. The first American to freefall over mainland China, Moose had taught the Chinese military to sky dive; a big assist to the Chinese government in their struggle against the Japanese. The Chinese had recognized his help and decorated him a hero, so Moose was an idol to the Chinese women. Dozens fussed over him—a swashbuckling, green-eyed Yankee superman. Their candle-lit massages were bonus compensation.

Cottle and Moose traveled to Wyoming three days before their scheduled rodeo competition, ostensibly to practice with their world-class horses. Moose arrived supremely confident. He had the calculated business instincts of a gator in a turtle pond, had planned this competition, and expected to win. Cottle had been driving a desk too long to beat him.

Cottle had accepted Moose's challenge for one simple reason: He never turned down free land. Riverfront was a bonus.

In Cheyenne, it was hard to keep secret who these two men were, nor did the press want to. Once the newspapers dug into their past, the story was big news throughout Wyoming, Colorado, and western Nebraska. Cottle was fabulously wealthy, a man of the earth who tilled the soil. Moose was a swashbuckling renaissance man. He had graduated from high school in three years, college in three, and grad school in one. He had blown through his Ph.D. in management in less time than it took to rearrange the dorm furniture.

By age twenty-nine, Moose was the C.E.O. of a regional grocery chain and took them national. The stock warrants, issues, and options had made him wealthy. So, he quit working and roamed the world—on a Harley Davidson, his preferred mode of transportation. He hunted lots of things with eyelashes, especially at night.

Moose also loved to fly. He had learned on Piper Cubs and Cessna four-seaters; then graduated to jets and barrel rolls, screaming power dives, and sonic booms. Often his flights required a co-pilot, since one reason Moose flew was so he could leap out and freefall into unsuspecting people's backyards.

Moose had skydived on every continent except Antarctica. Scores of photo albums housed shots of him with his chute, posing with surprised homeowners from Sudan, Madagascar, Iceland, Uruguay, and Tibet. His greatest jump, in 1953, was forty miles from Stockholm. Fickle Swedish winds had blown him onto a picnic table. He landed butt-first on top of a cake at the celebration of a divorce decree for a thirty-three-year-old fashion model. A dozen martini-drinking girlfriends then unbuckled him from his chute and invited him to stay.

He did. For five days.

The local press devoured the story of Cottle and Moose, the men featured on TV, radio, and the paper every day. Everyone in Cheyenne chose one or the other to root for, split fifty-fifty. The wire services picked up the story, too, and news teams descended on Cheyenne.

Neither Cottle nor Moose pretended to be a pro cowboy—at best they were gutsy amateurs—but everyone could relate to challenging a pal. Lines formed quickly at the advance-sales window and the demand for tickets exceeded the supply. Scalpers doubled, then tripled, their money, especially on the Brahma bull-riding. The townies were eager to watch a pair of millionaires get stomped.

One look at the long lines and the rodeo promoters quickly capitalized on the tenderfoots' popularity: posters, signs, memorabilia in hastily assembled souvenir booths. Cottle fans received a red pin badge with a potato graphic, Utley's a blue badge with an antlered moose head. Every day, the rodeo promoters featured a different giveaway.

A raucous crowd greeted the loudspeaker announcement that Moose Utley was in the chute for the men's first event, calf roping. When the calf was turned loose, Moose dug in both heels and his horse exploded out of the chute. Moose whirled his lariat overhead in hot pursuit. He threw a perfect loop over the scampering calf's head, the horse stopped, the rope stretched taut, and yanked the calf off its feet. Moose hopped down and ran to tie the little guy's feet together. The knot slipped and he had to retie it, costing him several seconds. But he finished with a flourish and raised both fists in triumph. The crowd roared. A good number, twenty-eight seconds.

The pressure shifted to Cottle, but he didn't feel it. He was outside the arena eating a chili dog, interrogating the counter clerk about the dog's meat/fat ratio and the rodeo's lack of Idaho potatoes.

He finished scarfing down the meal and wandered over to the cowboy entrance to get ready, late on purpose. He didn't want to deal with nervous time.

As luck would have it, he'd made a shrewd choice on his rodeo horse, which is why he had been so willing to overpay to get him. Veteran cowboys lived by one rule: Whenever possible, leave all major decisions involved in chasing a smaller animal to the bigger one you're riding.

When his calf scooted out, instead of running straight, it zoomed a hard left. Cottle's horse didn't miss a step and pinned the calf in a corner. The little critter just stood there and Cottle's lasso easily circled the neck.

The horse backed, tightened the rope, and Cottle hopped down. The calf offered no resistance and Cottle quickly tied all fours together and stepped away. Nineteen seconds. The crowd roared.

Moose watched with his arms folded at the railing next to the livestock chute. He bent his head and spit in the dirt. Done in by a timid calf. "You insolent little veal patty," he mumbled. "We shall meet again. And when we do, I'll be holding a fork."

Cottle's win in the calf-roping competition was played up big in the newspapers. He attributed his success to the fact that he ate a lot of potatoes, and was careful to point out that potatoes make you strong and ward off your adversaries.

Steer wrestling, he edged Moose again, by less than a half-second. Hundreds of cheering fans rose and hurled potatoes to the arena dirt floor. The rodeo clown dove to safety inside his clown barrel, only to get drilled on the noggin when he stuck his head out to prairie dog the situation.

Cottle beamed. Potatoes were everywhere! A record harvest! The crowd cheered and he bowed deeply to all four corners of the stands. *God love you,* he thought. *I can sell an extra ton while I'm here.*

"You're killin' me, brother," said Moose when Cottle exited the ring. "Spud you!"

"Got lucky," replied Cottle. "Ain't it a stinker when a friend gets lucky?"

Moose rode flawlessly the next evening and swept barrel racing in three straight races. Cottle didn't clinch it and his fans exited sadly, walking around with potatoes in their pockets, lumpy pants.

Cottle's lead was now two-to-one. Only the bull-riding event remained. He didn't expect to last eight seconds on the back of a wild-eyed 1,600-pound tornado, but he didn't expect Moose would, either. Cottle's strategy was to land soft enough to survive, his head not sticking in the dirt like a lawn dart.

Rodeo organizer Rip Quigley took the men aside an hour before the event. "Normally, rodeo bulls are assigned randomly to all cowboys," explained Quigley. "But since some of these would launch you from Cheyenne to Chicago, we think you're safer if we assign them."

"Fine by me," said Moose. "The calf I roped had a mean streak. Can't I just ride *him?*"

"Be a man, you mouse," said Cottle. "Find his granddaddy."

Accompanied by the bulls' livestock tender, Quigley walked Cottle and Moose back to the pens where the animals were housed. He pointed to two. When Moose stared over at one of them, a midnight black monster, the bull stared back, contemptuously chewing its cud. Then the bull peed like a fire hydrant and never broke eye contact.

"What's his name?" asked Moose, nodding toward the bull.

"You don't want to know," replied the tender.

"I do," said Cottle.

"Crush," the man deadpanned. "Stomped the last guy flat, like a mallet on a crab claw. You could hear the ribs break."

"More than we needed to know, my good man," said Cottle dryly. "Who gets him?"

To assign the bulls, Quigley flipped a coin. Cottle won the toss and took a smaller bull, Beauregard Skywalker. The look on Moose's face caused Cottle to laugh. "Headed to the gallows, Moose?" he kidded. "You want first or second?"

Moose waxed philosophical. "I love my family, my bills are paid. I've ridden one other bull in my life, broke my collarbone two days before the senior prom. Therefore," he said, "I'll go first."

When the competition got underway, the arena was packed, standing room only.

Moose thought of many things as he got assistance strapping in atop the massive Brahma, wedged inside the chute. The rodeo assistants secured his grip and yanked extra tight on the flank strap, agitating Crush's manliness. The bull angrily slammed both sides of the loading chute, eager to dislodge the annoying trespasser.

Moose's universe was very small. He closed his eyes, blessed himself, and raised his arm. "Ya-hoo!"

The gate swung open and the crowd roared. The five-year-old Brahma determined to launch Moose into rodeo folklore. Crush lunged out and Moose determined to hang on.

The bull whirled left, then right, and bucked so high that he made the front page of tomorrow's paper. The only part of Moose that made the paper were his ostrich boots, the rest of him had sailed out of camera range.

A great ride, all five seconds. The doc woke Moose with smelling salts, and stuck a wooden tongue depressor into his mouth.

"He's breathing, right?" asked Cottle anxiously.

"Yes," nodded the doctor. "I'm just checking to see if he swallowed his bowels."

Moose's glazed eyes stared at the doc. "How long did I last?"

"Five seconds. Helluva ride," replied the doctor. "The guys in the back thought you'd stay glued to the fence when the door flew open. You've got a lot of balls."

"Not so sure about that," whispered Moose hoarsely. "Could you check to see if they're both still there? Sure don't feel like it."

"Check the clown barrel," teased Cottle. "Thought I saw a pair flyin' that way."

Moose looked at Cottle and blinked drowsily. "Your turn," he mumbled. "Have fun."

Watching his pal get launched to the emergency room didn't do a lot for Cottle's confidence. He leaned down and patted Moose on the shoulder. "Tight about givin' up that land, ain't you?"

Cottle's ride was less exciting. Beauregard Skywalker whirled in a violent circle as soon as the gate flew open. Cottle sailed off, rolled when he hit the ground, and scrambled out of reach. With the score tied two-to-two, he'd take his chances in the tiebreaker.

They waited three days for Moose to recover. Winning the prized Idaho riverfront parcel came down to their traditional method of friendly battle: Indian wrestling. They had done this a thousand times as kids. Right foot square against right foot, left feet back for balance, right hands gripped tightly. Miss Cheyenne Rodeo yelled, "GO, PLEASE!"

This proved to be their ultimate battle and lasted two exciting minutes. Cottle lunged in to make Moose stumble backward. Moose swivel-hipped sideways and pulled Cottle toward him, then past him. Cottle lost his balance and it was over. Moose Utley won.

They sold their rodeo horses back to the cowboys they'd bought them from, for half what they'd paid. Bruised but happy, the pair flew back to Boise and relived the week in laughing detail, already scheming their next challenge. Cottle swore to get revenge.

Moose wasted no time in building a gorgeous cabin on his new riverfront property. Named it Cheyenne Lodge. The two friends spent many happy days there, flyfishing for trout and revisiting the day Moose had ridden the bull for five seconds and his ostrich boots were in the newspaper.

Meanwhile, Cottle dove right back into his work, convinced that what post-World War II America really wanted was to relax. He was especially intrigued by a new invention: the electric freezer. With no more need for door-to-door ice delivery, trips to the market could be reduced. Protected from spoilage, homemakers could stockpile whatever they chose. Potatoes were a staple. Freezers would fill with them. Given the option of eating what they had or making an extra trip out, people would eat what they had. Potatoes could be stockpiled; consumption would increase.

To test his theory, Cottle gifted his assistant a freezer. The day it was delivered, she invited her girlfriends to see it. Each went home and told her husband she wanted one. Any husband who didn't comply faced a very unhappy wife.

This simple neighborhood test reaffirmed what Cottle had suspected: that sooner than most people thought, nearly every home in America would have a freezer. Women would demand it.

Cottle urged his scientists to figure out how to turn a billion pounds of raw potatoes into a billion pounds of skinned, sliced, bagged, and frozen ones. The hard part was protecting texture and taste.

Once they figured it out, Cottle tacked on extra profit into each step and turned his salesmen loose. While they were off chasing orders, he and Moose took a week and balloon-raced across Europe. It had been two years since the rodeo.

Cottle returned to stunning news. His men had sold a thousand tons of frozen sliced potatoes, with back orders for hundreds of tons more.

On top of a tall stack of phone messages was one from a longtime friend in southern California, who had shared Cottle's vision that consumers wanted a more leisurely post-war America and would pay for convenience. Cottle called the man back immediately. In ten minutes, the two decided that what stared them in the face was the chance to shape a fast-food nation.

Cottle sat down that night to a medium-rare sirloin steak with a perfectly baked potato. As always, he ate slowly. No consumer in America would escape for long. He was now the sole supplier of french-fried potatoes to McDonald's restaurants. America had just transformed from an eat-at-home nation to a country of drive-thru convenience, another sonic boom of success over America's social landscape.

Sales climbed. Two billion pounds grew to three. To maximize sales, his team hammered out a complex distribution strategy. Then he sprung Ronald McDonald upon the unsuspecting nation.

Cottle's empirical expansion threatened to swallow up the humble tater grower, burying him under an avalanche of spreadsheets and lawsuits; an android tycoon held hostage, cross-eyed with budget decisions, legal consults, and rancorous labor meetings.

Moose refused to lose his friend that way. For decades, he mapped out intriguing challenges. Every four years they competed in a new event with high-dollar toys: hunting big game in Fairbanks, Alaska; Cottle dropped a trophy bull moose from the cabin porch at thirty-below. Spearfishing for grouper, wrestling black marlin off the Australian coast, pistol-shooting hyenas in Africa, capturing giant rattlesnakes in the Arizona desert. Racing bicycles Canada to Mexico, motorcars around the oval in Indianapolis, jet cars across the salt flats of Utah. The need for speed, adrenaline, exhilaration.

Their games escorted the men to old age. Cottle now in his nineties, Moose in his late eighties, side-by-side they ventured into a new big money world: Thoroughbred horse racing.

In rural North Carolina, zip-code heroes varied according to the size of the code. Most often they came from high-school athletic fields or community do-gooders, folks who owned little but needed even less and happily tried to brighten the lives of others.

Miss Louise was one of these. For thirty-nine years, she'd fed every kid who passed through the cafeteria at Possum Drop High. Every day of those thirty-nine years, she had shared a bubbly smile and a cheerful word for each child.

Possum Drop was a farm town and farm folks knew how to share. Over the years, Miss Louise became as much a part of Possum Drop High as its giant, pink-eyed, scaly-tailed namesake-mascot painted outside along the length of the gymnasium wall. Miss Louise was an institution.

She'd no children of her own, but she loved everyone who came through her food line, as though her own blood ran through their veins. So when the school district changed from buying fresh food to cheaper prepackaged crap just to save a few bucks, Miss Louise started arriving at five a.m. instead of six to process the donated meat and vegetables she needed each day to provide for her kids.

Daily she pieced together something nutritious, tasty, and hot for all the children who had left home hungry and returned home at the end of the day to bare cupboards. Possum Drop was a town of the poor and for many of its children the only square meal they ate each day was poured from the business end of Miss Louise's stainless steel ladle. Miss Louise had been born to cook country vittles, and she was never happier than when her ladle scraped the empty bottom of her big stew pot.

She was just as famous for her biscuits and birthday cakes. Every child received his or her own chocolate birthday cake, complete with a flickering candle and big enough for four slices. Most of the kids took theirs home to share.

Miss Louise lived a very private life in a modest trailer near the school. She had never married, not been squired around town on the arm of a perceived suitor. She had walked everywhere that mattered: school, church, the grocery, the library.

Since she kept to her own business, no one knew when she suddenly took sick, though rumors started when she went from pretty big to pretty small in just a few months.

Then one Tuesday morning, she fell to the school's kitchen floor and couldn't get up. She was unconscious when a cafeteria co-worker found her. She was rushed to the hospital but never woke up. She died three days later, two weeks shy of her seventieth birthday. Her passing was front-page news.

The photograph the newspaper ran was one of Miss Louise's favorites: smiling broadly, surrounded by her kids who were admiring the flowing blue ribbon she had won at the North Carolina Cafeteria Workers Baking Competition. She had taken first place nine years in a row for her secret recipe biscuits. "Possum Droppers" she called them.

The newspaper wrote that she'd cooked over one million Possum Droppers during her lifetime and had never burned a one. For thirty-nine years, she had left plates of Possum Droppers stacked high, waiting to be grabbed by hungry kids at lunchtime. And for thirty-nine years, she had left extra plates of biscuits for the poor kids to take home. The whole town had been raised on Possum Droppers. Suddenly, there would be no more.

When Miss Louise was laid to rest, hundreds of friends of all ages, races, and creeds crowded the church to say goodbye. A lot of tears that day, the most this small town had ever seen.

Nine days after Miss Louise's funeral, a young lawyer named Elliott Turner drove out to Melvin Trombley's vegetable farm on the edge of town to discuss a matter of great importance. He was the executor for Miss Louise's estate. After getting no answer from ringing the front doorbell, Elliott circled around back and saw a brown dirt-cloud way off in the distance. In front of the cloud was a shiny green tractor, the fancy kind with an air-conditioned cab. Elliott assumed that Melvin was behind the wheel and tilling the soil.

Because what he needed to discuss was important, Elliott began walking toward the distant tractor, which was a bit awkward since the rows were furrowed exactly the wrong width for Elliott's stride. He tiptoed the best he could to avoid mud on his Florsheims and dirt on his sharply pressed suit pants.

High up in the air-conditioned comfort of the cab of a spanking new John Deere Plowmeister tractor, Melvin Trombley bounced slowly but happily along. In his rearview mirror, he spied the only attorney in all of Possum Drop, North Carolina, walking quickly toward him through the field.

Uh-oh, he thought. *A lawyer.* A lawyer was never a good sight, no more than flashing police lights on the interstate. *He's totin' a damn briefcase. Why's he comin' for me? The truck's flat broke and so am I.*

Elliott was two hundred yards away but closing, wildly flailing the briefcase while trying to negotiate the fresh-plowed furrows. Melvin studied him in the mirror. He let Elliott close within sixty yards, then shoved the big tractor in gear and slightly sped up to stay ahead.

Let's see how fast you can run. He grinned as he watched the lawyer trot through the dirt to catch up.

Elliott was a kid, and had never caused Melvin trouble, but Melvin was a farmer who didn't care for lawyers. Farmers bought everything at retail and sold everything at wholesale and got stuck paying for freight both ways. Lawyers had it different. They sucked other people's blood. They slurped on take-home pay.

When Elliott had finally closed within hand-grenade range, Melvin reached the end of the row and quickly pivoted the tractor 180-degrees back around. The lawyer was just twenty yards away, his shoes and trousers flaked with the dark, rich Carolina soil.

Melvin revved his engine and chased after Elliott like a hound after a rabbit.

He laughed out loud, then killed the motor. The lawyer was here for a reason, a legal reason presumably. As much as Melvin didn't want to hear it, he figured he should. "Morning, Elliott," he called down cheerfully. "Didn't realize it was you. What brings you to row 206?"

"Morning, Melvin. Need to see you. It's important."

"What's up?"

"You and your brother Halvin, er, *Mountain*, are named as beneficiaries and co-trustees of Miss Louise's last will and testament."

"We get money?" said Melvin, astonished.

"Don't know," replied Elliott. "We need to read the will in my office. I need you to be there. It's up to you and your brother to supervise Miss Louise's final wishes."

"Tracking my brother down will be a problem," Melvin said. "He lives in New Zealand, sixteen time zones away."

"He can call in," Elliott replied.

"He'll hate that. For his sake, talk fast and skip the legalese. Phone charges from there to the States will cost him about four sheep per minute."

Miss Louise's simple life had enabled her to squirrel away quite a lot of stuff. At the reading of the will, Melvin sat next to Elliott; his brother conferenced-in from New Zealand on the speakerphone, the lawyer's office overflowed. Half the town was jammed inside, barely room to move, having heard rumors that Miss Louise was loaded and was spreading the wealth.

"Looks like a flea market," Melvin described to his brother. "People everywhere. Stuff stacked floor to ceiling."

"God bless her!" boomed Mountain. "Nice of her to give it all to me."

"Um, that's not the way this works," Elliott replied delicately, smiling at the frowning townspeople who heard Mountain's comment. "You are here to help administer the will, to execute her final wishes."

"Bummer!" boomed Mountain. "Wanted my brother to have to pay to ship it. As long as I get the recipe for Possum Droppers, I'll be happy. You all can keep the rest."

The crowd murmured. Every woman in town was hoping she'd get the recipe.

Elliott progressed through the reading, and there seemed to be no rhythm or logic to the mementos' dispersal. Yet no one belittled the dead woman. Her heart was bigger than all the Outer Banks.

In typical Miss Louise fashion, she had attempted to leave something to everybody. Virtually everyone who had ever attended Possum Drop High received something, a token of emotional significance. Every single thing in her doublewide trailer was assigned to somebody. Everything, that is, except her famous Possum Dropper recipe, the one thing she had kept for herself.

Two hours and seven minutes after starting, nearly every thing had been cleared out, including several items of Elliott's that he didn't remember awarding as door prizes.

Only Elliott and Melvin remained, with Mountain still on the phone. It had been a very long call on very long distance from New Zealand . . . and that meant Mountain needed a bundle from Miss Louise just to break even.

"I am gettin' the recipe, ain't I?" he boomed over the intercom. "I ate thirty thousand of 'em, so I reckon I earned it."

Elliott slowly rubbed his eyes with both hands. "No, Mountain," he said into the speaker, "no one gets the recipe."

"You kept it, didn't you?" boomed Mountain. "Rip his ears off, Melvin. Then his arms and legs. You gotta find it," Mountain then begged. "Life ain't worth livin' without Possum Droppers."

"Please. Mountain, don't interrupt," scolded Elliott. "This is important stuff."

"Better be," said Melvin. "If it ain't, you've got six hundred pounds of aggravated farm boys to answer to."

"Miss Louise left you boys some money."

"*Cha-ching!*" cheered Mountain. "Baby's got new shoes!"

"But it's not for you," Elliott interrupted, clearly irritated as he continued. "She trusted you two to be the custodians of her life's savings."

"Why us?" Melvin wondered. "She had thousands of people to choose from.

Surely she knew how worthless my brother is."

"Mine, too," chimed in Mountain.

Elliott leaned forward, his tone firm. "It was a very big decision for her, one she agonized over for a very long time. She even researched people, what they'd done since leaving school, how they've lived their lives. Miss Louise was as thorough as anybody I've ever seen, far more than people with lots more money."

"And she still picked us?" asked Melvin, surprised.

Elliott nodded. "She made her final decision two weeks before she died. All she told me was that you are your father's sons, that you'd do what's right—that you wouldn't drink it all away."

"That's encouraging," boomed Mountain. "It's nice to be trusted by dead people."

"Shut up, Mountain," scolded Melvin. "Be respectful."

He turned to Elliott. "How much did she leave?"

"Not enough to fulfill her dying wish. She's trusting you two to make that dream come true."

"Please tell me it's enough to cover this call," Mountain's garbled voice squawked. "What does she want us to do?"

"Miss Louise dreamed of setting up a scholarship fund for disadvantaged kids to go to college. She dreamed they'd have options. She wanted to get them out of the fields and into classrooms. If they want to farm, she wants them to be educated farmers. But if they don't want to farm, she wants them to be educated, so they can do whatever they want in life."

"Wow!" Melvin mused. "A scholarship fund? Colleges cost a lot of money. How much did she leave?"

"That's the problem," Elliott said. "$32,373.29. She gave away her mobile home. It's all you've got to work with."

"I KNEW IT!" thundered Mountain. "I *knew* it wouldn't be enough to cover this call!"

"This call would've been over an hour ago if you'd quit interrupting," Melvin scolded. "That's a big-hearted gesture, Elliott, for sure. But thirty grand won't get even one kid through college these days, much less several, will it?"

"Correct."

"What are we supposed to do? Did she say?"

Elliott leaned way back in his chair, stretched his arms; then leaned way forward, his mouth inches from the telephone speaker. *"Parlay,"* he ordered. "Our dearly departed and much beloved Miss Louise is counting on you two to parlay her money."

Mountain's voice boomed. "How the hell are we supposed to do that? I can't even parlay two sheep into three. How do we parlay a dead woman's life savings into a scholarship fund for needy kids? How do we do that?"

"She figured you'd ask that," Elliott said. He handed Melvin a sealed envelope. On it in printed block capitals were the words: Parlay Instructions.

"Take this home and study it," Elliott said to Melvin. "You may use my fax to send the instructions to your brother."

Melvin grabbed Elliott's brass letter opener, knifed open the sealed envelope, and extracted four pages. He secured his brother's New Zealand fax number, then Mountain hung up, to stop the long-distance phone charges.

Melvin could hear Miss Louise's voice as he read her wishes in silence. From time to time, he winced. Finally, he closed his eyes, tilted his head back, and stretched his neck by rolling his head round and round. When he stopped and reopened his eyes, he broke into a broad smile.

Miss Louise had a plan.

On the grounds of Keeneland's famed horse auction arena, the only man ever to win the Kroger Bag-Off three years in a row danced alone as he mucked a temporarily vacant stall in Barn 6. An earpiece threaded through his shirt to the portable yellow music player on his hip. The relentless pounding rhythm of rapper Mo Munny helped the tall, thin twenty-year-old black man greet the Lexington sunrise. His head bobbed furiously as he raked.

Deacon Truth had arrived at Keeneland a week before the sale, having retired from the grocery business with nothing left to prove. Three times, he'd bagged contest groceries against all comers in Kroger Nation . . . and three times he'd whipped them all.

Deacon was proud of it. Beatin' 'em once was an accident, they said. The second time, a coincidence. But three times; three times in a row? Three times in a row is the absolute truth, brother. *Winning the Kroger Bag-Off three times in a row is the proof of truth. The Deacon Truth.* He grinned widely, his head nodding in affirmation.

Deacon Truth was two years removed from high school, which he proudly had finished without a police record. He had graduated number 360 of 364, and was the only senior in the history of Taft High to try out for freshman basketball; he had complained angrily when he got cut. *I offered leadership. Name one team that ever won a thing without leadership. Even the damn Pistons had leadership.*

He had not been a good student, but he had lots of street sense. Against all odds, Deacon had survived the hardscrabble upbringing in the baddest part of town—without getting shot, stabbed, framed, busted, or convicted. Twice he'd been picked up and released because he was black, tall, and thin. Cincinnati cops did that. Proving his innocence was the tax he paid for living in the hood.

Never afraid of working, Deacon started looking for a job the day he turned sixteen. He bounced around a couple of restaurants, bussing tables, washing dishes, until Kroger hired him the summer after his sophomore year. Ever talkative, it didn't take long before Deacon's chatterbox persona became as much a part of the store as its huge neon sign that hung out front.

Barely ninety days into his fledgling Kroger career, Deacon entered his first Bag-Off, for a very specific reason: the winner got $500, plus a huge trophy inscribed Mr. Cincinnati. No one in Deacon's family had ever won a trophy, so the trophy alone was a pretty good incentive. The Bag-Off challenge was simple: Each contestant had to race the clock to properly bag a variety of grocery items, for safe transport according to the principles of proper baggery.

Deacon shocked the Kroger nation by winning the regional finals by enough time to do a victory pirouette and celebratory split on the shiny wax floor before the final horn even sounded. He was pictured in the paper that way, dancing, along with the caption: *"Kroger names Mr. Cincinnati."*

Deacon took pride in the title and carefully printed it in big block letters in black magic marker along the crossbar of the bicycle he rode to and from work. One month later, he won the national title. He didn't trust the oversized ceremonial check and during the presentation ceremony asked to be paid in cash.

For a while, Deacon was happy working at Kroger. Everybody had to eat, so sooner or later all the pretty girls in the neighborhood would come through the checkout line. As a famous bagger, customer service was now Deacon's number one priority. He zoomed back and forth among the registers in a determined effort not to overlook a single beautiful lady. He missed very few. And he always carried a pretty girl's groceries to her car, even if she was in the "10 Items or Less" lane.

Charming as he was, dating cost money and neither Deacon nor a restaurateur considered forking over a fistful of dough a charmable situation. Romantic dinners did accelerate the love process, but money was always tight. Deacon's effervescent smile faded every time he stared through the candles at a big-haired date who ordered, then ignored two days of pay. He agonized when a nibbler pushed the fancy food around the plate with the silver fork, playing but not eating. Feigned fullness created a duel: his make-believe smile battling theirs. From his toes through his lungs to both steaming ears he wanted to bellow to the heavens, *"Who you tryin' to impress, girl? EAT IT! Eat that fancy-ass 24-carat fu-fu mystery meat or I'll ram it down your throat!"*

But he never said a word, not even when they ordered dessert and played with it, too. Order big, eat small, dab the corner of pursed lips with the linen tablecloth, and excuse herself to hide in the women's room to reapply six coats of fire truck red lipstick. Every time a nibbler strode away, Deacon ignored her long legs, curvaceous butt, and click-clacking stiletto heels. Instead he'd stare, transfixed, at eighty-percent of dinner untouched on her plate. These are the killers, the ones who tease, the ones who never surrender more than a handshake. Pretty girls demand more money than ugly girls. They knew it and he knew it. His was a paycheck-to-paycheck life and yet he kept making the same mistake, over and over and over again. The tease was an addiction and he was a romantic rube whose paycheck was always shot two days after receipt.

After his third consecutive national bagging championship won him only a fifty-cent raise, and his promotion to Assistant Store Manager was bypassed without so much as a serious interview, Deacon felt disrespected and his heart told him to move on. Before heading home to break the news to his domineering mother, Deacon hid behind a loaded stock-skid on aisle nine, popped opened two bottles of Advil, plucked out the cotton balls and plugged one in each ear, because quitting a great company at age twenty was not Momma's idea of Harvard. The cotton proved a good idea.

Early the next morning, Deacon plopped into the back row of a slow Greyhound bus and stared out the window ninety miles down I-75 from Cincinnati to Lexington. The horses were selling and, where there were horses, there would be rich white people. *Millions* of them. They would flood the auction grounds as far as his almond eyes could see. If there was one thing centuries of blackness has tattooed into society, it was that rich white people never had a problem paying poor black people to do things the rich white people didn't want to do. Surely there would be work for a young man willing to hustle.

When Deacon first stepped onto Keeneland's immaculate grounds, his jaw dropped. The place was an emerald paradise, thousands of acres perfectly manicured, bordered by endless straight lines of white four-board fences. To a Cincinnati city boy, sprawled before him was a botanical garden, dotted with countless massive oaks, their canopies soon to burst into full autumn color: red, yellow, orange, and brown. The view was the same in every direction.

Lookee here, he thought. *Lookee here what white money and black labor can team up to build: endless green, baby, in the yard and in the bank.*

Whistling, Deacon quickened his stride. He'd find work. He could smell it.

The guy who hired him was a white guy, no more than thirty, who wore a crisp, starched shirt. The fellow had a blonde buzz haircut and spoke with a slow Kentucky drawl.

Old money, Deacon thought. *Hires and fires. Never bagged at Kroger.*

"With 5,000 horses for sale," the man said, "for the next three weeks pitchforks will fly like pistons. It's hard work. Sunrise to sunset. You got a problem with that?"

Deacon shook his head. "Nossir."

"Most of the barn labor is Hispanic. Very few speak English. You got a problem with that?"

"Nossir," Deacon replied. "I love everybody."

"No booze, no smoking, no cussin', no drugs. You got a problem with that?"

"Nossir. I get high on life, sir."

"You be on time, work your ass off, and keep to yourself. Never piss off a looker. You got that?"

"Yessah, yessah, yessah," Deacon chanted, a trick he'd learned from an old Sidney Poitier movie. "I be all that and much more. All good things, sir. Work hard and earn my money, sir. Just like at Kroger. I won the Kroger Bag-Off three times in a row, sir. I'm Mr. Cincinnati. Got the trophy to prove it."

The man seemed unimpressed. "Well, Mr. Cincinnati," he grunted, "come meet your new dance partner." He waved at Deacon to follow him toward a storage shed, where the man pulled open a door, reached inside, and grabbed a long-handled rake. He tossed it to Deacon, who caught it on the fly.

"Here you go, Mr. Cincinnati," the man said. "Let's see you win Mr. Barn 6."

Barn 6 was one of the ten largest of the forty-nine spread around the Keeneland campus, close to the sales pavilion. Throughout the course of the auction, eighty percent of the horses that came through this barn would be gaveled down to new owners. By the sale's final yearling, Deacon would personally clean up after $38 million, paid for via wired funds from buyers on five continents. His take was considerably less.

Deacon knew nothing about the value of the yearling horses that surrounded him. All he knew was that they loved to poop, and seemed to do so the moment they stepped onto his freshly strewn straw. Grenade launchers where their guts oughtta be. The need to clean was relentless.

The sale yearlings didn't stay on the grounds long, three days tops, but they reminded Deacon of the kids at Taft High: unpredictable.

Some kicked at him, others bit him. One snatched the Reds baseball cap right off his head, then dropped it in the water bucket. Deacon let him keep it.

Most of the youngsters were well behaved when paraded for prospective bidders but a few didn't handle the commotion well and had unusual ways of showing it. One gray colt got physically excited every time he was led outside, way beyond anything Deacon had ever seen in the locker room. His eyes bugged out at the colt's prodigious masculinity. How does he run dragging *that* thing around?

The gray colt got no reward for showboating his masculinity. Posed in his overt state of macho virility, he could barely walk and couldn't demonstrate his gait. Nobody would write a six-figure check for a horse they couldn't see walk. The owner smacked the colt's dangling boyhood, first with the back of his hand, then with a stick. Deacon winced.

Through all the fuss and menial labor amidst the buzz of activity relentlessly swirling during very long days, Deacon remained upbeat. Being at Keeneland was like being allowed to browse in Cartier without the cops following you. Much to see, lots of girls, and tons to learn.

Deacon hustled through his chores, kept his eyes and ears open, and continuously processed the sights, sounds, and smells. He whistled while he worked, could out-chortle a mockingbird, although he'd lost a girlfriend once because her momma insisted that only crazy people whistled.

A lot of beautiful girls walked by Barn 6 and Deacon smiled at every one. Many were younger than their hundred-year-old escorts. The girls didn't seem to mind that the men's bodies had morphed into plump moneybags.

That first day, everybody delivering the horses was white. The second day, things changed. Deacon saw a real Arab sheikh up close, who arrived with an entourage of advisors and security. In two days the sheikh flew in, would spend $50 million, and fly back out. A million dollars an hour.

The day the sheikh stopped at Barn 6, he looked at three horses and eventually bought all three, including the one Deacon liked the best. The colt was a son of the legendary Storm Cat and the early buzz throughout the backside stables guessed on how many millions it would take to buy him if someone with deep pockets decided to take on the sheikh. Deacon didn't know much about horses but everything about this shiny, coal-black colt exuded class. The horse was doted over by an attending crew as if he were a movie star. The sheikh took one look at the impressive animal and nodded to his entourage. He spoke aloud the colt's future name—Albacoa, in honor of a famous oil field.

After the sheikh's visit, a whirling blizzard of relentless motion by the team's pre-sale makeup team filled the hours leading up to the colt's turn in the ring. When the mighty yearling was led from Barn 6 to the sale ring, Deacon joined the group for the processional march. The muscular colt was led inside and a noticeable buzz filled the air.

The sheikh sat in his customary seat, fifth row center, and didn't move until the ping-ponging bids of others reached three million dollars. Then he arched an eyebrow, an arch for another half-million.

Deacon was spellbound by the drama. *A hooker on Vine Street in Over-the-*

Rhine arches hers for twenty dollars!

During four minutes of spirited bidding, the sheikh arched early and often, until the gavel finally fell at $6.9 million. Albacoa was headed to the Middle East.

Even after the sheikh left, Barn 6 remained a very hot barn throughout the first week of the sale to billionaires and jetsetters, since the sale's best horses were front-loaded to sell during the first four days. Deacon watched a whole lot of ultra-rich white people spend hundreds of millions of dollars.

"It's like a fireworks show. Six digits, *seven* digits. The digits are dollars, Momma," he reported over the telephone. "The auctioneer talks so fast ain't nobody got a clue what he's sayin'. Spotters barkin' and wavin' like they're flaggin' down taxis. They're faster than street-corner dealers with the cops closin' in."

Then Deacon embellished the facts just a little further. "It cost one lady $10,000 to sneeze, Momma. When she covered her face, the floor man yelled out a bid." When his mother said nothing, Deacon laughed and kept on prattling. "It's amazing, Momma. There's horses here that have sold for more money than my old Kroger store made in a whole year."

His mother said, "That's nice, son. As soon as the sale ends, you crawl back to Kroger and beg for your old job back."

Though he was working fourteen-hour days, Deacon whistled when he started and was still whistling when he stopped. This was a good business and it beat stocking shelves. He liked meeting all the Barn 6 visitors, and he enjoyed trading small talk, especially with those who didn't treat him like a toad.

At the first streaks of sunrise on the morning of day four, Deacon was whistling his lungs out when two old men came by. It was barely six o'clock. One of the men was noticeably older. Deacon guessed 200. The younger had the long-wrinkled face of a cypress tree.

Both men were talking animatedly. Deacon smelled money. They weren't showy, but they were draped in nice threads and they both wore good shoes. He judged men by their shoes. Cheap guys wore cheap shoes; players wore limousines. The cypress tree's boots looked like ostrich and ostrich cost big money.

"You work here?" ostrich boots asked.

"That's a stupid question," the older man barked. "*Of course* he works here. It's six in the morning. He's in a barn. He's got horse dirt on his shoes and he's holding a dung shovel. Put the clues together, Einstein!"

The old fellow slowly extended a shaky hand to Deacon. "Sorry, my good man. My associate is off to a slow start this morning. Spending money does that to him, I'm afraid. It tightens up his brain. Sort of an allergic reaction."

The friend protested. "That was an ice-breaker, J. L. Just being polite."

Deacon laughed and shook the old man's hand. "I'm Deacon. Welcome to Barn 6."

"Glad to meet you, Mr. Deacon," the older man said. "My name's Cottle. The rocket scientist here is Moose Utley. We're from Boise. We don't want to talk to anybody yet. Just want to look at a couple of horses. Came early to skip the sales pitch."

Deacon leaned on his rake. "Sorry, Mr. Cottle. I ain't allowed to show the horses. Only the owners and their people can show them. If you come back at eight o'clock, they'll be here. That's when the showin' starts, eight o'clock."

Moose Utley persisted. "You don't need to take them out of the stalls. We just want to see them. The two we're interested in are both are in Barn 6, or so we're told. A chestnut colt by, I think, a son of Storming Cat. Hell, I forget his name—but I'll recognize it when I see it. The other's a bay colt by Looking for Gold or something Gold."

These clues didn't resonate to Deacon. "Well, there's signs on the stalls. If they're here, we'll find 'em. But all you can do is *look*, okay? My skinny black butt will be dropkicked to Cleveland if I mess with somebody's horse. All I mess with is *their* mess, if you know what I mean."

Cottle smiled. "We acquiesce to the rules of a civilized man," he said. "Looking is fine. We thank you for your kind assistance, Mr. Deacon."

"I don't know what acquiesce means," Deacon answered, "but if it has anything to do with touchin' 'em, you can't do it."

Cottle chuckled. "Moose doesn't know what it means, either," he said. "I like your candor, Mr. Deacon. You speak to be understood."

The trio slowly shuffled slowly down the long corridor of the barn's front row, examining each stall sign carefully. From the comments the old men exchanged, Deacon guessed that the pair knew more about horses than they let on. At the end of the row, Cottle paused in front of a stall where a curious brown horse stuck his head out to take a look.

The three men studied the colt's breeding chart. "Colt by Tale of the Cat," Deacon announced. "He's a bay, a grandson of Storm Cat. And Storm Cat is *money*. That much I know. Is this one?"

"Yes, yes," Cottle affirmed. "This is the one." He pushed Moose Utley aside. "Get out of the way so I can see him."

Cottle moved within a foot of the colt and stared intently at the young horse's profile, mapping it to memory. He stared a long time at the colt's right eye, but made no effort to touch the animal. The colt had large eyes, bright eyes, and he didn't flinch, which surprised Deacon. Most of these skittish youngsters were bottle rockets set to launch. This one was different. He had a calm demeanor that seemed to match the old man's personality.

With a shaky slow smack on the colt's shoulder, the old man got the colt to turn. "Nice rump," said the old man said. "Plenty of cushion for pushin'. He'll do, Mr. Deacon. I'll take him."

"He sells today," Deacon offered. "He goes in the ring around eleven."

The old man smiled. "I'll take him."

"You hafta take him now, Mr. Cottle. You ain't got no choice," Deacon replied.

"Why's that?"

"You acquiesced him. Is that how you say it? *Acquiesced*. You broke the rules. You touched him. Touch him, buy him, the code of the brotherhood."

Cottle smiled and turned slightly toward Deacon with a twinkle in his eye. "You slay the girls, don't you Deacon?"

"Only on payday, sir. But, yessir, I'm in the game on payday."

Deacon didn't doubt the very old man's intent to buy the brown colt but said nothing as the three turned the barn corner to search the long row of back side stalls for the second colt. When a man don't have a whole lot of time left on earth, he ain't gonna waste any lookin' at horses for no reason. Waking up before dawn to torment barn workers ain't why Old Money is here. No doubt that both these old guys are loaded.

The other horse the men wanted to see was in the far corner stall, a small black colt, the son of Seeking the Gold, a top stallion from famed Claiborne Farm. This horse, Deacon knew, was worth major dough. Two Seeking the Golds had already come through Barn 6 and each sold for a half-million. A colt by this stallion this far back in the sale was unusual.

Moose was relieved but impatient when they found him. "Finding, Seeking, Needing, Wanting, Paying More for Gold, whatever," he said with a dismissive wave. "I was told he's a looker. "

This black colt was the exact opposite of the first bay, small and ultra-skittish, and very high-strung. He neighed loudly, disapprovingly, as Moose stepped up for a closer look. Several other yearlings hollered, too, and rising commotion echoed through the barn. Scared, the little colt retreated to the back of the stall and stood motionless facing the corner.

"My God, he's gone!" Cottle needled. "He's hiding! Where'd he go? Behind a bale of hay?" Cottle was laughing so hard he could barely eke out the words.

Moose snorted in protest, then bravely announced, "Looks plenty good to me."

"Admit it, Moose," ribbed Cottle. "You have no clue what you're looking for."

Moose scowled. "I know *exactly* what I'm looking for," he barked. "I'm looking for a horse with a lot of heart that will finish one nostril in front of yours. This one will."

"Never!" Cottle teased. "For God's sake, man, lookit him. Box turtle legs and a cartoon body. I've got lawn gnomes taller than him."

"He's so small, the jockey will have to run alongside."

Deacon had to turn away to avoid laughing.

Moose squinted at Cottle and pointed toward the colt's facing posterior. "Tell it to his butt, Cottle," he urged. "The same view your jockey will have the day our two horses meet. You might know potatoes, but you wouldn't know a fast horse if he rang the doorbell with a trophy in his teeth."

Cottle motioned a crazy sign, circling his right temple with his index finger. "You're nutso, Moose-o. The only way you'll ever get a trophy out of this little pygmy is if I duct tape an extra one of mine to the crown of his head."

"In your dreams, Potato Head," groused Moose. "We'll have to double-back to find you."

"That the best you got, Moose? Wanna know what's funniest of all? The sight of all the spiders that'll go running once you dust off that cobwebbed checkbook of yours to pay for him. Watching you fork over the dough will be the highlight of my week. My year. My decade. My . . ."

"My, my, my, what a spirited debate," interrupted Deacon. "And it's barely six o'clock! The Marines ain't done the first pushup of the day and you two are already getting' after it like Fred and Ethel."

Both men laughed, and thanked Deacon for helping them find the horses. With a twinkling eye, Cottle pressed a $50 bill into Deacon's palm and made him promise to spend it on a pretty girl. "Whether it's horses or women, Mr. Deacon, a feller's gotta have *taw*."

Deacon stuffed the bill deep into his jeans pocket and fingered it as the visitors shuffled away in search of breakfast. Seven days ago he was loading groceries into beat-up Saturns for quarter tips and fake phone numbers. Here he was getting fifty dollars for pointing at horses. Sorry Mom, Kroger will have to wait.

He grabbed his rake and started whistling. Mr. Cottle was right. A man's gotta have *taw*.

Deacon decided to invite a hot Latina to help him spend his new fortune. Several prospects came to mind, topped by a young Columbian girl named Lolita over at Barn 12.

Later that morning, she agreed to go out after work and help Deacon invest his taw in a bit of human horsing around. Thanks to Mr. Cottle, Deacon had a mighty fine time dancing with Señorita Lolita. Best of all, he had enough *taw* left over so they could go out and dance some more the next night, too.

At lunchtime, one of the trainers he'd befriended explained to Deacon that all 5,000 horses in the sale fell somewhere within a bell curve of desirability. During the first few days, the super deluxe blueblood pedigrees were sold. Then the auction team worked its way back through the four-legged middle majority. The last few days would move out the back-end of the herd. When the final horse was sold and the last of the transactions settled, well over a third of a billion dollars would have changed hands.

"Once the big-money people with the two-comma checkbooks are gone, budget-conscious dreamers comb the stables in search of a gem," the trainer said. "Watch them. You'll see what I mean. They're all in search of the next Cañonero II."

"Cannon who?"

"Cañonero II," the trainer repeated. "He won the 1971 Kentucky Derby."

"What'd he cost?"

The trainer smiled. "Take a guess."

"Twenty grand."

The trainer smiled again. "Twelve hundred dollars, Deacon. The Derby champion, bought right here, for twelve hundred bucks."

Deacon whistled. "That's all? Shoot, that ain't much, is it?"

"No, it's not," the trainer said. "Nowadays, twelve hundred bucks won't cover the cost of a good seat to watch the race."

The first week of the sale came to a close and the trainer was right. The sheikh came, bought, and went, and soon the Rolls Royces in Keeneland's parking lot were gone, too, replaced by SUVs, eventually by sedans, then pickup trucks. As the first thousand yearlings passed through the ring, Deacon noticed that the average sale price steadily tapered off. One hundred thousand dollars was now a rarity, a good sale instead of a weak one.

As the prices slipped, Deacon took the trainer's advice and studied the change in clientele; the ultra-rich replaced by the very rich, then the simply rich, then the wealthy; finally the carefully conservative, the leveraged, the bottom feeders and the overextended. But their dreams remained the same. Sellers dreamed of top-dollar received, buyers of a star that emerges from its catalog page and gallops to history and a blinding fortune.

Deacon liked that about this business. Keeneland was selling dreams. The horses were the currency.

With the sheikh's prized Albacoa settled in his new home, munching hay in the Middle East, and Mr. Cottle and Moose Utley back in Idaho, sunrise at the barn quieted down. Deacon still had plenty of work, but a more comfortable routine allowed him to meet some of the repeat buyers who trolled the barns for every new wave of less expensive yearlings. Some of the visitors were outgoing and talkative; others quiet, only nodding hello. Some had their noses buried in their auction books scrutinizing the pedigrees; others wanted to inspect every animal. Some, finicky over the price they were willing to pay, scribbled cryptic notes inside their thick paperback auction guides.

"Agents and pinhookers," an old groom explained to Deacon. "Agents who buy for rich folks. They get a commission on what they buy. The pinhookers are different. They spend their own *jack*. Ain't near as much fun as spending the rich folks' money and getting paid to do it."

Deacon nodded. "Amen to that. How do I get a job like that?"

The groom shrugged. "I ain't figured it out in thirty years. When you do, come tell me. Owners are tough to find, especially good ones. If the agent overpays or pisses the owner's money away, even a dumb owner figures it out. We lose a lot of owners that way. Good ones who love the game and got stayin' power are scarce. It's a tough racket, Deacon. It's a lot tougher to make money in this business fair and square than it is by cheatin'. Cheatin's easy money. You know what that means."

Deacon nodded. "Lots of sharks," he said. "What about the pinhookers? What's their gig?"

"Gamblers," the groom answered. "They buy weanlings to sell as yearlings or yearlings to prep and resell as two-year-olds to owners who want to race right away. Pinhooking is a tough business." The groom leaned on his rake. "You can lose your ass and I mean your *complete* ass, Deacon."

"Why?"

"Everybody wants a pretty horse, Deacon. Pretty sells. But speed is what matters. You got to have speed. Ugly is equal to pretty once the stopwatch gets involved. A pretty horse that can't run ain't worth half a ugly one that can—and it don't matter *what* the pinhooker spent to buy the pretty one in the first place.

"Guess wrong and a pinhooker gets wiped out. Then again, guess right and they can make a year's worth of pay on one deal. Buy low, sell high, brother. Pinhooking for a livin' takes balls. It's a four-legged crap shoot."

"How many of my Barn 6 horses been bought by pinhookers?"

The old groom stroked his chin. "Hmmm . . . You never know for sure," he said, "but after the first few days it's probably one out of four, maybe one out of three. The rich people buy first. They keep theirs to race. Then the regular people show up. They need to make a buck. They buy to resell."

The groom paused for a moment and nodded toward a nearby family of four inspecting at a chestnut filly. "Owners are everything," he said. "Never forget that, brother. The horses are great, the jockeys are great, the trainers are great; the horny little groupie girls are extra-great . . . but without owners there ain't nothing here but empty stalls and we'd all be bagging groceries for a living."

Deacon's eyes widened. "Baggin' groceries? I'd rather ride a goat to K-Mart than bag groceries."

The groom laughed. "We better get back to work or we might be ridin' double."

In only seven days, Deacon Truth was already a million miles from his career in the food-service industry. He took the groom's advice and made extra effort to be nice to prospective owners. Hundreds of millions of dollars were flying through this place. There had to be an angle for him to grab a tiny sliver of the action.

The next day, returning from an afternoon trip to the snack shop and sucking on an orange Tootsie Roll pop, Deacon spied an unusual-looking couple across the way in front of Barn 7, eyeing a bay colt with a white star on its forehead. The Asian woman looked fabulous, so Deacon sauntered over to say hello.

The man next to her was squat and powerfully built. His bald head glistened under in the Indian summer sun. He wore an expensive charcoal-gray, double-breasted suit, with all the buttons buttoned, a stiffly starched white shirt and red tie. Good shoes, too, fine black leather with a radiant shine. The shoes looked Italian. The man looked very familiar.

"Good afternoon," Deacon said cheerfully, pointing his orange lollipop toward the couple as he walked up. "You're Telly Savalas, ain't ya? I love *Kojak*, man. Watch it all the time. You love lollipops, too, don't ya? Or is that just actin'? I got a grape, if you want one." As he spoke, Deacon quickly fished for his extra lollipop. As he did so, he never took his smiling face off the Asian woman. She was a perfect ten. He'd fumble for a month if it meant he could stare at her longer.

The perspiring bald man paid little attention. "You have me mistaken. My name is Bonk, Otto Bonk."

"Apologies, Mr. Bonk. My bad. Come to think of it, you don't look nothin' like him. He's fat, you got muscles. You dress better, too. We got nice horses in Barn 6, too, if you'd like to see them."

"No, no," Bonk said impatiently, waving Deacon off. "This one. Only this one."

Deacon thought the man's abrupt manner was rude; as if Bonk confused a friendly black man's social pleasantries with a sneaky soft-sell sales pitch. He ignored Bonk's curt dismissal and pointed his lollipop toward the colt. "Who is he?" He smiled broadly at the Asian beauty as he asked, hoping she might answer.

"Niño de Siphon," the attending groom answered in Spanish. "He by Siphon. *Brasil*, Siphon. Good Brasil horse, Siphon bueno."

Deacon just nodded. This was a stocky, powerful colt. If horses played football, this one would be a linebacker. Deacon whistled long and low to show his admiration.

"Why this one, Mr. Bonk?" Deacon asked. With 2,000 fillies and colts left to choose from, Deacon was curious why this man was so zeroed in on this particular yearling.

Bonk, on the other hand, was irritated the motormouthed black kid was bugging him. He ignored Deacon, instead asking the groom to walk the colt a second time. As Bonk ignored him and studied the colt's easy, ambling gate, Deacon decided that the reason the couple was considering this particular horse was because Bonk's wife told him to.

The woman, tiny and immaculately dressed, remained silent. Deacon took a good long look, wishing she'd lift her eyes to his. She had perfect posture, her face partly hidden under an elegant, flowing hat. She wore a custom-tailored pink suit trimmed in white, and was smothered in jewelry. *This lady wouldn't get ten feet in the hood. She'd be somebody's 401-K.*

Bonk nodded to the handler that he'd seen enough. As the groom returned the colt to his stall, the woman whispered something to her husband that Deacon couldn't hear.

Deacon wished the couple a polite farewell and ambled back to Barn 6, where he sat in the shade and slowly sucked his lollipop. Bonk and the woman left soon after.

The next day, Deacon watched the Siphon colt being boarded inside a horse trailer. The couple had paid $80,000 for him, tricked into a fake bidding war against team bidders planted by the seller. Deacon whistled. The colt wasn't worth half that much.

"It happen," shrugged the groom who'd showed Bonk the horse. "Money. Always money. Money make men do bad things to each other they no do weethout the money."

Deacon nodded. "You're right. Taw ain't got no conscience. Taw makes sinners out of church-goin' people."

Day by day, Deacon Truth's fascination with the horse business grew. Money flew everywhere, and a superstar horse could emerge from any stall. While the best ones usually sold during the first couple of days, he heard a hundred stories of great ones that slipped back into the middle of the auction.

Anxious to learn, every answer spawned a dozen more questions and he chatted up virtually anyone who would talk, including a wrinkled old leather-necked trainer from California named Rigby Malone. Malone was in Lexington for the duration of the sale and came by the barn often, since every three days brought a new wave of horses to inspect. Over an early breakfast, he explained to Deacon more about Keeneland and this sale's importance to the history of the sport.

"A weanling is still a baby, Deacon. Colts and fillies grow and develop quite a bit between their weanling and yearling season. People buy on promise. Same holds true for the birthday after that, which is doubly important because that's the year the money starts. People pay for runners at two. When they're three, things really heat up."

"How come?" Deacon asked, as he tried, unsuccessfully, to reach across and spear one of Malone's sausages. The trainer deftly blocked him.

"Because three-year-olds race for fame. Five thousand yearlings sell through this auction ring in fifteen days, Deacon; one-seventh of all the foals registered the year this crop was born. The majority of good and great ones are *here*. But just one will emerge. Only one will be the best three-year-old on the first Saturday in May. Derby Day. The Kentucky Derby changes lives, Deacon. It's why this business exists."

"How else besides the taw, Rig? Money I understand. What else matters?"

"Way beyond the money is the fame, Deacon. Immortality. Winners live forever. Frozen in time, forever young. Draped in a blanket of roses that capes the soul."

"That's a pretty poetic thing for a hardboot like you to memorize, Rig," teased Deacon. "You eatin' that sausage or hidin' it in your pocket to impress somebody?"

Malone ignored his young companion and kept talking, comparing Keeneland and its horse auctions to Yankee Stadium and the World Series.

"Once you decide to trade sausage for books and read the history of American horse racing, you'll learn that most of the greats have passed through *these* gates." He recited a roll call of historic sales graduates. "Secretariat, Seattle Slew, Affirmed, Citation, Whirlaway, War Admiral. They all walked these grounds. Keeneland isn't located off Man o' War Drive for nothing."

"I didn't know Man o' War was a horse," admitted Deacon. "I was wonderin' about that. Couldn't understand why they'd named the road after a jellyfish. Can I have your toast?"

Malone surrendered the toast. As Deacon munched, he thought about the people who scooped up after all of those famous horses. Maybe one day he would brag about Albacoa, the sheikh's horse. Surely some of those who looked after the legends were ambitious, like him. Maybe they went on to graduate from day labor and pipe dreams to nice shoes, sleek cars, and swimming pool homes. That's what he dreamed of. He didn't interrupt as the old trainer droned on and on. Rigby had made his already. He lived in L. A. in a fancy house with more fine art than wall space. No way Rigby knew what it was like to be young, black, and from Taft High, 360th out of 364 in your class, mucking stalls for chump change a day.

As the sale slid into its final week, endless cavalries of nervous young horses still clip-clopped all over the place. With plenty to do, more to learn, and endless processions of new folks to meet, Deacon schmoozed a lot of owners and trainers, hoping to find permanent work.

The auction's final wave of horses vanned in three days before the sale's completion. Rigby Malone had taught him the fundamentals of conformation and Deacon learned to recognize which horses would bring decent money, and which ones wouldn't. One in Barn 6 seemed retarded. When Deacon dropped its lead rope, the horse stopped. Deacon could've gone to dinner and a movie, come back and the colt would still be there. It was none of Deacon's business to mention this to potential buyers so he never said a word. The colt showed well. He was handsome and obedient. Since the horse didn't take an I.Q. test as a condition of sale, the new owner wouldn't learn of his unique behavioral peccadillo until after the check cleared. *Caveat emptor,* brother. Buyer beware.

Despite the noticeable drop-off these final days, waves of lookers still milled around, giving each horse a sniff; everyone looking for a bargain.

Rigby Malone swung by for a second look at a short, powerful bay filly. "No, no, no," he judged. "Pretty little girl, but back at the knee. Wouldn't outrun you, Deacon."

Deacon didn't say a word. He might not look it, but he was fast.

Then Rigby noticed a big, gangly midnight-black colt in the stall beside the filly and asked Deacon to pull him out and walk him. The colt had big feet, three were white. He was tall but strode easily.

"Big horse, big engine," said Rigby as Deacon walked the colt past. He shielded the sun with his white cowboy hat and intently watched the colt move.

Deacon returned the horse in front of Rigby and posed him. Rigby flipped through his guidebook to check the pedigree. A foreign horse, fossilized parents, shrouded in anonymity. If the colt couldn't fly like Pegasus, he'd have zero commercial value. Pass.

Rigby Malone had been around horses his whole life, fifty years in the business. He'd seen 2,000 horses during this sale. A couple hundred he studied more closely. From them, he would bid on eight or ten. He might buy three, or none at all. He wouldn't compromise on what he wanted.

"Experience forces you to say no," he told Deacon. "Projecting what a horse will be like in two years is never easy. Sometimes you guess right. Most of the time not, no matter how picky you are, which tells you how damn difficult a business this is."

"How do guys survive?" asked Deacon.

"The industry feeds on the money of the impulsive and the stupid, Deacon. Quick wallets feed the slow wallets, if you know what I mean."

Deacon nodded. "Back home we call that *yourn*. What's mine is mine and what's *yourn* is mine."

"Precisely," nodded Rigby. "Gotta run, brother. More barns to cover, a hundred more to scout." He said goodbye and hustled off.

In many ways, Deacon thought the man was like himself, only older, fatter, and whiter. Rigby Malone was a people reader, his life a blend of street smarts and baseline thoughts. They talked easily, every conversation natural, unforced. The old trainer even remembered Deacon's name, and Rigby Malone never remembered names. He called every man "Roland" and every woman "Honey."

Although Rigby didn't plan to bid on anything out of Barn 6, whenever he passed by he waved. Once he whistled. Deacon waved back and whistled even louder, mimicking Rigby's note precisely, which made Rigby laugh.

By the next-to-last day the auction had blown through $350 million worth of horses and empty stalls remained empty because no more horses arrived to fill them. The crooked-legged filly Rigby Malone had dismissed brought only $6,500. The owner gladly took it. She was gone from the grounds an hour after the gavel fell. Deacon started asking around if any of the local farms needed help. Several did, but preferred experienced grooms. Deacon remained upbeat and optimistic. All he needed was one person to say yes.

Unfortunately, he had lots of time to ask. Barn 6 was nearly empty.

12
NAPKIN MATH

Deacon's workload wound down as the sale neared its end. Since the big black colt in his barn was slated to be ninth from last to sell, Deacon would still be working right up to the sale's final day. No one had asked to see the New Zealand colt since Rigby had taken a look.

To pass the time, Deacon started talking to the goofy, inquisitive yearling. Some of the horses hid in their stalls and slept. Others nervously paced. Not this guy. He was wide-eyed and alert, always watching the action around him. *At least he's not a retard,* thought Deacon.

No taw in his wallet, tapped out until payday, and Miss Lolita still hadn't learned English; so there was nowhere to go or reason to leave early. Deacon stuck around, whistling and working as the once-bustling stable area darkened into evening's quiet.

Five minutes after the security spotlights turned on, a giant-sized man with wild, disheveled strawberry blonde hair walked up to Barn 6, accompanied by his wife. The fellow looked about thirty-five and stuck out his hand, a massive paw twice the size of Deacon's, with a powerful, bone-grinding shake that caused Deacon to wince.

Damn, these white guys need to learn some brother shakes. Brothers don't try to hospitalize each other. Unless it's a gun sayin' hello.

"Howdy, my friend. Melvin Trombley's the name," the giant said with a warm southern drawl. "This here's my wife, Shelley. Sorry we're late."

"We're from North Carolina," Shelley added. "Drove the whole way non-stop."

"Except for potty breaks," Melvin corrected. "Hers mostly," he added, nodding toward his wife.

Shelley shot him a withering look.

"Everybody stops for 'em," Deacon replied. "White and black, rich and poor. A universal necessity, especially all the way from North Carolina. It's uphill. Uphill makes you go, too."

"It does?" asked Melvin. "No wonder my wife had to go so much."

"I'm sure she kept stoppin' to break up the drive. Women are smart that way. Guys, shoot, we drive from here to Mars, never stop, kidneys explode before we stop. Girls are smarter than that."

Shelley smiled at Deacon for defending her. "We're here to buy a horse in the memory of our late Miss Louise."

"She's a famous cafeteria worker back home," Melvin added. "She cooked special biscuits. You got a fast one here we can look at?"

Hold on to your wallets, Mr. and Mrs. North Carolina. You are exactly what Rigby Malone was talkin' about.

Deacon walked the Trombleys through Barn 6 and showed them the five remaining horses, three fillies and two colts.

"Which do you like best?" Melvin asked Deacon.

Deacon scratched his head. "Well," he said slowly, not telling them he didn't know much more than how to clean up after their business ends, "I'm partial to the big black colt with the white feet. He's my favorite."

"How come?"

"He's got a personality. From New Zealand. He neighs funny."

"Neighs funny?"

"Just kiddin'."

Melvin pondered the news. "My brother lives in New Zealand. I thought they only had sheep over there?"

"Down there," his wife corrected.

"Whatever." The giant man continued. "Miss Louise didn't mention anything about New Zealand in her instructions."

"How much will he bring?" Shelley asked Deacon.

Deacon shrugged. "Prob'ly not much. When people look a lot, they pay a lot. When they don't, they don't. Ain't nobody been lookin' at him. He and me have spent more time alone than most married couples."

Melvin juggled the auction book and multi-page letter from Miss Louise. "Here he is." He pointed to the colt's page in the auction book, but confusion clouded his face. "You know what all this stuff means?" he asked Deacon. "This horse junk and breeding stuff? It's hieroglyphics to me."

Deacon looked at the book, then up at Melvin and shrugged. "Ain't a clue. Come back in the mornin'. I'll find somebody to help you."

Melvin stuck out his massive hand again to Deacon, who winced at the thought of what was coming. "Well, thank you, sir. We appreciate your kindness."

As Melvin crunched Deacon's hand, Shelley poked her husband in the ribs. He grunted, reached into his pants pocket, pulled out a crumpled $5 bill, and gave it to Deacon.

Deacon grabbed the bill left-handed and shoved it into his pocket. "Thank *you*, Mr. and Mrs. Trombley." He'd remembered their name, which caused Shelley to smile. "Enjoy your evenin'," he added. "I'll be here all day tomorrow. Feel free to come back for another look. They look faster in the sunlight."

"They do?" asked Shelley.

"Just kiddin', ma'am." Deacon laughed. "Horse joke. Where you guys stayin'?"

"The Fairfield Inn," replied Shelley. "Know where it's at?"

Deacon nodded. "Close by. Downhill all the way. Ten minutes, tops."

After the short drive to the hotel, the Trombleys shared a six-pack of Miller Light and a delicious dinner of radiator chicken, cooked in tin foil with Idaho potatoes, onions, and carrots. Melvin turned on the hotel TV, but Shelley had a better idea and turned it off.

The next morning, the pair rose early in a great mood. Shelley wanted to hustle back over to Keeneland at first light but her early start forced Melvin to miss the hotel's free continental breakfast. Facing the choice of a full day or a wasted half-hour while waiting for a free donut, Shelley dragged Melvin by the ear to the car. Miss Louise's dream and the hopes of a whole town were riding on their decision. She had no intention of screwing up because Melvin was too tight to pay a buck for pastry.

Deacon didn't hear them approach. His music player was cranked up to *Mo Munny*. The sun was barely up and he was engrossed in his work, whistling.

Shelley walked up from behind and tapped him on the shoulder. Startled, Deacon whirled around, rake at the ready. When he saw it was the Trombleys, he greeted them warmly. "Yo, Trombleys! Good mornin' to *you*. Welcome back! What's with you early birds today? You are the third ones come lookin' already."

Shelley was surprised. "But it's barely six o'clock."

"Right," chimed in Melvin. "Six o'clock. When most normal people would be eating a free breakfast."

"Rigby Malone came by," Deacon said importantly. "A big-time trainer from California. Went off to get coffee. Said he'd be back later. A pinhooker from Florida, too. Beady-eyed like a weasel, dressed bad—like a refugee from the Poconos. Hooked a fish in the bar last night. Got new-owner jingle to spend but didn't say how much. I never trust beady-eyed guys with cheap shoes. He wore cheap shoes. When you're walkin' around, if you see a weasel dressed in cheap shoes, that's him."

Melvin quickly glanced down, as did Shelley and Deacon. Melvin wore cheap shoes. He had very large feet and these were comfortable. They'd also been on sale.

"I like *your* shoes," Deacon assured Melvin quickly. "Yours is nice shoes. Very nice shoes. Weasel-eyes wears cheap *ugly* ones. Not half as nice as yours, Mr. Trombley."

After the backpedaling extrication, Deacon quickly switched topics. "How many horses you like so far? Today's the last day. Ain't no more after this."

Shelley nodded. "We do have a decision to make. Right, Melvin?" She stared at him until he nodded too. She asked Deacon, "Which horses did the others look at?" She lowered her voice, leaned over close, and whispered, "I don't want to get in a bidding war, but if we have to, we will. We have thirty *thousand* dollars." After revealing her secret, Shelley pulled back and solemnly nodded.

Deacon whistled long and low, but he didn't say a word. He didn't have the heart to say that thirty grand might be a ton in Possum Drop, North Carolina, but here people spent that much for wine.

Melvin interrupted. "Anywhere around here to eat?"

"I'm sorry, Deacon," Shelley apologized. "Melvin's always hungry. He eats like a hog in a trough."

Deacon pointed toward a water tower two-hundred yards away. "Over there. Backside cafeteria, where the workers eat. Introduce yourselves to Rigby Malone. Rig's an old, burly dude with a tanned wrinkled face and short sandy hair. He's wearin' a beat-up white cowboy hat that's been stuck on his head since the seventies. Tell him I sent you. He might help you out."

They walked off to hunt pastry, Melvin faster than Shelley. Deacon watched them until they disappeared from view.

This would be a long and bittersweet day. He'd get paid at the end of it but Deacon hated to see this gig end. As he mucked out the big black colt's stall, he whistled *Taps*.

Melvin waited for his wife at the cafeteria door. They entered just as Rigby Malone was finishing an off-color joke to a circle of men he obviously knew. The group exploded in laughter at the punch line, just as the couple approached.

Timing right for a perfect exit, the old horseman broke from the group and stepped into line for a cup of black coffee. He reached for a white Styrofoam cup, and Melvin and Shelley each pushed the other toward him.

"Pardon me, sir," Shelley said, tapping him gently on the elbow, "are you Mr. Malone?"

Rigby didn't recognize them but nodded.

"Mr. Deacon sent us. Said you might help us sort through some horses this morning?"

Rigby sized them up, pausing briefly to look at Melvin's shoes, which were gigantic. "What are those boats?" he asked with a nod. "Eighteens?"

"Nineteens," Melvin said. "Ain't easy to find good ones without spending a whole lot of money."

"Same with a horse, my friend," Rigby said. "Deacon sent you? It'll cost you a coffee." His hand paused over the cups; the size would depend on who was buying.

"We can handle that," Melvin said enthusiastically. Rigby grabbed a large.

On a small tray, Melvin carefully balanced their three coffees and three sprinkle-covered chocolate donuts. They sat at a corner table by the east window. Visible in the distance were a dozen young horses, each being groomed for the sale's final day.

Rigby found the Trombleys a likeable pair who knew nothing about Thoroughbreds. They were pigeons. They'd run wherever he scattered the seed. Since Deacon had sent them, he would help.

On a paper napkin, he gave the Trombleys a quick schooling in equine mathematics: the expenses connected to buying a yearling at auction, developing him, and getting him to the starting line late in his two-year-old season. He explained item after item and their smiles grew tighter and tighter. Everything he listed was a direct subtraction from Miss Louise's nest egg. The balance remaining was rapidly shrinking.

When Rigby flipped the napkin over to gain more space to write, Melvin and Shelley looked at each other worriedly. By the time he finished, he'd estimated that they had about $12,000 to buy a horse.

"But you gotta take him out of state," Rigby added. "Out of state you can duck the sales tax. Otherwise, deduct another $700 or so."

The Trombleys sat stonily silent and stared at the napkin. Rigby had used big block numbers, easy-to-read, and each one screamed. The total at the bottom, he had underlined twice and circled. *$12,000*. It would cost more to get Miss Louise's horse ready to race than they could afford to pay for him in the first place.

Rigby watched his new friends closely. "Everybody new to the business is shocked by its expenses," he said gently. "But racing has an economic reality, a right of passage. No sense sugarcoating what you're getting into. There's a reason it's called the sport of kings. It ain't for the average Wal-Mart shopper.

Horseracing has turned a lot of billionaires into millionaires, and millionaires into working men.

"Million-dollar horses cost the same to keep as cheap ones," he continued. "It's upside-down to you, because you don't have a million to spend on a horse. But regardless what you spend on a horse to enter the business, don't kid yourself. It ain't no nickel game. It's a dollar game. It's horse racing, not dog racing; and it takes a whole lot of dollars to play. *Wheelbarrows* full."

He smiled gently at Shelley, who looked near tears. "Speed costs money, honey," he said softly. "The thing we're trying to figure is, how fast can you afford to go?"

"It looks like $12,000 worth of fast, Mr. Malone," she answered quietly.

Melvin picked up the napkin and stared at it for several seconds, then folded it and gently placed it inside his shirt pocket and looked at the trainer. "You're shootin' straight, right? Ain't perfumin' the pig?"

Rigby nodded. "Bank on it."

"Then let's go find the fastest $12-grand sum-gun out there," Melvin said and stood. "Shaken but undeterred, we shall persevere." He leaned down and kissed his wife on the forehead. "C'mon, Shel. Let's prove Miss Louise trusted the right folks."

The three adjourned to patrol the barns in search of a horse they might be able to buy for the money they had left to spend.

As they walked, Rigby explained the challenge they faced with such a limited budget. "You won't get a superstar. Everything we look at will have flaws. But we'll find the best $12,000 horse we can, one that has something to work with."

Three hours later, following a morning-long cram course in horse-ology, Melvin and Shelley were cross-eyed from looking at yearlings. All the horses looked the same, until Rigby explained things the couple hadn't noticed.

"How do you do this, Rigby?" Melvin asked. "I mean, day after day, horse after horse, sale after sale? You must see a billion horses."

"I love it Melvin, that's how I do it. I love everything about it. Being right, guessing wrong, seeing something in a horse other smart guys miss. Watching them grow into champions and proving me right, and smiling in the winner's circle. It's my life, Melvin. I can't imagine anything else. I pity the suits. I really do."

At ten a.m. it was time for Rigby to skeedaddle off to meet a client. Onto the back of his business card, he scrawled five hip numbers and handed it to Shelley. "Here you go. The auction numbers of the ones I'd bid on, in numerical order. Don't get carried away on any of them," he warned. "It's easy for first-timers to get suckered into overspending. *Don't*. Picking a horse is part science and part art. What it *ain't* is emotional. Never let emotion poke a hole in your savings account."

Then he looked straight at Melvin. "That's doubly true for you, big fella."

Melvin looked at Shelley. "We'll not get in a bidding war with anybody."

Shelley laughed. "Bidding war? We don't have enough for a skirmish."

Rigby nodded. "Good. Each of these five yearlings has pluses and minuses. Start with the first one and hope you get it. If not, move to the second. If not, try for the third. Same for the fourth. Bid your limit, then stop.

"These five are the only ones selling here today that you want," he added. "If you get one, great. If not, that's okay. You're always better off saving your dough than blowing it. There are always other horses." Rigby politely doffed his weather-beaten cowboy hat, shook hands, took a deep bow, and sauntered away.

Rigby disappeared around the corner, and Melvin let out a deep exhalation. "Wow! Are we lucky, or what?"

"Not yet, we aren't," Shelley warned. "We have less than an hour before the first of these five goes into the ring, and we've still got stuff to do."

The Trombleys established their credit account with the Keeneland business office, then stood motionlessly at the back of the nearly-empty auction arena, like Chinese Terra Cotta Warriors. The first of the final day's 400 horses entered the ring, an average-looking filly by a stallion named Louis Quatorze. She sold within minutes for $9,800. When the gavel fell, Melvin dug his elbow into Shelley's ribs. This might work out after all. However, in quick succession the next three horses went for more than $12,000, one for $39,500, which was a crushing blow to their optimism.

"What the heck?" whispered Melvin. "That one ain't even on our list. I'm worried," he added.

"Have another donut," Shelley hissed back.

Thirty minutes later, the first horse on Rigby's list was led into the brightly lit auction oval. And Shelley poised for action. This was a gray colt by a stallion named Skip Away. They remembered what Rigby had said when they watched him walk this morning. "Skippy's horses don't get respect in the sales ring, but Skip Away was a runner," she repeated. "Rigby said he was a real competitor. That's what he told us to look for: a horse with a good body and the genes of a competitor."

For whatever reason, the bidding on this colt was slow and the auctioneer had to back it down to $2,000 to get started. That was never a good sign if you were selling, but wonderful news if you were buying. Four people in the crowd seemed willing to get involved. In $500 increments, the figures on the tote board inched up to $9,500, then slowed.

Melvin, caught in the moment, suddenly waved both arms and hollered, *"Twelve thousand dollars!"* He was so excited, so wildly animated with enthusiasm, that everyone in the place turned to look. Even the auctioneer commented into the microphone that finally a man of equine expertise had seen in this horse what the others had not. A woman in the front row figured Melvin must know something and raised her hand.

"$12,500 in the front," the auctioneer reported. "Back to you, sir. Thirteen?"

The crowd turned to see if Melvin was going to bid $13,000. Instead, they saw his wife ball her fist and punch him in the meat of his upper arm.

"OWWWW!!!" He grimaced.

"I take that as a no," the auctioneer called out. Moments later the horse was gaveled down for $12,500 to the lady up front.

And so it went. During the next several hours, the Trombleys were outbid three more times. They were down to the final horse on Rigby's list. Since he was selling near the end of the sale, they left the arena to stretch their legs and visit the restroom. In the hallway, an elderly woman came up and touched Shelley on the wrist. "Lovely punch, dear. Made my day."

Melvin unconsciously rubbed the arm where his wife had slugged him, while Shelley thanked the woman for her compliment.

After sharing a small soda, they walked back to Barn 6 to take one final look at the last horse on Rigby's list. Melvin broached the idea that maybe they should raise the ceiling on what they were willing to spend. They could cut expenses on the trainer or where they boarded the horse. If they didn't buy something, they'd have wasted their time and a whole bunch of money driving all the way out here for no reason. And they'd still have Miss Louise's dying wish to deal with. Not doing something a living friend asked you to do was one thing; disrespecting the final wishes of a deceased town icon was something neither of them wanted to contemplate.

Shelley dismissed the idea. "We can't cut expenses, Melvin. It is what it is. Rigby said $12,000. Not one dime more."

When Melvin kept whining, she stopped and looked at him. "You can raise the figure under one condition, Melvin. Anything more than $12,000, *you* have to come up with. How much extra you got, Mr. Wall Street?"

Melvin emptied his wallet and pockets. "$116.42." He looked at her with a pitiful visage. "Can you cover the gas home?"

"Sheesh Almighty, Mother was right!" Shelley rolled her eyes. "*Yes,* Melvin! But only if you load up on free donuts before we check out of the hotel. If I pay for gas, there's no money for food. It's your call, moneybags."

"I'm using the extra $116.42."

"Don't start whining when you get hungry, or so help me God I'll pull the car over and kick you out." She ended the debate with the look only a wife could deliver.

They arrived at Barn 6, which was nearly empty. Out front, Deacon was brushing the tall gangly colt with the three white stockings. For the sale's final day, Deacon had been promoted to groom.

The horse stood placidly and never flinched. Deacon worked quickly, whistling softly, brushing every square inch of the black hair. He didn't waste time on the back end, since the colt had a bob tail rather than a full-length one.

"Hey, Deacon," Melvin greeted. "Remember us?"

"Sure do, Mr. and Mrs. Trombley. Got one yet?"

Shelley shook her head. "No luck so far. Mr. Malone gave us five to bid on. We missed out on the first four. The last one's here in your barn. The black colt with the white feet."

"This is him," Deacon said. "Wanna brush?"

Shelley looked surprised. "How do you know? I didn't tell you the number."

"He's the only one left," Deacon said. "And he's black with white feet. Must be the one. How much you got to spend on him? Thirty thousand, right? You'll get him for that."

"Twelve thousand, Deacon," Shelley replied.

"Plus an extra hundred and sixteen if we need it," Melvin added. "The rest Mr. Malone said to save for expenses."

Deacon whistled low and long. "You want the five back that you gave me last night? I'll give it back if it helps."

"No, that's okay," Shelley answered with a smile. "You keep it."

Deacon was glad, because he'd already spent it. "That weasel guy is gonna be on him. He came by a third time, 'bout an hour ago."

"How high will he go, Deacon?" Melvin asked, glancing at Shelley. She looked concerned. Returning to Possum Drop empty-handed would cause more gossip than they cared to create.

Deacon shrugged. "He didn't say. Maybe he likes this one 'cause he thinks nobody else is lookin'."

Melvin pointed at the horse's butt. "His tail's gone. Where'd it go?"

"No tellin', Mr. Trombley. He ain't never had a swisher since he's been here. But look on the bright side, it's one less thing to slow him down."

Melvin nodded. This kid sure knew a lot about horses.

When the time came to walk the colt over, they all went together. The

Trombleys' hearts thumped, but the yearling acted like he couldn't care less. He ambled along, flipping back and forth his stubby little tail and swinging his head side-to-side so his bright wide eyes wouldn't miss a thing.

Less than fifty people were sitting in the bidding arena when the colt entered the ring. Deacon nodded toward a man in a plaid jacket near the center aisle. "That's Weasel Eyes. If you can get past the jacket, check out his shoes."

The auctioneer started low. This time, Melvin let Shelley do the bidding since she thought the best strategy was acting like you didn't care about getting the horse. She made her husband promise to shut up and sit on his hands.

Three people bid and the price quickly ran from $5,000 to $10,500, then stalled. The third bidder, a girl with mousy blonde hair in her early twenties, dropped out when Weasel Eyes bumped it up to $11,000. Shelley offered up a $100 increment, which did little to chase off the inconvenient man in the ratty jacket. After ping-ponging back and forth a c-note at a time, Weasel Eyes loudly announced he was going $12,000.

The Trombleys looked at each other. Melvin's boot-heel was pounding the floor like a piston. He dug into his jeans, pulled out his pocket money, and waved it high in the air. *$12,116.42!"* he boomed.

"Now *there's* a commitment we rarely see in the ring," deadpanned the auctioneer. "We have a bid for $12,116 and how many cents? Forty-two cents? Dare anyone go higher?

"Going *once*," he dramatically intoned. "Going *twice*." He picked up his gavel. Shelley excitedly squeezed Melvin's arm. They were going to win!

"Twelve-three," Weasel Eyes called out. "I'm in for twelve-three."

Melvin's gasp sounded like a highway blowout.

The auctioneer looked at the Trombleys. "We have a bid for $12,300," he called. "Are there any others?"

Melvin looked balefully at his wife to stay in. She dug her nails into his forearm, and he assumed the broken skin meant no.

"Twelve-thousand, three hundred dollars, going *once* . . ." the auctioneer said slowly, "Going *twice* . . ."

"Twelve-five," boomed a different voice two rows behind the Trombleys.

The voice sounded familiar, so they turned around to see. Rigby Malone; and sitting next to him, laughing, was Deacon Truth.

The Trombleys stared at Rigby wide-eyed.

"Nice biddin', Mr. Trombley," Deacon chortled. "Way to confuse the other guy."

"I'll take it from here," Rigby whispered to Shelley. Then he looked at Melvin. "Shush it up, will you, Foghorn?"

Shelley smiled. "Thank you, Mr. Malone." Turning to her husband, she made an animated zip-your-lips pantomime.

Weasel Eyes turned around and looked at the new bidder, too. He knew Rigby Malone. If Malone bluffed him up, he'd be on the hook to spend more than he wanted for a horse he didn't need, so Weasel Eyes declined and the colt was gaveled to Rigby Malone for $12,500.

As soon as the hammer fell, Rigby leaned toward the Trombleys. "Here's the deal," he said. "I don't want that horse, so I'll sell him to you for your $12,116.42. In exchange, I'll train him for you at my place back in California. But to do that, I'll need the rest of the money we talked about this morning, escrowed, so I don't have to worry about gettin' paid. That's your choice. Take it or leave it."

Melvin beamed. "Brilliant idea, Rigby, sir. Ingenious. Take, take, *takin'* all the way."

"Thank you, Mr. Malone," Shelley said, tears welling in her eyes. "Thank you for making Miss Louise's dream a reality."

"It ain't a reality yet," Rigby replied. "Here's the deal: I'll train him and I won't shoot him full of drugs like ninety percent of the other guys. I will make all decisions on when and where he runs, up until he wins his first race. After that, we decide as a team. If you're good with that, we've got a deal."

Melvin and Shelley looked at each other and grinned, then turned to Rigby. "Mr. Malone," she said, "on account of the Fairfield Inn has a real big breakfast buffet with very little security, and on behalf of the wonderful memory of Miss Louise and all the fine people of Possum Drop, North Carolina, we *accept* your most generous business offer."

Rigby smiled. "Good. Have Keeneland wire the money to my account. You can do that here. Second, think up a name for your horse. Don't need it now, but we'll need it once he goes into training. Let me know and I'll send in the papers."

"Wow," said Melvin, "we never thought about naming him."

"Deacon's a good name," Deacon offered. "Call him Deacon. Deacon's a great name. A fast name. Ain't no way a horse can avoid being a winner with a name like Deacon. Deacon the Destroyer. Demon Deacon, like Wake Forest. If you don't like Deacon, how about Mr. Cincinnati?"

Shelley smiled politely. "Deacon is a *lovely* name," she said. "Perhaps a middle name."

"No way you're namin' him Deacon, are you?" asked Deacon.

"No, they ain't namin' him Deacon, you motormouth," Rigby snorted. "You want Deacon Junior, dig up your own twelve grand."

"I think the best thing is for the people of Possum Drop to name him," Shelley said. "This is a horse for the people. Let the people name the horse."

Melvin beamed. "Ain't she somethin'? Beautiful *and* smart, both. How did I get so lucky?"

"That's a question we've all been wonderin'," agreed Deacon. "It ain't the shoes, that's for sure."

They all laughed and walked back to Barn 6 to visit the horse. The foursome stayed for an hour, telling jokes and reliving the excitement of the sale. Shelley petted the colt so much that Deacon warned her his hair would rub off. She believed him and stopped instantly, mid-stroke and wide-eyed, as if jolted by electricity. Her reactive panic set off a new gale of laughter and caused the colt to bob his head and neigh loudly.

The colt stayed overnight in his stall. Early the following morning, Rigby loaded him into a westbound van for southern California. Before he boarded, his proud new owners took turns petting the big colt's muzzle. Deacon stood quietly nearby, his belongings stuffed inside his bulging gym bag. The bus back home wasn't due to leave until noon, so he had come to say goodbye; he'd hitch a ride to the station.

Rigby had developed a liking for Deacon Truth and paused by the driver's door of his pickup.

"Hey, motormouth," he called out to Deacon. "How you feel about L.A.?"

Deacon grinned, every sparkling tooth proudly on display. "Hate to have to paint it, love to get to see it."

"You want a job? Don't pay shit and the boss is a crotchety old asshole."

"Damn you're smooth, Rig. Talked me right into it. I'm in, baby."

"Climb aboard. You're on the team."

As Deacon ran up to give Rigby a hug and to hop inside the cab, but Rigby pointed toward the van. "Back there. With them. I can't stand that rap crap and I ain't driving two feet listening to it much less two-thousand miles. Back there, you can crank it up. But don't piss off the horses."

"You'll learn, Rig. You will learn. Mo Munny speaks the truth. He is the voice of the street. You will be a believer before we reach the Mississippi."

"Deacon, if I hear so much as one note of that crap between here and the Mississippi, you are goin' in it head-first when we get there."

"Yes, sir. I hear you. Mo can wait. He's the gospel in L.A., too."

Deacon grabbed his gym bag, ran back, and leaped inside the horse van. For three endless days, he would ride five feet from the three yearlings Rigby had collected during the sale. Two-thousand miles in a vented, smelly horse van wouldn't be fun, but it sure beat a Greyhound bus back to Kroger.

He stuck his hand out the side window and waved to the Trombleys as the van rumbled away. Then perched on a bale of hay, he fished out his headphones and leaned back against the front van wall, closed his eyes and nodded to the beat, turning up the volume to drown out the thunder of the pickup's big diesel motor.

For the first few hours, the adventure was new and exciting. Then the novelty wore off. Restless, now and then Deacon stood up and stepped to look out the side windows, watching as Kentucky turned into Tennessee, then Arkanas. Morning slipped into afternoon and finally faded into early evening.

Finally, fourteen hours after leaving Lexington, Deacon felt Rigby downgrade gears, slowing to make a careful wide turn. Soon the large boxy horse van graveled to a stop. Deacon slid open the vent window and looked outside for clues about where this man had taken him. Econo-Lodge. Oklahoma City. The Cincinnati street kid was two planets from home.

Rigby pulled open the back doors. It was cold, colder than Deacon had imagined it would be. Rigby's orders were cloaked in steam.

"C'mon, Deacon. Off your ass," Rigby grunted. "Feed and water the horses. Water 'em good. Let 'em graze over there." He pointed to a small grassy knoll to the left of the parking lot. "Twenty minutes. Hose out the van, too. While you're doin' that, I'll check us in and order a pizza."

Deacon said nothing. After fourteen hours on the road with three nervous horses, the Econo-Lodge looked like the Taj Mahal. He did his chores, then folded up and wolfed down half a pizza and nearly fell asleep standing in the hot shower. Within minutes of hitting the pillow, he was snoring.

Seven hours later, day two began. Again Rigby drove all day and well into the night. When he finally rumbled to a halt, Deacon looked outside. Under the hotel floodlights, he spied a neon sign. Flagstaff Motel. Arizona.

When he finished watering the horses, it was ten p.m. He craved a hot meal, but Rigby ordered another pizza and Deacon was too tired to argue.

Deacon woke early, before Rigby, and stepped outside to check on the yearlings. The rising sun illuminated the most spellbinding thing he'd ever seen: the southern rim of the Grand Canyon sprawled before him. As he stared, he slowly pinched himself.

Kroger was nowhere in the picture.

13
• SOMEBODY PLEASE SHUT UP • THAT ROOSTER

Few men surrounded by a million dollars worth of art, specially bred horses, and roosters born to fight, would perch on a toilet in an unfinished bathroom in an old ranch house. Such was the morning ritual of Rigby Malone. Thanks to one fast gelding with a big heart and a boxcar full of talent, a horse that started winning at two and kept winning for eight straight years, Rigby lived the good life. His great champion won so many races, and so much money, that it took two Brinks trucks to cart it all to the bank.

Besides a handful of yearlings, also wandering Rigby's backyard was a white pygmy goat named Josie that he had taught to ride a skateboard, plus a cat too fat to mouse. The fat cat, Calvin, had a ferret do his dirty work, which worked out fine since the ferret didn't eat mice; she just liked catching them. Another part of Rigby's backyard menagerie was a docile black burro named Fast Eddie, who'd been in the family twelve years and was housebroken. Like Rigby, the burro liked to watch the cockfights.

The private joy of Rigby's personal zoo was his small collection of magnificent roosters. Cockfighting was a bit of Mexicana he had brought to the burbs of La-La Land. Ostensibly the birds were raised for export, though in most cases that meant they were exported from one side of the thickly hedge-shrouded yard to the other.

Rigby bred and raised the roosters to be gladiators, to fight to the death. He enjoyed the barbaric sport every bit as much as the Mexicans who worked for him, several of whom had been with him a decade or more. Aside from the sporting spectacle, the fighting cocks kept the troops happy, since the losers went home with his workers, destined for the stew pot. Since team bonding translated into no turnover, fast horses, art on the walls, and a Rolls Royce in the garage, Rigby Malone knew he'd be hatching eggs until the Man Upstairs decided he was due for a final ruling on life's photo finish.

Ruffling feathers, thought Rigby, was a small price to pay for team unity. He was a tough guy and had the street smarts of an alley cat. He did virtually nothing the same as other horse conditioners on the Santa Anita back side. Approaching his sixty-fifth birthday, the craggy sandy-haired horseman had amassed his fortune by sticking to what he knew best: guessing right on young horses, and developing them into talented-enough runners that whenever he hissed "CHEESE!" they showed their teeth to the winner's circle photographer. Rigby's view of the world was eccentric compared to the traditionalists he competed against, but he continued to thrive—and without taking an easy shortcut, the tip of a veterinarian's needle.

He lived one mile from Santa Anita's stables in Arcadia, had grown up around the track, and spent more hours in the barns than in school. He did well for a disinterested student but quit the first day he was legally able.

By forty, Rigby was wealthy enough to purchase three houses, side-by-side. He made a couple calls and got a zoning variance to string all three backyards together so he could step out his kitchen door and teach his yearling bundles of wild-eyed potential how to become allowance and stakes winners.

In front of each home, Rigby planted overflowing gardens of cactus. The plants were all shapes, sizes, and varieties. Rumors placed their value in excess of a quarter of a million dollars. Rigby never discussed them.

When it came to running his business, Rigby was neither an optimist nor a pessimist. He was a realist, and that realism was as much economic as equine. A fixture at every major yearling sale, Rigby was notoriously picky about which horses he bought to develop. Rigby had great discipline, and much of his long-term success came from knowing that winning the financial game sometimes meant losing the bid.

Having his yearlings close by was tremendously important, since getting a young horse to behave with a saddle and rider required endless patience. Some horses broke quickly. Others challenged him every step of the way.

A monster for detail, he patiently taught the yearlings the smallest of things, like how to stand motionlessly with perfect posture and wait. Most learned that their life was easier if they caved in and did as they were asked. Those that didn't, he got rid of. If they fought him, and some did, they'd fight the jockey. And if they fought the jockey, they'd never consistently win.

Rigby Malone's training style was to let a young horse be a young horse—until it was time to become a racehorse. Each yearling stayed in a stall behind the house until it was grown up, broken, well behaved, and old enough to earn the right to join Rigby's other competing racehorses at Santa Anita. The three new yearlings from Keeneland maxed the backyard capacity at six. Five were big-boned, big-bodied, and well bred with an athletic presence. Five were colts. The biggest backyard challenge as the boys grew older was keeping them away from the filly, in order to guard against creating an instant broodmare.

Rigby preferred buying, breaking, training, and racing his own horses, but from time to time he'd bend that rule when a rich new owner with deep pockets and high aspirations would swing by. The rich ones all wanted the same thing, a silver cup for a mantel.

He told every one the exact same thing he'd said to Melvin and Shelley: "Speed costs money. How fast you wanna go?"

Typically the rich man's answer was "very fast." The tremendous sums these owners would trust him to spend enabled Rigby to select and purchase far more expensive bloodstock than he would risk on his own. The trainer fees and agent commissions he earned from the rich guys made it worth his while to take them on as clients.

The Trombleys were an anomaly. As a rule, bargain basement owners and final session leftovers were poison ivy, irritants to be avoided. Had they not paid him up front, he would never have gotten involved. He housed only a faint glimmer of optimism that the Possum Drop horse might someday grow into something profitable. He wouldn't risk a nickel of his own money finding out, but since these folks paid in advance, he'd do his best with what they'd bought.

Upon returning home from Kentucky, Rigby explained to Deacon the backyard training setup and left it up to him to settle in the three new yearlings. After he did, the pair climbed into Rigby's old Rolls Royce and slowly tooled over to Santa Anita to check on his racing stock. He was anxious to get there, since he never liked leaving his two-dozen racing Thoroughbreds for an extended period.

"Anything that can go wrong, will go wrong, Deacon. Sure as the world."

"No way, boss. You worry too much. Can I borrow the car? It matches my new L. A. criteria."

"Touch this car and a coffin will match your new L. A. criteria."

Rigby's employees were fiercely loyal and famously close-mouthed. When he introduced Deacon to his other five men, all Mexicans, each greeted him with a first name and limp handshake.

"You guys like Mo Munny?" chattered Deacon, showcasing his bright and sunny disposition. "He ain't Mexican, I know. Touch the groove, let your bones internalize the vibe."

"Loco," one said. "You loco." The other four laughed.

Rigby treated Deacon to a hot breakfast of pancakes and sausage at the track's back side cantina. Deacon ordered a double-stack. As the kid attacked his mound of food, Rigby wondered where the skinny rail would put it.

"L. A. is different than other cities, Deacon. Much different."

"In what way?"

"Women for one," Rigby explained. "There are more beautiful women in this town than the rest of the planet added together. Half of what you see ain't real, the boobs and all, but the half that *is* real is really unreal. Understand?"

Deacon nodded. "Clear as crystal on a sunny day. It's exactly what I rode a month in the back of a horse van to see. Can I have your orange juice?"

"No. Buy your own."

"When can I meet one of the unreal ones?"

"Pretty girls love fast horses, Deacon. The quicker we win, the faster you'll meet them."

"When's the first race?"

"That's not what I meant. First you've got to get set up. A place to stay. My wife and I will put you up in our backyard cabana house. But do us both a favor. Be discreet, okay?"

"Deal," Deacon grunted, reaching his fork toward Rigby's sausage. "You gonna eat those?"

"Eat your damn pancakes," Rigby replied, swatting his hand away. "You can stay at my place but be cool. Sneak them in, sneak them out. My wife won't like you whorin' around. Get sloppy and you'll need to go the badges-of-shame route, like the rest of the guys."

"Badges of shame?"

"Keys to each other's apartment. The team shares, Deacon. Hotels are expensive. And traceable. This ain't Cincinnati. In this town a man needs a lot of hideouts. You'll find yourself waking up in a lot of unusual situations."

Deacon laughed loudly. "I hear married guys wake up in them, too."

Rigby nodded. "Yep. And they're very expensive extrications, I assure you."

Deacon nodded several times. "Swimmin' in women with badges of shame. Here I am," he mused, "just rolled into town, smell like a horse trailer, and I love this place already. How lucky can I be? Got a boss, a crib, a love coach, and almost got a Rolls. All on the very first day! God knows how good it'll be once I'm surrounded by buxom starlets who love me for me."

Rigby laughed. "That'll *never* happen, Deacon. This is Los Angeles. Girls like that don't exist. They'll love you, all right, but for a million reasons other than you being you." Rigby chuckled again as he reached for his coffee.

Deacon paused his fork. "What's so funny?"

"This town is twenty-four seven, non-stop, complete and total bullshit. Los Angeles is three things and don't you ever forget it: hype, bullshit, and mirrors. Everybody uses everybody. But that's okay because everybody knows the rules. Wherever you wake up, whoever you're next to, and whatever preposterous situation you find yourself in, never take it personally. It's just L. A."

"Hype, bullshit, and mirrors," Deacon repeated. "I can deal with that. I'm great at the middle one."

"Get good at the other two and you'll fit right in."

The check came and Deacon excused himself to go to the toilet. He hid inside long enough so that Rigby could pay the tab and tip.

Rigby waited by the door and resumed talking as they walked to the car. "Money and horses go together, my young friend. And pretty girls love fast horses. Not as much as money, but they're a very close second."

Rigby put an arm around his young friend's shoulder. "You'll love it here, Deacon," he said confidently. "A week ago you were shoveling manure in Kentucky. Now you're here, in L. A., in the horse business, soon with a buck or two in your pocket. Mark my words, skinny man. If you can't get laid here, you can't get laid anywhere."

Deacon smiled again. "How big's the TV in my crib? Got a wine bar? Need a Jacuzzi, Rigby. Stereo, too. Bose speakers. Big ones. Four is good, eight is better."

Rigby stopped as he unlocked the car door and looked across the roof at his young charge. "There are only four great mysteries in life, Deacon." He paused for effect, then raised his hand to count. "The first three are when you die, how you die, and whether you'll leave footprints or buttprints in the sands of time.

"Our team leaves footprints. The other trainers and teams can leave buttprints. We leave footprints. And those footprints lead from our barn straight to the winner's circle."

Deacon held up three fingers. "That's only three, Rig. What's the fourth?"

"Since hearses ain't built with luggage racks, the fourth is most important of all."

"Which means?"

Rigby grinned broadly. "Which means, my young friend, that we're not here for a *long* time, but we are here for a *good* time. The fourth great mystery of life is whether you'll ever get laid above your social class."

Rigby poked himself in the chest. "I did," he said proudly, "and I married her."

It didn't take long for Deacon to settle into his new life, every sunrise bringing with it a new friend. Quizzical by nature, his days were consumed by the sights, sounds, and creatures of this new world—big time horse racing and the Santa Anita sizzle. Almost immediately, he was enraptured.

In addition to caring for the backyard yearlings, Deacon's bartered pool-house bungalow deal also required cactus tending, which he hated. Even Mo Munny couldn't save Deacon from the pain of a prick. He got stuck at least once every damn day.

He soon had wheels, an old ten-speed bicycle won on a bluff in a payday poker game. He put the bike to good use, shuttling back and forth to Santa Anita. He also pedaled to pick up smallish girls for dates; bigger ones proved a greater challenge.

One morning Rigby spied Deacon sneaking out a big Latina out of the cabana. He watched as Deacon struggled to pedal her home, the girl's ample bottom spread the entire width of the bicycle's crossbar. Deacon had to stand up in the pedals to get them turning. He'd worked up a sweat just leaving the driveway.

When Deacon returned, the old trainer ribbed him mercilessly. "Quite a sight this morning, you two emerging from that den of sin. Side by side, you and her looked like the number 10."

"Bite me, Rig," retorted Deacon. "A man's got to do what a man's got to do. Cull too many and you'll cull out the best you'd ever have. Big girls need love, too, Rigby. Remember that: Big girls need love, too."

"Tons of it," Rigby needled. "Keep it up and you'll need fatter tires for that bike."

As the days passed by and Rigby watched Deacon acclimate, and for a thousand reasons he couldn't quite put his finger on, Rigby grew to believe in this kid. Deacon was capable of bigger things than mucking stalls and bathing claimers. Rigby silently rooted for him. This kid might someday step beyond the boundary of his skin color.

Deacon hustled, so Rigby encouraged him to network. "Around back the horses are king," Rigby told Deacon, "but the real kings are up front in the clubhouse, the gamblers and suits. You're a natural cross-pollinator. It's your gift, son. Take advantage. Mingle. Work the crowds. This is a networking industry. Meet as many people as you can."

Personality, knowledge, and connections would pave Deacon's access to power. He quickly proved Rigby right. His gregarious nature enabled him to chat up instant friendships with the track regulars—rich and poor, working and retired; black, Mexican, and white. His nearly photographic memory enabled him to assimilate into any social circle, laughing with millionaires as easily as two-dollar railbirds.

Three months after arriving, two weeks into his first race meet, Rigby's favorite jockey committed to a different trainer's horse the night before a Grade III stakes. Deacon urged Rigby to replace him with a lightly raced apprentice named Lorenzo Callas. "Zo's the man for this spot," Deacon insisted. "He's a light hand and won't fight the horse. C'mon, man, we're 20 to 1, morning line. Zo gets us five less pounds, too. They'll help, Rig. C'mon, give him a shot. These two are a perfect pair."

Two things Rigby Malone did not like were root canals and apprentice jocks. For some reason, he listened to Deacon's sales pitch, and bought it.

It was a smart investment. In the featured ninth race that day Lorenzo Callas snuck up on the outside and won in a photo finish. The winner's share for Rigby was 60 percent of $150,000. Callas earned 10 percent of Rigby's winnings: $9,000, which equaled nearly four months' pay. Callas tipped Deacon $900 for getting him the mount.

By the time the happy crew made its jubilant way from the winner's circle back to the stables at the rear of Santa Anita, a large tan Winnebago was parked outside Rigby's office, with three buxom lovelies awaiting, the Rigby Malone Celebration Society.

Each of Rigby's stable hands took turns disappearing inside in the Winnebago, leg-wrestled with a shapely aspiring starlet, and emerged blissfully disheveled a half hour later. Then went through the line again.

Fast Eddie, the good luck burro, watched through the camper window, his nose against the glass. Rigby stood nearby, happily doting over his troops. He loved winning, never more so than in an upset; and he applauded each man as one by one they happily staggered out of the camper.

Rigby sent Lorenzo Callas in, too. These perks didn't happen in Panama. When the jockey emerged, he shook Rigby's hand vigorously. "In Panama, I get fifty bucks," he said. "Here is better."

Deacon talked his way into an extra helping of the conjugal friendships. He finally extricated his happy self from the Kama Sutra yoga entanglement of a redhead named Boom Boom, and emerged like a peacock to thundering applause. Fast Eddie brayed.

"You have streeted it up for a brother!" Deacon crowed. "I now understand Rule Four!" Deacon squeezed Rigby in a happy bear hug. "Life is once again worth livin'!"

Officially indoctrinated into the Rigby Malone incentive program, that Saturday stakes race also opened the door to Deacon Truth's true calling. He had learned a lot about life on the back side of the track; but to reach the real money he needed to work the owners.

He began matching less-established riders with small-string owners and small-stable trainers. Blue-collar opportunity broker, he billed himself. Connecting owners, trainers, and riders who need to win on weekdays.

Coupled with his weekly wage, Deacon earned enough that, for the first time in his life, he had disposable income. Encouraged by Rigby to save some, he did: twenty cents on the dollar, investing instead of pissing it away. Blowing a wad on a longshot chance to bed a money-grubbing beauty queen fell into the "pissing it away" category.

Six months after leaving home, Deacon Truth now had life in the palm of his coconut-brown hand: paying his way with a job he loved, surrounded by a circus of characters he cared about and who cared about him.

Deacon's favorite four, the "Odds Quad" he called them, became his inner circle. Esther Gormay, an old Hollywood actress, he nicknamed Gallopin' Gormay, since she was owner/operator of the love house Winnebago.

"If this bus could talk," Esther bragged. "you'd never believe the Hollywood bigshots who've climbed aboard and dropped their pants between races."

Esther liked Deacon Truth and coached him on the business realities of Los Angeles. "Everybody in this town sleeps around, Deacon; especially the suits. Let nothing surprise you. Suits eat ego food. They have ravenous appetites. Feed the suits and they'll buy whatever you're selling."

Esther's endless stories of her sexual peccadilloes with the armies of rich and famous enraptured Deacon. Four decades and the money that went with it, that's how she had lived her life.

"I got hooked for good in 1969," she said, her well made-up brown eyes glimmering. "Majestic Prince won the Santa Anita Derby that day. Won the Kentucky Derby, too."

Deacon hadn't heard of Majestic Prince. "Is he a sheikh or a horse?"

"Horse."

"Did ya win a lot?"

"Not a dime, honey. But I did meet the most generous man. I went home that night with $3,000 cash. That's when I knew I loved this track."

Deacon's three other Odds Quad pals lived far more modest lives. Mung Fu was a "horticulture technician."

"Back home, we call yo ass a gardener," Deacon said. "But we had to take a field trip over to Whiteyville to see you. No gardeners in the hood, 'cept in the basement."

Mung Fu looked puzzled. "Basement?"

"Reefer," said Deacon. "Basement herb of the streetcorner."

Delmer Smithers, called "Toker" by everyone, a belching, beer-bellied man with the eyes of a basset hound and a waddle to match, was head of the post-race cleanup crew.

"Toker's got the most thankless job in the whole place," Deacon said to Mung Fu at lunch one day. "He don't wanna be nuthin' but who he is, and he's happy doin' what he does. The track should cherish a guy like that. Shows up every day, happy to aim a leaf blower and bag ten tons of other people's trash."

Mung Fu said that rumors persisted that Toker smoked pot during his nightly duties.

"So what?" Deacon protested, defending his pal. "He's a Vietnam vet. Reefer don't make nobody a bad guy. You wanna meet a bad man? Ride a convertible through east L. A. Toker's as good as the Pope, compared to the brothers you meet on the street."

Deacon's best pal was Pez Perez, a Mexican-American his own age. Son of illegal immigrants, fruit pickers and migrant farm workers, Pez valeted cars. He spoke impeccable English and hustled his butt off.

In contrast to Deacon, Pez was shy, so theirs was a practical friendship. Pez showed the skinny black ghetto kid the ins and outs of the neighborhood. Deacon helped Pez hustle up girls. Deacon wasn't picky, but Pez was. Most of the time, Pez picked out who he wanted to meet and left it to Deacon to do all the talking. Pez got the pretty one; Deacon took the easy one.

Deacon admired his pal, because Pez worked very hard, was conscientious, and wired $300 a month back to Mexico to support his relatives. His parents were laborers and earned very little, and neither spoke English. Pez had no interest in that lifestyle; three hours in a strawberry patch as a kid had cured him of that. He had knuckled down in school and graduated on time. His ambition was to answer the call of the satellite dish and remote control as soon as he could be Anglicized enough to buy one.

Pez was shuffling cars at Santa Anita for two years before Deacon arrived. Thanks to Pez, Deacon got to drive through In-N-Out Burger in a Porsche the first week of the race meet, a Ferrari the second, a Lamborghini the third.

"At the rate we're goin,'" Deacon bragged when he called home to his mom, "I'll be takin' a helicopter by the end of the month."

The Odds Quad were Deacon's surrogate family, each of whom helped him sprout different roots in smoggy Arcadia.

Tightly tucked up against the San Gabriel Mountains, where estate homes and Botox injections were as common as mosquitoes in a swamp, Deacon took the first few steps of an exciting new career.

Within months, his fortunes would skyrocket.

14
LIVIN' LIFE IN LA-LA LAND

The limousine ride from Los Angeles International Airport was a long one, well over an hour. The freeway's bumper-to-bumper traffic mesmerized Tuki Banjo. Back home in Cambridge, three cars had defined a traffic jam. Here a million of them rolled inches apart, creeping along a six-lane highway, like a giant steel centipede, brake lights blinking like Christmas bulbs.

Talking with Mitzi Cleater came easily, to Tuki's relief. She was relaxed and non-threatening, and the warmth and accent in her voice made Tuki feel comfortable. By the time the chauffer exited Interstate Highway 210 at Sierra Madre, Tuki decided that despite the obvious Americanized riches, Mitzi was still very much a Kiwi.

The fashionable estate was tucked high into the snaking hills of the mountains. The massive hilltop home rose like a castle and sundown ushered in evening darkness, the expansive blanket of orange haze replaced by twinkling lights.

However, walking through the massive doorway of Mitzi's palatial home, Tuki felt more discomfort than awe and stepped self-consciously through the enormous foyer. Her hard-heeled shoes echoed on the mottled gray-and-white Italian marble under vaulted ceilings that soared thirty feet. Beautiful paintings with accent lights covered the walls. A grand crystal chandelier hovered above her, cold and imposing, not warm and inviting like the old pohutukawa tree back at the farm.

Mitzi walked past Tuki, tossing a set of car keys to her. "Here, darling. These go to the yellow Mustang out in the drive. You do drive, don't you?"

Tuki caught the keys in midair. *Technically, yes,* she thought. How hard could it be? The traffic only moved five-miles-an-hour. She nodded.

"Never run a company, dear. Relentless, conflicting demands and a horribly busy schedule." Mitzi chatted as she quickly shuffled through her mail. Two-thirds of it she tossed in the trash.

The next morning, five minutes into Tuki's inaugural expedition with the yellow Mustang, she met her first American policeman. By noon, she'd met another. Neither had a sense of humor. She got lost twice and never got close to Butterfly World, her intended destination.

She arrived back home that night with a pair of tickets, one for running a red light, the other reckless driving. Over dinner, Mitzi suggested a driver.

Tuki shook her head. "Will figure it out on me own, thanks. Not friendly, your constables. But no worry. Tomorrow I'll do better."

"They're all gruff and grumpy," said Mitzi, "even the young ones. Drunk with power. It's no bloody wonder they act the way they do, though. It's not as though people break the law so they can get caught and give them donuts."

Tuki was surprised. "Like donuts, do they?"

Mitzi nodded. "Famously. Take it a little easy on the gas tomorrow, eh? And don't zigzag without the turn signal. Drivers hate that. Causes road rage."

"What's that?"

Mitzi pointed her hand like a pistol and pretended to pull the trigger.

Tuki had never heard of such a thing, people cruising streets, shooting bad drivers. Back home, they honked.

Mitzi held up her right hand and solemnly wiggled her little finger. "Pinky swear. Turn signal, safe driving."

Tuki wiggled her little finger back.

The next morning, Mitzi had to leave early for a meeting way down south in La Jolla. "Sorry, darling; but I'll be home very late, if at all. I'll call and let you know." She sighed as she hugged Tuki goodbye for the day. "PowerPoint and roundtables. Dreary things, business meetings. Avoid them as long as life allows, dear. They cause wrinkles."

Clueless about what Mitzi meant, Tuki nodded anyway. The prospect of being alone in this cavernous place didn't bother her. She had bunked twenty-four to a room at the orphanage. An evening alone with a cricket serenade would be a sweet symphony.

Shortly after Mitzi left, Tuki drove the Mustang down the hill to re-explore the neighborhood. Two minutes down the winding road, she yanked the car across lanes and jammed on the brakes in front of Howie's Ranch Market.

Three minutes later, she emerged with an apple, orange juice, and large bag of chocolate donuts; then breakfasted at nearby Mt. Wilson Trail Park. Swinging back and forth on a leather-saddled swing, she munched the apple and planned her day.

She flipped the core under bushes, breakfast for a rabbit; and continued to swing, while casually watching two orange-winged monarch butterflies flutter past. She sipped the orange juice, thick with pulp and more rich than the watered-down stuff at home. *Cleanse the system, cleanse the soul. Only fruit before noon.*

Then she waved goodbye to the butterflies, who soared up toward the treetops and drifted away to the east. Impulsively she hopped off the swing and ran to the fence, where she watched them flutter in the air currents until they finally vanished.

Since the butterflies went east, she would, too. She tossed her empty juice container into a nearby trash bin and headed back to the car.

The bottom of Sierra Madre fed into the interstate. Tuki worked her way over to the far left lane, then slowed like she would in New Zealand. The other drivers zoomed all around her, flashing their headlights, honking their horns and tailgating her with wild gestures.

"Emotional blokes, these Americans," she murmured.

She spied a small green road sign painted with a horse and exit arrow, and impulsively veered a hard right—from the farthest left lane, in bold defiance of the commuters. A cacophony of car horns screamed at Tuki as she weaved toward the exit ramp.

She followed the horse and arrow signs, slowly winding through tidy, shop-lined streets. Downtown Arcadia.

At a fork in the road, a giant Jumbotron screen welcomed patrons to Santa Anita Park. It read 9:19 a.m. as Tuki drove past. She aimed the Mustang toward a few dozen cars parked in a cluster in front of the massive, faded-green, track-front buildings. Judging by the hustling workers unloading trucks, it appeared to be a race day.

A uniformed security guard quickly approached Tuki's Mustang.

"Good morning!" she greeted cheerfully.

"No parking, lady. Can't you read?"

She offered him a donut. He took one but made her move anyway.

She did. Then donuts in hand, not deterred from her goal, she set off on foot.

The entrance gates she tried were locked. She caught the attention of a passing maintenance worker. Two donuts got her in. Two more got her a ride on a golf cart to the far side barns and horses.

Tuki thanked the golf cart driver, a portly graying man in a security uniform. He mumbled his thanks, mouth full, and clutched the half-eaten donut in his left hand and shook goodbye with his right.

As Tuki watched the jolly man step on the accelerator and putter away, she thought, *Bloody amazing! Enough donuts and I could take over this country.*

"Hey, girl! Where you goin' with those donuts?" hollered a tall, thin black fellow.

"Wherever they'll take me," she hollered back.

"They'll take you right over here." He waved her over with a broad smile.

Tuki was surprised. She'd never spoken to a black man before, much less fed one.

"Deacon Truth," he said, holding out his hand.

"Tuki Banjo."

"Kooky Banjo? You a musician?"

"*Tuki* Banjo," she repeated politely, stuffing a donut into his hand. "It's me name."

"Pleased to meet you, Tuki Banjo. What you doin' here?" Deacon took a huge bite of the donut, nearly half of it, and waited for an answer.

"You know bloody well what I'm doing," she answered. "I'm feeding a black man. I'm from New Zealand and I've never done this before."

He licked his fingers. "You're doin' a great job, Tuki Banjo . . . but you need more practice."

She dutifully handed over another donut.

He nodded gratefully. "Thanks, but don't overdo it. I'm liable to follow you around."

Deacon toured Tuki throughout the stables, introducing her to people everywhere they went and she spent the entire day at Santa Anita shaking hands.

She enjoyed herself very much and returned to the track the next three mornings.

Then on the fourth morning, she traded three powdered raspberry jellies for a jaunt atop a stable pony. Deacon walked alongside and she rode out onto the historic track where early morning workouts were underway. Up close, she thrilled to the sights, sounds, and smells that paying customers couldn't experience. *The best slice of America yet.*

On the fifth morning, Rigby Malone arrived at his barn, his first day back from a weekend vacation in Las Vegas with his wife. He was late, almost nine o'clock. The workouts should be finished. The barn should be buzzing. Where was his chief assistant? Where was everybody?

And who was that tiny redhead hosing down his seven-year-old bay gelding, Toner Phoner? Why was she messing with his horse?

He marched right up to the freckled pixie. "Who the hell are you?"

"Who are *you?*" she said without looking up, still hosing the horse.

"Never mind who *I* am," he blustered. "That's *my* horse you're drowning."

She still didn't look up. She reached down and scrubbed the gelding's chest. "You must be Mr. Malone," she said softly. "Seashells and balloons to you, Mr. Malone. They told me you'd act like this."

"Like what?" Rigby stepped on the water hose to stop its flow.

She then looked over at him. "All huff and bluster. Like you're mean—even though you're not."

Rigby stepped off the hose, and stuck his nose in her face. "Why the *hell* are you bathing my horse?" Then he stepped back, crossed his arms, and rumbled, "Is that *blustery* enough for you?"

She folded the hose in half to stop the water, and looked Rigby Malone in the eye. "Me name's Tuki." She stuck out her hand. "I work 'ere. It's me first day and I'm doin' a bloody good job. Is it too early, sir, to inquire a raise? Donuts are expensive in America."

"A raise? Who hired you?"

"I did, sir. Yesterday. You seemed one woman shy, so I signed on." She wiggled her hand, signaling she wanted to shake his.

Who was this little twit? He clasped her hand and squeezed really hard . . . She squeezed back.

Eye-to-eye, they both power squeezed, neither backing down. For a runt, she had a powerful grip.

Finally Tuki laughed and let go. "They said you'd do that, too."

"Where *are* they?" he asked suspiciously. "Locked in a stall, lured in by a trail of pastry?"

"On the track, sir. A tractor problem shoved everythin' back. They said you won't work the horses with a crowded lot, that you insist on a freshly harrowed surface."

"That's right. I never work my horses in someone else's tracks. You can finish what your doin'," he said. "I gotta go find my team." He spun on his heels and headed over to saddle up his personal stable horse.

"He's bathed too, Mr. Malone," Tuki called out. "I gave him a happy scrub."

Rigby nodded and kept walking. *A happy scrub! Jesus H. Christ!*

Rigby's auburn gelding, purchased a decade ago for $35,000, had changed his life. The horse had won six Grade I races, nearly $7 million.

The gelding hated retirement and missed the action of the track, so Rigby had methodically prepped him to adjust to his new role as stable pony. The gelding traded tail-flying workouts against the clock for the daily rigors of lugging around a walking load twice as heavy as the exercise riders and jocks he formerly carried.

Now, as Rigby tightened the gelding's girth belt, he was preparing to swing a leg aboard a horse that was fresh off a happy scrub, courtesy of a pint-sized, funny-talking foreigner. As Rigby climbed aboard and found the stirrups, he glanced at the little pixie. She waved, then put her thumb over the water hose and sprayed it playfully toward him.

Serves me right for leaving town, he thought, ducking. Rigby turned his horse toward the track and rode over to the main dirt oval to check on his fillies and colts. He sat atop his horse for a half-hour, studying each animal intently as he or she cruised past.

After watching the final workout, Rigby rode slowly back to the barn and dismounted onto a tree stump that was set outside the dilapidated shed that served as his office. He walked inside and grabbed his tattered spiral notebook. Standing over his cluttered desk, he took a stubby pencil and made meticulous notations: which horse had worked, which hadn't, which were on schedule, which had slipped.

It took two full hours of concentrated study to get caught up with where each of his two-dozen runners stood in fitness and preparation. He checked for any recent changes in the racing secretary's condition book, noting which races had been cancelled, which added.

Getting a horse sharp for a specific race began with the race date. Prepping a horse for a race that no longer existed was a waste of time. Missing the chance to ready a horse for a newly announced race could be a lost opportunity. Careless mistakes cost money.

From the race date, Rigby worked backward day by day. Fanatically disciplined to his process, he left nothing to chance. Every horse entered at Santa Anita was prepared, conditioned according to a carefully mapped-out and monitored fitness plan.

It could take a hundred little things to make one significant difference in a race between equal horses. Rigby could accept getting beat by a better horse . . . but not a better-prepared one. If you ran a horse that beat Rigby Malone's, you had earned your money.

After a few days, Rigby let the new girl exercise a couple of his horses. In the saddle, she looked confident and fearless, which surprised him. His world was full of fancy practice riders, especially women. Rigby didn't like apprentice riders and teens. He was doubly skeptical about women.

However, the girls worked hard and cheap, so he hired them occasionally as exercise riders. Jocks were generic and interchangeable during workouts, but once the races got underway, the pros separated. Strength and experience were vital, so Rigby hired only male jockeys to ride the races.

Tuki Banjo's value was a blend of work ethic and versatility. She showed up early, stayed late, and rarely spoke. Though petite, she was well-muscled and steady in the irons. An unexpected bonus was the girl's inner stopwatch, her uncanny ability to judge pace and time. From a trainer's perspective, she was brilliant, and Rigby grew to rely on her to work a perfectly, regardless of his training objective. This alone made her meager salary worth paying. She also was quite willing to pitch in and help with any of the endless chores that needed to get done around a racing stable. Rigby noticed but never uttered a compliment.

Within a week, Tuki had exercised nearly all of Rigby's twenty-five horses, several on long gallops. Rigby didn't know if the girl aspired to ride for money, but didn't care, and he never asked. Few females were strong enough, tough enough, or resilient enough to win at this game's highest competitive level, and racing at Santa Anita was world-renowned. As long as she did her work and caused no trouble, she could stick around.

After five straight mornings of stuffing his face with Tuki's free food, Deacon announced, "I'm tired of donuts." He invited her to join him and the Odds Quad at the Rose City Diner for breakfast.

He plopped down in the booth with his four friends and energetically offered up his reflective thought for the day. "What could a cross-eyed man and a cross-eyed woman possibly see in each other?"

"Sex," purred Esther. "Loud, angry, glorious, sloppy, sex. With lots of playful spanking."

Mung Fu laughed and raised his hand. "Where to meet cross-eye girl?"

Deacon tried again. "If an old bag walks along holding an old bag and somebody says, 'Lookit the old bag,' how does anyone know which one they're talkin' about?"

"That's obvious," Esther said. "It depends on her makeup."

Deacon looked at her blankly and shook his head. He then segued to his favorite TV show. "Last night, did ya see it?"

Pez Perez bit. "See what?"

"*Jeopardy!*"

Tuki had no clue what they were talking about.

"Let me guess," Pez replied. "Rerun season. You knew all the questions."

Tuki looked at Pez blankly.

"You don't know? Deacon lives and dies by Alex Trebek."

She still didn't understand. "Translate?"

"The host of *Jeopardy!*," Deacon said. "My favorite show. They give you the answer, and you have to guess the question."

Tuki was confused. "What's the need for that?"

"For what?" Deacon replied. "A question if you already know the answer?"

"For watching television."

"He doesn't just watch it, Tuki," Pez offered. "He worships it. During rerun season, he goes to Wal-Mart and watches it on forty TVs at once."

Tuki was puzzled. "Why? Watchin' one telly is silly enough. What do you need *forty* of the buggers for?"

Pez looked at Deacon. "You want to tell her, or should I?"

Deacon waved his pal to continue.

"Deacon loves to act like a brainiac in public," Pez explained. "He stands there shouting out all the right questions, from the beginning of the show to the end. He draws a crowd. They cheer and applaud. By the time the program ends, they think Deacon's a freakin' genius."

Tuki turned at Deacon. "A bloody genius, are you?"

He shrugged. "This is L.A., Tuki. It's all hype and bullshit and mirrors. Never forget that."

"I cherish your wisdom." She arched an eyebrow and pointed to him. "Sittin' next to a genius, am I? Is this our little secret or do your bicycle girls know how bloody brilliant you are, too?"

The group laughed and proceeded with breakfast, then aggravated the waitress by making her split the check six ways, a lot of work for breakfast tips. Tuki handed hers to Deacon, who grumbled but paid it. Since she was driving, she added two chocolate donuts to go.

"You ain't full?" asked Deacon.

"In case of emergency."

Deacon held the driver door open for Tuki, and invited her to go over and see Rigby Malone's backyard yearling operation. "You gotta see the new ones," he said. "One of them is drivin' Rigby nuts."

It was a six-minute drive from the restaurant, which Deacon filled by telling Tuki about his experiences at Keeneland, meeting Rigby, and how he ended up in California. He embellished the recollection of his interactions with the sheikh and Albacoa, the sale-topping yearling he looked after.

Tuki gasped when she heard the multi-million-dollar price tag. "Are Rigby's worth millions, too?"

Deacon shook his head. "Rigby brought home nice horses," he told her, "but none for big money. He said that first class only costs a nickel more in most things, but not the horse business. In the horse business, goin' first class costs a million more."

Tuki looked shocked. "A million U.S. dollars? My God."

Deacon never blinked. "Rigby owns four colts and one filly. The other colt is a big oaf named Ooty. He was in my barn, too. The owners paid Rig in advance to break and train him, but Ooty is makin' Rig earn that money." He chuckled. "Ooty's headstrong as hell, just like Rigby. The two of them are havin' a 'failure to communicate'. Cool Hand Luke," he added. "The warden said it to Paul Newman."

"Paul Newman? The popcorn man?" Tuki recognized the name. "Mitzi popped some just last night."

"The popcorn man," affirmed Deacon. "I'm sure he'd be proud you know him."

Tuki sighed wistfully. "Failure to communicate. Me bloody specialty. Ooty's the name, is it? That's a funny one."

"The owners had a contest and the townspeople named the colt after a small mountain town in southern India, where Miss Louise's favorite tea grew."

"Miss Louise?"

"A popular old lady. She died, and her last wish was for her life savings to buy a horse and win scholarship money for the kids of Possumville. From what I heard, her only vice in life was her daily fix of Ooty tea, Chammo-mammo-ming-lang or whatever it is that old white women drink."

"Chamomile," corrected Tuki.

"If you say so, girl. Brothers don't sip tea. We don't even chug it. C'mon." He climbed out of the car. "Time to check out the family. Rig says that raisin' horses is like raisin' kids, except you shovel the diapers. These new ones are *nice*. High-heeled diamond nice, as Mo Munny would say."

He led the way around the corner along a slate walkway. "They're around back. Watch out for the damn cactus. They'll stab your ass if you don't watch out."

Fast Eddie, the burro, ambled up. "Pet him," Deacon advised, "or he'll holler 'til you do."

Tuki did as instructed, and Fast Eddie followed her, nudging her back.

Deacon grinned. "He'll climb in the car if you let him. Never got the memo he ain't people."

Tuki met each young horse in its own stall. Big, beautiful, athletic.

"Big engines," said Deacon. "Rigby says that if two horses have equal talent, the bigger engine wins."

"These are now two years old, right?"

"Right," replied Deacon. "Turned two January first."

"It's August first back home."

"That means you're either seven months behind or upside-down," teased Deacon. "Which is it?"

"Neither," she retorted. "We're five months ahead, Mr. Genius."

As they went from stall to stall, Tuki petted each young one and breathed into its mouth when it came close enough. The fifth, a wild-eyed auburn colt, skittered away and refused to come over. "Is this Ooty?" she asked.

"No, but don't take it personal. He's psycho. Hates everybody. Got a bit of Jack Nicholson in him. Rig loves that. Loves big colts with the ego of a crazy man."

Tuki looked for the sixth stall. "Over here," Deacon said, waving her to follow. "The 'Dog House' is around the corner. Ooty stays in it. He bit the snot out of Rigby the first time Rig turned his back. Be careful around this one. Don't get too close." Deacon chattered on like a Michener novel.

They turned the hedge corner. "Here he is. No tail, neither."

Tuki didn't answer and Deacon turned. The only one standing was Fast Eddie. Tuki was on the ground, unconscious, her face flushing crimson.

Deacon panicked. A black guy in Arcadia, towering over an unconscious white girl, a burro his only alibi. Not good.

He raced to a nearby rooster cage, flung open the door, reached in and grabbed the water dish. The agitated cock fiercely pecked at him.

He spilled half the water while scrambling back to Tuki's side and dumped the rest on her face.

She blinked. Her eyes fluttered. She looked up at the horse, then fainted again.

"White girls are crazy," he muttered, then slapped Tuki's pale cheeks softly, terrified at getting caught like this. "Ain't no sister *ever* pass out, except maybe from meetin' Denzel."

Again Tuki came to. She pulled herself up, quivering, and pointed to the tall, black yearling. Her voice trembled. "I b-birthed him, Deacon," she whispered slowly. "His mum died in me lap. Lenslugger, I called 'im."

Deacon looked down at the pale redhead. "You stutter nonsense, girl. You need a donut or somethin'. This here's Ooty."

Tuki scrambled to her feet and rushed over to the stall. Ooty snorted and pawed at the ground. Fast Eddie brayed, the other horses neighed, and the roosters crowed.

"For God's sake!" Deacon hollered. "You are all off key! *Shut up!*"

Reunited with the colt now named Ooty, Tuki whispered to him, "I promise I'll never leave you again." She smothered his muzzle with kisses, and he let her, which surprised Deacon.

"He must like you," Deacon said. "I expected him to rip off your face, like Hannibal Lecter."

He smiled and stepped forward. "Dang, Ooty, lookit you. Gettin' some love without spendin' a dime. You are a role model for brothers everywhere."

That night, Deacon switched sleeping quarters with Tuki so she could stay close to her horse. When Mitzi arrived home late and flipped on the light switch in Tuki's room, she screamed at the shirtless black man in the bed where the Kiwi girl was supposed to be. Her bloodcurdling shrieks of terror filled the house as he chased after trying to calm her down, clad only in boxer shorts.

Tuki's evening was far less eventful. She rose early and was bathing Ooty at sunrise when Rigby came out with a mug of coffee.

"Let me guess," he said gruffly. "A happy scrub."

Mr. Grouch again. Tuki didn't bother to look up. "Seashells and balloons to you, too."

"Back at ya," he grunted. "Congratulations. As of today, you are now assistant trainer of all imported, tailless colts. You can tend to Ooty but I warn you, I'm a monster for detail. If you take him on, I'll ask you to pay attention to a thousand little things. Each is important." He took a sip of coffee and then pointed the mug at her chest. "Never challenge me, Tuki. To me, this horse is like any other. Either he adapts to my methods or he'll be moved to another barn. As of today, he is the worst prospect I've had in a decade. That said, Miss Seashell, think you and your balloons can handle that?"

She didn't flinch, pausing only to brush the breeze-blown hair off her face. "Yes, sir," she said. "He is one hardheaded, bloody pain-in-the-arse, but he is special. You'll see."

Rigby stared at her for several seconds, then took another long sip of his coffee.

"Prove it," he said. Without waiting for a reply, he turned and went back into the kitchen, the screen door banging behind him.

Tuki bit her tongue and returned her attention to Ooty. Reunited with her foaled baby, despite the mean old man, had made her new life infinitely better. Butterfly World would have to wait.

After Xao Yan Li's three-day guest appearance with the Seattle Symphony, she wanted to visit Ellery Point and meet the men who had crafted the most perfect bow she had ever touched.

Trapped in the rain and rush hour traffic, Otto Bonk fumed while his wife stared out the window. It was hard for Otto to get in the Christmas spirit, rolling along at ten miles an hour. It took three dreary hours to arrive at Ellery Point.

They met the four bowmakers at seven p.m. at Lonnie's Restaurant on Katalpa Road. Otto ordered two bottles of Dom Perignon, not what the locals typically gargled. The six clinked their glasses to the magic wood of pernambuco, and savored the tingle of the elegant French champagne.

Small talk turned to dinner talk, then over coffee and dessert, Otto smiled at his wife and tapped his water glass four times quickly. "One ping to honor each of you," he said with a broad smile. "Xao Yan Li has a small gift of gratitude we hope you will appreciate."

In succession, the bowmakers politely accepted the thin rectangular gift-wrapped packages that Xao Yan Li shyly presented to them.

"This is most kind of you," Lionel George said humbly, "but your visit means more than any material thing."

"That is precisely what Xao Yan Li wants to discuss," said Otto Bonk. "She has a very special announcement."

Xao Yan Li nodded shyly. Then she slowly looked each man in the eye and nodded. She felt deeply indebted to the artisans who had grafted the Brazilian wood with melodic perfection.

"Old bow not play right," she said. "New bow . . . *you* bow . . . perfect. Perfect bow. Xao Yan Li play new bow. Only new bow."

After a pause she added, "Never fro against wall. Promise!"

The bowmakers laughed.

Lionel George was delighted she had chosen to keep it. "We thought you came here to return it. This news is certainly an honor for all of us."

Xao Yan Li shook her head no. "Play bow. Always. No return."

Otto Bonk stood, kissed his wife on the cheek, and raised his champagne flute. "Returning the bow is no longer an option, gentlemen. The *Tourte* has been sold." He watched their stunned faces. Selling a Tourte was like selling a Rembrandt. *Nobody* did it.

Saul Lewis's mind raced and his stomach churned. *My piece of hand-selected wood, my work, replacing a legendary Tourte? My God. What did the Tourte bring?*

He was not bold enough to ask, but he wished Lionel would. A quick glance sideways told him that Lionel wouldn't pry. None of them would. Here they sat, dying to know, but none rude enough to snoop. *Ours is a small universe,* Saul thought. *Soon the answer will orbit its way to Ellery Point. Lord God, the world will know we replaced a Tourte!*

Whatever the mystery amount turned out to be, all four bowmakers knew it would take a log cabin's worth of bows to match it.

Otto Bonk hoisted his champagne flute in another toast, and Xao Yan Li urged the bowmakers to unwrap their gifts. "Open! Open!"

They did. Each small wooden picture frame housed a print of the same photograph.

"It's a horse," Saul Lewis noted dryly.

"A brown horse," D. C. Lee added.

Nathan Pillsbury politely chimed in, "And a fine brown horse it is."

Then they three turned to Lionel George, who was marveling at the pernambuco frame. He looked up at Xao Yan Li. "Your horse is very handsome, indeed."

She shook her head no and swept her arm past all of them. "You . . . You horse."

"His sire is a great champion from Brazil," Otto Bonk added. "Xao Yan Li picked this colt herself. He's a Thoroughbred racehorse. She thought the four of you might enjoy a sporting diversion."

"I live on a houseboat," said Saul. "Is he good with knots and steady on his feet?"

Otto Bonk chuckled. Xao Yan Li didn't get it and frowned with misunderstanding, causing Otto to instantly stop. He held up his hand.

"Don't worry," he said to the four craftsmen. "You four are the registered owners, but the legacy of Mr. Tourte has taken care of the bills. Your sole responsibility is to root for him when he's racing. He won't go into serious training until later this year. Hopefully he'll win you lots of money."

Otto smiled and politely nodded toward his wife. "Xao Yan Li has given your horse a special name. You may, of course, change it if you wish."

Otto turned to his wife, and she enunciated carefully. "He name Per-nam-bu-co!"

As Xao Yan Li shared each slow syllable, the bowmakers smiled and nodded.

Again Otto lifted his champagne flute. "To Pernambuco! May you all be rich and famous!"

Lionel George nodded and clinked glasses with Otto, Xao Yan Li, and his three partners. "Rich is good. We don't need famous, but rich is good."

Outside after dinner, the four bowmakers paused before splitting up.

"Can you believe this?" said D. C. Lee. "I show up hoping for a free dinner and leave with a horse, a Dom Perignon buzz, and my work in the hands of one of the world's great violinists. How obtuse is that?"

"Our work over a Tourte?" echoed Saul. "I wonder what they got for it?"

"I like my frame," chimed in Nathan Pillsbury. "I'd like to stick the bill from the restaurant in there to remind myself how the other half lives."

Lionel shrugged. "Maybe the horse will show us how the other half lives."

"A horse has the same use as a sixth toe," Saul snorted. "If the nag makes a dime, it's found money."

The next morning, all four were elbow-deep in wood shavings and hand-

planing pernambuco blanks. Horse or no horse, there were bows to make and
bills to pay.

Luckily for the bowmakers, the colt Pernambuco matured quickly. His racing
debut as a two-year-old came six months later, at Seattle's Emerald Downs on
July Fourth. Three of the four bowmakers ferried across Admiralty Bay and
Puget Sound in Lionel George's antique yellow Volkswagen Beetle to watch
the race. Including the boat rides, it was a three-hour journey.

Saul refused to go. "I am not wasting a day of my life traveling six hours to
watch an animal run around in a circle. Spending a day immersed in a cloud of
gamblers' smoke appeals to me about as much as sucking the tailpipe of a city
bus."

As it turned out, Saul missed getting his picture taken. Pernambuco zoomed
out to an early lead and won by eight lengths. The five-furlong race for maiden
two-year-olds was worth $16,000. As winners, the men shared 60 percent.

"No way Saul made that much today!" Lionel crowed. "I like this. I like this
a lot."

A mistake in the program had listed the handsome young colt's *owner* as
Bo Makers, but it didn't stop all three of them from beaming broadly in the
winner's circle. As the muscular bay colt, the image of his champion father
Siphon, posed like a statue beside them, he wasn't even breathing hard.

Trainer Olin McCully beamed as he proudly pet the horse. "Look at him,"
he said. "This one's special. He's ready to go right back to the starting gate and
win again."

"Let him!" urged Lionel. "Twice more if he's up to it!"

The news of Pernambuco's effortless victory quickly spread throughout
Washington's racing circles, a two-year-old with a boatload of talent stabled at
Emerald Downs. Despite the attention, Pernambuco's trainer refused to rush the
horse and waited six weeks before entering him again.

Again the bowmakers ferried over to watch. Again Saul refused to go,
this time saying he needed to shampoo the carpets of his houseboat's living
quarters.

Again the other three got to smile and say "Cheese!" after Pernambuco glided around effortlessly and won by six lengths against seven new opponents.

Trainer McCully was ecstatic. "He could've moonwalked the last furlong on his hind legs and still won by daylight."

This time, the bowmakers won 60 percent of $20,000 and agreed unanimously that they really enjoyed racing. Each man's share was the equivalent of selling a bow—free money—without having to invest two tedious weeks earning it.

During the drive home, the men agreed not to tell Saul he'd won, unless he asked; and they knew an elephant would rollerblade down Washington Street wearing a tu-tu before he ever would.

"Unless Flipper swims up and *eek-eeks* the news," said D. C. Lee on the ferry, "Saul will never know he's just won another three grand."

Five weeks after his second victory, Pernambuco won a third time, and it was obvious the horse had too much talent to stay in Seattle. He was good enough to chase bigger money at higher levels.

"He's the best two-year-old I've ever seen, much less trained," said Olin McCully. "If I don't screw him up, this one has a chance to do something."

A perfect three-for-three, McCully decided to rest Pernambuco until November. Then it would be time to crank him back up to compete at the start of the new year. He called Lionel and told him Pernambuco's initial race as a three-year-old should come against tough competition in a Grade III stakes race outside San Francisco. "It's got a $100,000 purse," he said. "Sixty-grand to the winner."

Lionel's face was blank as he re-cradled his kitchen telephone and did the quick math. *Sixty grand, divided by three grand a bow, divided by four bowmakers.* "Five bows a man," he mumbled. "We've got a horse running for five bows a man."

Olin McCully believed Pernambuco had the talent to aim for southern California's prestigious Grade I Santa Anita Derby—though so did a hundred other horses already stabled there. Stretching out to longer distances, higher levels of competition, and tactical racing had caused dreamers and pretenders to fall like autumn leaves. In the 120 days spanning January through April,

McCully would give the horse every chance to prove he had the staying power to chase history.

While Pernambuco was earning newspaper headlines as a two-year-old in Seattle, Ooty was still growing, still gangly and surly. His trainer, Rigby Malone, thought the black horse wouldn't amount to anything beyond a claiming race fill-in or a lifelong back-of-the-packer. Based on his traditional yardstick of speed, form, and conditioning—a five-eighths of a mile time-trial with Tuki in the irons—Ooty showed the skill and patience of a chimp racing a stock car in the Daytona 500.

After the workout, Tuki jogged Ooty over and asked the trainer what he thought.

Rigby looked down and spit a long, slow drip of saliva on to the dirt, smoothed it over with his boot, then looked up and squinted. "He runs like a wildebeest."

"It wasn't *that* bloody bad," she protested.

"You're right. There *was* a positive. He beat the tractor by five."

Tuki didn't like Mr. Malone's blunt negativity. "Phar Lap lost his first four races, eight of his first nine."

"That was in the '30s. This is today, and today this horse couldn't beat *any* of them. And they're dead."

Unconvinced that Ooty was anything more than an oat-chomping imposter, and to prove that he was right and Tuki was wrong, Rigby entered the foreign-born colt in a five-furlong maiden race to be run on Halloween. Surrounded by seven other inexperienced two-year-olds, Ooty loaded into the starting gate with post-time odds of 40:1.

Tuki thought they were way too high.

Rigby thought they were way too low.

Rigby was right. Every cantankerous step of the way Ooty fought the jockey. He lost by thirty-six lengths.

The jockey, a track veteran, had a succinct message after he steered the stubborn colt over by Rigby and Tuki and slid off. "He don't wanna run, Rig. This one is awful short on the *want to*."

"He is not," defended Tuki. "He'll do better."

Rigby challenged her. "Tuki, the man just raced a horse that ran like his bones and muscles are duct-taped together. No horse short on the *want to* will ever amount to anything bigger than the pile of dung he produces."

"He needs more work, Mr. Malone. Give him a chance, will you? It was his first bloody race."

He shrugged. "Still not convinced, are you? Okay, we'll wheel him back. You got two weeks to find his *want to*."

"Fine," she sniffed, "but I want a different rider. That guy is bloody awful."

Two weeks later Ooty raced again, with a different rider and against a smaller field. The jockey gunned Ooty straight to the lead, but the colt immediately dropped back; and he ran all over the track, covering six furlongs during what was only a five-furlong race.

After it was over and Ooty was circled back to the Tuki and Rigby, the new jockey hopped down and gave a one-syllable report, "Slug."

Tuki was puzzled. "What's 'slug' mean?"

Rigby shrugged. "Could be one of two things: rifle or invertebrate. Neither's good."

"Pick one," the jockey suggested. "They both fit."

Although Rigby had been paid in advance to train this horse, he was starting to think the colt's career path should include dude-ranch tourists at forty bucks an hour. Burning through the old lady's life savings on this lollygagger gnawed at him. *These Possum Drop farmer folks are lighting cheap cigars with hundred dollar bills.*

He mulled over what to say to the Trombleys during his post-race report, and with crossed fingers, phoned them. Melvin answered on the first ring. Rigby could read the excitement and expectation in Melvin's voice. Every owner answered every post-race call with it.

"How'd we do, Rig? Win some money for Miss Louise?"

"He did better this time, Melvin. Sixth."

"That's good, ain't it?" Melvin asked positively. "Last time he got eighth. Good job, Rigby. Keep doing what you're doing, so he'll keep getting better. We've got confidence in you both. Next time will be the one. You just watch, Rigby. We know you can do it."

Hard talks with soft owners was a miserable part of the job. Rigby chose his words carefully. "Sixth don't turn a profit, Melvin . . . but we'll keep trying. We'll do our best, Melvin. He's got some talent." Rigby winced at his little white lie. Gutless. It was only a six-horse field. Why was he dicking around? *Just tell them it won't work,* he told himself.

16
SUNSHINE SUPERMEN

The best racehorse Luther O'Neil had ever received to train was unloaded from the shipping van, two minutes before the second best horse he'd ever received to train; and both had arrived due to a common racing reason: he knew somebody who knew somebody, who was somebody who wanted to get into the biz. Racing Thoroughbreds was a very big business, but its major tracks orbited a very small world . . . and black trainers were rarely the recipients of such good fortune as this.

The toughest routes to the big races—the major league preps—were California, New York, and Florida. From this stiff competition only a few horses in each state would emerge good enough to compete at the Kentucky Derby. Florida's blend of a robust stakes schedule, good purse money, longstanding racing tradition, and wonderful winter weather appealed to many horsemen. Into that world had entered J. L. Cottle and Moose Utley . . . and into their wake had come Luther O'Neil.

Luther owed his good fortune to Moose Utley's recent Bahamas bonefishing trip. As Moose's guide had poled their boat across the expansive flats of north Bimini, Moose had mentioned his quadrennial sporting challenges with J. L. Cottle. Horse racing was next on their agenda. Moose forgot to mention that the yearlings he and Cottle had bought cost upward of a million dollars each.

The bonefish guide, an old Bahamian named Anvil Sanders, had had a dabble or two on the fortunate side of racing years before in South Florida, and he recommended Luther O'Neil.

Moose liked the soft-spoken fishing guide, so he took the man's advice and looked up Luther O'Neil as soon as he returned to Miami. He invited him to lunch at Joe's, Miami's famed stone crab restaurant.

"If I told the guide what the yearlings cost, he might've doubled his rate," Moose said, smiling.

Luther nodded. "No worries about that, Mr. Moose. His rate'll be the same as long as you know him." He grinned. "Mine, too.

"But I gotta tell you," Luther continued, "I never had a great horse. Had some good ones and trained 'em good, but there's guys here with bigger stables who can buy a hundred of me.

"I lived here fifty years, Mr. Moose, and I'll die here, so if you want me to train your horse I need to take the Florida trail. I'll do my best. I'll treat 'em better than my own."

"I sense that about you, Luther, and that's all I expect. Do your best and shoot straight. Tell me what I need to hear. Not what I want to hear."

"Yessir. That's the way I like to be respected, too."

Talk between the men was open and easy. By the time they finished their key lime pie, Moose was sure he had the right guy.

Moose picked up the tab and tipped the valet to bring around both men's cars. While waiting for his flight at Miami International, he called Cottle.

"You trust him?" Cottle asked.

"He's an underdog. Been one his whole life. He's in a white and Hispanic world. Probably hanging on by his fingernails. So, yes, I trust him."

"Call him," Cottle said. "Tell him my horse is going to him, too."

In honor of potato folks everywhere, Cottle had christened his pricey two-comma chestnut grandson of Storm Cat, *Spudcat*. Shortly after Spudcat settled into Luther's training barn at Palm Meadows in West Boynton Beach, it was obvious the handsome colt had a lot of his granddaddy in him, not unusual for male relatives of the globe's priciest stallion. Spudcat was a confident, impressive athlete.

Despite the ribbing Cottle gave Moose over his own smaller yearling, as the colts turned two, it was obvious that Moose's colt had a lot of talent. Smaller than Spudcat, Moose's dark, sleek colt had instant acceleration and could fly.

Moose named him Hundo, in honor of a close friend, his World War II co-pilot, who lived for screaming barrel roles and shrieked like a madman whenever he performed them.

Hundo was the first of the two colts to race. Luther started him at a summer race at Calder Race Course in North Miami Beach.

After a perfect break, a quick lead, and winning by a full length, the jockey returned, grinning. "He's a rocket out of the gate, Luther. Like he knew when the gates were going to open."

"Reactions like that are special," Luther reported to Moose on the phone that evening. "Can't teach reflexes, Mr. Moose, and your little guy's got 'em. You got yourself a racehorse."

"Good," Moose replied. "Glad to hear it. You earned yourself a dinner at Joe's. Take a lady friend, one who likes a martini. Have fun on me." He added with a laugh, "Then have fun on her."

Luther chuckled. "Yessir. You're the boss."

Luther O'Neil had been traipsing through Gulfstream Park's barns for a lot of years, thirty-three Florida Derbies in a row. Word quickly spread that he had been handed not one, but two, terrific young prospects. He had never trained a million-dollar yearling before, much less two. As a trainer, his biggest win had been a Grade III stakes. The only horse he'd ever trained that was good enough to enter a Grade I had pulled up midway with a bowed tendon. He'd had a career of small-money claimers and longshot prospects, with hopeful traits but unchangeable limitations. Now, gifted with twin miracles, Luther took no chances, so he monitored their every move.

During the conference call update after Hundo's first win, Luther told his two bosses, "The good ones, they understand winnin'. And they understand losin'. Some have a killer instinct. Others give up; they don't got the heart.

"Losing can be habit formin', Mr. Moose, Mr. Cottle; so pickin' the right spot and the right competition is crucial. Each horse is born with a will to win; but it has to be nurtured, some more than others.

"Emotionally, they're like boxers," continued Luther. "Only so many championship fights in each. The body and the mind both take a poundin'."

"In that case, Luther," said Moose, "keep the two apart as long as possible."

"Yes," agreed Cottle. "Wait 'til the time is right."

"Was hopin' you'd say that. Keep 'em apart, then see what you got. Hundo was ready today. Spudcat needs another couple a weeks."

"You make the call," Cottle said. "That's your decision."

Luther felt three more gray hairs sprout as soon as Cottle said that. Pressure. Damn, it was heavy.

Nevertheless, Cottle wondered if he'd made the right choice in a trainer. Leaving a million-dollar asset in the hands of a stranger ran counter to the life Cottle had lived.

After this bugged him for several days, he phoned his best friend.

"What are you worried about?" Moose replied. "All that time you were learning about potatoes, Luther's been working with racehorses. Seems to me you two have something important in common."

"What's that?"

"Work ethic. You outwork your competition. Don't punish him for being like you."

Cottle smiled. "Thanks, Moose. You always know the right thing to say."

"Course I do."

"Oh, Moose? One last thing."

"What's that?"

"Better put goggles on that Shetland pony of yours. Hate for Spudcat to kick dirt in his eye." *Click.*

As Cottle leaned back in his deep leather chair, he reflected on what Moose had said. Cottle had ridden thousands of miles on horseback, overseeing his land, inspecting his mushrooming herds of beef cattle. Sixty years after starting with a dozen head, the herds stretched farther than he could see—too numerous to count. He owned the cattle, the dirt beneath them, the potato fields, and the fertilizer plants that produced the nutrients that maximized yields. All of this earned him billions. He'd done it by hiring good people and trusting them to do good work. Moose was right. Yes, Cottle knew a lot about horses but not a lot about racing Thoroughbreds. The guy he had hired did.

Eyes still closed, Cottle swung around toward the big bay window, and let the sunshine warm him. *Here he sat, smart enough to build four billion-dollar companies from scratch, and he's relying on a hired hand to share secrets about how his horse was feeling on Tuesday. This was smart?*

Slowly Cottle broke into a broad smile. *Yes, this was smart. Moose had already figured it out. His best chance to beat me is to trust a true horseman. Delegate. Empower. Stay out of the way.*

Whoever won this one would gain custody of their old, camelhair suitcase with the bullet-hole reminder of Marrakech, the stack of memories inside it, and the trinket that had fueled their rivalry for decades. *Poor Moose! All that good advice . . . but he'd never beat Spudcat.*

Two weeks to the day after Hundo's debut victory, Spudcat raced for the first time, and won by three lengths. Within minutes of the race's conclusion, Cottle's office phone in Boise started ringing, six different trainers trying to unhook Luther's relationship with him and Moose. Cottle despised badmouthers. After fielding the last of the intrusive calls, he dialed Luther in Florida and conferenced in Moose Utley.

"Luther," Cottle said evenly, "these other trainers say you're a dumb black man, that you don't know what you're doing, that they could do a better job. In view of these opinions, Moose and I have a question."

"What, sir?"

"Are you?"

There were several seconds of silence at the other end the line.

Then Luther quietly responded, "Those are harsh words, sir. Mean words."

"Easily spoken by men pretending to be your friends," Cottle said pointedly. "What's your answer?"

Luther answered slowly. "My answer, Mr. Cottle, is I don't know the answer. How smart I am is for others to judge. For you and Mr. Moose to decide."

"Anything else?" asked Moose.

"Just one other thing, Mr. Moose. Maybe it's the answer you want, maybe not. Smart or not, I am a *proud* man, sir. Proud of the work I've put in, the job I've done; proud I wake up when a cricket chirps 'cause all I live to do is keep your horses healthy and strong."

Cottle interrupted. "Luther?"

"Yes, sir?"

"Good answer."

"Beautiful, Luther," chimed Moose.

"You're my man, Luther," Cottle confirmed. "You're my trainer. You hear me? Right, Moose?"

"Absolutely," reaffirmed Moose. "You handle the horses, Luther. We know how to handle circling buzzards and backstabbing nitwits."

The next day a story appeared in a national newspaper about clandestine racism in Florida horse racing, with Cottle speaking out. The meddling trainers quit calling.

Buoyed with confidence, Luther O'Neil developed the two best colts he'd ever seen, bluebloods, purebred fliers. The colts consumed his life, and his determination was laser-focused.

Luther O'Neil's mission as J.L. Cottle's trainer was simple and straightforward: prepare Spudcat to beat Moose Utley's horse. Moose Utley's assignment, of course, was just the reverse. Prep Hundo to wax Spudcat.

Like everyone who'd ever bought a racehorse, Mr. Cottle and Mr. Moose were motivated by the flickering dream of racing glory. Luther had warned them that there were a lot more broken hearts and legs in racing than silver cups and *happily-ever-afters*.

Long odds meant nothing to Mr. Cottle and Mr. Moose. They had defied the odds their entire lives.

At this stage, the odds were 50/50: J. L. Cottle versus Moose Ultey. *Mano a mano*. Spudcat versus Hundo. *El caballo contra caballo.*

17
HAPPY NEW YEAR!

On New Year's Day, Deacon Truth knocked on Rigby Malone's half-open office door. Rigby was studying his notebook, looking for winners. Deacon stepped inside and sat down in the wobbly chair by the desk.

"Happy New Year," Rigby grunted, not looking up. "What's your resolution? Mine is to win enough to pay the help."

"That's what I wanted to talk to you about," Deacon said. "I want to be a jockey agent."

"What makes you think you can do that?" Rigby asked, still not looking up.

Deacon shrugged. "How hard can it be? Other people do it."

Rigby then closed his notebook and looked at Deacon. "The good ones have phone numbers of big-time trainers and owners. More importantly, they rep a great rider." Rigby paused. "All you got is me."

"I got a couple guys rides in December," offered Deacon. "You know, connected them with trainers in a bind."

"Anonymous horses and riders might help pay the rent, Deacon, but you'll need a big name if you plan to change your tax bracket. Getting one will be a pisser."

"What's the best way, Rig?"

"There's no agent prep school, Deacon. Many are former jocks, retired by choice or broken bones. Other has spent years establishing connections. You're neither, and you ain't white. So your objective is simple: Network your ass off. Be positive, visible, and accessible to as many people as you possibly can be. Sell whatever decent rider you can onto a decent horse in every race possible.

It's a tough road, brother. A very tough road."

Rigby stood up and walked to the dirt-streaked window. "Only the agents of superstar jocks can be picky, Deacon. You can't. You need to outwork everybody—be doggedly persistent. Most important of all," Rigby concluded, "you need your riders to win. Winning fuels everything."

Deacon sat in the chair, thinking about Rigby's advice. "The work don't bother me, Rig. You know that. I ain't got nothin' else to do but work. I want to *be* somebody, Rig. When I was growin' up, my dad told me that in order to *be* somebody, a man must prove he *is* somebody."

"Your dad is a wise man," replied Rigby. "You two close?"

"Used to be," said Deacon quietly. "Lost him three years ago. I miss him sometimes."

Rigby walked over and put his hand on Deacon's shoulder. "You always will, son. You always will."

Deacon's new job required long inglorious hours, starting before sunrise, and a lot of thankless effort. Few blacks had ever shagged down rides, so every day was a struggle.

Jockeys who wanted help finding rides paid him fifteen percent of what they won and looked at him as an employee, not a friend. If Deacon couldn't hustle a jockey a mount, preferably on a horse with a decent chance to win, *Poof!* he'd be gone. Deacon soon learned that agents were like mushrooms. When one disappeared, two more popped up.

Deacon was entering a tough business—but he trusted his personality. He had people skills. He was a *connector*. He was always facilitating relationships.

"I am an equal-opportunity people person," he liked to say when meeting new people, "for rich and poor alike." Happy by nature, the words came easily. Some believed him. Some didn't. When things got tough, he sought out Rigby for empathy. He rarely got it.

"That's the way the cookie crumbles," Rigby said bluntly.

"Then I'm leavin' crumbs all over the damn place," grumbled Deacon.

"You want a Kleenex?" scolded Rigby. "Or do you want your rake back?

You knew it was hard, Deacon. So it's hard—big deal. Quit bitchin'. If building a book of business was easy, then hell, *I'd* be doin' it."

January first also had signaled the start of the new three-year-old racing season, which would culminate in May with the run for a blanket of roses at the Kentucky Derby. From there, Baltimore's Preakness Stakes; then Long Island for the Belmont, the final leg of the Triple Crown. For established horsemen, the New Year was time to dream. For guys like Deacon Truth, it was time to scratch out a new beginning.

Six days later, Deacon was searching at sunrise for free food, preferably a warm cinnamon sugar twist. He had a good idea where to look and bee-lined toward Rigby Malone's barn. Tuki was already at Ooty's stall. Did the girl ever sleep? Deacon spied a box on the railing. There they were! Chocolate, jelly, and cream-filled, fresh from the bakery! *I love this girl!*

Three donuts and thirty minutes later, Deacon walked out to the training track alongside Tuki and Ooty. He leaned against the railing and watched their workout. Their motion was effortless.

She belongs on that horse, he thought. *Rigby ought to put her on him in a race and see what happens.*

Deacon saw a boatload of talent in the girl. Star power. If this funny-talking girl could ride as well as he believed, she could win. He could sell the heck out of her. The media would sell her to everybody. Her appeal would transcend the betting windows. She could be a celebrity.

Hype, bullshit, and mirrors, he mused. *That's what sells in L.A.*

After several days of coaxing, Tuki agreed to get an apprentice jockey's license—only in case Mr. Malone ever asked her to race Ooty. She would ride no other horse. This business had killed her mother, and she had sworn a thousand times she'd never race for money.

As she studied the license papers, Tuki heard a demon laugh, with it a haunting vision of a black horse tumbling, both her and her mother flying.

The horse had three white stockings. She ignored the premonition and quickly scribbled her name.

"Happy now?" she said to Deacon, stuffing the papers to his chest. Then she strode out, back to the barn.

Deacon suggested she talk to some of Santa Anita's other female jockeys. Tuki sought them out for snippets of advice. The first scrounged hard for a dozen mediocre mounts each week. "You have to fight, honey," the woman said. "Riding here is no tea party. When the bell rings, no one's your friend. They test you. Protect yourself and protect your horse. But whatever you do, don't screw up. Women jockeys have clawed for decades to earn respect. One stupid move would slide every single one of us right back down the mountain. I repeat, *don't screw up.*"

Deacon's confidence in Tuki was greater than her own, so she was mortified by the machinations of his bombastic ad campaign. Before she had even ridden a single race, he was billing her as the *Diva of Dirt* and the *Smurf of the Turf.* Handbills printed with her picture and a promise of greatness were taped to light poles everywhere. Hundreds more he had Pez stick on the windshields of cars parked in the owners lot.

The turf writer covering Santa Anita for the *Daily Racing Form* called it the greatest hype job since 1973 when Bobby Riggs and Billie Jean King lobbed tennis balls in the Astrodome. "I don't know if the woman can ride," the reporter wrote, "but I do know Deacon Truth can sell."

Deacon convinced Tuki she needed to get experience on other horses before climbing aboard Ooty in a live race. He framed his reason perfectly. "You'll only hurt Ooty's chances if you're not comfortable in a money race. Don't ride for me. Do it for Ooty."

"You are bloody nonsense," she replied. "You're so full of it, your shoes should squish. But you may have a point." Reluctantly, she agreed to ride a few races.

Deacon amped the promotion. "Third on Thursday . . . Free on Friday." On Thursday, any owner or trainer who saddled Tuki in the third race would get a free ride in any other race on the card; and any owner who put her on a horse on Friday would have their jock mount refunded if she didn't win.

As he expected, Deacon was flooded with requests for all the early races on Thursdays and the full card on Fridays. With multiple horses from which to choose, his ability to put Tuki on a contender dramatically increased. None of the calls came from Rigby. No way in hell Rigby would trust his athletes with a novice.

Deacon's bombastic promotional gimmickry paid off. Tuki placed third and second on her first Thursday; and won on her third try on Friday, on a horse that went to the post as the fifth betting favorite. She wheeled right back into the next race and won again. Rigby watch both victories through binoculars from the upstairs clubhouse, but said nothing.

Deacon Truth turned a small profit—and with it bought lunch for the beat media and hyped Tuki's story. He hit the mother lode. The next morning Tuki Banjo's picture was splashed onto the sports page of the *L.A. Times*. Then because of the newspaper coverage, three radio stations called. Deacon booked Tuki onto all three. At first, she flatly refused and relented only after Deacon promised never again to commit her without permission.

Several veteran jockeys in the colony resented Tuki's instant notoriety and conspired to teach her a lesson. Rigby got wind of it and warned her. "If they come at you, fight back. If you have to, knock one of those sons-of-dogs over the rail. Do whatever you need to do—but never risk your horse."

One glance at the icy intimidation stares from jockeys on both sides of her in the starting gate told the story. *Rigby's right. They're bloody comin'.*

As the race unfolded, four jockeys pinched her in, then boxed her out of contention. Inexperienced riders were fragile, the four determined to find Tuki's emotional trigger. She would fold. They'd seen it before.

Tuki was trapped and had no choice but to slow and swing wide to escape them. When she did, she effectively rode herself out of the race. She finished last and earned her first chorus of boos, but she bit her tongue and said nothing. It *was* a bad ride.

On her way to the women's dressing room, she ignored the male jockeys' taunts. Rigby was waiting when she emerged. "Don't say it," she said, holding up a hand. "Dumb ride."

He swatted her hand away, stood nose to nose and barked, "What were you thinkin'? You knew what they were planning."

"I was thinkin' that they knew what they were doin' and I didn't."

Rigby was fuming. "What did you learn?"

"I learned that the bloody truth of this business is I hate it."

"Then quit. Muck stalls and play with a garden hose. *Happy scrub* your life away!"

"I'm not going to bloody quit," she replied indignantly. "I'm going to beat their bloody arses. Next time they try that bloody trap on me, I'll knock one over the rail. Like you said. Shoulda done it this time."

Rigby nodded. "Good. Glad to hear a 'triple bloody' answer. Tells me you must've gotten the point. You wasted a race, but learned something. Now go home and get some rest. It worked today, so they might try it again tomorrow."

They didn't, but her initiation continued mid-week in a $36,000 allowance race. A quick glance at the tote board showed her 50:1. When she loaded into the starting gate, eight of the greatest jockeys west of the Mississippi sandwiched her in. Santa Anita's fabled A-team.

Her thoughts flashed to her mother. Had her mom ridden against men like these? What had she done? Why hadn't Rigby Malone provided advice?

The bettors wondered, too. Tuki broke a half-length slow in the explosion of dirt-kicking hooves, then urged her horse to keep up. Hopelessly pinched behind two horses and nowhere to go, she was trapped. Mousetrapping greenhorns was child's play for the veteran jockeys. She finished eighth, crossing the finish line with tears of failure. She'd been outsmarted, outclassed, and outridden. As she circled back to dismount, angry fans foghorned their displeasure.

Rigby was waiting and, much to the amusement of the veteran riders nearby, he let her have it. "That ride," he hissed, "was DUMBER than letting a three-year-old hold a tomato!" He inhaled deeply and lowered his voice. "That was a *stupid* ride, young lady, maybe the stupidest this track has seen since the Nixon administration."

"I gather you didn't like it," she shot back, her arms folded defensively.

The Nixon reference meant nothing. She'd never heard of the guy. But the snickers of the jocks cut deep. There were a thousand easier ways than this to live a life.

As she was stewing, Deacon walked up. "Seashells and balloons to you, Mr. Truth," she mocked. "Thanks for a glorious opportunity."

She walked away and sulked alone in the locker room. She pondered her options, quitting one of them. Before this race, she'd believed she could compete. Now she knew she couldn't. *These blokes make instant decisions. I ponder choices. If I don't get better, I'll never win.*

That night, back in her room, Deacon phoned but Tuki didn't pick up. She listened as he left a message. "Two trainers dropped us. Changed their minds after watching this afternoon's mess. But you picked up a ride in the first race."

She picked up the receiver. "Who's the bloody crazy man?"

"You mean besides me, for repping you? Rigby. He said you ride too good to be that bad. He also said you probably won't ride that dumb twice in a row 'cause it's almost impossible for *anybody* to ride that dumb twice in a row."

"That's encouraging."

"Rig's all heart, Tuki. You know that. Except for his mouth. He also said if by some freak chance you do ride that dumb again, it's only the first race and you won't spoil the rest of his afternoon." Deacon paused, then continued. "It's a small field going two turns. Five horses. They can't gang up on you. It's a good spot. You can win this one."

"Did he apologize for yellin' at me?"

There was another pause. "Does he ever?"

"No."

"Answered your own question."

Tuki did win, by two lengths. She'd gotten a great jump out of the gate, forced an early pace, then dropped down on the rail to save ground and energy. She'd patiently stayed in touch with the two leaders, who'd locked up in a premature move, and bided her time as the four- and five-year-olds gobbled up the middle furlongs. The pace was good but not consuming. Two hundred yards from the finish line, she made a quick and decisive move. A fresh horse beneath her, she shot to the front in a blink. Her lead stretched to a length, then two, and widened as she crossed the finish line.

Inwardly, Tuki was ecstatic. Outwardly, no emotion. *It was just a good spot.* The best-prepared horse had won the race. She had made no blunders.

Rigby had dropped a few shillings on his horse at the betting window; Tuki's slump had boosted the odds. In addition to the winner's share of the purse, he pocketed a little gas money for the Rolls.

He felt the girl had a lot to learn, but her win boosted confidence and her commitment to the craft grew even stronger. She patrolled the barns every morning at 4:30, never left before the work was done and every horse was cared for. Fourteen-hour days, seven days a week. Never missed a day. Maybe it was time for even a snot-wiping curmudgeon like him to believe in her.

Deacon kept hustling up rides; and the more Tuki rode, the more frequently she won, and on better horses. Deacon was making money, so was Rigby.

Tuki was earning quite a bit now, but she couldn't care less. She lived off what Rigby paid her as a stable hand and saved the rest.

Within a month, she returned the Mustang car keys to Mitzi and replaced the car with a rebuilt 1957 Harley-Davidson Sportster, same as her parents in the photograph she treasured. Her mum's Sportster had been the first of its kind in Australia. Her mum had shared that detail on the back of the picture, the only sample of her mum's handwriting she had.

Tuki's motorcycle half-helmet was pink, with Ooty's picture laminated on the back. The gas tank was pink, too, with another picture of Ooty. That she could take the motorcycle apart, work on it, and reassemble it, added to Tuki's ever-growing folkloric status among the young and hip in southern California. She and the bike were a common sight on streets throughout Arcadia. Deacon started referring to the pink Harley as "Tuki's taxi."

For all her enjoyment of the motorcycle, however, life was never better than when sailing on thundering hooves. Nothing compared to a horse race, she discovered, no smile wider than the ones she wore in the winner's circle.

Rides came easily and wins started to pile up, too. Several times she won twice in a day and once she won three. Deacon bet her she'd win four at least once during the meet.

The idea of four wins in a day made her laugh. "Four? In one day? Drinking your breakfast, are you? What if I don't?"

Deacon rubbed his Afro vigorously. "You *don't* win four, I shave my head and dress like a white person on the last day of the meet. Rigby picks the clothes. He's the whitest guy I know."

"And what if I *do* win four?"

"You shave your head and dress like a white person, too."

"But I *am* a white person," she giggled.

"Not a normal one," he replied. "You don't worry about material things enough to be a *normal* white person. At least not in America."

On Tuki's nineteenth birthday, she proved Deacon prophetic and won five races. To fulfill her pledge, she had her head shaved. Deacon, of course, staged the shearing so it was televised live on L.A.'s prime time sports news. Tuki scrunched up her face throughout the ordeal, refusing to watch, as her red locks drifted to the ground. One hour later, Deacon's cell phone rang and Tuki Banjo was booked for an appearance the following day on *The Tonight Show starring Jay Leno.*

At the taping, when her cue came to walk on-stage, she meekly inched out into the bright lights of Leno's set. She wore a custom-sewn silk shirt, a birthday gift from the Odds Quad. A local silk-maker had quilted together all seven colors of the rainbow—violet, indigo, blue, green, yellow, orange, and red.

She greeted host Jay Leno quietly, shyly holding out her hand, saying, *"Seashells and balloons, Mr. Leno."*

"Where?" he asked, puzzled. "What are you talking about?"

"Me way of saying hello," she said quietly. "Nice things, they are. Happy things." Too nervous to look at the famous star, her eyes wandered everywhere.

Leno blinked. Twenty thousand interviews he'd done. First one that featured seashells and balloons.

A motorcycle buff, Leno asked about her bike. Then he showed a film clip of

Tuki winning five races in a day. He asked about her bald head and kidded her about her colorful outfit.

"Me colors match me mood," she replied. "Different color for different emotions. Me friends gave me this. Had it made, they did."

Leno waved at the shirt. "Look at those colors! You look like a flower shop!"

The studio audience, including Deacon backstage, howled.

Not knowing what to say, Tuki bowed her head and buried her face in her hands.

"C'mon, c'mon, don't be shy," he encouraged, reaching over and putting a reassuring hand on her arm. "If each color represents an emotion, what's the whole shirt mean?"

Tuki sat up quickly, ramrod straight. "It means I'm bloody petrified!"

Leno nearly fell off his chair, laughing.

The following morning, Tuki Banjo was the new "It" girl coast-to-coast and the bald-headed pixie with the perfect Hollywood name was deemed a "must-have" guest for every TV talk show in the nation.

Among those watching Tuki's meteoric ascension was a Santa Monica animal rights activist named Ginger Bredman; at fifty, still Botox smooth—a faded soap-actress hanging onto her youth as if clinging to a treetop in a rising flood. Ginger stroked her four cats while watching Tuki Banjo's appearance on the Leno show. She jumped at the TV screen when she saw the film of Tuki whipping a horse down the stretch. *"Those poor horses! This cruelty must stop!"* Always looking for a cause, Ginger had found one. Where Tuki went, so did cameras. So would Ginger. Equine emancipation would soon come to Santa Anita.

Millions more had watched her, too. With the light-speed fanaticism of the celebrity-hungry media, Tuki Banjo was a star. Endorsement offers flooded Deacon's fax machine. Among them, a six-figure attempt from an aspiring suitor, determined to romance the nation's hottest new female athlete. Almost overnight, college students from coast-to-coast were awash in Tuki colors, so Mitzi capitalized and launched a line of *BanjoWear* products splattered with seashells and balloons. They flew off the shelves like godwits.

Tuki cared little for the frenzy, though she toyed with the press whenever possible—just to drive Deacon crazy. The only time it backfired was when she suggested that he spend his time on something more worthwhile than dialing for dollars.

"Like what?" he asked.

"Do something for kids," she said. "Hold a bloomin' contest or somethin'."

"I can see it now," Deacon said and waved an arm wide across the sky. "Spend the Day with Tuki Banjo."

"Kids only," she said. "No bloody adults. Kids, I'm in. Adults, I'm out."

Deacon loved a challenge. The answer to this one, however, seemed hidden. "What kind of contest?"

"You figure it out," she said over her shoulder, while heading to her motorcycle. "Earn your money, Jeopardy Genius!"

The next day Deacon's contest was splashed all over the paper, the Santa Anita racing program, and the local airwaves. A folded copy of the *L.A. Times* was in Rigby's office, displaying a story about how teenage girls, who shaved their heads and mailed their hair as donations for wigs for children with cancer, could win a day with Tuki Banjo. The best essay would determine the winner. When Rigby came by Ooty's stall and showed it to Tuki, she was flabbergasted.

"He bloomin' did it," she gasped. "He actually bloomin' did it."

"I'd enter," kidded Rigby, "but I hate writin' essays."

"Let that be a lesson to you," Deacon bragged to Tuki at lunch. "Never leave the room. *Never.* I am the idea man, baby. That's why you love me."

He got down on one knee and took her hand. "You know why I love you? 'Cause when some little baldheaded Tuki Junior comes to spend a day with you, you will make sure that little girl loves every single minute. *That* is why I love you."

He stood and dusted off his pants. "Now go win a race or somethin', will you? Last night I ended up somewhere I shouldn't have, and my American Express card did the tango with an Argentinean girl."

After work that evening, an enterprising interviewer rode up alongside Tuki on a rented Harley Sportster while Tuki waited at a red light. He asked for a quote and she gave him one.

"The press is annoying," she called out, eyes straight ahead, loudly gunning her throttle.

"Can't use that," he answered over the din. "Need something I can use."

"Fame is pollen in the wind."

"I don't get it," the reporter replied.

"Then go with the first one."

Without waiting for the light to change, Tuki gunned the throttle, made a quick illegal turn, and thundered off, leaving him boxed in traffic. Ticks, fleas, chiggers, mosquitoes, the media were. Not a butterfly among them.

Ten days after the contest was announced in the *Times*, Deacon's "Spend the Day with Tuki" promotion had received 29,436 large envelopes full of human hair. The positive press created a sonic boom of publicity. The contest blossomed to life, a noble purpose.

Tuki Banjo was now a Hollywood insider and with fame came instant riches. Thanks to Mitzi, she was now just two degrees from Kevin Bacon; they shared the same financial planner.

The sudden celebrity complicated life immensely, her fishbowl life stealing her privacy. Even Rigby's neighbors rented their tree limbs to paparazzi who shot invasive photos through long-lens cameras. Gossip columnists fed the public every rumor imaginable. The thirst for all things Tuki was oceanic.

Tuki despised it all, refused to watch the silly box, and rarely looked at a paper. She distrusted everyone tied to the swirling insanity and soon was arguing with Deacon, angrily rebuking the right of the media to intrude on her life. "Why can't you let me keep me life bloody simple, Deacon—true to me core beliefs? All the rest of this nonsense is buggery."

"Money ain't buggery," he protested. "The money is *real*. Call Kevin Bacon! Tell him to ask your accountant if all that money you're sittin' on is real or fake?"

She wasn't listening. As she wheeled away on Ooty in Santa Anita's morning darkness, 5:08 a.m., Deacon's cell phone rang. Tuki knew who was calling:

Someone who wanted her for something intrusive.

"Answer that and I pity you," she called back over her shoulder.

He mimicked her sardonically. "*I pity you.* You don't pity me on payday, do you?" he yelled back.

Ooty's morning workout was steady but unspectacular. Although Rigby still thought he was a big galoot, Tuki believed in him. He had grown from a spindle-legged orphan to an uncoordinated yearling, then gangly at two years old. Now, having turned three, he stood seventeen hands tall at the withers, his chest deep, hind-end thick.

Rigby wasn't impressed. "Scared armadillos move faster than that horse," he complained.

Tuki didn't argue. "Somethin's troublin' him."

"Take him back out," Rigby suggested. "Stand him wide of the far turn. Let him watch the others. Maybe he'll understand the business he's in." With that, Rigby spit on the ground and walked away. Damn horse. Still short on the *want to.*

Tuki did as he suggested. She walked Ooty back onto the raked loam and they stood at the edge of the turn as horses surged past, exhaling loudly. Ooty was a smart horse. He was also stubborn. Until he decided to compete, he wouldn't. She wondered if Ooty's lack of confidence was due to his bob tail. After twenty minutes watching the workouts, she turned him back around and slowly returned to the barn.

The next morning, as Tuki fussed over Ooty as she bathed him, Deacon sneaked up to scare her.

"Seashells and balloons, Mr. Truth!" she called out loudly, without turning around.

He laughed. "Dang, girl, you're good! What's up this morning with Tuki Banjo, Superstar?"

"Today, Mr. Businessman, a wee experiment. But, first, here you be." She handed Deacon a warm box of donuts she bought for the crew. "Trade you," she said. "I'll hold your phone. Take a few."

Still warm, the donuts smelled delicious. He made the swap. "Don't drop that phone, girl. My whole life is in it."

"Really?" Tuki turned and tossed it toward Ooty's water bucket.

"Aahhh!!!!" Deacon raced after the phone, diving in mid-air, missing by inches.

Splash!

"Oops." Tuki giggled. "Me aim was off. Sorry."

Deacon collapsed onto a hay bale, his head in his hands. His entire contact list—*gone*. "My phone," he moaned. "My phone. My phone is . . . "

"Taking a bath," finished Tuki. "Methinks his tail is making him self-conscious."

Deacon looked up. "How you plan to fix that? Call Dr. Phil?"

Tuki ignored Deacon's prattling satire. "We'll grow it. Long and lovely."

She finished brushing Ooty, then held up a small mirror to his face. "See how handsome you are, Ooty? The fillies will stampede you, Mr. Handsome. No cell phone necessary for you."

Deacon rolled his eyes. "He's a *horse*, Tuki. He ain't no shrink-thinker. He don't care how he looks. He eats, he poops, he runs, he sleeps. He lives in a box! C'mon girl, inhale deep!"

"Shhh!" she whispered, with her finger to her lips. "If he thinks he's handsome, he'll do better. It's all in the mind. Yes, he's a horse, but he's still a male. A porcelain fragility, you men have."

Deacon stood up and shook his head. "You worry me, Tuki Banjo," he said as he walked away. "You're harder to figure out than algebra."

After Deacon left, Tuki grabbed the shopping bag she'd brought from home and walked her four-legged friend to the canopy of a ninety-year-old oak, the tree that had shaded Seabiscuit and four Kentucky Derby winners. For two hours, Tuki wove into Ooty's bobtail braids of the longest strands of straight black hair donated by the contest fans.

When finished, she held up the mirror and urged Ooty to look at himself. He tested his new tail, swishing it back and forth, and kept swishing.

"I knew you'd like it," she said, kissing him on the forehead.

Then they clopped two hundred yards back to the stable, passing a dozen fillies and mares, showing off his new tail. Tuki kissed Ooty again on the nose and departed for the day. He stood in his stall, looking out, nickering at several fillies that paraded past.

For the next ten days, Tuki took the mirror to Ooty's barn and fussed over him. One morning, she arrived with a camera and an oversized straw sombrero with the ears cut out. Ooty ate it.

"Okay," she noted. "No hats."

The next day, she tried a pair of custom-made polarized sunglasses, modified to fit as half-cup headwear. Ooty seemed to like them.

"Sensitive eyes, have you?" she teased. "Or a more mysterious look for the ladies—a foreign colt of international intrigue?"

Tuki customized a second pair for race days; with the mirrored reflector lens, he would see forward but the other horses wouldn't see him.

"That's the way he prefers it," she told Deacon, who looked on in disbelief. "He likes the look."

"What look?"

"Being invisible. He likes it."

"He likes being invisible? How do I explain that to the press?" As he walked away, he muttered, "Girl, I am gonna need a *bodysuit* of invisible if you don't cut this craziness out."

The final piece of Ooty's ensemble was a handcrafted screw-on "earring" with the design of a fern leaf, the national emblem of New Zealand. Ooty didn't seem to mind it at all. When he looked in the mirror, he cocked his head to the right.

Tuki realized he was left-eye dominant, like people, one eye more than the other made sight-driven decisions. So she put the "earring" on Ooty's right side.

Convinced she had propped up Ooty's self-esteem, Tuki convinced Rigby to flank his stall with fillies. "Ego food," she told him. "Feed him."

Without a word, Rigby did. Six months of training sure as hell hadn't worked. This petite baldheaded Kiwi orbited a solar system of her own. If she thought having filly neighbors would make Ooty run faster, so be it.

She then asked Rigby to enter Ooty in a seven-furlong maiden race three days away. He didn't see the point but didn't argue. Some things weren't worth debating, especially involving those two.

Ooty's race was third on the card, a field of eight, of which none had ever won a race. When Tuki was announced as the rider, Ooty's morning odds of 20:1 dropped to 9:1.

Rigby saddled the horse and Tuki screwed the good-luck fern-leaf earring to the base of the colt's right ear, then secured his reflective visor in place and showed Ooty his handsome self in the hand-held mirror. Tuki was fashionably decked out in Miss Louise's custom-designed racing silks: cornstalk green with PDHS in capital letters stitched broadside onto the yellow school bus sewn across the back. Possum Drop High School had never been so regally advertised.

At the call *"Riders up!"* Tuki kissed Ooty on the muzzle and whispered, "I love you, you handsome son of Flossy McGrew." He swished his hair-extended tail and nodded—or so Deacon later swore to reporters.

When Tuki steered Ooty away from the paddock, the colt was alert and on his toes. Theirs was not the typical pre-race paddock procedure that a million previous horses had undergone when preparing to race at Santa Anita; so fans and photographers took snapshots of each their every step, and kept clicking as Tuki steered Ooty to their place in the processional line, fourth of eight.

Ooty walked peacefully and Tuki replayed her strategy in her mind for the hundredth time. She knew who would set the pace, who would stalk the leaders, and who would close. Four of the other horses had ability, three didn't. What she didn't know was whether all the horses would do what they were supposed to. There would be dozens of decision points requiring immediate reaction. She, however, expected Ooty to battle.

A small mid-week crowd watched in the bright California sunshine. The bell rang, the gates opened, and the eight eager young horses took off down the back straightaway. Tuki rode along, letting Ooty pick his own pace.

For the first half-mile, he ambled leisurely behind the others, still eighth by twenty lengths. With a quick loving touch high on his neck, she signaled him that it was time to go home.

With three furlongs to go, he dug in and lengthened his long stride, eating up dirt with every flying stride.

Three outclassed horses were quickly reeled in. The other four gamely held on. One furlong to go, 220 yards. Ooty was fourth, trailing sixth lengths. Tuki urged him on. He could pick off at least two if he kept charging.

One wobbled from fatigue; Tuki guessed he would veer to the rail to save ground. She stayed in her lane, the four path, and urged Ooty to run down the other two. Crouch fatigue burned her thighs, but she didn't move an inch in the saddle.

Ninety yards remained. The fans in the stands rose to their feet. Tuki clutched her whip but didn't have to use it. Ooty was closing like a cannonball.

Fifty yards. She leaned forward and whispered, "C'mon, boy. Catch him!"

Ooty strained to the lead, zoomed up on the outside, within a head, then a nose, and was still flying at the finish. The crowd roared!

Had they won or lost? Tuki had no idea.

Upstairs in the clubhouse, high above the finish line, Rigby and Deacon lowered their binoculars. Whether or not he'd been wrong about this horse, Rigby knew he had just witnessed something extra special. To his view, Ooty's jockey had stolen the race. He turned to Deacon, an odd look on his face. "You know, Deacon. I've got a funny feeling about this race."

"Me, too," replied Deacon. "I got a funny feelin' I just made a whole lot of money. Enough to rent a Winnebago! Is *that* the funny feelin' you mean?"

"No," said Rigby, "not that. Something is telling me that someday you'll be telling your children about this horse, this rider, and *this* race."

"*This* horse?" crowed Deacon. "*This* horse? This horse you said couldn't beat a tractor?" Deacon grinned broadly. "What you just *saw* was a superstar doin' the supernatural! We just saw Tuki Banjo Superstar come from twenty lengths back to *win?*"

Rigby nodded. "She earned her money. If the photo holds, she just won a race she had no business winning."

"I agree with you completely, Mr. Malone, sir. That girl deserves a *raise!*"

"Can't afford a raise, Deacon. Didn't have a dime on them."

"What?" Deacon stared at Rigby in disbelief. "No money on them? You didn't bet the Rolls? Tell me you're lyin'."

Rigby rolled his tongue in his cheek wistfully and slowly shook his head.

"Not to place?" Deacon pressed.

"No. And I'll save you the breath; not to show, either. Nada, zero, zipska. I had him last by half a mile."

The crowd roared, signifying the posting of the official results. Rigby glanced at the board. Ooty's lunge to the wire had gotten the job done. He had won by a flared nostril.

As Rigby and Deacon hurried down to the winner's circle, Rigby chided himself for not betting on his own team, especially with 9:1 odds.

"No money on your own horse," Deacon needled. "With Tuki Banjo Superstar in the saddle? Why you do somethin' dumb like that? You got so much money you don't need any more?"

Deacon continued his exaggerated dramatic panache. "Oh, lookee here, a whole *pocketful* of tickets!" Deacon fanned open a dozen winning tickets from his suit pocket. "Want one?"

Deacon needled Rigby mercilessly at the winner's circle. "You gonna call Melvin and tell him you didn't bet on his horse? Need me to dial the number?"

The next day in North Carolina, the photo finish made front-page news in a special edition of the Possum Drop *Herald-Tattler*. Ooty's win was the town's best news since Marilyn Piggley delivered triplets in 1964. The paper showed a box score of Ooty's lifetime earnings. So far, one-third of what he'd cost. He was in the game.

After three straight convincing wins in Seattle, a talented three-year-old colt from Washington finished a hard-charging second in the season's first graded stakes race at Golden Gate Fields in San Francisco. Stumbling at the start, he broke poorly but was much the best the rest of the way. Two days later the colt arrived at Santa Anita, three barns over from Ooty.

Deacon and Tuki stood alongside trainer Olin McCully and watched the powerful colt's first work. Pernambuco was striking, heavily muscled. "He flies like a godwit," Tuki said, impressed.

McCully had no clue what a godwit was. He assumed it was religious and thanked her.

While Deacon stayed behind to talk to McCully, Tuki walked over to Rigby's office and reported the news about Pernambuco. He was less than thrilled to hear about a thousand-pound godwit moving into the neighborhood. "It's always somebody," he muttered. "As if it ain't hard enough to get them ready when you've got a good one, in come the shippers."

She put a consoling arm around the old man. "Don't worry, Mr. Malone. There's much money to be won. We'll get ours."

"Thanks for the philosophy lesson," Rigby grunted. "But horse races are like fishin' trips. Ain't no fun when the other guy lands the big ones."

Rigby turned his attention back to his battered notebook. Somewhere inside its ragged covers had to be hiding a miracle. To him and every other trainer in the business, the new year meant a new dream: to win the Kentucky Derby, America's race. The 1998 winner, Real Quiet, had cost burger-joint owner Mike

Pegram less than a new Subaru, just $17,000. The victory was worth millions. Pegram had earned another fortune already, selling McDonald's hamburgers and Cottle's french fries.

Owners like Pegram, with millions invested, tended to trust only proven trainers who'd shown they could win "two comma" races, Grade I showcases with million-dollar paydays. His friend and bloodstock agent, trainer Bob Baffert, had purchased many horses on Pegram's behalf, but Real Quiet was by far the least expensive. Baffert had nicknamed the skinny horse "The Fish" and put some meat on him. Once he did, Real Quiet won the first two legs of the Triple Crown and nearly took the third.

Converting potential into talent was a trainer's job, and some guys Rigby Malone had competed against were better at it than others. For three-year-olds, only one of those Grade I races was run at Santa Anita; and only a handful of horses on the grounds were good enough to maybe make a splash on a national level. None were in Rigby's barn eating his oats. And no matter how hard Rigby studied the penciled notations in his notebook, a legitimate Derby prospect hid nowhere among the pages. He hated not having a rising star.

Pernambuco and a hotshot named Eracism seemed to be the two best horses housed at Santa Anita. Pernambuco's jockey, Wally Ball, had exercised both. He thought the Siphon colt, Pernambuco, was better.

Eracism was greener, experience-wise, but had a ton of speed. The colt's owner, thirty-three-year-old Silicon Valley billionaire Crofton Tate, had the resources to do whatever it took to keep his horse in the mix. He put a powerhouse team behind the horse, including trainer Durwood Lane, a long-time rival of Rigby Malone. The jockey was Othello Guidry, a sullen, tough-as-nails veteran with 6,000 wins. Guidry was as famous for his scowl as he was for his immense talent. He only smiled in the winner's circle.

Tuki's baptizing *Othelloism* came while working horses the morning after Ooty's exciting come-from-behind win. Guidry was steaming up during a sprint work and angry that she was drifting toward center-track. As he blew past, he swatted his whip at her. "Get back in the kitchen!" he shouted. "Men are working here!"

Rigby watched the incident and asked about it later that morning.

"He is not a nice person," she replied in a huff.

Rigby looked at Tuki like she'd whined about a fly in the ladies room. "Not a nice person? *Nice* doesn't matter in this business! *Nice* gets you unemployed. *Nice* gets you vet bills to pay, but no money to pay them. Sorry to crunch your seashells and pop your balloons, missy, but this is not a *nice* business."

He paused to let the message sink in. "This is pro racing, Tuki, at its highest level. Racing is a *results* business. Only winning matters. It's the sole reason people do this. Nobody mucks stalls at five a.m. because they dream of finishing second. People who make it are all here for one reason: They hunger to win."

"Still no excuse," replied Tuki. "He's bloody rude."

"Nobody hires Othello Guidry because he's *nice*. People hire Othello Guidry because he's the best there ever was out of a gate, half-a-length better than anybody else, including you. Guidry's won more races around this track by less than a length than the rest of you added together."

"Don't care. He's still a wanker." *Why is Rigby flying off like a bloody goon? Why defend a jerky pig?*

To buoy Rigby's irascible demeanor, on the second Saturday in January she went early to the stables and unlocked his cramped little office. Onto his desk, next to his old notebook, she placed two gifts: a new notebook, with the words Derby Plan carefully printed on the cover; and on top of the new notebook, a hand-carved wooden figurine, a six-inch horseman in a cowboy hat—holding a trophy.

When Rigby came in later and saw the gifts, he picked up the wood carving. Then he picked up the notebook and thumbed through its pages. From January one through the first Saturday in May each date was handwritten. Only three dates had anything else written on their pages. The Kentucky Derby. The Santa Anita Derby. The second of February. Carefully printed in calligraphy on all three days was the exact same message: Ooty Wins!

"Dizzy girl," he muttered. "One win in a maiden race and she thinks she'll win the Derby."

Later at the barn he asked where she bought the figurine.

Her eyes narrowed. "Bought it? I bloody well *carved* it, Mr. Malone. Me name is on the bottom!"

"I figured you carved that on after you bought it."

She swatted at him but he ducked. He never mentioned the notebook. As he walked away, she bit her lip. *Allergic to saying Thank you, are you?"*

That night at his kitchen table, from the moment dinner ended until ten p.m., Rigby studied the racing secretary's condition book and penciled notes inside his new notebook. He worked backward from the first Saturday in May, to the Santa Anita Derby Day the first Saturday in April, to the allowance race February second.

Deacon was right. They couldn't roll over and let Pernambuco or Eracism beat them. Miracles *did* happen. They were the soul of the business. The sweetest races were the ones he wasn't supposed to win in the first place. Like Pegram and Baffert and Real Quiet.

Rigby studied the racing schedule from every conceivable angle: allowance, graded and ungraded stakes, distances, surfaces, and purses. Dollars won in the graded-stakes would determine who ran in the Kentucky Derby, the top twenty earners making the field. If the field didn't fill, any owner with enough dough and ambition could pay a whopping supplement and take a shot. The Trombleys didn't have the financial resources to supplement.

We have to earn our way in. But how? Where was the path of least resistance?

He tossed his pencil down and buried his head in his hands. Surely he had a better option than Ooty. *What kind of pipe dream is this, anyway?*

Nothing had changed by sunrise, so Rigby picked up the telephone and dialed the Trombleys. Would they or could they take the risk and pay to ship Ooty around in search of softer competition? It was a dicey strategy. Some horses didn't ship well.

"We have to pick our spots," Rigby explained to Melvin, "be careful who we race against. Some horses travel and handle change okay; others hate it. At least you'll find out how good a horse you've really got."

Melvin thought about it. "The way we see it, Rig, Ooty has shipped from the bottom of the world to the top, and halfway around. If that ain't change enough, we don't know what is. You decide what's best. If we have to spend scholarship money, then I guess that's what we'll have to do. I don't rightly remember whether we covered this on the napkin or not."

"Better keep Ooty close to home, then," said Rigby. "Win or lose, we'll compete at Santa Anita."

Rigby hung up, feeling half the height of his carved figurine. The discussion had gone south as soon as Melvin mentioned rifling Miss Louise's college fund.

The next morning, Rigby tracked town Tuki and showed her the plan he had sketched out in the new notebook.

"Not a grumblepuss today?" she said cheerfully. "Nice to have you back."

"Seashells and balloons to me," he deadpanned. "Here's the deal: We'll build Ooty a foundation of experience for strength, speed, stamina, and confidence. It's a logical plan but it does not factor in the one other thing we'll have to have."

"What's that?" asked Deacon, walking up.

Rigby turned to him with a serious look. "Ten tons of good, old-fashioned racing luck. Without a leprechaun in the barn, we'll never get a shot at a big one."

Two days later, a wood-carved leprechaun stood next to the wood-carved Rigby near the old rotary telephone on his office desk. He was seated in his old chair when Tuki delivered it, mulling over how to beat the odds in a game where the odds are tough to beat even when things go perfect. In this business, there were no shortcuts to greatness. Mediocre trainers made excuses. Great trainers made fortunes; heroes made history in fifths of a second.

Sustained success demanded a daisy chain of skillful decision-making. He had to intimately know not only his own horse, but all the horses he had to beat. Prepping for the Triple Crown dream was always exhausting—for the horse and the people, especially when all were new to the challenge. There was no room for error in either judgment or execution. Only the rarest of superstar horses could offset a blunder in training.

Talent, luck, fate, and the weather all would filter out Santa Anita's racing pretenders from the contenders. Slowly but surely those with world-class talent would boil out from those with regional and zip-code talents. Eight-to-twelve horse fields of aspiring three-year-olds would weed out the undeserving; the teletimer would tell no lies.

Rigby saw no other horses on the grounds that were developing to the caliber of Pernambuco and Eracism. Those were the two to beat. So, he watched and charted their every move, tracking their works and recording their progress in his notebook. He knew every step they took, as well as if he were training them himself.

Rigby had raced in the Kentucky Derby twice, finished sixth and ninth, never close to winning. He didn't have a superstar horse this year, nothing close. He had three good three-year-olds in the barn, but no great ones. His best was a six-furlong sprinter who would never hold up in longer races against more talented horses. Aside from that, Ooty.

The more Rigby watched Pernambuco and Eracism, the more wistful he became.

Meticulously, he tracked the workouts and progress of his twenty-five horses, plus the top dozen that he thought had a chance to take the Santa Anita. Despite Tuki's optimistic confidence, Rigby dismissed Ooty. He was too green, too inconsistent, too unpredictable.

Or was he? With no other plausible options, Rigby mulled taking a gamble. He phoned Deacon and asked him to swing by the office.

Fifteen minutes later Deacon showed up. As usual, he was hungry.

"I'll feed you later," Rigby said impatiently. "Need to bounce something off you."

"Bounce."

"Does Tuki really think Ooty can do this? Or is she lost in space, lost in the romance of the horse?"

"That's a great question," replied Deacon. "Before she won on him, I was like you. I thought she was suckin' too much smog on her motorcycle . . . that believin' in that horse was a big L. A. overdose of hype, bullshit, and mirrors."

"What do you think now?"

"In *her* mind, Rigby, he's real. She really believes he can do it."

"What do *you* think, Deacon?"

"What I *think* is what I *saw*. And what I *saw* was Ooty winnin' from twenty behind. No normal horse can do that, Rig. Even if he had six legs it woulda been hard. She loved that horse to the finish line, Rig. That's the only reason he won."

"So you think he can do it?"

"He's your only chance, Rig. Your *only* chance. Can he do it? Probably not. Definitely not, if he don't get the chance. What's it cost you to find out?"

Rigby sighed. "I was afraid you'd say that, Deacon. I have trained a thousand racehorses in my career, but none like this."

"Ever seen a jock like her?"

"Hell, no."

"Then maybe they're a perfect pair." Deacon paused for several seconds before continuing. Rigby waited. It was obvious to him that Deacon had more to add but wanted to get the words right.

Finally Deacon continued. "Maybe it's time to stop fightin' what you got, Rig. Maybe you should worry less about trainin' him *your* way, and start thinkin' more about trainin' him *her* way."

Rigby took off his old cowboy hat and scratched his head. "You know, Deacon," he said slowly, "90 percent of what you say is pure noise. But the other 10 percent makes all 100 percent worth listening to."

"Is that your way of sayin' thanks?"

"Sort of," Rigby admitted.

Deacon broke into a broad grin. "How about that? A *compliment* from Rigby Malone! We need to record this historic moment. Write that down in your notebook, Shakespeare," he teased. "Put a star next to it, will you? A Tuki Banjo *superstar*."

Rigby decided to take Deacon's advice. Tuki knew the colt far better than anyone else, so he walked over to the racing office and entered Ooty into the allowance race.

Then he called Melvin in North Carolina. "A little longer race and better competition, but more money. Maybe we'll get lucky and win a year or two of college for somebody."

As Rigby listened to Melvin's response, he reached over, grabbed up Tuki's whittled leprechaun, and rubbed it on his shirt for luck. For better or worse, he was stepping up Ooty's competition.

East coast to west, similar choices to Rigby's were causing millions upon millions of dollars worth of dreams to evaporate. Only the best and the luckiest would win their way through the grueling four-month winter campaign. Of fifty-five major prep races, different horses would win about fifty. For them, the dream of glory would linger at least one race longer.

Young horses were still growing and changing physically and temperamentally from week to week. That's what Rigby was banking on, that Ooty was still filling out and learning. The colt loved to eat, so Rigby worked hard to convert the weight to explosive muscle. The colt needed to get better, quickly, but he needn't be the best in February or March.

Ooty won his allowance race easily. Again he spotted the field twenty lengths, and chased them down. He won by two. Had Tuki pressed him for more, she thought he could have won by five.

Deacon stopped by Rigby's office at dawn the next day. Rigby waved him in while he was on the phone. Without a word, Deacon put a winner's circle photo on top of the desk, along with a freshly sharpened pencil. He bowed deeply at the waist, dramatically swept his arm, and gracefully backed out, closing the door behind him.

Ooty's smashing win signaled that to make a run at Pernambuco and Eracism, it was time to accelerate the workload. The calendar was an unforgiving mistress, so Ooty's immediate challenge was not to be first to the Derby finish line. Rather, it was to survive the pounding it would take to earn a spot in the starting gate.

Rigby phoned the Trombleys daily with updates. "It's an uphill climb for any young horse to grow big enough, fast enough, strong enough, smart enough, and rich enough, quick enough, Melvin. In January, two hundred horses out here were in the mix. We're now in the final two dozen."

"What about the others?" asked Melvin.

"Behind us," said Rigby. "Scattered into obscurity. But I need to put him in boot camp if we hope to do anything. It's either boot camp, or we join the vanquished. It's your call, though, Melvin. What do you want to do?"

"Ten-*hut!*" Melvin snapped. "Forward, march! All the way, Rig. That's why we paid you all that napkin money."

"You're never going to let me forget that, are you?"

"No, sir. We still got it, too. Saved that napkin to check against your monthly statements. So far, you ain't too far off."

"It's not an easy road, Melvin," Rigby warned, ignoring the farmer's gentle zinger. "Horse racing teases us all with dreams of greatness. It just as easily floods the soul with heartache and disappointment. For all its beauty and elegance, racing is a sport of seductive cruelty. I gotta warn you, Melvin. Tighten the screws down on a young horse's training and injuries can happen. We're talking tough workouts and tougher races. Some horses can't take the pounding."

"Hang on a sec, Rig. Shelley wants to say somethin'." Melvin handed the phone to his wife.

"Hi, Rigby," Shelley said. "Thank you for all you've done for us. All of us here sure do appreciate it. You never met Miss Louise, but I guarantee you one thing, she challenged every kid in this town to follow their dreams. You honor her now and do the same, okay? We'll all sleep like babies here in Possum Drop if we try and fail, but we won't sleep worth a hoot if we don't."

Rigby smiled faintly. "Gotcha. We'll know more after another start or two. We'll need some luck, but maybe we can work our way into the Santa Anita Derby. If so, you two may want to come out."

"Money's tight, Rigby. We're in the middle of planting season. But you find a way to get Ooty there and we'll find a way to get there, too."

Rigby went right back to his notebook, plotting his next move. Chasing rainbows was a life-consuming commitment, totally focused on one distant, non-negotiable moment in time. Forgotten was Ooty's humble history. Regardless where a horse came from, once it was time to toe the line, Thoroughbred racing remained at its core a very simple game. Despite the pomp, pageantry, money, and blueblood tradition, plus the big-race media coverage, in the end every race is just a bunch of horses running in a circle. The fastest could come from anywhere.

Ooty needed work, lots of it. Rigby figured the colt needed at least two more starts before contemplating whether or not to enter the Santa Anita Derby. He needed some graded-stakes money, but Rigby wanted no part of Pernambuco or Eracism. So, he made a very unconventional decision and entered Ooty in a Grade III one-mile turf race that was absent the two biggies, gambling that the softer competition would enable Ooty to earn a $60,000 winner's share and get within one additional "in-the-money" performance to qualify for Churchill Downs.

"Graded stakes are the hardest races," he had explained to Melvin. "It's from these races that the best emerge. A mile, two turns, on the grass. It's a nine-horse field that's good, not great. These are tests Ooty's got to pass."

What Rigby didn't know was how well Ooty would race on turf. Some dirt horses adjusted, some didn't. He was banking on Ooty's New Zealand bloodlines—turf horses.

Before the race, Tuki beamed with confidence. "It won't matter if we race through a bloody supermarket," she whispered to Ooty as she prepared for her boost into the saddle. "We're ready, aren't we, big boy? We should've brushed your teeth to dazzle the camera in the winner's circle."

Rigby had brushed his teeth, but it didn't matter. Veteran jockey Othello Guidry leapt out to a quick opening quarter mile and Ooty dropped back. Guidry held his pace through a half mile and Ooty fell farther behind. When Tuki urged him to make a move, the turf didn't provide the same solid grabbing traction that she was used to. She had waited too long, and Ooty couldn't catch up. Both horse and rider were booed as they crossed the finish line. Ooty finished third, soundly beaten.

Rigby described the race real-time to the Trombleys over the phone, and the call was relayed live on the Possum Drop radio station. For two minutes, the whole town paused and cheered. When Ooty finished third, they went back about their business. Third was back-page news.

When Tuki trotted the colt over and hopped down, Rigby was visibly upset.

"Whadya learn?" he demanded. "Whadya learn? Besides the fact—once again—that Othello Guidry ain't *nice?*"

She looked up and replied quietly, "That a good horse can't overcome a bad ride?"

Rigby ignored the answer. "What else?"

"That he doesn't like the grass?" She guessed blankly.

"Grass, my ass! This was a winnable race, Miss Seashell! Your job is to *win* winnable races! Despite what you think, this ain't your horse. It's the owners' horse, and third don't get it. Third is like kissing your cousin. It ain't satisfying for nobody."

Deacon stepped up to lighten the tension. "Now hold on, Rig. Don't condemn the relatives."

Rigby ignored Deacon, his steely eyes remained fixed on Tuki. "You can love that colt all you want, but you just wasted a race, a race we had to win. We ran this race to win and get that money. Now we ain't got squat."

Rigby's face flushed. "All he is, is a one-run horse. He runs backward; first half slow, second half fast. All he's got is that one run. *You* must decide when it's time. Against good horses, there is zero room for error. Get that? Zero! Hesitate and I guarantee all this horse will ever see in those mirrored glasses of his is the ass end of Othello Guidry's horse. Get the message?" Rigby's face was flushed.

Tuki stood expressionless. "Yessir."

Stonefaced, Rigby turned to Deacon. "Any questions?"

"Nossir."

"Let me put that ride in language you'll understand, Deacon. I'll summarize it in two words."

Deacon shrugged. "Your game, boss man. Deal the cards."

Rigby moved to inches from Deacon's face and stared for several seconds, then hissed, "No Winnebago, Deacon."

"That's three words," replied Deacon quickly, mouthing and re-counting them on his fingers.

Rigby glared. "Focus on the first two, Deacon. You might want to slink back to the barn and apologize to the other guys on the team. Your rider just ruined their whole damn month."

"C'mon, girl!" Deacon yelled at Tuki in mock anger, playacting to the news that the starlets had been driven away. "You cost me some *love!* Lord help me, Tuki Banjo, I'll glue postage stamps on you and mail your fuzzy little butt back to New Zealand if you *ever* do that again!"

She gazed back and forth between Deacon and Rigby. "Seashells and balloons to you both," she said evenly. "I'm going to bathe the horse." She stomped off, Ooty in tow.

Exasperated, Rigby looked at Deacon and pointed at Tuki. "How the hell do I yell at somebody who ought to be winding up to slap me, but instead says fu-fu things like 'seashells and balloons?' What the hell is that? Whatever happened to good, old-fashioned arguing? You know, spirited, toe-to-toe hollering and debate? Loud differences of opinion?"

Deacon shrugged. "Call me when you figure it out. Sometimes I think that whatever's inside that girl's head rolls back and forth like a lava lamp."

Rigby called the Trombleys back. "I picked a bad race," he said.

"We won $15,000," Melvin pointed out. "We're thrilled with that."

"It should have been $90,000."

"Don't tell Shelley."

Tuki beat Deacon back to the barns and, tight-lipped, apologized to the crew. "I'm sorry, I cost you twenty minutes of *goosh* with your rental friends." She ran away when one of the guys good-naturedly lobbed a clump of dirty straw toward her.

After she finished bathing Ooty, Tuki refilled his feed bucket but the colt refused to eat.

Rigby had caught a ride up in a golf cart and hopped out, checking on the horse and jockey before heading home. A glance in the bucket told Rigby the horse was off his feed. "That means he's either sick or upset," Rigby said. "How's his temperature?"

"He's fine," Tuki said abruptly. "He's not sick. He's sulkin'. He knows he lost. The races are games; let the others think they'll win, then go run them down. He's a terrible loser. Gets it from his father."

Rigby nodded but said nothing A life of experience was screaming that she's nuts. One whispy thought said maybe she's right.

Tuki looked at Rigby. "Wheel him back soon, Mr. Malone. Put him on the dirt, grass, wherever you want. Short, long, it won't matter. He'll be on his toes, like a bloomin' track star. We'll be ready, I promise."

"Better be," Rigby grunted. "We're running out of sunrises."

At home that night, Rigby studied the charts and mulled upcoming races in the condition book. Today's third-place money didn't do any good. He'd wasted a precious start.

The following morning, Deacon showed up at barn with the ten remaining doughnuts from the dozen he'd purchased still warm in the box. "News flash, Rig," he said brightly as he barged in.

Rigby grabbed the box and hunted a Bavarian cream. He found one.

While the trainer savored his breakfast, Deacon asked, "You want the good news or the bad news?"

Rigby wiped his mouth on his sleeve and eyed Deacon. "Gimme the good news."

"There ain't no big horses coming out of the Big Apple this year."

Rigby grunted. "Bad news?"

"They'll have one soon. You remember that $7-million colt the sheikh bought when we got Ooty? Albacoa? Word is he's blitzed through Europe and is headed to the States. They say he's finally gonna deliver the sheikh his Kentucky Derby. A billion dollars of horses that man has bought and it looks like he finally got the right one."

Rigby shrugged. "Albacoa? He was a monster. I didn't hear he's coming over early. I thought the sheikh would run him in the United Arab Emirates Derby in late March, then decide. Today he's the least of my worries. Remind me then, when I've got a reason to care."

Rigby remained preoccupied with trying to figure out how to beat Pernambuco and Eracism. Both were very legit horses, good enough to stretch out and compete at the classic American championship distance of a mile-and-a-quarter.

Trainer Olin McCully had beautifully prepared Pernambuco, the bowmakers' talented speedster. He had picked his races perfectly and had earned enough graded stakes money to lock up a spot in Louisville.

Eracism was almost in, too. Regardless what Tuki thought of Othello Guidry, Eracism's owner loved him. Othello's first time aboard, Eracism flew out of the starting gate, grabbed an immediate lead, and held on to beat a hard-charging Pernambuco by a head, winning the season-opening Golden Gate Derby. The race was won at the start, when Eracism bolted clear and Pernambuco struggled.

Damn perfect pair, Othello and Eracism. Wish he was ridin' somebody else.

Despite the bad turf race, the only three-year-old in Rigby's barn with the physical tools to go long was Ooty. The big-bodied colt was strong and long-striding, able to eat up ground; but throwing him in against those other two right now would be like tossing a salmon to tiger sharks. As the Grade III turf defeat had proven, Ooty and Tuki Banjo were nowhere close to big-race ready.

Nevertheless, the colt showed promise. So, Rigby plotted an unconventional course for Santa Anita's biggest race, California's lone Grade I, one of only five American preps contested at racing's highest level. From it would advance only one or two horses good enough to challenge the best in the nation one month later. Rigby trusted what Tuki told him, and asked her for ideas on how best to get Ooty to peak at a mile-and-an-eighth on the first Saturday in April.

"Do what I said," she implored. "Race him. Short, long, in between. Won't matter. He's fit enough. He can handle it."

Rigby was skeptical. "How about if we're less ambitious? What if we aim for the Grade III on the Derby undercard? We duck Pernambuco and Eracism. All grades-stakes money counts. A win might sneak us into Kentucky."

"Race him," she repeated. "Booger-all on waitin'."

"Okay, we race him."

Though the strategy defied conventional training practices, Rigby subbed races for workouts, and Tuki's uncanny knack of measuring race pace enabled him to methodically tighten Ooty's conditioning. He raced the colt three times in eight weeks under seemingly odd circumstances: two low-level sprints on the grass, and a longer turf race around two-turns. Ooty won two of the three and earned nearly $50,000 for Miss Louise's scholarship fund. It wasn't graded-stakes money, but the Trombleys were thrilled. The horse had turned a profit.

Despite his modest success, however, Ooty remained one of Santa Anita's least likely suspects to blossom from anonymity to prominence. No one outside Rigby's team was following the horse closely. Rumors swirled that Malone had decided Ooty's future was as a turf horse, that he was out of the Derby hunt.

Rigby laughed when Deacon told him. "You didn't tell them we're running grass to save his feet a pounding, did you?"

Deacon shook his head. "I told 'em they were right, that you gave up, but I'm not supposed to say anythin' because you'd get pissed. You've got 'em buffaloed, Rig. Everybody thinks you're out."

"Perfect. We're right where we want to be, Deacon. Sneakin' through the grass."

Tuki quickly realized that Ooty never fought her when they started slowly and increased speed with each successive furlong. He ran his best after falling way behind, then charging up late—as if to prove he could do it.

His first win came when he rallied from way off the pace; so did his second and third. He won his next start, six furlongs on the turf, despite a thirty-length deficit.

Tuki gave up any notion of trying to rate Ooty near the lead. Whatever he decided, she went along. She resisted the urge to rush him, sailing along as relaxed as he was, playing a game with the others until it was time to chase them down. His late power and speed was exhilarating.

"When he goes, he flies," she told Deacon, "His feet don't touch the ground."

Rigby and the other Santa Anita old-timers had seen only one horse like Ooty before—a 1950s slingshot-closer named Silky Sullivan, who'd won a six-furlong race after falling forty lengths off the pace. Ooty won after falling behind by thirty, the track's greatest comeback in more than fifty years. And when he won, the way he won, the fans went wild.

Because of the sheer volume of work Ooty was sustaining, Rigby decided to bypass Pernambuco and Eracism in the marquee event, the Grade I Santa Anita Derby, and entered the undercard's mile-long Grade III race. In addition to the powerhouse rivals, the Derby field also contained three overmatched speedballs who would set a furious early pace; they would run out of gas, but combined with the two super-talented stalkers, its field was a bad mix for Ooty. There was easier money on the undercard.

Melvin agreed. "The napkin ain't lied. Your call, Rig."

On Tuesday of race week, everything changed. In Eracism's final workout, Rigby thought the normally sharp colt looked dull and tired. Then an hour later, word filtered through the back side that Pernambuco had developed a minor hoof bruise; with a spot in Louisville secured and not wanting to risk the horse's chances in the rigorous Triple Crown, trainer Olin McCully had scratched him.

Rigby saw an opening. Tuki didn't answer her phone, she rarely did, so Rigby had to go track her down. As usual, she was at Ooty's stall, carefully bleaching his jet-black mane a shiny platinum blonde.

"What do you think?' she asked Ooty, showing himself in the mirror. "I think you look *macho.* "

Rigby asked for a time-out by making a T-sign, and fought the urge to ask her why she was bleaching the horse's mane. "Think you can win the Derby on Saturday?"

"Not without a horse."

"What if you had a horse?"

"Which one?" She had already passed on two other mounts Deacon had brought her, opting not to unseat their regular riders. She had no intention of doing so now.

"Rock star, here," Rigby said, nodding toward Ooty. "Pernambuco just scratched. Eracism looked dull this morning. I think he'll bounce. You think you got enough horse? Your call. The other race is easier."

Tuki cooed, lifted Ooty's head, and kissed his muzzle. "What do you think, handsome? Up for some fun on Saturday? Show off your new mane? Get on the telly and let Mr. Eracism get a nice long look at your superfine tail?"

Ooty nodded. Rigby removed his cowboy hat and scratched his head. Fifty years in this business. A baldheaded girl asking the horse if he felt like racing. The horse agreeing. Rigby walked away, muttering.

He trudged two-hundred yards to the racing secretary's office, filled out an entry form, and handed it in. The clerk was surprised when he saw which race Ooty was entering.

"What made you switch?" the man asked.

Rigby looked at him for a several seconds. "The horse thinks he can win. Who am I to argue?"

With Santa Anita's most colorful jockey, Tuki Banjo, and the unconventional storybook-longshot Ooty, now featured in the season's biggest race, the track's public relations department cranked into overdrive. With perfect weather forecast for Saturday's race, the over-hyped media coverage emboldened track officials to predict a crowd of 62,000 fans—an all-time record.

Othello Guidry didn't care if only five people showed up. He intended to win and scoffed derisively to *The Daily Racing Form* when informed about Ooty's late entry. "That pair is made for each other," he said. "A bald girl on a horse with a toupee. How disrespectful is *that* to a dignified profession like ours?

"I just hope they like dirt for lunch," he added. "Come Saturday, Eracism and me are gonna serve plenty."

Pressured to deliver, Luther O'Neil's nights grew increasingly more fitful. These were new decisions he'd never had to make. The mirror told no lies, the bags under his eyes were sagging and creeping forests of gray framed the temples of his almond face.

Florida's robust racing schedule, with millions in purse money, had given him a matrix of options for Cottle and Moose Utley's colts; eleven major preps stretched over a span of four months, added to dozens of liberally scheduled allowance races. Gulfstream Park, south of Fort Lauderdale, was the hub of the action, where dreams were made and hearts broken, stamped by hoofprints in the circular dirt.

As the winter campaign began to unfold, three horses had emerged as serious frontrunners for the prestigious Grade I Florida Derby, the south's biggest stepping-stone to Churchill Downs.

Two of those three were Spudcat and Hundo. The third was a gray colt sired by Unbridled's Song, originally owned by a redheaded Palm Beach heiress and socialite named Katie Thwing. To honor her late father's fried-chicken empire and south Florida's heavily Spanish-speaking influence, she named the horse Marco Pollo. Trainer Puggsly Van Dorn looked like Mr. Peanut in his blue blazer, white shirt, red ascot, hickory walking stick, and monocle. Wherever he went—polo matches, race track, to sip martinis with the Palm Beach socialites—he never left home without Puggsly Junior, a miniature pug who greeted everyone with a full-speed head butt in the shin.

Marco Pollo had won easily the first big three-year-old stakes of the season, a

Grade III nine-furlong chase. Immediately after, the gray colt was sold privately to a slick New Yorker suspected to have mob connections. Tony Syracuse was rumored to have paid in cash a price in excess of $1 million. Puggsly Van Dorn was fired, replaced by the gruff, foulmouthed New York hardboot, Cy Raffone.

Luther O'Neil hadn't heard of Tony Syracuse, but he knew Raffone and he didn't trust him. "Never trust nobody whose vet spends more time hanging around his barn than the mice," he told a friend.

Two days after Marco Pollo's impressive win, Luther saddled Moose Utley's Hundo to a six-furlong Grade III victory in near-record time. Two weeks later, J. L. Cottle's Spudcat determinedly held on, winning the Grade III Holy Bull Stakes by less than a length. With veteran rider Billy "Yoda" Mann in the irons, Spudcat tired after a hard duel at the top of the stretch but gamely kept digging.

Immediately after, Yoda announced to the press, "This is a Derby horse. He's got talent and courage, everything a champion needs—and more. With experience, he'll beat everybody out there. Write that down. This horse is the one to beat. The trainer had him perfect."

Buoyed by Yoda's public praise, Luther was the happiest man in the winner's circle photo. Yoda Mann was not known for hyperbole.

With different horses taking the first three signature races of the young season, the Florida contingent loomed as the strongest class in the nation. Luther knew he had two of the country's best three-year-olds, and immediately began phoning distant connections. Who else had a big horse that was separating itself from the rest? A friend working at Santa Anita told him California had two, Pernambuco and Eracism.

"How good are they?" Luther asked.

"I could lie and cheer you up, Luther, but they're legit. Both got a real good shot."

"Any others?"

"No. They tower above the rest."

Luther's spirits brightened when he checked in with a friend who was tracking the young horses closely in Arkansas and Louisiana.

"We got two decent ones," the friend reported. "Let It Go Foul and Zorro's Tax Advisor. Both are pointed toward the G-II Louisiana Derby in early March."

"Can they advance?" Luther asked.

"Doubt it. In my opinion, they're regional heroes, the best of a very average lot. Both of their biggest wins were very suspect. Weak rivals and pedestrian times."

The worst news came when Luther dialed New York. Two more challengers from a tout he'd known thirty years.

"I hear you got two big ones, Luther," the oddsmaker said. "Congratulations! Keep 'em healthy, so I can see 'em. Up here we got Sherpa Warrior, a son of former Kentucky Derby winner Fusaichi Pegasus. He's impressive. But the bigger news ain't who we got, but who's coming."

"Who's that?" asked Luther.

"Albacoa," the tout replied. "Owned by that Saudi oil guy, Sheikh Mustafa Ali Ali Mumtaz. Destroyed the field four times straight in big stakes races in Europe and the Middle East. I hear he's a monster, a perfect genetic specimen. Word is, he's headed our way."

"Figures," Luther sighed and sagged. "All my life I dreamed of a good horse. Now I got two great ones, and what do I get? A sheikh and a freak. Superman flyin' over to race me. Damn horse'll probably fly hisself over without a plane."

Across the nation, hooves were churning and dirt was flying. Trainers, railbirds, writers, and gamblers were picking their favorites for the race looming several months away.

Twenty Thoroughbreds would eventually load the gates at Churchill Downs on the first Saturday in May. But which twenty? And of those twenty, only half had a chance of winning.

Luther O'Neil was determined that two of those would be his.

20
SLINGSHOT HERO

Prior to the featured Santa Anita Derby, Tuki had three mounts on the day's undercard. She rolled in on her motorcycle eight hours early and pushed down its kickstand at precisely 4:30 a.m. The first of Rigby's team to arrive, she cleaned Ooty's stall, walked him, bathed him, gave him a pep talk, brushed and teased his bleach-blonde mane, and re-braided his tale. She reminisced to him about the day he was born in New Zealand, the farm, his mom and his dad, and the starry night she had unlocked their paddock gates. She mused about how Ooty's life and hers had been destined to intertwine again, just like his handsome braids.

As she walked him toward the shade of the old sprawling oak, countless back side workers waved, calling out good luck. Ooty paid more attention to them than she did. She was lost in the past, talking of butterflies and godwits.

"Today," she cooed, "you will fly like both. Flutter like a butterfly at the start, then *zoom* like a godwit to the finish." To animate the word *zoom*, she made a jet plane motion with her hand.

Before leaving the stables to report to the jocks' room, Tuki stopped by Rigby's cubbyhole office. Deacon was there reviewing for the umpteenth time their game plan. Rigby was doing most of the talking.

"There's plenty of early speed," Rigby said. "The field should stretch quickly. The leaders won't have staying power. They'll set the pace for Eracism. What I don't know," he said, "is how aggressive Othello Guidry will be while he shadows the leaders. If he gets Eracism too far out front, Ooty won't catch him. My guess is Othello will get out quick and try to steal it early, especially if he senses that his horse is off."

Tuki sensed that this meant Rigby wanted her to stay closer to the early speed than she'd planned. "If I push him to stay too close, he'll fight it. He'll waste energy," she said. "He's happiest when he lets them go, then reels them in. I'd rather not change that if we can avoid it."

"You're right," Rigby replied. "Forcing Ooty to shadow Eracism won't work."

Deacon leaped on the opportunity. "She's *what?*"

"She's right, dammit. You're *not*, Deacon. *She* is."

"Don't turn crotchety-old-man on me, Rig," Deacon retorted. "I just wasn't sure I heard you right. I never heard you use those words before."

Tuki dug an elbow in Deacon's ribs to get him to shut up.

"Let's take a chance you're right about Eracism being tired, Rig," offered Deacon. "If he is, he'll bounce."

Tuki agreed. "A dull effort on Eracism's part makes the early pace irrelevant. If he's tired near the finish, Ooty will roll right past him."

Deacon grabbed Rigby's carved leprechaun and tossed it into the air, then caught it and pretended it was talking. "Say old chap," he mimicked with a bad Irish accent, pointing it at Rigby, "how high must you finish to go to Kentucky?"

"Win and we're in," Rigby said tersely. "Second, probably. Third's no good. But we ain't runnin' this one for second. We're running this one to win. Big races change lives. Let's steal one for Miss Louise."

"Winnebago time!" Deacon clapped. "You got that, girl?" He turned and faced Tuki. "Your agent's social life is wearin' *your* silks!"

Tuki feigned disgust. "All the bloomin' money I make you, and you can't get a girlfriend?"

"Okay, you two," Rigby concluded, "that's the plan. By race time, the owners will be here. It's one hell of a long way from Possum Drop, North Carolina to the winner's circle at Santa Anita. If they can travel this far, we can get 'em the rest of the way."

Tuki passed on the offer of a golf-cart ride to the front of the track and instead walked it, taking in the sights and sounds of the biggest racing day of her life. This year's Santa Anita Derby had everything: a field of fast horses, Hollywood star power, perfect weather, and an overflowing crowd of excited fans pouring in, anxious to bet a lot of money. Track officials had been ecstatic all week, saying to the media that they expected the track's biggest crowd since its 1930s heyday. Now, two hours before post time, the stands were already filling. She guessed they'd be right.

As the program's race card unfolded, Tuki had a terrific day. She won with her first mount, rode flawlessly to earn a second, then won again. The crowd noticed, and throughout the afternoon, the advance wagering odds on Ooty kept sliding.

Rigby was among them. He patiently waited in line to make his wager, and several fans asked what he thought Ooty's chances were in the big race. Normally he'd lie. Not today. "In 90 percent of races," he said, "the jockey won't determine the winner. But the 10 percent that it does, you gotta vote that confidence with your wallet. I'm emptying mine on a baldheaded jockey."

The national telecast meant Tuki had a quick interview before heading to the paddock to mount, but she wasn't in a talkative mood. When the interviewer asked what she expected during the big race, she smiled into the camera and said simply, "Seashells and balloons." The reporter kept holding the mike in front of her, expecting more, but she had nothing else to say. After several awkward seconds of silence, he finally said, "And there you have it."

Ooty had drawn the five post. Rigby and Deacon walked the horse around, joined by Melvin and Shelley Trombley. They delivered him to his saddle-up stall. Cameras clicked like invading cicadas as thousands of fans jammed the paddock area to see the entrants.

Next to them were Othello Guidry and Eracism. Ten feet away, Othello ignored Tuki, offering neither a handshake nor a good luck nod.

You're such a bloody child, she thought.

Rigby finished saddling Ooty and quickly reviewed the instructions. Deacon handed Tuki the horse's headgear, which she carefully buckled into place and secured the symbolic fern-leaf earring. Today he was running for his homeland.

Ooty was also running for Possum Drop High, so Tuki was wearing the green-and-gold silks with PDHS emblazoned across the back on the yellow school bus.

At the call of "Riders *up!*" Tuki asked Melvin for a boost. Excited, he nearly threw her over Ooty's back. Rigby caught her and helped her find the stirrups.

She steered Ooty to their place in line. Ten horses paraded single-file along the walkway from the paddock, through the opening in the overhanging grandstand, and out onto the racing oval. Every step was accompanied by countless shutter-clicks from cameras.

Tuki looked all around. The sights, sounds, and smells were magical.

Horses and riders leisurely paraded past the grandstand, then slowly circled back. After several minutes of warmup, they moved into position behind the starting gate. The crowd rushed to its feet and roared as the ten horses began to load one by one. Systematically and without incident, each horse stepped in.

After the door to Ooty's chute clanged shut behind them, Tuki had a short wait while the final five loaded in sequence. She talked to Ooty and rubbed his neck.

After the final gate clanged shut, she leaned forward and whispered, "Seashells and balloons, me darlin'. It's time to fly. Float like a butterfly, zoom like a godwit. Today, me love, you are the fastest in the world."

The bell rang and the gates flashed open. Tuki was in a perfect position for a clean break. The first hundred yards, Ooty grabbed the track with a smooth-striding rhythm. He settled in, loping along, letting the others race neck-and-neck for the early lead.

After the first quarter-mile, Ooty was twenty-six lengths behind.

In the stands, Deacon looked at Rigby. Rigby knew he was looking but refused to lower his binoculars. This was her race. Fussing over how she rode it would do no good.

Tuki kept the leaders in view and noticed Othello gunning Eracism up into the draft of the early speed. He was biding his time, waiting for frontrunners to fade. They'd gone out too fast and both Othello and Tuki knew it.

Ooty, meanwhile, decided thirty lengths was a fun-enough head start and, on his own, quickened his pace. He zoomed four increasingly quick furlongs and reeled the field to within ten lengths as the leaders rolled around the turn. They emerged around the bend, and spread out, facing the overflowing grandstand.

The crowd urged Ooty on, roaring louder with each stride. He was flying like the ghost of Silky Sullivan, and Tuki hit her timing mark perfectly.

Following two late furlongs run in twenty-three seconds flat, Ooty was eyeball-to-eyeball with Eracism. Only an eighth-of-a-mile to go. Tuki stole a glance to her left and waved a bent-hand goodbye to Othello. He gave her a quick middle-finger salute. Ooty left Eracism in his dust and barreled through the finish, winning by three.

Upstairs, Melvin hugged Deacon, nearly crushing him with a giant bear hug. "Didja see that, Miss Louise?" he hollered. "We got one!"

Shelley cried. "I could never dream of such a thing." She hugged Rigby tightly. "Thank you so much for this," she told him. "Miss Louise is dancing by the gates of heaven."

"I'll be dancin' in a Winnebago," mumbled Deacon. "Just as soon as I can get over there."

"What did you say?" asked Shelley.

"I said they'll be dancing in Minnesota." He smiled. "It's an old racin' term. Means you won a big race. Horse people say it all the time."

All around Santa Anita, the overflow crowd remained standing, thousands chanting, "Oo-ty! OO-TY! *OO-TY!*" The crescendo lasted for well over a minute, the pulsating echoes reverberating from the old grandstand.

The Trombleys joyfully accepted the champion's trophy in the winner's circle and jointly hoisted it high in the air. Melvin windmilled his free arm, urging the crowd to keep chanting Ooty's name.

At Rigby's nudging, Shelley stepped toward the microphone. She got too close and her jewelry caused ear-splitting feedback. Nervously she stepped back and collected her thoughts.

"Well," she stammered, looking around at the overflowing crowd, "they're dancin' in Minnesota."

"What the bloomin' 'ell does that mean?" Tuki whispered to Deacon.

He shrugged. "Maybe she's from there."

"We never won a trophy before," Shelley stammered, "but this one is goin' straight to the cafeteria at Possum Drop High in honor of Miss Louise. We thank ya."

Seconds later she was crying again, courtesy of the ceremonial winner's check she and Melvin held: $450,000.

As Tuki stepped down from the winner's platform, the television reporter who'd interviewed her before the race ran over and stuck a mike in her face. "Your thoughts on such a smashing victory? How does it feel to win the Santa Anita Derby? To represent California in the Kentucky Derby?"

She smiled and gave a thumbs-up to the camera. "Butterflies and godwits, seashells and balloons."

Again the reporter paused, expecting an explanation. Tuki stood with a frozen smile and said nothing.

"There we have it from the winner," the reporter summarized. "*Tukispeak*."

After the ceremony, while Deacon made best friends with every camera and print reporter he could find, Tuki went to shower and change. When the microphones finally shut off and the reporters drifted away, Deacon stepped behind Rigby and squeezed him in a ferocious bear hug. He held the old trainer close and leaned forward, whispering into Rigby's ear.

When Rigby nodded affirmatively, Melvin leaned over and asked Deacon what he'd said.

"I wanted to know if the Winnebago is around back."

"What Winnebago?"

"It's a business thing, Melvin," Deacon explained. "Whenever we win a big race, we gotta do extra paperwork. You know, tax stuff. The Winnebago is our portable office."

"Bummer," replied Melvin. "Sorry to hear that. Can I help?"

Deacon looked at Melvin, then at Shelley, then Melvin again. He shook his head sadly and draped his arm around the giant's shoulders. "Negatory, big man. Mighty nice of you to volunteer, but paperwork is tedious. Dullsville,

Melvin. Ain't no fun."

Deacon tapped Melvin's heart. "Thanks for the concern, big man, but don't you worry about us. While we're wrestlin' with paperwork, you need to go count your money. You just snagged almost a half-mil for Miss Louise's kids. Tell the banker you want singles to go."

Reminded about the purse money, Melvin and Shelley started dancing. Deacon winced. *God love you both but, man, do you two dance white!*

In a sprint, Deacon disappeared toward the barns.

21
WIN SOME, LOSE SOME

In Florida, Cottle's Spudcat remained a serious Derby contender. Moose Utley's smaller colt Hundo was showing great skills, too. Spudcat, in Luther's opinion, was ahead in his training and Luther wanted to sharpen his speed in a shorter stakes race.

"I don't think you want to race them against each other right now," Luther told his bosses. "They're not at the same place in their work."

"How's Hundo doing?" asked Moose.

"He's a speedball, a real professional. Works his little ass off. Improving all the time. That little colt is smart enough to play poker, once he figures out how to hold the cards."

"Then keep working him until it's time to beat the potato farmer."

"That'll be forty Sundays from never," Cottle retorted. "Mark it down."

The morning of the Florida Derby, Luther O'Neil woke early after a fitful night, nerves trumping fatigue. He rolled over and looked at the clock. Four a.m. Could be worse.

Shower, shave, in and out of church by five. Both of his big horses were running on the card, in different stakes races. Both were favored to win.

Spudcat, Cottle's million-dollar colt, was on the undercard in the seven-furlong Swale Stakes. An odds-on favorite, his entry had scared off all but five challengers. Plus, with riding legend Yoda Mann in the irons, Spudcat was never threatened and won easily—by five lengths under a hand ride. Yoda triumphantly stood in the stirrups as he crossed the finish line, proudly holding aloft his unused whip. For the first time in six years, he was advancing to

Kentucky with a real chance to win his second Derby.

One hour later, Moose Utley's Hundo was running in the $1-million Florida Derby. The ten-horse field was Luther's sternest test as a trainer against the stiff competition of the New York gangster's horse, Marco Pollo. Luther had little doubt that the competitor would lay off the pace and close with a rush. Despite the confidence boost he'd gotten from Spudcat's easy win, Luther was worried as post time drew near. Moose had trusted him with a great horse. He'd done his best to get the colt ready, but as he tightened the saddle straps he knew that horses do what horses want to do. On any given race day, Hundo could fly or fizzle. Luther prayed he would fly. He was terrified the distance might be too far, that Hundo might tire.

In the paddock, neither Cottle nor Moose seemed overly concerned about anything more than how the potatoes would be fixed for dinner. Their relaxed demeanor, however, did not stop Luther's beads of perspiration.

At the call of "Riders *up!*" Luther boosted up his longtime jockey, Piso Mojado. The plan was simple: break fast, get out quick, get clear, then stretch the field behind you. The race was a mile and one-eighth. A clear lead at the mile mark might be enough to hold off Marco Pollo's expected late charge.

The race did not go according to plan. Pressed the entire way, Hundo went too hard, too soon, for too long, and he had nothing left when Marco Pollo steered up on the outside. At the finish, the sold-out crowd rushed to its feet and roared, but Hundo had an empty tank and Marco Pollo won by a length. Owner Tony Syracuse was jubilant.

Fifty feet from Syracuse's celebration, Moose Utley stood quietly. Losing had never entered his mind.

Luther was devastated. On the biggest day of his life, his horse, the favorite, was unable to get the distance. Financially, finishing second instead of winning had cost Moose nearly a half-million dollars. Few owners could swallow this type of defeat.

Luther stood in the loam, waiting for Hundo to circle back—and expecting to be fired.

Piso Mojado hopped down. "He excited, he no settle," said Piso. "But he learn. He get better."

Luther nodded, but said nothing.

Moose Utley sneaked up from behind and wrapped the trainer in a surprise bear hug and lifted Luther off the ground. "This ain't the one that matters, Luther!" he boomed. "The *next* one is the one that matters! You're taking 'em both to Churchill!"

Luther blessed himself with a sign of the cross. "Thank you, sir. Ain't nobody gonna outwork us, Mr. Moose. Nobody. Nobody gonna outrun us, neither."

Moose nodded. "Pressure makes diamonds, baby. Win the next one and we're all famous."

Luther faked a smile. *Pressure bursts pipes, too. Please God, don't bust mine.*

Team Ooty was scheduled to leave California one week before the big race. His meteoric explosion across the finish line at Santa Anita had stamped him a West Coast hero, and national publicity had labeled him a legitimate threat to win the Kentucky Derby. The Odds Quad were not staying behind. They were heading east.

When the morning arrived to leave, they rendezvoused early at Rigby's barn, each arriving with rations they needed for the cross-country trip in Esther's Winnebago—2,000 miles of rumbling to Kentucky. Pez brought Mexican food, Mung Fu Asian, Esther salads, and Toker beer, pretzels, chips, and twelve bags of shell peanuts.

Fast Eddie the burro watched the commotion and brayed.

"Don't worry, Eddie," Rigby said and scratched the burro behind the ear. "We ain't come this far to leave anyone behind. You're going, the whole team's going. It's your job to keep Ooty company and help us win."

Also making the trip was Rigby's carved leprechaun, hidden away in his windbreaker pocket.

Rigby and Toker lifted Tuki's Harley into place on a motorcycle stand across the back of the camper. Rigby locked it securely into place, then hitched Fast Eddie's trailer to the rear of the motorhome. Well-supplied with hay and water, the burro clopped up the aluminum ramp. The pygmy goat, Josie, followed; Rigby also packed her skateboard, to guarantee publicity. The ferret and the fat cat would run loose inside the trailer. Rigby slid the ramp in, closed and checked the tailgate, then tossed in a hatful of mice to keep the ferret busy.

Deacon, Tuki, and Ooty had flown ahead to Louisville yesterday. Rigby would fly out later today, after the team had safely departed.

Rigby brushed his hands on his pants and walked over by Esther. "Quite a circus you've got there," he said with a smile. "Odds are three-to-one you'll arrive in Louisville with at least two more men than you're leaving with."

"I certainly *hope* so," she giggled. "If so, they'll be delicious." She hugged Rigby goodbye and kissed his cheek. Then she tossed the camper keys to Mung Fu, who tossed them to Toker. Pez Perez intercepted with a determined snatch, since Toker had already guzzled the morning's inaugural bottle of beer.

The Odds Quad waved wildly from every window of the Winnebago as Pez slowly pulled out.

"Look out, Louisville!" hollered Toker, leaning out a window. "We may not win the race, but I can guaran-damn-tee we're gonna win the party!"

Rigby shook his head and laughed as the merry gang bounced away. On both sides of the camper, large magnetic signs read, The Odds Quad—Derby or Bust! A smaller sign on the driver's door said, We Know Ooty Personally.

With determination, the Odds Quad rolled along: It wasn't easy caravanning a Winnebago full of lunatics, pulling a trailer with a braying burro, skateboarding goat, fat cat, ferret, and desperate mice. Nevada was sparse, Utah desolate. East of Vail, they barely made it up and over the 11,000-foot crest of Colorado's Continental Divide; but made up time crossing the Kansas flatlands. Throughout the three-day journey, passing drivers honked and waved.

Two-thirds of the way to Kentucky, they faced a crisis. While waiting for Esther to emerge from the ladies room, Mung Fu checked on Eddie and the rest of the trailer's menagerie.

"We have problem," Mung Fu reported tersely.

Esther looked surprised. Nothing was wrong five minutes ago. "What do you mean? What kind of problem?"

"Ferret in heat. Ferret die—if no Mr. Ferret *soon*."

"You're kidding," said Toker. "Hell, I'd have died ten years ago."

"Are you sure?" Esther asked Mung Fu. "You're not joking, are you?"

Mung Fu shook his head. "Need Mr. Ferret. Soon. Or Mrs. Ferret die."

Esther sighed. "Well, that certainly is an annoying and inconvenient quirk of nature."

"You better not kill Rigby's ferret," Toker warned. "He'll kill us if we lose his ferret."

Esther ran inside the gas station. Through the bulletproof glass, she imparted the urgent need to find a male ferret. The black gas station clerk behind the glass hadn't seen a white customer in four months, much less one in urgent need of a hairy rodent.

"All sold out," he said facetiously. "Sold my last one not twenty minutes ago. But if I was you, I'd get back in that thing and keep goin'. This is East St. Louis, lady. A Winnebago full of white people is *Christmas* to the brothers what live 'round here. You best find what you need in the phonebook and get goin' . . . or whatever you got in that trailer is gonna be barbecue by sundown."

Esther quickly scanned the yellow pages, tore out the page she needed, and ran back outside, where three sinister looking fellows were studying the camper. She brushed by. "Good morning, gentlemen." She stepped up onto the running board to climb inside. "Love to chat, need a ferret. *Toodles!"* She slammed the door and locked it, gunned the engine, ran a red light, and rumbled to the interstate.

Forty miles down the road they exited and found the exotic pet store. When the salesman heard they were desperate for a male ferret, he doubled the price. Esther offered to barter inside his private office, but Pez coughed up the cash. He also bought an extra dozen mice. He tossed the ferret and mice inside the trailer. Fast Eddie brayed loudly, and the Odds Quad were rolling again.

They arrived in Louisville very late Tuesday night, four days before the Derby. Pez won a quick game of rock-paper-scissors, so Mung Fu and Toker had to fork over a hefty sum for a secure parking spot inside a fenced lot adjacent to Churchill Downs. Several large vehicles, mostly TV trucks, were already there. It was past midnight when he finally parked next to a CBS van and killed the ignition. "Made it," he announced. "I'm hittin' the rack." He plopped in his bunk and was asleep in minutes.

A half-hour's work remained, so Toker volunteered to feed and water the animals while the others went to bed. Despite the tent city all around, Churchill Downs was quiet. Toker sat on the tongue of the trailer and rolled a fat joint, lit it and inhaled deeply, then snorted the blue smoke for an extra boost. Two seeds popped in his face, jolting him.

Ahhh, my first Kentucky buzz. One more hit and he'd water the animals. *Better do it now, before I forget.*

One hit turned into five. He swilled a beer as he smoked. Guzzled it and popped the top on a second.

Finally he stood up, joint dangling from his lips. He unlatched the doors and swung open the burro trailer. The wave of small animals flew at him. *Oh shit, they're attacking!*

The mice jumped onto his pant legs and shirtsleeves and ran for higher ground. The ferrets leaped, clawing at his shirt, snarling and biting at the mice. The cat meowed, the goat walked off the trailer, and Fast Eddie peed, his urine splashing Toker's hand. Toker wasn't sure if it went in his beer or not. *You little bastards!*

Trying to keep the chaos contained, Toker jumped into the trailer and frantically pulled the doors behind him.

Trapped in the pitch black, the mice scurried to hide in the dark. One stayed on Toker's head until he swiped it off; the mouse ricocheted off the aluminum trailer wall.

The aroma of animal poop and urine was gagging, so Toker inhaled a deep drag off the stubby remainder of the joint and held his breath until he had to breathe again.

He slid open the trailer door's small window and cocked his head sideways to look out. Ten feet away was Josie the goat, chewing on the cables of the TV van. "Hey," he called softly through the vent, "cut that out!" Josie ignored him.

He took a final deep hit of the joint and felt the door for a way out. No handle. Trapped in a damn donkey trailer. Now what? *Welcome to Louisville.*

Oh, screw it! They'll find me in the morning.

His slid down to a sitting position, with his back against the rear trailer door. Might as well have a second doobie. He rolled and smoked it in silence, down to a nub, and extracted a roach clip from his pocket. Expertly he snorted the rest. "The ashes of a noble warrior," he mumbled to Fast Eddie.

As Toker drifted off into the Zombied recesses of a deep, stoned sleep, a mouse hid inside his pant leg.

Pez found Toker in the morning when he swung open the trailer's back doors, looking for Fast Eddie, who was supposed to be tied up outside. Toker tumbled out backward. "Mornin'," he grunted, leaning on an elbow. He squinted up at his rescuer. "Cool in there, dude. You should try it. Lots more fun than sellin' Christmas trees."

"You smell like a landfill," said Pez, waving his hand in front of nose. "Walk through a car wash, will you? But hurry. Deacon's treating us to lunch."

The team spent the day exploring historic Churchill Downs, the fulcrum of a city turned upside-down, buried in an avalanche of preparation. The place was swarming with technicians, media personnel, vendors, and concessionaires, all preparing for Saturday.

Newspeople reported on every conceivable thing: The search for outfits, the hunt for perfect hats, parties of the rich and famous, race predictions, weather reports, gossip—and the rising price of tickets, cardboard billets of historic currency. Three days before the race the grandstand seats had traded hands for four times their face value. The best seats sold for thousands; as the race drew closer, prices were expected to escalate.

Deacon and Tuki had been in Louisville for several days already and Deacon's reaction was similar to other first-timers pulled inside the vortex of the spectacle that is the Kentucky Derby. He was hooked immediately.

"We gotta do this again next year. This ain't no nickel-dime flea market. This is *real* money, Tuki. Derby dollars flying like confetti."

"When's the post-position draw?" she asked. The surrounding noise meant zero to her.

"Noon, the museum."

"Meet you there. At the barn if you need me."

He shook his head as she walked away. New Year's Eve in Times Square and the girl don't even care.

Rigby had been in town for two days, and volunteered to pick up Melvin and Shelley up at the airport. He tossed their bags inside the trunk of his rented Escalade and hustled behind the wheel. "Gotta hurry," he said. "You are featured guests at a really big event, the post position draw."

"What's that?" asked Shelley. "Do I need to dress up?"

"You look great," replied Rigby. "The draw is where they randomly assign horses and positions in the starting gate."

"What's the big deal, Rig?" asked Melvin. "Why does that matter?"

"To us, it don't," he answered. "But for everybody else, it can mean the difference between a good shot and no shot at all. With Ooty's running style, it won't matter where he starts. We'll drop back and reel 'em in."

"How about the other biggies?" asked Melvin.

"It's a long run to the first turn, which gives the jockeys some settling time. The contenders will want to get out quick and clean. They'll want the shortest straight line they can get."

"Where do you want Ooty to be, Rigby?" asked Shelley.

"Outside. The race is run in a circle, so the wider the circumference, the farther the distance the horse has to run. The shortest distance is around the rail, but the rail is the easiest place to get boxed in."

"Boxed?" asked Shelley.

"Trapped. Against great horses, you can't get trapped."

"That's what you pay the jockey for, right, Rig?" said Melvin.

Rigby turned his head toward the big man and nodded. "You're catching on. You got a future in this business, Melvin."

"Farmers, Rig. Our future in this business is feedin' the participants."

Deacon and Tuki were waiting outside the Churchill Downs museum when Rigby valeted the car. They greeted the Trombleys warmly. The five quickly huddled near the front door to finalize their strategy.

"The dead-zones trainers want to avoid are the ones in the aux gate and the inside hugging the rail," said Rigby. "The rail only works if you've got enough balls . . ."

"Guts," corrected Deacon.

"Right," agreed Rigby. "Guts. The rail works if you got the guts, and speed, to risk getting trapped in order to get out fast, ahead of everybody else."

"What's the aux gate?" asked Shelley. "You said aux gate."

Tuki handled that one. "Fourteen go out of the main gate. The other six from the auxiliary gate, a second gate they bring out for everybody else."

"Why don't trainers want it?" asked Shelley.

"The winner traditionally comes out of the main gate," said Rigby.

"Poppycock," said Tuki sharply. "The race is far more traditionally won by the fastest horse."

"I'm willing to go out there," Rigby warned, "but, Tuki, you can't get lazy. Every step matters. We can start there, but you gotta get inside quick, and save ground as soon as possible."

He turned to Melvin and Shelley. "You two own the horse. I'll do what you want. Once those gates open, twenty will explode forward and storm toward the turn like a cavalry. It's a stampede, let me tell you."

"What does the outside add, distance-wise?" asked Melvin.

"We spot the rail horse six lengths, Melvin. If Othello starts from the rail and gets out quick, and we don't, Tuki's got a big problem trying to catch him, 'cause he ain't gonna wait."

"He might not have the chance to pick inside," said Deacon. "He might get stuck with a bad draw."

"Possible," nodded Rigby. "That's why we're here. To watch the others sweat."

"No worries," Tuki chimed in. "We've got the winner."

Rigby looked at Tuki sternly. "Braggadocio is okay sometimes, Tuki, but this is a humbling business that chops braggarts off at the knees. If we go out wide to the aux gate, history says we probably won't win. The aux gate ain't Siberia, but a lot of horsemen say you can see it from there."

"It's a miracle we're even standing here, Rigby," said Shelley. "The gate doesn't really matter to us."

"But we *are* here," he said. "What I'm saying is the aux gate is an unconventional, odds-against choice."

"You really think the bloody gate matters to Ooty and me?" Tuki interrupted, agitated. "We'll start from the bloody parking lot, if we have to."

"Now, now, calm down," Deacon said firmly, glaring at Tuki. "No need for 'double-bloodys'. Let's all play in the sandbox together, shall we?" Turning to Rigby, he asked, "Sum it up, Rig. Where you wanna be, inside or out?"

Rigby looked at Melvin, who looked at Shelley, who looked at Deacon, who looked at Tuki.

"Out," Tuki said firmly. "Avoid the bumper cars."

"This event got food inside?" asked Melvin. "I'm hungry." He turned and marched into the museum.

"I'm glad we don't have to do this before every race," Deacon said to Rigby as the two brought up the rear.

"Feed him?"

"No. Screw with a 20-horse draw."

Rigby nodded. "Once a year is just about right. Same with a twenty-horse field."

Since the post-position telecast was the horsemen's most important pre-race Derby event, its build-up and excitement was a show all its own. The hot, bright klieg lights of television were new to the Trombleys and the surrounding whirlwind of behind-the-scenes preparation mesmerized Melvin. "Where are we, Rig, relative to the track?" he asked. "This museum, I mean."

"Three hundred yards from the finish line," Rigby replied. "Win the race and you'll be back here Saturday night, signing autographs. The winner's party is right here."

Shelley nudged Melvin and nodded toward the new arrivals.

"Money and bright lights both draw moths," Rigby said. "As do fast horses. People cling like remoras to Derby contenders. Pick your simile or metaphor, folks. We'll all have a dozen new best friends by the end of the day."

"I'll take one," volunteered Deacon and sat next to Rigby. "A pretty one! I've only got three requirements: Look good, smell good, act *bad*. A girl like that will make my trip."

"A mannequin would make your trip," snorted Rigby.

"I'm in Louisville," justified Deacon. "The three-river rule is officially in effect."

"What three rivers?" asked Rigby, puzzled.

Deacon grinned and help up three fingers. "Cross three rivers on a trip away from home and there *are* no rules for love."

Rigby clapped Deacon on the back. "That what's I like about you, Deacon. Always thinking of others when it's time to strut your bantam rooster mating dance."

Deacon laughed. "I don't know what that means, Rigby, but thanks anyway. Three rivers, baby. Deacon Truth, gangster of love."

Tuki couldn't contain herself. "*Prankster* of love is more like it."

Shelley giggled. "Melvin's one of those, too."

Rigby knew the other horsemen and interrupted to point several out.

"Odd, ain't it?" said Melvin. "A roomful of strangers assembled from God knows where. All this fuss for a two-minute race. Then we all vanish back to where we came from."

"Don't wax esoteric, big man," Rigby implored. "You'll ruin your farmboy charm."

"I ain't waxin'," Melvin replied. "I'm just sayin'."

The TV people hurried to get the draw ceremony ready to begin and Melvin asked, "Where's the sheikh?"

"Not here," said Rigby. "Sends his people to undercard events like this."

"Will he be here Saturday?"

Rigby nodded. "He's here now. Just not *here* here."

Deacon elbowed Tuki, whose eyes were closed. "Check this out, girl. Look around! We got potato man, sheikh people, fiddle makers, dotcom billionaires, underworld gamblers, *everybody*. Plus, we got *their* people *and* their people's people. Check it out!"

"Deacon?" she asked.

"What?" "Shut up."

"Look at the Japanese dude," Deacon implored, instantly resuming. "I heard about him. He's big time, a silk baron or somethin', got 100,000 geisha girls."

Rigby sat up. "What! Who's got 100,000 geisha girls?"

"Just kiddin', Rig." Deacon grinned. "He's only got a few hundred. Oh, my God, I don't believe it!"

"What?"

"Lookee there, in the corner, a group of brothers! How sweet is that, a brother in here besides me?"

"Keep looking," teased Rigby. "A brother owns Blackula, one of the entries; and another brother trains two of the favorites." Rigby looked across to where Deacon was staring. "That's the fellow who owns Blackula."

Deacon let out a low whistle. "Check out the posse. African garb, voodoo beads . . . think they got the elixirs? Who's that white girl next to them, Rig? Next to the fossil in the suit?"

"Samantha Stevens," replied Rigby. "Cosmetics queen. Rich ancient husband bought her a fringe pretender so she could say she started a horse in the Derby. No chance."

Melvin leaned over and nodded toward the temporary stage. "Who's that, Rigby? The serious guy in the brown suit? He keeps checking his watch. Is he a TV guy?"

"That's Burton Anderson. He runs Churchill Downs. He'll host this circus, if it ever gets started."

The television taping was late getting underway and Chairman Anderson was perturbed. He didn't like delays, especially during Derby week. He had run this place for thirty years and studied the room with the wooden smile of a political mannequin.

This year's field defied the sport's blueblood tradition. It was, by far, the oddest assemblage of contestants in the Derby's storied 130-year history. Future-book wagers were 16 percent ahead of the previous best. Ticket demand was at an all-time high. A record crowd would flood the track on Saturday and jam the betting windows. He didn't like these unseemly recalcitrants, but collectively they were brilliant for business.

Anderson glanced again at his watch. Ten minutes behind schedule. An aide came up and whispered in his ear. Anderson narrowed his eyes as he listened. An animal rights protestor had hired a couple of comedians to hide inside a horse costume and disrupt the event. The jokers were prancing around outside the museum, blocking the entry of credentialed media. Doubly annoying was the video camera the woman protester was wielding as her insurance against illegal mistreatment. Some old has-been actress with nothing better to do. In the old days, he'd have tossed all three of their asses into a dumpster. Nowadays, they had rights. Anderson whispered a terse reply to the aide, who then rushed back outside.

When the protesters were finally dispatched, the doors were locked to prevent further disruption.

Deacon nudged Tuki, who seemed to be sleeping. "Showtime. Pay attention, quiz at the end."

Rigby leaned over to Melvin as Chairman Anderson stepped to the podium. "Watch close," he whispered. "You are about to see Lady Luck bitch-slap some very rich people. She'll bury them in post positions where they've got no chance. Cruel as hell when it happens to you. Fun as hell when it happen to a jackass."

The television camera's red light came on and the program director pointed to the host, Chairman Anderson, who welcomed the race participants and the TV audience to historic Churchill Downs and the traditional Kentucky Derby Post Position Draw.

Anderson briefly explained the rules. "The draw involves a series of random selections, matching each horse in the field with an assigned number, one through twenty.

"There are nineteen rounds of random rolls with these large dice; each die is numbered one through twenty."

Anderson paused and held one aloft. "Following each random roll of the dice,

Miss Kentucky, Charlotte Owens, will reach into this rose-red velvet box and remove, also at random, the official entry slip of one of the twenty horses."

He smiled toward Miss Kentucky and nodded. "Welcome, Charlotte. We are honored to have you with us."

Resplendent with a sparkling tiara, red ball-gown, and elbow-length white gloves, Miss Kentucky smiled and waved a royal greeting to the crowd.

Deacon whistled, which caused a ripple of laughter through the audience; and a TV flunkie wearing headphones stepped menacingly toward Deacon, pantomiming him to hush.

Anderson scowled at the disruption, then smiled woodenly into the camera and continued. "After the selection priority is determined, one through twenty, those numbers will dictate the order in which each trainer selects his or her preferred post position. The selection order runs low-to-high, number one having first choice. Number two chooses next. Number twenty is assigned the sole remaining open gate."

Urged by the TV flunkie with the headset to pivot, Anderson turned stiffly and swept an outstretched arm toward a giant one-minute clock timer. After several seconds, he turned back to the camera with a tight smile. "Once the selection order is determined, each trainer—beginning with whoever drew number one—will have one minute to pick his or her preferred post position."

Tuki tapped Rigby on the shoulder from behind. "Smooth, he is," she whispered, "like a cactus."

Anderson gripped the podium with both hands, preparing for his big finish. "Owners, jockeys, trainers, handlers, ladies, gentlemen, and race fans around the world," he summarized dramatically, *"Good luck!"*

Melvin leaned over to Rigby and whispered, "The super-duper dice machine looks like a bingo basket."

"Normally is," Rigby whispered back. "Brought it from his living room."

Tuki nudged Deacon. "A bit much of fluff, don't you think? Quite a bloody fuss."

He waved her to be quiet. "Pay attention," he whispered hoarsely. "You win, and I get to hang with Miss Kentucky."

Having finished with the rules, Chairman Anderson carefully poured the twenty dice-like "pills" inside the wire-mesh tumbler. He secured the lid and turned the handle several times to demonstrate the tumbling fairness of the mixture. He then extended the honor of selecting the pills to the governor, who stepped forward and cranked the handle several times until a single pill tumbled down the exit chute.

The governor then handed the pill to Chairman Anderson and politely deferred to Miss Kentucky. She reached her white-gloved hand inside the red-velvet box and withdrew a single entry slip. Smiling, she turned the slip over to the chairman, who stepped forward to announce the horse and its selection priority.

Rigby nudged Melvin. "The fun begins. If we get first pick and I go way outside, the media will shred my flesh."

"Number nineteen," Chairman Anderson called out, causing the audience to groan.

Deacon laughed. "Check it out. Nobody wants this pick."

"Selecting nineteenth will be . . . "

The raucous crowd, growling its growing discontent, ignored the TV flunkie's imploring windmills to pipe down; and as the chairman attempted to announce Miss Kentucky's selection, they drowned him out. They hooted, hollered, whistled, and pounded on the chairs like tom-tom drums. Sounds of African jungle instruments wailed mystical voodoo refrains. Loudest of all, from the back of the room came the thunder and trumpets of what sounded like scores of stampeding elephants.

Tuki giggled. "It's a bloody migration!"

Mortified that his traditionally dignified ceremony sounded like a frat-house initiation, Chairman Anderson raised his right hand in a futile attempt to throttle the noise.

The nineteenth and second-to-worst position went to the cosmetics lady, whose late addition to the field didn't belong anyway. The crowd collectively exhaled and broke into an explosive cheer.

Melvin clapped as he watched. "This is great," he said. "Definitely worth the airfare."

Shelley leaned in. "Is this fair, Rigby? The way they do it, I mean."

Rigby nodded. "Very. Plus it adds dramatic theater to an otherwise boring ritual. Give the man credit. Anderson was smart to think of it."

The governor wheeled the pills through ten rounds of choice; none of the first, second, or third picks tumbled out. Miss Kentucky picked her white-glove way through the first ten selections; the names of four pre-race favorites also remained inside the velvet box.

Following the twelfth pick, someone outside pounded loudly on the front door. Race officials assumed it was the animal rights protesters and ignored the intrusion. The selections went on, and the coveted first pick remained unassigned.

The final pill tumbled out—marked with number one. Miss Kentucky, not a math major, soon became the first to learn that the race officials should have answered the banging door. Elbow-deep, she fished around inside an empty box. She smiled with pageant-tested determination and kept fishing.

"Houston, we've got a problem," whispered Melvin to Rigby.

Rigby nodded. "Told ya. Best free theater in America."

Frantically Miss Kentucky then searched with both white-gloved hands. Nothing. Still smiling, she finally surrendered, pulled both arms back out of the box, turned to Chairman Anderson and, with dazzling big teeth, upturned her empty hands and giggled. "Oops! No horse!"

Only nineteen entry slips had been in the box. The crowd exploded, and the blacks were furious since they had been first in line to pick.

Arms folded, Rigby watched impassively. He had pulled sixteen. No man's land.

Chairman Anderson blanched and blamed the TV guys for messing up the draw. The TV headphone flunkie loudly retorted, "Bullshit!" The TV mike caught it and the audience howled. Many jumped to their feet shook their fists, demanding an explanation.

Deacon joined in and urged the audience on.

"Your agent is quite distinguished," Rigby noted dryly to Tuki.

"You've trained him well," she replied.

Rigby kept watching Burton Anderson, who was shell-shocked at the podium: his dawning of realization that split-second when he realized it was all screwed up. It was beautiful.

Melvin followed Rigby's gaze. "He looks like a farmer who spent all day plowing dirt, only to see it washed away by a deluge."

Rigby nodded. "Poor bastard worked all year building the thing right and *ka-boom*—instant implosion."

Finally a security guard unlocked the museum door and in rushed a clerk from the racing secretary's office. In his hand he waved an entry slip. The clerk ran straight to the podium on-stage and handed it to Chairman Anderson. "It was under the table," he stammered, struggling to catch his breath. "Thought you might need it." His message boomed out clearly through the microphone, setting off another explosion of chaos and noise.

Following an extra-long break, the crowd finally simmered back down. The broadcast returned to a smiling Chairman Anderson.

He reloaded all the pills back into the tumbler, all twenty entries safely back inside the velvet box. Anderson nervously straightened his tie, then solemnly announced, "Do over." They would start again from scratch.

The owners and trainers who'd gotten low numbers the first time now were back in the mix with everyone else. Yet the redraw was a reprieve for those first doomed to lousy posts.

"Splendid programming," Rigby commented dryly, nodding at Melvin and Shelley.

"Oops! No horse!" mimicked Deacon. People seated around them laughed loudly. As the post-position re-draw ended, one of the few in the room who seemed happy was Rigby Malone.

Melvin seemed crestfallen. "Twentieth?"

Rigby put his hand on the big man's shoulder. "It's perfect, Melvin. We'll let the rest play smash 'n' crash. We'll drop to the rail and bide our time. Then we'll reel 'em all back in. We got what we came for, kiddies."

"Think so, Rig?" asked Melvin anxiously.

23
IN SEARCH OF A BOWL
OF POTATO SOUP

Friday night parties blanketed the city, and caterers turned every cocktail weenie into a five-dollar bill.

In the presidential suite at the hundred-year-old Hilton, Sheikh Mustafa Ali Ali Mumtaz met with a small group of very nervous men who'd assembled at his request. One of the planet's richest men and Albacoa's owner, Sheikh MAAM had invited them over to talk horses.

At precisely five minutes to six, Rigby Malone and Melvin Trombley knocked three times on the suite's double doors, paused, then knocked four times more. The sheikh's valet opened the door and ushered them inside.

Tony Syracuse was already seated at an exquisite mahogany table, drumming his fingers. Rigby didn't know Tony personally, but he'd seen him surrounded by bimbos at the post-position draw. He had seen a hundred guys like this before. They came and went; they never stayed. He judged Tony Syracuse to be all about angles, and not a horseman. The slick New Yorker probably hadn't stepped in horse poop once, much less a million times.

Across the table were three bowmakers. Rigby knew that four men owned Pernambuco, but one of them had never seen their horse run. If the third choice in the Derby wasn't reason enough to show up, then four girls in a Jacuzzi wasn't enough reason to get wet.

Rigby's discussion earlier in the day with the sheikh's people had gone deeper than what he'd shared with Melvin. He only told the farmer they were invited to an important pre-race meeting and dinner. In fact, Sheikh MAAM wanted to buy Ooty, and he wanted to buy all four of the other top contenders.

Another loud knock at the door echoed, followed by a booming voice. "IT'S COTTLE! Open the damn door! I'm ninety-five years old, and every minute means something."

J. L. Cottle and Moose Utley, the final two invitees, had arrived.

"Glad to be here," Moose said warmly as he shook hands with the others. "Cottle and me don't generally meet people worth more than he is."

"Should be a fun evening," added Cottle.

Neither man was phased by Sheikh MAAM's spectacular wealth and didn't care about what part of the desert the sheikh came from. The guy hailed from Planet Billion and very few breathed such rarified air. Cottle had more dough than most countries. If this guy had more, then Moose and he sure as hell wouldn't need to reach for the dinner check.

After all eight horsemen were settled around the table, a second aide escorted the sheikh into the room. Sheikh MAAM was dressed in casual clothes rather than traditional robes, which disappointed Melvin and the bowmakers. They'd expected him to look like Prince Feisal in *Lawrence of Arabia*. Also, the sheikh was younger than they'd expected, mid-forties.

He walked around the perimeter of the table and politely introduced himself. When he reached Melvin, the farmer held up a disposable camera and gestured hopefully. The sheikh laughed and nodded. Melvin handed the camera to Rigby, who took two pictures. The bowmakers then wanted one to show to their fourth partner, Saul. Rigby snapped a shot of all three with the sheikh.

The sheikh then stepped to the head of the opulent table and nodded for the men to sit. "Thank you, gentlemen, for coming," he said in perfect English. "I am honored by your presence and honored to be in your company in conjunction with the wonderful event that brings us all together: sportsmen united with a shared love of the horse."

Moose nudged Cottle under the table at the sheikh's unemotional matter-of-fact tone. *That* came from ruling a nation bubbling over with oil. Cottle never took his eyes off the sheikh, listening politely but wondering when the man would quit slatherin' on the butter and bring on the main course.

"We are new friends," the sheikh said, "bound by this occasion, yet businessmen nonetheless." He looked around the table, making eye contact with each man.

Then he nodded to his closest assistant, who presented Shekh MAAM with five envelopes embossed in red wax with the sheikh's official seal. On each envelope, in florid calligraphy, was written a horse's name.

Moose watched the sheikh hand out the envelopes. The rich ruler remembered each owner by sight, and their horses by name.

No one opened his envelope. Lionel George nervously twiddled the bowmakers'.

The sheikh milked the moment, smiled, then resumed. "Inside is an offer to purchase. It expires at midnight. Each is affixed with an executed check in certified funds. The money is yours if you so choose."

Moose piped up, "What if we want more time? Say until five minutes *after* the race tomorrow?" With a wide grin, he looked directly at the sheikh.

The others chuckled. The sheikh's expression didn't change. He raised his hand politely. "Midnight, Mr. Utley. One other thing, should you *all* decide to execute the agreements, there will be a $5 million bonus."

"A million bucks a guy?" Tony Syracuse groused. "Big friggin' deal. Winning the freaking race is worth more than that, especially considering the babes that go with it."

"Five million *per man,* Mr. Syracuse. Twenty-five million added to what is in your envelopes right now. But, remember, *all* of you . . . or no bonus. One out, all out."

Melvin raised a hand politely. "Lemme ask you somethin', sir, just so I'm clear, Mr. Sheikh, sir. If we want to sell, whatever's in this envelope is ours, right? And if everybody sells, we get what's in the envelope *plus* $5 million more?"

The sheikh nodded. "Precisely, Mr. Trombley."

Cottle did the quick math in his head. What the sheikh was saying made no sense at all. "Why you doing this?" he asked. "Why throw so much money at a fistful of horses, when you've already got a billion dollars worth of better ones back home?" Moose nodded in agreement.

Tony Syracuse's eyes widened with a vision of millions dancing on its tippy-toes.

Rigby Malone leaned forward. "I'll answer that. Sheikh MAAM has been the world's greatest celebrant of the Thoroughbred for the past twenty years."

"That doesn't answer the question," said Cottle.

"I'll answer it if you'll let me," Rigby retorted. "For the last two decades, Sheikh MAAM has traveled the globe supporting our industry with more money than any ten men added together. That money keeps farms running and people working. Those jobs raise families."

Cottle nodded. "I understand. So do I, by the tens of thousands. I still see no relevance."

"You're a great man, Mr. Cottle," said Rigby, "and have been for decades, but the sheikh ain't got twenty more years." He paused and looked over at the sheikh. An almost imperceptible nod signaled Rigby's permission to continue. "He's ill. And the only race the sheikh ever really wanted to win, and hasn't, is this one."

The sheikh held up his hand for Rigby to stop, but Rigby continued. "It may not be my place to say, but this might be his last shot. And I respectfully request, gentlemen, that news of his illness will stay in the room."

All eyes turned toward the sheikh. He rose stiffly, nodded to the men and excused himself from the table. He whispered briefly to his aide and left.

"Dinner must be rescheduled," said the aide with a polite bow. He quickly followed Sheikh MAAM out of the room.

The sheikh's second aide stepped forward. "Please consider this most generous offer," he said, then he exited, too.

Cottle's envelope sat in front of him. Moose stared at Hundo's carefully printed name. The bowmakers and Tony Syracuse were eager to rip theirs open.

Melvin turned to Rigby. "What do you think we should do?"

"Manage by fact. See what he's offering. We wouldn't be here if there weren't big numbers in the envelopes, *plus* $5 million more per guy if everyone goes in. That's huge money. Ridiculous money. Think about what brought you here in the first place, Melvin. If money's part of it, then maybe it's time to head to the cashier's window."

Tony Syracuse scoffed. "*If* money's part of it? You nuts, Malone? Money's part of everything."

Cottle shoved his unopened envelope to the center of the table and sighed. "I don't need more money. I need *less* money. I'm ninety-five years old. I need more time, more fun—not some bag of Middle East payola."

Tony Syracuse saw his $5 million bonus sliding away and pounded on the table. "You friggin' nuts, old man? You out of your friggin' mind? For Sicily's sake, at least *open* the envelope and see what it says." He tore open his own and stared at the check. Then he turned it to the others dramatically. "*Four* million! *Four* friggin' million dollars! That's *eight* million total!"

"Nine million," bowmaker D. C. Lee corrected. "Four million plus five million is nine million."

"Right, maestro. *Nine* million! Where's a freakin' pen? Whose got a freakin' pen?"

Tony's animation made the others laugh. The bowmakers reacted like the Marx brothers and reflexively patted their pockets a hundred fruitless times.

Moose interceded and tried to calm down the volatile Italian. "Win the race and your horse is worth three times that." He turned to the bowmakers. "Open yours. See what the *Santa of the Sands* brought you."

Lionel carefully cracked his wax seal and peeled open the back of the envelope; he wanted to save it as a souvenir. He carefully removed the folded letter that held the check. "I can't stand it," he said. He closed his eyes and slid the papers toward Nathan Pillsbury. "Tell us, Nate."

Nate slowly unfolded the documents, then showed the check to D. C. Lee and grinned. "Five million. A million more than Tony's. A pretty good trade for a violin bow."

Lionel exhaled deeply, then opened his eyes. He looked at Nathan Pillsbury and D. C. Lee, and all three looked across at Tony Syracuse. Lionel asked dryly, "You find that pen?"

With a dramatic flourish, Moose Utley impulsively tore off the short end of his own envelope for Hundo and emphatically blew it open. With two fingers, he extracted his check and letter and flicked them open.

Cottle watched his friend's eyes. "Forty bucks," he teased.

Moose stared at his letter, but his thumb hiked up.

"Ninety bucks," Cottle said.

Moose held the check out for the others to see. "So far, the sheikh likes Pernambuco the best. Four million."

Melvin shot a nervous glance at Rigby Malone. "I can't stand it, Rig. I gotta know. I gotta know."

"Then find out," Rigby urged, patting him on the shoulder.

Melvin tried to open Ooty's envelope carefully but his fat, stubby fingers quickly abandoned finesse for function. He closed his eyes and pulled the letter out. When he finally looked, the letter was upside down. He fiddled with it and Rigby stole a glance. Three million. Not bad for a clearance sale yearling.

Melvin's hand shook and the letter fluttered. He exhaled loudly. *"Gawl-mighty!* Miss Louise can rest in peace! Three million dollars!"

"Three plus five more," Rigby corrected. "Eight million for the kids at Possum Drop High."

Flushed red, Melvin gushed. *"Everyone* can go to college! I can't believe it."

Cottle had made no move to open his own envelope. He assumed it was more of the same. He studied each face around the table. The sheikh had read them right. Each had a price. But why now? The sheikh had known of these horses months ago; and for a sick guy, he looked fine. Cottle's instincts screamed. Another piece was out there. The puzzle wasn't complete.

He put both hands on the chair's sturdy armrests and struggled to stand. He finally rose and looked at the men. "Shallow men believe in luck," he said. "Strong men believe in cause and effect. I'm hungry boys. I'm going to think about this over a bowl of potato soup."

Tony Syracuse leapt to his feet. "You can't eat SOUP! No friggin' bowl of soup in the world is worth $50 million! We gotta sign this, pops. We gotta sign now! *Then* you can have soup. I'll even *buy* your soup. I'll buy all the potato soup you can eat for the rest of your life!"

"I appreciate the offer," Cottle responded while shuffling to the door. "I assure you, I can eat a lot of potato soup. I also assure you I will return."

Rather than get a bowl of potato soup, Cottle went to the movies. Movies helped him think; they always had. He wanted some private time. He also wanted to leave the others to talk things through at a deeper level, not knee-jerk to their wallets' first impulse. Every one of them had a chance to win the world's greatest race. After all it took to get here, suddenly they wanted to walk away?

The sheikh was purchasing their manhood. Cottle preferred to tell the rich man to go sit on an oil well.

He also realized that, aside from him and Moose, none of the others was financially free. Costing each owner five million bucks was not something he took lightly. As the movie's final credits rolled, he still hadn't made up his mind.

After three hours, everyone except Moose began to panic. He said little, preferring to watch the others and listen. To them, the sheikh's payoff was a lifetime of riches. To Moose and J. L., it only meant that after four years their bet was a push, an unresolved tie.

Moose would just as soon leave the sheikh's money on the table, but thumbing his nose at the others' dreams was cruel. He wouldn't trade two used pizza boxes for Tony Syracuse, but he didn't want to squash the bowmakers' retirement assurance, nor barricade the realization of Miss Louise's dying dream.

He glanced at his wristwatch. Well past nine. Assuming Cottle made it back before midnight, he decided to support whatever his friend chose.

Cottle returned at 10:15, pounding on the double-doors. "Open the damn door! I forgot the secret code!"

Tony Syracuse leapt up, ran over, and yanked the doors open. He pretended Cottle was a friend and warmly welcomed back the old man.

"Stuff it, Syracuse. You annoy me." Cottle waved dismissingly at him and made his way slowly toward the table. He had raised pigs with better manners than Tony Syracuse. Before he sat down, Cottle looked at him disdainfully and added, "You think with your mouth, and you behave like you're hornier than a pen full of billy goats. A bad combination, young man. Even if we take the taw, you'll piss yours away in a month."

Tony froze and the bowmakers laughed. So did Melvin, who liked Cottle and pulled out his yellow disposable camera to snap a quick picture.

They all reseated and Cottle looked each man in the eye. "What will you do with the money?"

Syracuse ignored Melvin, who'd raised his hand. "I want to sell, Cottle. We all want to sell. Money's money. I can parlay this ten-fold. Who knows, maybe I'll buy a potato ranch." He cocked his head sideways and winked.

Rather than challenge the insolent, blustery Italian, Cottle looked at the bowmakers. They also wanted to sell. Lionel George deferred to D. C. Lee to explain.

"We're not rich people, Mr. Cottle," said D. C. "Far from it. And we're not horse people. We're just four guys who got lucky. The money would secure our future. Some of it would also go a very long way toward funding a trust account for pernambuco reforestation in Brazil."

As D. C. spoke, both Lionel George and Nathan Pillsbury nodded.

"Me, too, Mr. Cottle," added Melvin. "Sellin' is best. Right, Rigby?"

Rigby minced no words. "There's twenty horses in the race. Only one winner. If everyone gets a clean trip and an honest ride, the sheikh's horse is probably the best. If not, one of you guys might win. Ooty won't. In this field, at this distance, as much as I'd like to say he can win, he can't. Take the money, Melvin. Possum Drop doesn't need a trophy. Possum Drop needs college graduates. What mattered to Miss Louise was that her kids end up winners. The horse is a means to an end. Thanks to the sheikh, you've reached that end."

Melvin stared vacantly, nodding. When Rigby finished, Melvin agreed. "I'm in. I'll sign. Thank you, Rigby . . . and thank you, Mr. Sheikh. This is a historic day for Possum Drop, North Carolina."

Three teams in. The $25-million pooled bonus now sat squarely on the two old-timers. Moose ran his fingers through his hair. "Dang, boys! I don't wanna sell. I wanna win the Derby!"

The others deflated.

"But," he continued, "I *will* sell if you really need the dough."

Upon hearing *these* words, they re-inflated.

Moose turned to Cottle, who locked eyes with Rigby Malone and stared at him for ten full seconds. Then Cottle slowly began to smile. He saw the final piece of the puzzle. He broke eye contact with Malone and glanced at his watch. 10:50. Way past bedtime.

Moose slid Spudcat's envelope over and nudged it against Cottle's wrist. "Check out the number, J. L. At least look at the number."

Cottle pulled his hand away, as if the envelope were poison ivy. "No need." He slowly shook his head. "Taw don't mean nothin'. I came here to race a horse . . . and I'm *racing* a horse. Sorry, gentlemen, but I'm not selling."

Everyone exploded. Tony Syracuse cursing loudly, pounding his fist violently on the table.

Cottle ignored him. He leaned over and whispered to Moose, who nodded back. Then Cottle rose shakily and shuffled to the door.

Syracuse lunged toward Cottle but Melvin jumped up to protect the old man, quickly blocking Syracuse's path. Syracuse struggled with the giant, determined to keep Cottle from leaving. Syracuse finally broke free and grabbed a spindly wooden chair. He flung it angrily across the room, exploding the fragile antique into splinters against the opulent double doors. Cottle was safe by a matter of seconds.

Moose tried vainly to calm the men down. "Let's talk through the situation," he pleaded. "Sort it out."

"Pound sand, sidekick!" Tony Syracuse yelled. "You're in on it, too." Syracuse kept cursing, refusing to listen, and his face flushed purple. Moose knew Syracuse would never listen. He gave up and tried the others.

The bowmakers were civil. "One year ago, we had nothing," Lionel George shrugged. "Today we get a million apiece, after taxes? We're okay."

"Me, too," added Melvin. "Three million bucks is a whole lot of money in Possum Drop. It's about as much as the whole city budget. We can help *busloads* of kids with $3 million."

Rigby Malone saw things differently. He was incensed. "How can that old fart blossom live with himself?" he demanded. "How can he sleep? Ruining kids' lives, destroying their futures? How the hell can a man have so much money that it pollutes him to the point where he quits caring about others?"

"Sing it loud, cowboy. Say it proud!" yelled Tony Syracuse. "I'll sing the refrain, word for poetic word!"

Moose let the men finish venting their feelings, and then tried to explain why Cottle chose what he did. Syracuse wouldn't shut up.

"Ah, the hell with it," Moose muttered.

At midnight, escorted by both aides, the sheikh re-entered the vacant room to collect his signed contracts. All the documents were on the table, all unsigned. One envelope unopened. The sheikh flipped it over. Spudcat. The only blank check in the bunch.

His jaw tightened. He had underestimated the potato farmer. "Get Malone on the phone!" he hissed. "Find him! *Immediately!*"

24
DERBY DAZE

Tuki traded her hotel room to Esther and slept in the Odds Quad Winnebago. She arrived at Ooty's barn well before sunrise and spent the morning there, much of the time in his stall, talking to him and reading aloud.

When she was tired of reading, she brushed him. As she did, she chided Ooty for biting and kicking her two years ago. After securing and reweaving his tail extensions, she carefully polished his racing visor, shining the mirrored lens.

Deacon arrived at seven a.m., with an orange juice for her from the cafeteria, the *Courier-Journal* under his arm. He read aloud what a columnist wrote in the newspaper's special Derby Day edition.

> *Today, we witness racing's perfect storm: rich, poor, young, old, experienced, novices. Farmers, sheikhs, bluebloods, and woodcarvers. We've got good guys, bad guys, and rumors of late-night meetings; and the dying wish of a cafeteria worker from a town named after a pink-eyed marsupial. If you can't find someone to root for, you can't find a bonnet in the clubhouse.*

Tuki didn't listen, so Deacon entertained her with what he'd learned during last night's "Jeopardy!" broadcast.

She still ignored the babble. "What are you hearin', Deacon? Who's got the horse?"

"Albacoa. Seven or eight have a chance. He's the consensus."

"Ooty's the one," she said quietly. "Albacoa's second."

Deacon nodded. "How long you stayin'?"

"'Til ten. This is me sanctuary. Rest of the place is a bloody insane asylum."

"Be on time for the press conference and photo shoot, okay?"

"No worries," she said, still brushing Ooty.

Deacon paused at the doorway. "Do me one favor today, okay?"

"What?"

"Don't call Churchill Downs an insane asylum."

She sighed. "Must I fool them one more day?"

"Please do," he said. "Come sundown, it'll all be over. They'll all be gone."

"Come sundown, so will I," she mused softly.

"You've got three races on the undercard," he reminded. "Report straight to the jocks' room from the photo shoot."

"I know, I know, I know," she said and shooed him away. "Off you go. Leave me be. Amuse yourself. Go find a look-good, smell-good girl."

He rolled up his newspaper and fired it at her. "Great minds think alike, Pastry Girl. See you later."

Rigby arrived shortly after Deacon left, two reporters one step behind.

Not those people! Tuki cared for the press even less than she did Othello Guidry. She ducked behind Ooty's stall wall and sat cross-legged on the straw, safely hidden.

"Word on the street is you were involved," one of the reporters said to Rigby. "Care to comment?"

Armed with paper and pen, the two men pinned Rigby against the barn wall, barely six feet from Tuki. She stayed crouched down, hiding and listening.

"I don't know what you're talking about," Rigby replied evenly. "But why should I. You're the press. When you got nothin' to write, you make stuff up."

The second reporter took a turn. "There's a very strong rumor circulating that the sheikh tried to buy five top contenders last night during some midnight maneuvering."

"Then go ask the sheikh," Rigby barked. "Or are you bothering me because you can't get to him and I'm easy to find?"

"Is it true you were involved?" the reporter persisted. "We have confirmed reports you were there."

"Who?"

"Doesn't matter," said the first reporter. "The meeting took place, you were involved, and the sheikh made an offer to buy all the contenders. Is that correct?"

"Hell, no." Rigby snorted. "I don't know what you're talking about—which makes three of us! Why on earth would I be involved in a deal like that? Makes zero sense. Listen to yourselves! On the eve of the Kentucky Derby—a race I've never won—I am trying to sell the horse I've trained all the way from a rummage sale to the starting gate? *Bullfeathers!*"

"Word is you were in line for a 10 percent commission. Your job was to bring the principals together, the sheikh buys the contenders, and tosses you 10 percent for helping."

Tuki's eyes widened and she strained to hear more. She quietly rose to her knees and moved slightly closer, cupping her ear to hear every word.

"I get 10 percent for winning *today*," Rigby replied testily. "That's plenty good enough for me. And I plan on collecting. *Every damn dime.*"

Tuki smiled. *Good. He knows Ooty will win, too.*

"C'mon, Mr. Malone," the reporter persisted. "Isn't 10 percent of $40 million more than 10 percent of the winner's share of the purse? Isn't $4 million a little bigger payday than $120,000?"

Rigby's voice rose. "Bullshit!" he yelled. "Bullshit on this story, bullshit on you, and bullshit on you both for trying to take me away from my work. Now, if you'll excuse me, I've got a Derby to win. Interview over. Beat it," he ordered icily. "And don't come back. Go find someone else to leech your lives off of!"

Tuki peeked over the stall door and waited until the men were safely gone. Rigby's back was to her. She stood. He was visibly upset. "Mornin', Mr. Malone," she called softly. "What's new?"

Startled, he wheeled around. "You heard none of that," he barked. "All bullshit. Total fabricated bullshit, you hear me?"

She nodded. "Total, is it? As you say." Rigby's face was flushed bright red, like a stop sign. She'd never seen him like this.

He pointed at her and his voice trembled as he spoke. "You've got one job to do today, you hear me? Know what that is?"

"Win."

"You're damn right, you *win*. And after you do, I'm gonna shove that trophy right up their ass."

"It's not the trophy's fault," Tuki said quietly.

Rigby stormed off.

Tuki kissed Ooty on the muzzle. "Tomorrow will be better, me love," she whispered. "Tomorrow our lives go back to normal."

The reporters tried unsuccessfully to phone the reclusive fourth bowmaker, Saul Lewis, to get his take on the rumor that his "friends" had cost him millions of dollars. Despite several attempts, they couldn't reach him. Saul had unplugged his telephone.

Surrounded at their hotel while trying to eat breakfast, Melvin and Shelley Trombley denied knowing anything either. "We don't know nothin' about nothin'," he announced. "Do we, honey?"

She shook her head. "Nothing," she echoed. "About anything."

Race morning unfolded the way every Derby Day always has. Since just after the Civil War, the first Saturday of May had been a celebrated Kentucky spectacle. An American tradition for over 130 years, the race was the only sporting event in the nation that drew fans wearing their finest fashions.

The record crowd in excess of 150,000 flooded toward the track. On this Derby Saturday, Louisville's unemployment rate hovered at *zero*. Money turned over everywhere: T-shirt hawks, ticket scalpers, parking lot attendants, and short-order cooks, all hustling to earn two weeks' pay in less than twelve hours.

Moose and Cottle rumbled up to Churchill's clubhouse valet shortly before noon on a rented Harley Davidson Ultra Classic Electra Glide. Cottle sat in the sidecar, wearing aviator goggles. A cluster of TV cameramen and reporters circled them; two helped to extricate the folded-up billionaire from the confines of his passenger seat. A quartet of security guards hustled up and escorted the two old men through the bowels of the grandstand to the clubhouse elevator. When the doors closed, Cottle looked at Moose and deadpanned, "Maybe we *shoulda* taken the taw." Moose laughed.

Cottle and Moose exited their elevator and slowly made their way toward their fourth-floor suite on the famed Millionaire's Row. Down below, Churchill track officials were hidden away, meeting with security. The weather forecast was bleak, a big thunderstorm predicted to roll in about race time. On rainy Derbies past, slop parties had broken out, immaculately dressed VIPs victim to volleys of mud-pies hurled by drunks in general admission.

Despite the ominous forecast, the fans kept coming. The infield, at forty bucks a head, was expected to strain capacity. The more crowded it became, the worse the behavior. Tens of thousands were drinking beer for breakfast. With no way to protect a small city of people in a monsoon, the infield would be a quagmire.

Around back in the stables, Rigby ordered the rent-a-cops to stay busy checking credentials. He wanted them to shoo away all press and curiosity seekers. Most trainers loved the pre-race attention, since the buzz and publicity were always great for business. Few horsemen were lucky enough to stand in the shadows of the famed twin spires, centerpiece participants in the world's most famous race. Only the superstar trainers could expect to return.

Derby Day should be the thrill of a lifetime but not today. Rigby Malone's horses had won tens of millions of dollars over the past four decades, but today he was under siege by the prying press. He stood in silence outside Ooty's stall, arms folded, a scowl on his face, oblivious to all the surrounding commotion. In a few hours he was saddling up a Derby favorite, his first real shot to win after fifty years of dreams.

Tuki and Deacon refused to comment on last night's rumors; but when they arrived at the jockeys' press conference, Deacon had to push their way through the room overflowing with reporters,

"My God," Tuki protested. "Lookit all the bloody people. Let's get out of here."

"Three hundred easy," whispered Deacon. "All waitin' for you."

"Lock the toilets," she whispered through a tight jaw. "Let's see who's truly committed."

She walked onto the stage to join the other jockeys, every step illuminated by strobing camera flashes—a cult of the curious clamoring for attention. The back row was full; she had to sit in the front. She looked out at the sea of anxious faces. Jackals and hyenas. *Pitiful. A willy-nilly spectacle.*

Tuki had learned that dealing with the media was part of the business of horse racing. But, today, facing a record number of journalists from thirty-five countries, she wanted to duck under the table. Better a barn and the eye of a horse than an overflowing pressroom and the lenses of cameras.

All twenty jockeys were present, so maybe the reporters would focus instead on Hall of Fame veteran Riley Biffle, who was riding the sheikh's pre-race favorite, Albacoa. Perhaps Yoda Mann, who'd won this race before and was on the second favorite, Spudcat. Or even the legendary sourpuss, Othello Guidry, on Eracism.

Unfortunately the press only wanted her. Yes, she was bald and liked it. Had stayed that way in support of the cancer kids. Yes, Ooty liked his mirrored sunglasses. Yes, his braided tail was her idea. And yes, she really did believe that how the horse felt about himself had a lot to do with how well he ran. No, her mum's fatal accident in a twenty-horse field on a black horse with three white stockings hadn't entered her mind. Thanks for the reminder.

"Please," she finally implored after the barrage of questions, "ask the others something, will you? They're all here because they've earned the right to be here. I'm only here because me horse has."

A reporter standing in the back called out, "Care to comment on the story going around that the sheikh tried to buy your horse?"

Tuki didn't like the question and glanced at Deacon. He zippered his lip.

"Don't know a bloody thing," she replied. "Next."

A lightning buzz blitzed the room. The sheikh was arriving. His motorcade was rolling up out front. The reporters and photographers flushed like a live hand-grenade had rolled toward the stage.

When the press left, the jockeys marched toward the museum to pose for the race's traditional group photograph. Tuki fell in near the back of the line. Where the path narrowed, she stepped in front of Othello Guidry. Guidry spun her around and jabbed her in the shoulder.

"All about *you*, isn't it?" he snapped. "Let me tell you something, you little fruitcake. *You* don't belong here. This ain't no Down Under trail ride. Don't screw up, you hear?"

Without giving Tuki a chance to respond, he quickly stepped ahead of three other riders so he wouldn't be next to her in the photo.

Across town, animal activist Ginger Bredman, ex-actress still vying for the camera, wasted no precious time in scrambling to get ready. Her pre-race demand at the Post Position Draw to stop the race and halt the cruelty to racehorses had been ignored. She would not be ignored today. Once she pulled this off, she would be a headline story in every Sunday newspaper around the world.

The more paparazzi photos she was in, the more publicity she'd receive. Getting in the frame was all that mattered. Stars, semi-stars, and former stars— all drawn to the lenses of cameras. The magic hour was ten a.m. Celebs dawdled upon arrival—needing to be noticed, photographed, worshipped.

With one last look, she studied herself in the mirror: wide hiding hat, oversized sunglasses, full-length muskrat coat passing for mink, black stiletto heels, matching clutch purse. Perfect.

Traffic was bumper-to-bumper to the track. Blocks away, locals were parking cars on their lawns for $20. She scouted an exclusive private lot across from the entrance and forked over $50. Guaranteed global TV coverage five feet away, her car tucked between a Winnebago full of oddballs and a news van with a satellite transmitter.

She freshened her lipstick in the mirror, carefully adjusted her wide floppy hat, and puckered her lips to a kiss. Time to seduce the cameras.

"Nobody remembers who finished second in the Derby."
Hall of Fame jockey Steve Cauthen (winner 1978)

Track chairman Burton Anderson, arms folded, stood staring out his office window, alternating his gaze toward the gray clouds above and the swelling crowd below. He thought he'd seen it all in his long run as uncrowned emperor of these hallowed grounds. But today, with two hours to post time, he was hosting the largest audience of his life.

He pondered the reporter's question. "What do I hope for today? A safe trip and fair race for all, and a record day at the window."

"Who do you like?" asked the reporter.

"Kentucky's native son," Anderson replied indignantly. "Othello Guidry. Eracism will pull the upset. Just you wait and see. Othello Guidry, born in Frankfort, Kentucky—our great state's capitol—home to compete in the granddaddy of all horse races."

Anderson continued. "A couple years ago, he told me that when Derby horses are loading, there is no other sound in the world like the clanking closure of the Churchill starting gates. He said you can't describe it to anyone who hasn't heard it. They wouldn't understand it." He paused. "I, of course, am a Kentuckian. I understand *exactly* what he means."

By law, the track would keep one dollar out of every five wagered; the fans would divide the rest. Today, Anderson's track would win big—really big.

Owners and trainers, and great riders like native son Othello Guidry, faced a far more uncertain destiny.

"The legend of the Kentucky Derby says she's a teasing mistress," Anderson concluded to the reporter. "She flirts with all, but chooses only one. Today that *one* is Othello Guidry."

Two hours later, in the first race on the card, Othello Guidry crossed the finish line a winner. Watching from his office window, Chairman Anderson smiled broadly and shook his fist with pride. *Today's your day, Othello. Run the table for the Commonwealth of Kentucky.*

One by one, the day's races were held and the afternoon inexorably crept toward a dramatic climax. Anderson spent much of the afternoon staring out the window. Gray clouds lowered, darkened, and sagged . . . but the rain held off, failing to release its imminent monsoon.

Tuki Banjo rode twice on the undercard, in the third race and the fifth, but did not win. The rail was fast, six feet out was dead. Otherwise the track seemed fair, as several closers rallied for a win. After the fifth, she retreated to the jocks' dressing room. There she'd stay until the feature race, when it was time to return to the paddock in Miss Louise's school bus silks.

When the time finally arrived for the Derby horses to report to the paddock, the Trombleys joined Rigby Malone and Deacon Truth on Ooty's long walk to the front saddling area. Tens of thousands of spectators jammed the clubhouse rails on their left, and pressed against the infield's tall, confining, temporary chain-link fence to their right. Too many to heed called out "Good luck," snapping photographs with every step.

Deacon smiled to the fans and waved. The rest of the team walked quietly, the late afternoon sun peeking through a hole in the heavy gray clouds, casting a faint elongated shadow of the twin spires across the freshly harrowed dirt in front of the finish line.

Rigby pointed it out to the Trombleys. "Superstitious?" he asked.

"No," answered Melvin, shaking his head. "How 'bout you?"

"Just one," replied Rigby. "My lone superstition is that it's always lucky to have the fastest horse." As he spoke, the shadow disappeared, swallowed behind the heavy sagging clouds.

"Smell the rain, Rig?" Melvin said. "It's comin'. Gonna dump *big*."

"Can't wait," the old trainer grunted. "It'll flush away the imposters."

Rigby was oblivious as his team neared the tunnel that led to the paddock, where thousands of fans were packed shoulder to shoulder, anxiously waiting to watch the horses saddle up. The betting windows were jammed forty deep, the sheikh's Albacoa favored over Spudcat and Pernambuco but not by much. With no clear-cut choice, the lure of extraordinary payoffs hung in the air.

Rigby glanced up one last time at the gray sky, the clouds blackening, so low he could almost touch them. A downpour was imminent.

Fifty yards away, hidden in the quiet privacy of her dressing quarters, Tuki was ready; tapping her open palm gently with her whip, staring out the window, waiting for her horse. When she spied him, she smiled. Melvin was carrying the saddle. Cradled in his massive arms, the saddle and stirrups looked as small as a band-aid. One step outside and she'd be through the looking glass, marching through that sea of insanity that was the gambling public, every fan yelling advice. A pro jockey didn't need advice. She needed a horse with courage . . . and she had one.

As she emerged from her dressing room near the laundry, she bumped into Othello Guidry. He was following three other jockeys leaving the men's locker room. He shoved past her, breaking her stride. Off-balance, she brushed against the nearby wall.

He's such a bloody child, she thought, suppressing the urge to confront him. A phalanx of uniformed police was waiting and escorted the jockeys to the nearby paddock. Tuki walked to stall twenty. She ignored the urgent screams of the thousands of fans who craned their necks to see her and tried to get her attention. Deacon and the Trombleys greeted her warmly. Rigby was busy saddling Ooty. His back to the crowd, the fans had let him know that the star had arrived.

"What's wrong?" Deacon asked. "You look ticked."

Tuki waved him off. "Not worth knottin' your knickers over."

She looked skyward. Heavy rains would change everyone's strategy, because mud would add a monumentally unpredictable dimension to the race, especially with such a large field. She walked over to Ooty and kissed him. To her trainer she asked, "Same strategy in the slop, Mr. Malone?"

"Same one," he grunted, double-checking the stirrups. "Finish first."

"What's the big deal about the rain?" wondered Shelley. "It's the same for everybody, isn't it?"

Deacon shook his head. "Some horses love the mud, others don't. The ones who don't, they won't try very hard. They'd rather be in the barn." He nodded down the lane toward the other owners and trainers. "Some of these guys don't know what their horse will do if the rain really opens up."

"Are we worried?" Melvin asked anxiously.

"Not unless it rises over our bloody head," answered Tuki confidently. "Pernambuco will be fine, too. He grew up in the rain in Seattle."

"What about Albacoa?" asked Shelley.

Tuki shrugged. "No way to know. Doubt he's ever run in it."

"He'll hate it," predicted Deacon. "Royalty hates mud coats."

Tuki stepped out and looked down to where Albacoa was being saddled. The normally unflappable Sheikh MAAM was nervously checking the sky; though his jockey Riley Biffle, seemed less concerned.

Tuki stood next to Deacon and nodded toward Biffle.

"Don't look too worried, does he?" said Deacon. "Arms folded, standin' like a statue, impassively starin' out at the sea of faces staring back."

Rigby walked up and joined the conversation. "He learned long ago that he can't control the weather. He expects to win. He and Albacoa will dodge lightning bolts if God decides to hurl them. Riley ain't got no intention of finishin' second. He's the one we need to beat."

Rigby handed Tuki a small cloth and yellow squeeze bottle. "Here," he grunted. "Put a coating of this stuff on his visor."

Tuki looked at the bottle quizzically. "What is it?"

"Rain-X. Clear silicone oil. Water beads up, rolls off. Easier to see the butts he's passing."

Tuki smiled. "I'm impressed, Mr. Malone. Think of everything, don't you?"

"Yep." He pressed into her palm a small fern leaf, symbolic of New Zealand. "Tuck this in your helmet lining. You're riding for them today, too."

The cry of "Riders *up!*" signaled that it was time to go. The crowd roared as the jockeys mounted their horses. Tuki kissed Ooty's forehead, then stood sideways and waited for Rigby's boost up into the saddle.

He turned his back to the others and said quietly, "Before you go, there's something I need to tell you."

"I know, Mr. Malone. *Win.*"

"No," he said quietly. "Something else."

She looked at him expectantly.

"Ours is a . . . " he started, struggling.

"Spit it out, Mr. Malone. The others are leaving."

"What I'm tryin' to say is that you've taught me a lot. About people and other stuff. A guy like me, my age, I'm set in my ways. Don't learn a lot. Nothin' that matters."

"And?" she asked.

"I wanted to thank you for that. That's all. Thanks."

She smiled. "Seashells and balloons to you, too, Mr. Malone. Now hoist me up, will you? We've got a race to win."

He leaned down, grabbed her shin, and pulled Tuki up onto Ooty. Once on the horse, she smiled and waved an excited little wave to Deacon and the Trombleys as she led Ooty to their place at the rear of the procession. The clouds were nearly black now and sagging. But she didn't care. She stroked Ooty's neck lovingly as they walked along. "Seashells are happy on the beach or under water, me love. Let it pour. Let the tide roll in. It shan't slow us down. Not today. Not a step."

Deacon stepped over to Rigby. "What did you say to her, Rig?"

"Told her she needed a new agent," Rigby replied wryly. He slapped Deacon on the back and waved for the Trombleys to hurry along. "C'mon, let's get under cover."

As the line of horses and riders began threading single file through the tunnel beneath the grandstand, Rigby impulsively broke away from his friends and hustled up alongside Ooty. "These ain't Clydesdales," he reminded Tuki he jogged to keep up. "They got big engines. Keep 'em in reach or you'll never catch up."

She nodded. "No worries, Mr. Malone. Straighten your tie. See you in the winner's circle."

Tuki then disappeared into the tunnel behind the inexperienced longshot owned by the cosmetics queen. "Let's get under cover," urged Melvin, who'd followed Rigby. "Heaven's dam is fixin' to blow."

A gauntlet of screaming fans lined both sides of the paddock tunnel, pushing and shoving against the hip-high railings. Slowly the horses and riders walked their way, single file, two hundred yards from the back paddock, underneath the grandstand, and out toward the main track.

The call to post was trumpeted, signaling the lead horse's impending arrival. As the ponies and riders emerged from the tunnel, the fans roared *en masse*. And as each colt stepped out onto the track, the roar grew even louder. Each jockey slowly steered their horse in a wide, sweeping left turn. The line of all twenty stretched out for more than one hundred yards and they paraded the length of the grandstand. As they strolled past, the crowd sang "My Old Kentucky Home," the traditional song of the Derby. Half the crowd knew the words by heart; the others followed karaoke-style, watching massive Jumbotrons scroll the lyrics. Thousands of native Kentuckians wiped tears from their eyes.

Deacon snickered to Melvin, "Never, anywhere, will you hear such a simple song sung so badly, so loudly, and so off-key, by so many white people."

"Stuff it, Deacon," Rigby growled. "If Mo Munny had written this, you'd be dancin' to it."

Last in the procession, Tuki was barely aware of the roaring din. She and Ooty were walking toward immortality—despite the remarkable road they'd both taken to get here.

Far from the chain link fence, buried in the infield, Pernambuco's invisible fourth partner, Saul Lewis looked up at the giant TV monitor. The horses had come onto the track. Which one was his? What number was he?

He winced at the chorus of off-key drunks warbling "My Old Kentucky Home." He craned his neck and strained to glimpse the horses, but he couldn't see anything around the large woman big enough to waltz with a grizzly. She stood on the tongue of a refreshment stand trailer hitch, posing for friends with Churchill Downs' famed twin spires in the background. Beer in hand, she was baring a naked, tattooed breast for the camera.

My God! thought Saul. *For this, I flew all night?* He hadn't told the others he was coming. He had planned to sit under shelter in the grandstand or clubhouse—but not at the cost of a week's worth of bow-making. Instead he bought the cheapest ticket he could find, general admission to the infield. So here he was, amidst the *hoi polloi*, an invisible microbe in a growing, bewildering spectacle. *What am I doing here? I live on a houseboat. Bend twigs for a living. How do I wake from this nightmare at Woodstock?*

Disgusted by the half-naked walrus, Saul asked an armed National Guardsman in army fatigues how he might go about seeing his own horse, explaining that he was part-owner of Pernambuco.

The Guardsman waved toward the surrounding sea of confusion. "Jump high, pal," he snickered derisively. "Just like all these other *owners* have to."

The fat woman climbed down and waddled away, so Saul climbed up on the trailer tongue to get a better view. He asked a nearby fellow with a program what Pernambuco's number was. Eight. Then he craned his neck to search for his horse. There he was! A slight smile creased his face. He watched as Pernambuco completed the long processional, turned around, and jogged out of sight. Saul climbed down. He kicked himself for spending so much to travel so far, able to see so little. He was doomed to watch the race on the Jumbotron, checkmated by the masses.

The pre-race procession ended and the colts peeled away from their stable pony escorts to go warm up. One was visibly distressed and frothing heavily. Tuki noticed him the instant he began acting up. Almost always, "washing out" meant trouble. She watched the rider, an inexperienced Panamanian who spoke no English, struggle to calm the colt. He would start inside, from the 5-hole, prime starting gate real estate.

Glad he's there, she thought with concern. *Won't get in our way.*

The outriders signaled the jockeys it was time to approach the starting gate. They loaded two by two, due to the large size of the field, starting with 1 and 11, followed by 2 and 12.

Tuki expected number 5 to balk at loading, and he did. Despite repeated attempts by the gate crew to push him in by the haunches, he refused. When the handlers tried to force him, he reared, neighed, and dumped the jockey who rolled quickly to avoid being kicked or stepped on.

While the gate team spent several minutes working to calm the agitated horse, Tuki walked Ooty in a large circle. Finally a gatehand blindfolded number 5 and walked him inside the gate. When the rear door clanked shut, the gatehand climbed up and out, and the jockey climbed in and maneuvered his way aboard the mount. Once he was safely in the stirrups, the gatehand reached in and removed the colt's blindfold.

The other jockeys were watching the jittery horse carefully. Now there was more to worry about than just riding a smart tactical race. Not only was the horse nervous, but this was the jockey's first Derby.

To Tuki's left, Othello Guidry waited stoically in the middle. His eyes were riveted straight ahead.

As the remaining colts loaded into their chutes, the temperature continued to drop and wind swirled. The air smelled heavily of rain. Tuki loved to ride in the rain—Ooty, too.

Hot dog wrappers blew in circles, and random drops began to fall. Tuki tested her footing in the stirrups, her stomach churning. She cycled through her mental checklist. She and Rigby had reviewed it a thousand times. All nineteen pilots to her left had multiple game plans. She had *one*: drop back, bide her time, then close like a rocket.

In moments, all twenty would blast off. One would find fame, the others forgotten.

The starting gates slammed shut behind number 19. Her turn to load. Ooty walked straight in and stood at attention, his ears up, ready to go. Tuki stole a glance at the packed grandstand and infield.

Get out quick. Get out clean. Save ground. She couldn't win the mile-and-a-quarter race at the start—but she sure could lose it.

The gate attendant scrambled out of the way and yelled, "Clear!" The crowd's rumbling roar doubled in anticipation. Ooty swiveled a hard look right, a thousand fans mirrored in his visor.

High up in the grandstand, Tony Syracuse's cheerleading squad of exotic dancers yelled their ample lungs out, rooting for Marco Pollo, synchronizing a shimmy dance and enthralling five rows of high school boys from Possum Drop High.

Tuki felt goosebumps, and thought of her mother. She patted Ooty's neck, leaned forward, and dropped her whip to the loam below. "Showtime, Mr. Ooty Lenslugger McGrew.

"Grab that!" she yelled to the gate hand, nodding toward the ground. "Don't need it!"

The gates flew open and all twenty Thoroughbreds blasted out, each jockey fighting to guide his mount to a settling position for the long run down the grandstand straightaway.

Blackula and Hundo got out perfectly. Spudcat, Eracism, and Pernambuco all within a few lengths. The leaders sprinted forward, every stride accompanied by rolling roars of the spectators, echoing from the infield and grandstand.

Two inside horses bumped each other off stride, neither a favorite. Two others were forced to check up and nearly stopped, all four left at the back of the pack, their chance of winning over.

Tuki watched them all out of the corner of her eye, biding her time.

Deftly, all the jockeys steered into the first turn. The pursuers majestically stretched forward, noses to tail, like a forty-yard rubber band.

Early speed created running room. Clear of traffic, the next challenge was navigating the field. Two turns at this distance demanded tactical speed, summoning strength and courage to outlast all others.

For an extra five strides she kept Ooty away from the inside trouble, then guided him safely to the rail to save ground, feeling a powerhouse beneath her. The leaders leaned around the first turn, blistering along neck and neck, Ooty twenty lengths behind. Never had he moved so easily. *It's our day, Ooty. Our* day. Fly like a godwit!

Blackula wanted the lead and took it. He zoomed to the front but Tuki knew he had no chance after an opening quarter-mile in a hopelessly fast twenty-two seconds. *He'll flame out*, she thought. *Doomed to fade.* Six lengths behind Blackula, ten horses bunched, including Albacoa. Four lengths farther back, seven more. The leaders stretched, straining under Blackula's too-fast pace. Ooty was still way back, alone along the rail. Tuki ignored the impatient railbirds who were hollering at her to hurry up. She was perfectly on pace and Ooty was comfortably gliding along.

The leaders reached the half-mile mark too quickly, forty-five seconds flat, Ooty now thirty lengths behind. Tuki stole a peek at the giant scoreboard teletimer posting the fractions.

"Right on time, big boy," she whispered. She had specific targets in mind and was hitting them all. Her inner clock was perfect. Secretariat had won this race in just under two minutes in 1973. The early pace of *this* Derby was far faster, and the early speed would never stand up. She held Ooty tight along the rail to save ground and energy, focusing only on the dirt before her.

Tens of thousands of fans in the overflowing infield, standing-room-only grandstand and packed clubhouse, screamed at Ooty and Tuki, who were gliding along with no seeming sense of urgency. Hundreds gave up and dropped their tickets to the ground or tossed them in the air in disgust.

Ooty's first half-mile had been perfect, each of the four furlongs quicker than the one before. Tuki's goal was two minutes flat, a faster time than the Triple Crown legends, Seattle Slew and Affirmed. For now, she would hold Ooty back two more furlongs, then they'd put down the hammer and reel in the pretenders.

The leaders entered the backstretch, maneuvering to avoid getting boxed in or to burn too much energy. The Thoroughbreds strained forward, urged by riders desperate to win.

The backstretch loomed ahead. More than half the race behind them, Tuki prepared to turn Ooty loose.

Suddenly there was a tremendous disruption in the cluster of horses ahead. At least three lead horses went down and jockeys went flying. Tired and pressured, the nervous number 5 had misstepped and fallen. The others behind him tipped, among them, Albacoa, who toppled into Eracism.

From the sixth floor suite high up in the clubhouse, Sheikh MAAM watched the train wreck through binoculars. His horse, Albacoa, went down. He closed his eyes and recited a prayer for the safety of all. When he reopened his eyes, Albacoa was up. But he was riderless and limping.

The sheikh retrained his binoculars. What he saw sickened him: the motionless body of a jockey lay twisted in the dirt, with blood spreading. The rider was not his. Still, a tragedy. The sheikh's jockey, Riley Biffle, wobbled uncertainly to his feet, then fell to his knees.

Othello Guidry, thrown off Eracism into harm's way, had bounced to a half-sitting position and was twice trampled by the stampeding field. He was left behind, as racing's injured always were, his lifeless form crumpled in the dirt,

Tuki watched the horror in slow motion as she and Ooty drew closer.

Guidry's broken legs were pointed in grotesque directions. She pulled up hard on the reins, hopped down, and ran to his side. He was face down, his skin blue. Hoof prints tattooed his torn racing silks.

She rolled him over. His nose was broken, his mouth full of bloody loam, blood streamed from both nostrils. He wasn't breathing.

She pried open his jaws and fished two fingers to clear his throat. His jaw reflexively chomped, cutting the skin and biting the bone of both fingers. She ignored the searing pain and with one hand pried open his jaw and with the other cleared his tongue. She bent over and gave him CPR. Every child at the orphanage had learned it. She had practiced a thousand times.

Othello Guidry gasped and sputtered. The paramedics rushed up and took control. The roar of the crowd told Tuki the horse race was over.

Having navigated the chaos in front of them, the four leaders flew around the final turn and lined up shoulder-to-shoulder toward the eighth pole—the final furlong.

Saul Lewis stared at the giant overhead monitor, watching every stride.

Marco Pollo took the lead. His jockey struggled to keep him tracking straight, but the tired horse started to drift sideways.

Pernambuco kept pace and then suddenly inched ahead. One hundred yards from the finish. Spudcat moved up alongside. Jockey Wally Ball deftly switched whip hands and tapped Pernambuco on the left rump, urging his horse to the finish.

Fifty yards. Four still in. Neck to neck.

On Pernambuco's inside, Marco Pollo and Hundo moved even. The crowd rushed to their feet, their cheers reverberating.

Five strides from the wire: Spudcat, Hundo, and Pernambuco head-bobbing side by side, Marco Pollo closing, all straining toward the finish.

Suddenly a woman ran onto the track by the finish line. She flashed open a fur coat, naked, except for her flesh-colored panties. As she posed, the four gallant Thoroughbreds lunged across the finish and the crowd exploded. Who had won? After a mile-and-a-quarter, no one knew.

"It's too close to call!" sang the track announcer into the broadcast microphone. No one heard him; his stoic baritone was drowned out by the roars of 150,000 as the bright "PHOTO" sign illuminated on the giant infield tote board.

In the clubhouse upstairs, the three racing stewards quickly huddled. No one was permitted to enter the locked room. When the leaders raced within twenty yards of the finish, as usual, the finish line photographer pressed the button that activated two remote control cameras. The main camera recorded the two-thirds of the track closest to the infield. The second camera shot the area closest to the grandstand. As each horse passed the imaginary finish line, he would break the reflected light beam, his time recorded to one-thousandth of a second.

Unfortunately for the stewards, when Ginger Bredman ran out and posed, she had tripped the electronic light beam emitted from a pole by the grandstand railing. The beam transmitted across the track, reflected off a mirror, and bounced back, creating the invisible finish line. As the stewards studied, frame by frame, the lunging horses' images, dead center in that invisible line was Ginger's provocative image. The race was a near dead-heat. Head bobs would determine their position.

"Who is that idiot?" wondered the chief steward in disbelief.

"I dunno," commented a second steward, "but I wish it had been her daughter. This one's got some miles on her."

The stewards intently studied the streaming sequence of dual-camera, finish-line photographs.

"There's no way to release an accurate photo of the finish without the naked lady," decided the chief steward. "She's smack dab in the middle of it."

As the stewards wrestled with what to do, the crowd below grew impatient. Were they cashing tickets or tearing them? Heading to the ticket window or the parking lot?

The stewards discussed the pluses and minuses of posting the photograph. Horse racing history and hundreds of millions of gambling dollars pended on the outcome, and teeming masses of fans below were growing increasingly restless. They had no choice.

"I need to call Chairman Anderson," the chief steward finally decided.

"And tell him what?" asked the second steward.

"That we gotta post a picture of a naked lady on an instant worldwide feed. We have no choice. It's the only way to show the official order of finish."

"Call him on the speakerphone," begged the second steward. "This is priceless."

On the far back side of the track, Tuki waited to make sure Othello Guidry was conscious. Assured by a paramedic that he was, she got a quick boost back onto her horse and galloped away, even though the winner had crossed the finish line four minutes ago.

Tuki urged Ooty to turn it loose; and ignored the pain of her bleeding fingers. "Let's go, Ooty! Show 'em what you've got!"

He took off down the backstretch, Tuki's blood dripping onto his blonde mane, and dappling her white racing pants with splattered spots of crimson.

The stunned crowd rushed to its feet. The race wasn't over.

Ooty gained his stride, every furlong faster than the one before.

Tuki kept him tight on the rail. They wheeled around the final turn and pointed to the long straightaway for home. Lining the ground along the rail were a hundred press cameras, clicking like cicadas, triggered by remote control.

The grandstand rolled a chant: "Oo-ty, Oo-ty! Oo-ty, Oo-ty! Oo-ty, Oo-ty!"

Down the lane he burst, his braided tail flying, his blood-spattered blonde mane whipping, his mirrored shades reflecting the thousands of fans in the infield and grandstand.

He rocketed past the quarter-pole.

High up in the stands, a small middle-aged man concentrated on every move Tuki made, tears streaming down his cheeks. For every bad decision he'd made in his life, hocking everything to travel halfway around the world was not one of them. This was his daughter, the one he'd never seen.

Tuki and Ooty streaked past the finish line to a standing ovation—the teletimer still running—and made racing history. Six minutes, forty-nine seconds. Ooty had run his blazing final quarter in a tick under twenty-two seconds—faster than the opening fractions of the race's early speedsters.

Tuki and Ooty zoomed through the finish and kept going, all the way back around to check on Othello Guidry. He was strapped securely to a rescue board, his arms and legs immobilized. He was alert and recognized Tuki when she rode up. As the four paramedics carefully lifted him up to the ambulance, his eyes met hers. He wiggled his fingers in thanks. *Busted up, but alive.*

She smiled and wiggled her own aching fingers back. "Seashells and balloons to you, Mr. Guidry," she called softly. "Many more Derbies ahead for you."

She turned Ooty back around to leave and noticed a small white butterfly hatching from the tilled track soil and flutter skyward. "Hurry," she whispered, offering encouragement. "Hide from the rain." All around the butterfly, bombing raindrops fell.

The light rain intensified, fat, cold drops, stinging like hail. Seconds later the heavens opened, rain pelting down in sheets.

Just then the results were posted and the OFFICIAL sign illuminated brightly on the massive infield tote board. Instantly the crowd exploded into a photo finish's patently singular chorus: shrieking ecstasy and baritones of despair, sprinkled with shouts of joy and groans of dismay. The sound of 150,000 winners

and losers. *Jockeys don't quit. Jockeys can't quit—never cheat the fans.*
Tuki never bothered to look.

26
I WISH WE WERE GODWITS

The fans ignored the cold, pelting rain and roared *en masse* when the official results were posted. Seconds later they cheered even louder when the official photo finish was displayed on every monitor on the grounds. Ginger Bredman, flashing in front of four straining horses, became an instant legend in racing lore.

Up in the owners' box, J. L. Cottle turned to Moose Utley and smiled. Moose looked back at him with a blank expression, then arched an eyebrow.

Cottle stuck out his hand. "You won, leg-humper. That little runt of yours got the job done. Hundo did it. Congratulations."

Moose nodded "How about that?" He broke into a slow, broad smile. "I win the suitcase."

In the quagmire of the crowded muddy infield, Saul Lewis sat drenched, sundown falling. On the tongue of the beverage trailer, sipping a Coca Cola, he bottoms-upped his paper cup. His drink was finished and crushed ice tumbled onto his nose. He grinned. Third was good. Third was *wonderful!* Two hundred grand, split four ways.

He knew precisely where his share of the money was going: Brazil, where he'd plant some *pernambuco*. Fifty grand would plant a whole forest.

The official order: Hundo by an inch, Spudcat second, Pernambuco third, Marco Pollo fourth. Three horses didn't finish. Ooty was officially seventeenth.

Debris and insults pelted down on Tuki and Ooty along with the cold, full raindrops; the cheers replaced by boos, cursing, and catcalls. Millions in wagers had been lost.

Tuki steered Ooty away from the rail to the center of the track, out of the range of projectiles. She stared straight ahead, otherwise oblivious as they continued the slow walk back to the finish line. Waiting in the driving rain by the finish line was Rigby Malone and the clerk of scales.

As Rigby took the reins, he looked up and asked, "What didja have?"

She smiled weakly. "I had a perfect horse, Mr. Malone. But you had an imperfect rider. Tell the Trombleys I'm sorry."

She slid off, kissed Ooty on the nose, and handed Rigby the reins. "Take care of him for me, will you?"

"Sure," he nodded.

"I wasn't talking to *you*," she replied to Rigby softly. "I was talking to Ooty *about* you."

Rigby chuckled. "Seashells and balloons to you, too, Miss Banjo."

Once she had weighed in and stepped off the weighmaster's scale, Tuki needed a phalanx of security to protect against angry fans demanding retribution for their losses. Four uniformed police officers formed a tight, protective diamond formation around her and escorted her quickly to the safety of her dressing room.

She stripped off her bloody, muddy silks and showered, lingering in the steamy water, ignoring the blood still dripping from her hand. She'd skip the press conference. Deacon could handle those jackals.

Afterward, she stared into the mirror while buttoning her violet satin blouse. *I wish I was a godwit. I wish Ooty was one, too. We'd soar away forever.*

Although Deacon was stalling the press, promising that Tuki was on her way, she cut through a side door of the dressing room into the laundry room. Chairman Anderson had arranged an undercover policeman to shepherd her safely off the property inside a rolling laundry hamper.

"In?" she guessed, pointing as the man stood ready.

He nodded.

She climbed in and hid beneath a layer of towels and silks. He then rolled the hamper outside to a van.

After quickly climbing inside, she saw J. L. Cottle and Moose Utley coming toward her, Mr. Utley clutching an old valise. The policeman wanted to close the rear doors, but Tuki asked him to wait.

Moose stepped forward and extended the case. "Please take this, Miss Banjo. Cottle and I want you to have it. We don't need it any more."

Cottle leaned in and nodded, and offered her a trembling hand. "You got some pretty big spuds for a girl." He kindly squeezed her hand.

Tuki studied both of the old men carefully, nodded back, and took the case. "Thanks."

Moose and Cottle stepped back, the policeman shut the van door, and drove her off the property.

They rode in silence for thirty minutes to the policeman's home, where his wife cleansed and bandaged Tuki's fingers. After dinner, she napped.

The policeman woke Tuki at three a.m. and drove her back to the dark quiet of the Churchill grounds, where she retrieved her Harley from the rear of the Odds Quad's Winnebago. She quietly secured the old men's valise with criss-crossing bungee cords, then silently pushed the bike a hundred yards before roaring it to life and throttling her way through the empty streets.

She headed out of town. Only one stop, the hospital.

"No note," she said to the night nurse who took the good-luck seashell and small yellow balloon. "He'll know."

Then Tuki Banjo thundered out of Louisville, pointing the Harley west; days later, northwest.

A hard ride. A perfect life.

In a couple of weeks, the godwits would arrive in the Arctic Circle and she would be there waiting to greet them.

Having said goodbye to Tuki, Moose and Cottle headed over to the Derby Museum for the winner's party. Three hours later, Hundo's victorious owner, Moose Utley, made one slow, final trip around the grounds to say goodbye and thank folks for their hospitality. Cottle shuffled along doing the same.

Cottle also matched the sheikh's offers and immediately purchased the other top contenders—Ooty, Pernambuco, and Marco Pollo. He assigned training responsibilities for all the horses to Luther O'Neil.

Sunday morning's newspapers thudded on Louisville's doorsteps, reporting this Derby's war of attrition: one horse fatally hurt, two injured, a rider in critical care, another trampled—still another quitting mid-race and costing fans an estimated $12 million in wagers. The quitter—Miss Tuki Banjo—had disappeared, whereabouts unknown.

Cottle and Moose checked out of their hotel. Cottle shakily put on his safety goggles. Steadied by the doorman, he slowly folded back down into the Harley sidecar, clutching Moose's trophy.

At every red light, they debated which sporting challenge they would tackle next. The only one they agreed on was Alaska's Iditarod, since that idiot Tony Syracuse would never surface for a dogsled race from Anchorage to Nome.

Deacon remained in the horse business, and the star-connecting spotlight the big races provided, booking races for a handful of riders until Othello Guidry recovered from his injuries and resumed riding. Deacon took over Othello's book and soon became the top agent in southern California. He made a great living and built a beautiful home in Arcadia, bigger than his behind-the-hedge neighbor, Rigby Malone. Deacon hired Mung Fu's landscaping company to look after his yard and shrubs, the only stipulation being that under no circumstance was a cactus allowed anywhere on the property.

Deacon had married a wonderful woman with a stylish flair for fashionable dress and a vigorous appreciation for her Neiman Marcus credit card. She bore him two motormouth sons, both like their dad. Othello went on to win a lot of big races, but nothing in Deacon's life approached Tuki's meteoric explosion onto the national scene.

Tuki's disappearance stymied the press, so over the following months and years, Deacon fielded countless calls from reporters. On the fifth anniversary of their famous Derby, he held a press conference and provided updates on the race's colorful participants.

He looked out at the dozen reporters and grinned. "I'll start with what I know matters most to you guys—the naked lady." The reporters, all male, laughed, and several applauded.

"I knew it!" he exclaimed. "You guys are *so* easy to read!

"The best thing that ever happened to Ginger Bredman was getting' thrown in the slammer. She got overexposed for *bein'* overexposed." Again the press laughed.

"Getting' busted for wearin' nothin' but a smile and a fur coat turned that old girl into a cult hero: radio show, cable TV talk show, paid appearances, signin' the finish line photo for twenty-five bucks a pop . . . That crazy lady has made a mint! She lives near us. Scared to open the door at Halloween, my wife is. Lousy babysitter, too," he teased, "but the boys sure like her."

The press howled.

Deacon was then asked about the bowmakers.

"Three of the four still make magic bows. I bought one of their special charity bows for my oldest son—four grand, the thing cost me! Didn't help a lick. When the kid played his cello, damn thing sounded like gutting a live bobcat."

Deacon looked out at the writers. "My magic bow died," he said sadly, shaking his head. "Kid used it like a sword. Lost a duel to Darth Vader and a light saber."

The press laughed again. "Did you buy him another one?" asked a reporter.

Deacon looked at the reporter like a dog watching television. "You crazy? Four grand! Bought the kid a trumpet."

"Whatever happened to the recluse? The invisible man?"

"Saul Lewis? Plowed every dime of horse money into pernambuco reforestation. Lionel George told me that Saul is still on the same boat, at the same dock, tied to the same slip, wearin' the old same clothes. Only Derby memory he kept is the framed horse photograph from Xao Yan Li. Sits on a shelf in his workshop."

Deacon paused, and then updated the reporters on the other three bowmakers. "Lionel George and D. C. Lee are still working. Invested their money, setting themselves up for a comfortable retirement. Lionel's sole extravagance is a customized license plate for his vintage, yellow Volkswagen Beetle, "Derby 3.""

"D. C. Lee got into real estate. Talked to him a month ago. Bought the bayfront building where he used to rent a room. Still shapes his bows there, and still runs outside to catch fish whenever the salmon and cutthroats migrate near the shore, within castin' range.

"The fourth bowmaker, Nathan Pillsbury, moved to Papeete, Tahiti," Deacon said. "Three years now. Bought a coffee bar and T-shirt shop near the cruise ship docks. Married a local girl. Livin' large, makin' a ton, according to Lionel."

Deacon paused and rubbed his neck, pretending to be pained. "How come he's in Tahiti with hula girls and I'm still bustin' my butt *here*, dealin' with you guys? Seems like those musical guys got things figured out a whole lot better than me!"

A young writer, obviously not a beat regular in the horsing world, asked about Luther O'Neil, the trainer who trained Cottle's and Moose's colts.

Deacon whistled long and low. "Luther? You kiddin' me? What a run he had! Hundo wins the Kentucky Derby, Spudcat wins the Preakness Stakes, and he puts a new rider on Ooty, who rallies from way behind to win the Belmont! Then in the fall, Luther sweeps the top four spots in the Breeders Cup Classic, a training superfecta unprecedented in racing.

"That man's 10 percent trainer's cut earned him enough to pay cash for a house on Star Island in Biscayne Bay. Nicer than my house! The rest he invested. Shoot, Luther's set for life.

"Still cheap though," Deacon grumbled, before flashing his dazzling, teasing smile. "Makes me pick up the check every time we eat. Remind me to buy him a wallet for Christmas, a big fat one with lots of room for dead Presidents. Something's wrong with the wallet he's got. It don't seem to work so good.

Deacon smiled broadly. "Next time you guys are down at Gulfstream Park, ask Luther about that fat livin', courtesy of the stallion shares Mr. Cottle peeled off and gave him. One for each horse! Any man who has tax problems 'cause horses are having sex is a shrewd brother, indeed." Again the press cheered.

"You guys are easy today," Deacon said. "All my one-liners are workin'. You can come back tomorrow, too, if you want."

"How about Cottle? We hear he's sick."

Deacon shared little. "He is a great man," Deacon said. "Note that I said that in present tense—he *is* a great man. That's all you guys should ever need to print about Mr. Cottle. For a rich guy who came to racing late in life, he played his cards perfectly. Bought all the principal characters in the most famous three-year-old class of all time, and with those horses came their breeding rights. Generated *millions* as soon as they were retired to stud. Tripled his investment, then headed off to Alaska to mush the pups in the Iditarod. Can you believe that? Five-hundred-years-old and the dude is wearin' fur hats, yellin' at sled dogs?"

One of the reporters switched subjects, and asked about Ooty.

"Ooty raced the longest," Deacon said. "Two more seasons. Retired when he was five. Othello rode him twice—never won a dime. Othello wanted him to break fast. Ooty liked amblin' along. Dumb experiment that was! Blame the jockey agent. Guess I didn't know the horse well enough," he deadpanned.

"Cottle bought him after the Derby, but he let Miss Louise's scholarship fund keep all of Ooty's earnings. Shoot, Ooty ended up winning twelve races. Nearly $4 million! With Cottle's purchase payment, plus all of Ooty's prize money safely invested in the charitable trust, Miss Louise's dream came true. Last I talked to Melvin, he said about forty kids from Possom Drop have used the money to go to college.

"How about that?" he added, "Small town kids chasin' Derby-sized dreams, all thanks to Ooty and Mr. Cottle. When my boys are seniors in high school, I'm movin' their asses and trumpets to Possum Drop. Let Melvin write the checks for college, not me!"

"Where's Ooty now?" asked the same reporter. "With the others?"

"He's sterile, so he ain't no good in the breedin' shed," replied Deacon. "Mr. Cottle shipped him to Melvin's farm in Possum Drop as a gift. The small town embraced its hero, and Miss Louise's and Ooty's portraits were carefully painted in great detail, fifteen-feet-high on the outside wall of Possum Drop High. They shoulda painted me, too, but I didn't have time to pose." No one laughed. Deacon blanched and quickly continued.

"Horse fans from all over still detour off the interstate to visit Possum Drop. Melvin said thousands have stopped by. They all want to feed Ooty dandelion roots. On sunny days, he's livin' large. On rainy days, he plucks them himself. He's doin' good, real good. Still ain't got no tail."

"Where's Tuki?" a magazine reporter called out. "She's stayed hidden all these years. Nobody knows where she is."

"She never rode in another race or granted another interview," said Deacon. "Allergic to microphones."

"There's a report circulating that she was kidnapped by gamblers," one fuzzy-cheeked reporter offered.

"Nonsense," scoffed Deacon. "She's off in Tukiville, livin' how she wants to live. Chasin' butterflies and godwits, pickin' up seashells, blowin' up balloons. Probably inhalin' some of the helium ones. You know—the squeaky voice thing."

The young reporter looked puzzled. "What's a godwit?"

Deacon stared at the kid for several seconds. "What's a godwit? Didn't do your homework, did you, young fellow? *She* is a godwit. Go look it up. *Learn somethin'*. Do that . . . and you'll know where to find her.

"Every year I've known her, she sends my family a Christmas card, postmarked from all over the world. Inside is a photograph: godwits in the Arctic, butterflies by the billions in Mexico. Last I knew, she's still ridin' and rebuildin' the same old motorcycle. Melvin said that that occasionally she slips back to Possum Drop to visit Ooty. Puts a seashell atop a fence post, with a balloon tied to the railing. Don't even knock on the door.

"She never forgets where she came from," Deacon told the reporters. "Every Christmas at that orphanage where she grew up, the holiday tree is surrounded by mountains of gifts with carefully personalized handwritten labels for every child. Every card is signed 'With love, Santa.' From what I'm told, the writing looks a lot like hers.

"Santa hangs out in Tukiville," Deacon concluded, a serious look on his face. "Make sure you write that down, okay? Santa hangs out in Tukiville."

28
FINDERS KEEPERS

Three Years After Deacon's Press Conference

Tuki rode the Harley the final few miles from her small northwest Washington farm to the graded road that snaked to Moose Utley's Sawtooth River hideout. The woods burst in canopies of yellows, oranges, and reds. Indian summer days were rarely more beautiful than those in Idaho.

The lengthy jaunt took a little longer than it might have, since this time the motorcycle was equipped with a sidecar and passenger. The pint-sized, freckle-faced rider was Tuki's adopted six-year-old daughter, Sadie. When Tuki slowed to turn at the drive, Sadie hollered, "MOM, *ARE WE THERE YET?*"

"YES, DARLING!" Tuki yelled back, with great relief that the magnificent log cabin was finally in view. She braked at the front porch, turned off engine, and looked at her impatient passenger. "Believe it or not, we *are* there."

Moose had heard the loud motorcycle coming before he saw it. When Tuki pulled up, he smiled approval. "'57 Sportster!" he marveled. "Fond señorita memories, earned in Mexico, with one of these. You have excellent taste in three-wheeled transport, Miss Banjo. Welcome to Idaho." He turned to the child. "And who's the gorgeous stowaway in the sidecar?"

"Mr. Utley," Tuki introduced, while helping her daughter climb out safely. "This is me daughter, Sadie. Sadie, this is the man I told you about. Say hello to Mr. Utley."

Moose bent over and held out his weather-beaten hands to gently make Sadie's acquaintance. "What a beautiful young girl you are," he said with a smile. "You look just like your mother."

"I'm adopted," Sadie announced proudly. "My mom is my second mom. I'm an orphan. Can't you tell? I don't talk funny like Mom."

Moose didn't flinch. "I *meant* your first mom," he said. "For that matter, your second mom, too. Moms are all the same in the love department, little lady. You are lucky to get such a special one." He studied the wide-eyed little girl. *Sheesh!* Banjo was gonna have her hands full with this one. A pint-sized Tuki.

He ushered them up the porch steps and inside the lodge. Tuki had changed, ten pounds heavier, shoulder-length red hair, the rough appearance of a woman who labored outdoors. She wore no jewelry or makeup, which was a shame. She was prettier with makeup. Had she married? He didn't ask. Why had she suddenly resurfaced in his life?

After a few minutes of social pleasantries, Moose suggested freshly baked chocolate chip cookies, then a walk on the grounds of his riverfront estate.

Paths lined both sides of the flowing Sawtooth River. They walked onto an arched wooden footbridge and paused at the crest. He scooped some green pellets from a fish feeder and poured them into Sadie's small, cupped hands. She turned and tossed the food into the deep water below, and squealed excitedly when a couple of trout rose up and ate the morsels bobbing on the surface.

Moose leaned back against the bridge railing and looked at Tuki. "How can I help you, Miss Banjo? What brings you all the way to Idaho to see an old man like me?" He studied her face, hoping she wasn't here for money. If so, it would be a very short visit.

Tuki had expected this question and rehearsed the answer . . . but her script zoomed away like a migrating godwit as Moose's steely eyes bored into her.

She didn't have to answer. Sadie's slow, sad voice beat her to it. "We're here because of Show and Tell."

Moose had great-grandkids Sadie's age and was well familiar with unexpected revelations. He arched an eyebrow and switched his glance down to the little girl. "Show and Tell?"

She nodded and put out her hand. "More fish food, *please.*"

She waited to explain until Moose refilled her small palm with more pellets for the trout. "Show and Tell at school," she repeated. "I took a picture of Mommy in the paper. My teacher said Mommy's famous. Mommy says she's not famous. Then Mommy said we had to visit you, because Finders Keepers isn't real."

Moose feigned surprise. "Not real? Since when is Finders Keepers not Losers Weepers? That's news to me. But what does Show and Tell have to do with Finders Keepers?"

Sadie gave her mom a long *do-I-have-to* look and Tuki nodded. Sadie frowned, then dug into her jeans pocket and pulled out a small maroon velvet pouch. Moose recognized it immediately.

Carefully the six-year-old untied the drawstring and stuck her tiny hand inside. She pulled out a gold coin in a protective plastic case and a folded note and reluctantly handed both over to Mr. Utley.

"Here," she said, "I found this. Mommy said it's yours and that Finders Keepers isn't real."

Tuki winked at her daughter. Sadie cared far more for the coin than the wink and hated to give it up. Reluctantly, she handed it over. Then she stared down at the swirl of hungry trout circling in the sparkling green water below.

Moose took the coin. "Where did you find this, Sadie?"

"In the old suitcase with the hole in it. Mommy said it's a bullet hole. She said you shot your suitcase. The nickel was under all the newspapers with Mommy's picture." Sadie smiled weakly. "You were in the pictures, too. You looked a lot younger, though."

"So *that's* why you're here?" Moose smiled and stroked his chin. "A Finders Keepers problem that grew out of Show and Tell? Hmm. This *is* rather complicated. The suitcase was a gift to your mom from me and my friend, Mr. Cottle. We wanted her to remember a great time in our lives. Your mom was a very special part of that. Tell me, Sadie, why were you looking in the suitcase?"

The little girl looked at her mother, who nodded. "Go ahead," Tuki said. "Tell Mr. Utley."

"Do I hafta?"

Tuki nodded. "Hafta."

Sadie wrinkled her face, confession not easy. "I was looking for birthday presents," she admitted. "The suitcase was under Mommy's bed. I thought maybe there were presents so I opened it. I saw Mommy in the paper but she didn't have any hair. She was in the paper a lot! I looked at all of Mommy's pictures and I found the gold nickel. So I took it to schoool."

"Show and Tell?" Moose added.

She nodded. "Uh-huh."

Moose smiled kindly. "Good for you, birthday girl! What did your Mommy say when she saw the coin and the note?"

Sadie shook her head. "I didn't tell her. I found it. It's mine."

"Ahhh," he nodded. "Now, I get it. *Finders Keepers.*"

Sadie nodded. "Finders Keepers."

Moose pondered the child's dilemma for a several seconds. "Hmm. Hunting for birthday presents? A centuries-old tradition. A gentleman never asks a woman her age, but I promise I can keep a secret if you'd care to tell me which birthday you were celebrating."

"I'm six," Sadie announced proudly. She held up five fingers on one hand and the index finger on the other. "Can I feed the fish again?"

Tuki nudged Sadie, and the child quickly added, "Please?"

Moose scooped out more fish-food pellets and poured them into Sadies's cupped hands until they overflowed. She giggled, then turned and cast the bounty into the gurgling water below. The three of them stood at the railing and watched the hungry trout rise for several of the pellets while the rest drifted downstream.

Moose broke the silence. "Well, Sadie, six is an important age. This is a tough one. We need to think it through. Can we do that over lunch? The trout have eaten and so should we."

With a gentle smile, he held out his hand. The little girl took it and held hands with the old man all the way back to the lodge.

Over sandwiches, Moose steered the conversation back to the gold coin. Years before, when he'd handed Tuki the old valise after the Derby, the battered bag had been stuffed with newspaper clippings, magazine articles, photographs, and the Derby program. The stories had chronicled the long march from Keeneland's yearling sale, through the prep races, all the way to Churchill Downs.

"Cottle and I made scrapbooks about each of our skirmishes," Moose explained, "to archive a great friendship."

"What's archive mean?" asked Sadie quizzically.

"To save it, sweetheart," Tuki said. "Mr. Cottle and Mr. Utley were best friends."

"Like you and me, Mommy?"

"Just like you and me."

"That's right," Moose nodded. "Best friends. We were going to make a scrapbook, so we could go back and look at the pictures whenever we wanted. Instead we decided to give everything to your mom."

"I'm not a saver, Mr. Utley," Tuki explained. "Memories matter. Things don't. When you and Mr. Cottle gave me this case, I kept it not because of what was in it but for your kindness."

Moose nodded. "Eight years. Like yesterday, isn't it?"

Wistfully Tuki forced a smile. "A million years some days, an hour ago on others. Ooty and me were alone at the finish line that day, Mr. Utley. All bloody alone. Imagine that, can you? Sittin' there, on a horse I loved; surrounded by 150,000 screaming strangers. Some loved us, most hated us—every bloomin' one of 'em yellin' at us. Even today, eight years later, me knuckle scars are a daily reminder." She paused and looked at her hands and rubbed the scars. "Who but me ever left a race in a laundry truck?"

She looked away for several seconds and then looked back at Moose. "Your kindness touched me deeply, Mr. Utley, yours and Mr. Cottle's. I never thanked you properly, nor did I ever forget. I opened the case once to see what was inside, but I never looked through it. I never turned a page. I never saw the coin. It would still be hidden there if Sadie hadn't snooped under the bed."

Moose sat back and smiled. "How did you find out?"

"Because of Show and Tell. Sadie's teacher phoned and asked if I'm the famous rider who quit the Kentucky Derby."

"What'd you tell her?"

"The truth, Mr. Utley. I told her I stopped—but I bloody well did *not* quit."

"Precisely!" Moose's palm smacked the table in affirmation. "A great answer, Miss Banjo. Good for you—because that's *exactly* what happened!

He leaned forward. "Did you read the note J. L. put in with the coin? '*You gotta have taw.*' That was his motto. Truer words never written. Next to J. L.'s ability to make billions out of dirt, his second greatest gift, rest his soul, was his ability to speak volumes with very few words."

Sadie tugged at her mother's pant leg. "What's taw, Mommy?"

"Money, honey. I guess Mr. Utley and Mr. Cottle wanted the coin to be me good-luck piece. Me sendoff dowry."

Moose looked Tuki in the eye. "I assume, then, that's why you're here, Miss Banjo? Because of the coin?"

Tuki nodded.

"To return it?" he guessed.

She nodded again.

"You know what it's worth?" he quizzed.

"Yes."

Moose studied the girl carefully. Tuki Banjo was eight years older and had collected a child, but inside she hadn't changed a bit. Once she got an idea in her head, it stuck like a barnacle.

Again he leaned forward. "Let me tell you about this particular gold piece, Miss Banjo. It was J. L.'s originally, not mine. Extremely rare, even the day it was minted. He had purchased it for a very large sum, using the proceeds from his first government check for his initial shipment of wartime spuds. Double Eagle, that's what this is, a 1933 Double Eagle $20 gold piece. They were minted for less than one hour."

"Twenty dollars!" cried Sadie. "I'm rich!"

"Shhh, darlin'," glared her mother, "let Mr. Utley finish."

"It was the Great Depression," Moose continued, "a struggling time in America. President Franklin D. Roosevelt took the country off the gold standard and banned the coin just as production was scheduled to begin. Only a few left the Mint.

"The government eventually recovered all but one," he added, winking at Sadie. "J. L. Cottle's."

"The one I got?" Sadie interrupted.

Moose nodded. "Precisely, my dear. The one *you* have. The President knew he couldn't muscle the guy who had fed the Allied troops, so J. L. got to keep his. And now *you* have it. The very same one!"

Sadie looked pleadingly at her mother. "Can I keep it, Mom? *Please?* It's special! You heard Mr. Moose."

"No," Tuki replied firmly. "It's not ours. You know the rules. We do not keep things that don't belong to us."

Moose held up his hand. "Almost done," he said. "Please let me finish. J. L. was a very sharp man, the sharpest I've ever known. Always one step ahead of everybody, even the President. He never talked about it, but I think he knew he could pull it off, even before he bought it."

"Is it still the only one?" asked Tuki.

Moose nodded. "By all studied numismatic opinions, this gold piece that Sadie took to Show and Tell is the only one of its kind, and it's generally considered the world's most valuable coin. That's why he and I always battled for it. A few years ago, it was appraised at $7.6 million. We ping-ponged that thing back and forth for decades."

"Why'd you fight over it?" asked Sadie.

"A good question, Miss Sadie. An easy answer. The things that matter most to rich people are the things there are only one of."

"It's worth more than that now," Tuki said quietly to Moose. "That's what a Seattle coin dealer told me."

"We knew what we had, Miss Banjo," he said. "And we knew what we gave away. That day at the Derby, J. L. realized he was near the end of the line and he admired—hell, we *both* admired—the courage it took for you to do what you did. In our view, you earned it. What you did took a lot of guts."

Sadie looked up. "What did you do, Mommy?" She'd never heard *this* story.

"Shhh, honey. Let's not interrupt Mr. Utley."

"J. L. was also right," Moose added, "when he wrote what he did about the taw. As you go through life, you *do* gotta have taw. He and I had plenty, more than we needed. That day we both ended up leaving with even more, which, of course, meant nothing to us.

"You, on the other hand," Moose added, "didn't have much—yet *you*, Miss Banjo, never hesitated when faced with a courageous decision. Everything you worked so hard to achieve, the chance of a lifetime, gone forever. Neither he nor I thought it was right, that you leave with nothing. That's why we gave you the suitcase. For us, it was a ten-second discussion."

Tuki sat up stiffly, uncertain what to say.

Moose enjoyed her discomfort. "J. L.'s also the one who figured out how they'd sneak you out. That's how we found you. It was all him." He winked at Sadie. "My friend liked your mom a lot, Sadie. He always said that she has a lot of spuds for a girl."

Sadie looked at Tuki and wrinkled her nose. "What are spuds, Mommy?"

"Potatoes, honey. Spuds are potatoes."

"You have a lot of potatoes, Mommy?" Sadie asked, puzzled.

"Truckloads, darlin'. You got a box of 'em yourself." She grinned at her daughter and tousled her hair.

Sadie frowned as she swatted Tuki's hand away. She had spuds?

Tuki nodded gratefully to Moose. "Thank you for your kindness, Mr. Utley, but we don't want your property. We're here to return it."

Sadie crossed her arms and scowled.

Moose nearly laughed at the extreme display of the little girl's displeasure. She'd grow to be a hardheaded one, just like Banjo. Few actions this woman took in life didn't swim against the current. For several seconds he though about Tuki's determined ride all the way to Idaho, just to return something worth millions.

He interlocked his fingers behind his head and closed his eyes for several seconds, pondering her request. Finally Moose bounced back forward and stared at her. His scowl was furrowed, his voice emotionless. "Unfortunately,

Miss Banjo, returning it is not an option."

His reaction startled her. "And why not?" Tuki had not ridden for two days expecting a debate. Other words were slow to come.

Sadie, meanwhile, was grinning broadly.

"Never joust with the desire of an absent friend, Miss Banjo. It's bad for the soul. The coin was a heartfelt gift from friends. He and I took turns owning that gold piece for sixty years. All along we had intended to give it to a worthy custodian. *You* are it. If you don't want it, assign it to young Sadie's future."

"That's a great idea!" squealed Sadie, clapping her hands excitedly. "That means I can have it! Right, Mommy?"

"No dear."

"Overruled!" Moose boomed. "Of *course* you can have it!" He snapped his fingers and rose from the table. "Better yet, young lady, you've inspired me! Excuse me for a moment. I'll be right back."

He shortly returned with the silver, twin-handled, foot-tall winner's cup from the Kentucky Derby, on its lid a Thoroughbred. He presented it to Sadie. "In honor of your sixth birthday, Miss Sadie. An extra special present, just for you."

Sadie grabbed the silver cup with both hands.

"The top comes off," Moose then demonstrated, "a secret hiding place for your special coin."

"Mr. Utley," Tuki protested.

He waved her to be quiet. "Sadie, the next time you have Show and Tell at school, take in this trophy. Tell them all about the day your mom could have won the Kentucky Derby but, instead, she stopped to save a man's life."

Sadie's eyes widened. "Mommy! You never told me *that!*"

Tuki started to protest, but again Moose stopped her. "History will treat me just fine, regardless whose mantel this trophy sits on. Be proud of who you are, Miss Banjo . . . and be proud of what you've done. Honor those who honor *you*, in the spirit in which such moments arrive."

Moose then stood. "The trout are calling me, Miss Banjo, and the road is calling you. I assume Miss Sadie is not in school today, courtesy of the 'possum flu.' If so, I am now a co-conspirator and I cannot bear the guilt."

"What's possum flu, Mommy?"

Tuki laughed. "Pretending to be sick, sweetheart. Faking it to get out of school."

Moose smiled as he held open the door. "Thank you for the visit, Miss Banjo. Old codgers like me don't get many visits from beautiful girls, much less two at a time."

Outside at the Harley, Sadie rummaged through the sidecar and proudly emerged with two presents.

Moose chuckled. "A beautiful seashell and a yellow balloon! You *are* your mother's daughter! They are wonderful gifts, darling. Thank you so very much." He leaned over and hugged her goodbye. "Don't forget to take your trophy to school."

"I won't, Mr. Moose! Thank you for letting me feed the fish."

"I'll tell them you said goodbye. Ride safe, okay?"

Mother and daughter climbed onto the motorcycle, buckled their helmet chinstraps, roared it to life, and waved goodbye.

It was two days back to their sixty-acre broodmare farm in northwest Washington. Sadie marched inside and cleared a place for the trophy on her bedside nightstand. Inside the trophy's hollow center cavity she carefully placed the gold coin and Mr. Cottle's note. She also put in a pellet she had saved from Mr. Moose's fish feeder.

She climbed into bed and pulled up the covers, touching the trophy one final time before putting her head on the pillow. She closed her eyes and counted the trout in the river. In moments she was fast asleep.

Six Months Later

Tuki was happy hidden in Washington, tucked away with a dozen broodmares and their babies. Being granted permanent resident status in the United States had enabled her to adopt Sadie, despite being single. Tuki loved America and hoped to stay.

Six months after visiting Moose Utley, a naturalization letter arrived in the mail. Her interview was officially set for thirty days from the date of the letter.

Tuki was so excited that she raced down the stone path that bisected the milkweed beyond the back patio. Joyously she waved the instructions in the air. "A bloody citizen!" she screamed as she danced. "I'm goin' to be a bloody citizen!" Several monarch butterflies flushed from the bushes and fluttered past as she plopped onto the morning bench and reread the appointment letter two more times.

Sadie was practicing her violin when she saw her mom run back. She stopped playing, carefully put down her instrument and pernambuco bow, and zoomed out to investigate. "What is it, Mom? Are you famous again?"

"Better than that, darlin'. Much better than that! Mum is going to be a citizen!"

"What's that mean?" Sadie was perplexed. "I don't get it."

"You know how Mum is from New Zealand? Now Mum is going to be from America, too. Isn't that wonderful?"

"But you're already here. How can you be *from* here if you're already here?"

"It's complicated, Sadie. We need an ice cream to celebrate!"

"Hooray for America!" Sadie cheered. "I love America, too, Mommy." She hugged her mother tightly.

Tuki telephoned only one person with their exciting news, her busy former agent Deacon Truth.

He whistled at the news. "I'm happy for you, Tuki, I really am. But between work and home, I can't swing the trip. Sorry, girl. Great news, rotten timing."

"That's okay," Tuki replied, her excitement haltingly subdued. "Knew you're busy. Didn't expect you to come. Just wanted you to know. "

"Don't go puttin' no big Tuki guilt trip on me," he pleaded. "You know what time of year it is. Stakes time! Othello has some big rides lined up back east, on some monster horses. Rich new owners, too. People we need to keep close. You know how the business works, baby. You gotta have taw. This year we got lots of it on the line."

"I understand, Deacon," she answered, a twinge in her voice. "Seashells and balloons to the fam."

"Balloon beaches to you, too," he replied. "I'll tell Rigby when I talk to him. He'll get a kick out of it. He always said you'd end up pouring margaritas at a wood hut in rural Mexico. Call me again girl, as soon as you've sworn allegiance to that bed-hopping Thomas Jefferson—once you are a genuine, official, certifiable, *real* American."

"Sure," she said softly. "Goodbye." Deacon hung up. She kept the phone to her ear for several seconds after the line went dead. Then she gently re-cradled the receiver.

Seattle's federal courthouse was a tall, shiny, building on the downtown corner of Stewart Street and Seventh Avenue. The morning of her appointment, Tuki had trouble finding parking, then she arrived to an overflowing waiting room, friends and relatives of America's next wave of naturalized citizens.

"Do we have friends here, Mommy?" asked Sadie.

"Not yet, darlin'. Maybe we can make some. Mummy's late. We have to hurry. Our appointment is on the second floor."

Tuki nervously pushed the elevator button several times. Ahead loomed an interview relative concerning her moral character, disposition, and emotional attachment to the United States. She worried she'd say something stupid and blow the whole deal. She pushed the elevator button again. Sadie pushed it several times, too.

"It don't get here no faster, lady," said a scruffy-faced fat man.

"Pardon?" The unkempt man eyed her closely, making her feel uneasy.

"Pushin' the button over and over," he said. "It don't get here no faster."

"Oh, of course," she replied, glancing at her watch. "C'mon, dear." She grabbed Sadie's hand. "Let's take the stairs." She pulled her daughter along, Tuki's heels clattering loudly on the wide marble steps.

Sadie complained loudly. "Stop, Mom! My shoes hurt. Can I take them off?"

"No time, sweetheart. C'mon, can't be late. Help me find room 213."

Tuki pulled Sadie down the hallway. She searched anxiously, alternating glances between door numbers and her wristwatch. Found it. Two minutes early.

She paused at the door, took a deep breath, and reached for the doorknob. As she did, the door flew open and the doorjamb smacked her forehead. When she looked up, there stood Deacon Truth in a custom-tailored suit flashing a pearl-toothed grin.

"Where you been, girl? It's eleven o'clock! Didn't I teach you it's unprofessional to be late?"

"Deacon! What are you doin' here? And how on bloody earth did you find us?"

"I'm me," he said. "That's how I found you. I figured there had to be free food in this party somewhere."

Tuki hugged him tightly, and Sadie tugged on his pant leg. "I know you," she announced. "You were in the pictures, too. Mom said you like girls."

"You know too much, Mini-Tuki. Pipe down, will you? I'm married now."

"Are you a friend of Mom's?"

"Yes, I am. I'm Deacon. Surely you've heard of me? I'm famous. I'm Mr. Cincinnati!"

"You're not famous," challenged Sadie. "You're just a guy." She looked at Tuki. "Told you, Mom," she sang happily. "Told you we'd see a friend today."

Tuki touched her forehead for blood or a lump but felt neither. She hugged Deacon again, tighter. "I am so flippin' happy you came. Thank you so-o-o much!"

"I brought a couple of friends," Deacon said, leading the way into the interview room. "Hope you don't mind. They wanted free food, too."

Waiting in a dark blue suit, crisp white shirt, and red silk tie was Othello Guidry. In his hands, two seashells and a pair of yellow helium balloons. He handed one each to Tuki and Sadie and politely hugged Tuki. "Congratulations, Miss Banjo. This is a wonderful day for you, I'm sure. And a wonderful day for America, too."

Tuki recognized the shell Othello Guidry gave her. "This is the one I left at the hospital. Me lucky one."

He nodded. "My lucky one, too. It was a tough road back, hard and painful. At times, when I doubted I'd make it, I'd look at that little shell and think about what happened. It kept me going."

Othello quietly looked away to regain his composure. "I vowed some day to return it. Thank you for saving me, Miss Banjo." He wiped a tear from the corner of his eye.

"Thank you for coming today, Mr. Guidry." Tuki's own tears welled. "Having you here means more than you realize." She smiled and wiped the tear. "You've proved me right, you know."

"How so?"

"I knew all along you weren't a wanker."

"What's a wanker?" wondered Sadie loudly.

"Scared to guess," said Othello. "It doesn't sound good."

"Toe cheese," said Deacon. "As far as you two are concerned, it's toe cheese. Stick close, kiddies. I've known her a long time. I'll handle the translations."

Behind Othello, the Trombleys were beaming. Shelley handed Tuki a worn leather halter with Ooty's name engraved on the brass plate and a locket of hair from his mane. Tuki took them eagerly.

Melvin handed over the horse's mirrored sun visor to Sadie.

She grabbed it but stared at his blue dress shirt. "You're shirt's dirty," she announced, pointing to the white powder and jelly stain of a dropped morning pastry.

"Free continental breakfast," he admitted sheepishly.

"He still eats like a pig," Shelley said wistfully, shaking her head. "The man is incapable of safely passing through a buffet line."

As Tuki gently fingered the halter and looked fondly at the visor, she asked, "How's Ooty? He's all right, is he?"

"Oh, he's fine," replied Shelley happily. "Nothing bothers him."

"How about Rigby?"

"He couldn't come. We phoned him after Deacon called us, but he's busy with his yearling wrestlin'. Made us promise to tell you he's here in spirit."

As she listened, Tuki gently shook her head. The image of Rigby Malone cussing and wrestling with stubborn young Thoroughbreds was timeless.

Waiting impatiently behind the Trombleys was a pair of teenage girls, half-a-head taller than Tuki, both brunettes, each holding a hand-carved wooden figurine.

It took several moments. Then Tuki burst into tears. "Angelina! Angelica!"

The girls giggled with delight. Then they bounced up and down excitedly and chanted, "Picklehead on hol-i-day!"

She rushed over and buried her face between them. They were Sadie's age the last time she saw them. "My God, look at you two," she managed. "All grown up and beautiful! And so tall! I feel like a bloody midget," she sputtered, causing the others to laugh loudly.

Behind the beautiful twins stood their mother. Cushla Roberts, patiently waiting, timidly handed Tuki a small, framed photograph of a happy sixteen-year-old Tuki Banjo thumb-spraying bath water from a garden hose onto the face of the very pregnant Flossy McGrew; the old mare's head back, her mouth wide open, her teeth and pink tongue showing—her belly sagging, with Ooty.

Tuki stared at the picture and flashed back to the farm, Okataina. The twins, her picture books, her room over the barn. "God, how I loved that mare," she whispered. "Had to grow to love her son, that's for bloody sure."

Sadie tugged on her mother's dress. "Why, Mommy? Why didn't you love him, too?"

"He bit me every Tuesday and Friday," she said. "Just like I bit the family."

"Now, now," soothed Cushla. "You never hurt the family. You were *part* of a family."

Tuki looked at the floor, searching to find the right words. Head still bowed, she said quietly, "I'm sorry I was so difficult."

Cushla embraced her warmly. "Don't you be so silly," she whispered. Then she nodded toward the twins. "You were cherry cheesecake compared to those two."

Tuki laughed. "Doubt that. Arrived at your door with me black eye and blue vocabulary. Dialed it back a bit now. Too much anger, I had. Got a daughter of me own now. Relive it as a parent, don't you? God takes what we've dumped on others and dumps it back on us. Speakin' of 'im, God only knows where I'd be without you, Cushla. Nowhere I'd want to be, that's for sure."

Cushla waved off Tuki's apology. "I just hope you'll forgive Truck and me for being so hard on you." She kissed Tuki's cheek and pulled her close. She nodded toward Sadie. "It all flies by so quickly."

"Like a godwit, does it?" Tuki said with a gentle smile.

Cushla laughed. "With its tail on fire." She turned and waved the twins over.

Angelica held her carved figurine in front of her face and mimicked a ventriloquist. "We wouldn't have missed this day for anything."

Angelina did the same. "Yes," she added in a high-pitched mimic. "We always knew we'd see Picklehead on holiday. But we never realized *we'd* be the ones on holiday!"

Tuki shook her head. "Tell me you sang the Picklehead song all the way across the bloody Pacific. I'll bet the passengers were parachuting out the exit doors.

"Whatever you do," Tuki pleaded in a hushed tone, "please don't teach it to Sadie! I can't handle ten sonnets of it, much less ten hours of it."

Everyone laughed, and Sadie looked up puzzled. She tugged on Deacon's suit coat. "I didn't hear that. Teach me what?"

"The New Zealand national anthem," lied Deacon. "You're an American. You don't need to know no Kiwi folk song. What you need to learn is Mo Munny. Learn some social values, girl."

"The moment Deacon called us with the news," Cushla volunteered to Tuki, "We wanted to come cheer you on. Truck couldn't make it, but he does want you know he finally got his motorcycle."

"But he wrecked it," blurted Angelica. "Mum took it away." After sharing the news, Angelina and her mother exchanged a spirited high-five.

"Serves him right," laughed Tuki. "Tougher than mule steak, that man. At least he was to me."

Again everyone laughed.

A caseworker called Tuki forward. Seeing the large gathering of happy friends, the caseworker smiled. "It appears this will be a very brief interview." Five minutes later Tuki Banjo was approved for U. S. citizenship.

The group celebrated with a festive lunch at the Painted Table, then strolled up First Avenue through Seattle's famed Pike Place Market.

In mid-afternoon they returned to the courthouse for the swearing-in ceremony.

Sadie rode on Deacon's shoulders and proudly and loudly led the cheers as her mom became a U.S. citizen. Deacon whistled like a flock of mockingbirds, urging the others to applaud louder and louder.

Afterwards everyone went sightseeing at the top floor of the Space Needle. From the observation deck she could see all of America. Melvin bought a disposable camera from the gift shop and took photos of Tuki with her arms spread wide, her face glowing, the spectacular hulk of Mt. Rainier looming majestically in the background. They took a group photo, too, then others. One posed Tuki sitting astride Melvin, who was down on all fours like a horse. She held aloft a hand-printed cardboard sign that read "U.S. Citizen" while Othello held another that said "OFFICIAL."

As the sun began to set, the group boarded the car ferry to ride across Puget Sound, heading southwest toward Tuki's farm. The twins handed popcorn to Sadie to feed the seagulls. The birds screamed, wheeled, and dove their way behind the ferry, relentlessly demanding more.

"Yo, Melvin!" Deacon hollered over the droning throb of the powerful diesel engines. "Nice limousines on those feet! Got to commend those shoes! Far better than the swamp trompers you were wearin' the first time I met you."

Melvin grinned and snapped a picture of Shelley and Deacon.

After the ferry docked, Deacon phoned the restaurant and reconfirmed his order. When he rejoined the group, he was fuming. "Can you believe they make a brother do that? Reconfirm a takeout order? Is that a Washington thing? Othello, do they make you do that everywhere you go?"

"Never, Deacon. Then again, I'm a jockey. You never let me eat."

Deacon looked at him in mock disgust. "Be grateful, brother. I am your *manager*. Think of all the money you save."

They picked up the dinners en route to Tuki's farm. Othello had only a small piece of grilled king salmon and a side of steamed vegetables.

Melvin was shocked. "Is that all you got?"

Othello nodded. "Welcome to my world, big man. This is a special occasion. Tonight I'm livin' it up."

Mountain scratched his head. "Ten dollars must last you all week."

"Don't mind him, Othello," Shelley chided humorously. "Melvin spills more than most people eat." Studying her husband's mountainous portion, she added, "Looks like he got the rest of your salmon."

"Plus the entire school the fish was swimming in," Deacon added.

The rural Washington summer night glistened with twinkling stars as the group approached Tuki's farm. The small farmhouse was dark, except for two yellow porch lights. Also glimmering was a light in the barn. "Must've left the bloomin' thing on all day," fumed Tuki. "Bloody electric bill."

"C'mon, Miss Priss," she said to Sadie when they got out of the car. "Race you to the barn. Loser does the dishes!"

Tuki ran slow and Sadie zoomed past her, to everyone cheering. Sadie creaked open the barn door and slipped inside.

As Tuki jogged up, Sadie poked her head out. "FINDERS KEEPERS!" With a happy giggle, she ducked back inside.

When the light stayed on and Sadie didn't reappear, Tuki opened the door to find her. She was greeted by one hundred helium balloons, a white pygmy goat curled asleep on a hay bale, and a gray-faced burro. The burro was watching a familiar-looking, heavy-set old horseman who was brushing a black horse—a horse with three white feet and a stub of a tail.

Brush in hand, the heavy-set old man turned and winked at Tuki. "Where you been?" He waved toward the barn full of balloons. "Ever hear a burro bray on helium?"

Tuki sprinted past Rigby Malone, straight to Ooty. She hugged her beloved horse's neck, breathed in his mouth, and smothered him with kisses. He nickered happily.

She turned to Rigby enthusiastically and hugged him. As she did, Ooty nudged her in the back with his muzzle.

She immediately pivoted back around with an effervescent glow. "Jealous, are you, Handsome? No worries," she cooed. "I am a one-colt woman. Yesterday, today, tomorrow. Forever."

"Hey, what's the matter with me?" protested Rigby, puckering his lips. "Ain't you gonna breathe in my mouth, too?"

Tuki laughed and gave him another tight hug. As she did, everyone else stepped inside, cheering as they brought in dinner. They all dined in the barn, using hay bales for tables and chairs.

Midway, Melvin excused himself to the restroom, and Josephine the goat sprang to life, waddled over, and ate Melvin's dinner—paper plate and all. She was curled back atop her bale of hay when Melvin returned.

Melvin scratched his head, certain he'd left his plate where he'd sat. His dinner was gone. He looked heartbroken and eyed Othello suspiciously. "You eat my food?"

"Still working on mine," Othello said, showing his plate, still holding a tiny portion of fish. "I still got an hour's worth to savor."

The goat burped, the burro brayed, and everyone broke out laughing.

The Trombleys gifted Ooty to Tuki and left him on her farm. They left the following morning for the airport in a very crowded Town Car. They shared it with Rigby, Othello, and Deacon, who impressed the driver with all the questions he remembered from the previous night's rerun of "Jeopardy!"

Cushla and the twins remained at the farm for an extra week and went to Show and Tell along with Sadie's mom and Ooty. Sadie got an "A" and all the children wanted their picture taken with the famous horse and jockey, while Sadie proudly hoisted aloft the Kentucky Derby champion trophy.

Tuki's life had come full circle. She was happy, and squeaked out a living by delivering well-bred baby horses and raising them for auction. The best of her bunch, she shipped each fall to Keeneland.

Soon after Show and Tell, Sadie became enamored with her mother's heirloom silver stopwatch and spent countless hours with her mom, timing horses at the training track.

When a writer stopped by the pair and asked Tuki how her daughter had learned to guess time so well, Tuki turned to Sadie and smiled. "What's the secret, kiddo?"

With a broad smile and a front-tooth missing, Sadie said, "Seashells and balloons. That's all it takes, right, Mom?"

Tuki nodded with a twinkle to the perplexed reporter. "Seashells and balloons," she repeated. "Now off you go," she waved politely to the reporter. "Off like a godwit."

"I love you, Mom," Sadie said, hugging her tightly.

"Me, too, darling," said Tuki, hugging her back and kissing the top of her head. "More than all the seashells in all the world. And all the balloons, too."

"Pinky swear?" her daughter asked, wiggling her little finger.

"Pinky swear, my darlin'." Tuki smiled as she locked fingers with her little girl. "Seashells and balloons forever."

THANK YOUS & REALLY SPECIAL IMPORTANT STUFF

A special "seashells & balloons thank you" to the many friends who have supported this project:

Donna Brothers, Steve Cauthen & Chris McCarron. There's a reason very few athletes can sustain career excellence as world-class jockeys: The combination of courage and skill that's required to win at the sport's highest level eliminates all but the very best. These three have demonstrated excellence throughout their careers and have always taken the time to help me better understand life through the goggles at thirty-five miles per hour. "Thanks" seems humbly insufficient.

Skip Dickstein. The top equine photographer in the nation. A button-pushing genius.

Chris English. A craftsman is a skilled woodworker who's happiest when surrounded by wood shavings. Hats off to this artisan and craftsman.

The wonderful people of Hertford, North Carolina—especially Tommy Harrell & Fannie Hunter. Tommy is a perfect friend. Each of Fannie's handwritten letters has brightened my life. Theirs is an extraordinary zip code.

Bruce Headley. Wherever he goes, a thousand stories walk along. A great horseman, Bruce was a gracious host and tremendous help during the research phase of this story.

Lisa Johnson. Throughout the lonely rollercoaster ride of the creation process, every storyteller needs a cheerleader. Thanks for being Tuki's.

Ole Kanestrom. Anyone whose truck breaks down in rural Mexico, and decides to stay for a few extra weeks so he can play a violin barefoot atop a desolate sand dune, is good by me. One of the great bowmakers of Port Townsend, Washington, who welcomed me into his world.

Stacey Lane. My favorite designer, who recently learned that *Feng Shui-ing* a house can get very complicated, very quickly.

Charol Messenger. Editors are like dentists; writers need them more than want them. Mine's a a monster talent in a pint-sized package. Best of all, she's a great teacher and I'm lucky and grateful to have her.

Don Morehouse & Bruce Seymour. Thanks, men, for teaching me how the finish line cameras work. I'll never protest another photo finish . . . unless my horse is short.

Lonnie Owens. Very few small-farm horsemen ever breed a starter good enough for the Kentucky Derby or Kentucky Oaks. Lon Boy has sent colts and fillies to both. He is also one of the nation's top bingo strategists and pickleball players.

Temple Rushton. Many thanks for living the life and keeping my filly healthy, happy, and running in the right direction. May your next horse be The Big One.

The fabulous work of Russ Rymer. To learn more about the history and facts behind the pernambuco story, make it a point to read this man's beautifully written work. His words will usher you places every reader dreams of going.

J. L. (Scotty) Scott. Moose Utley ain't got nothin' on this guy.

Richard Scott. The happiest friend I've ever known. Rich lives his life in the cockpit and on the dance floor. Grinning like a boy with a frog in his hands, he's drawn to women like Superman to Lois Lane.

Paul Siefried. A gifted bowmaker and industry spokesman, whose support of high-road ensemble comedy is greatly appreciated. Better music is made where better craftsmen make it.

Mark Simendinger. A great brother, better father, and lousy skier.

Raine & Don Simplot. Instrumental to the story-shaping process, their candid opinions about what worked—and what didn't—helped shape a far better fable.

Jack Simplot. Creator of one of the greatest life stories in modern American history, meeting and listening to Jack was one of the ultra-special days of my life.

Junior & Miss Galaxy. Thanks for lending me the time to create the characters that built a fun story, wrapped around an industry I love that never makes sense two days in a row. *MWYADAETM.*

Note: For information on how to purchase handmade pernambuco bows crafted by the great bowmakers of the Pacific northwest, as well as to learn more about the preservation initiative to save the trees, visit: **www.tukibanjo.com**

SAVE THE MAGIC, SAVE THE MUSIC

The world's dwindling supply of pernambuco trees is a very real crisis facing everyone who appreciates classical music. The wood's rigidity, flexibility, density, beauty, and ability to hold a fixed curve make it a unique material with which craftsmen can work. Two-hundred-and-fifty years after it was first introduced to the music world, no comparable substitute—either organic or man-made—has been found.

Pernambuco is a slow growing, medium-sized tree that requires thirty years to mature from a seedling to a size suitable for harvest and bowmaking. Today, roughly 90 percent of previous tree stock has been eliminated due to clear-cutting for farming and urbanization.

The fledgling International Pernambuco Conservation Initiative (I.P.C.I.) was formed to work in partnership with the Brazilian government in order to promote the protection, regeneration, and sustainable use of pernambuco. Artisans from around the world have joined the I.P.C.I. to raise awareness and funding. In its initial year, the reforestation effort was able to fund, plant, and irrigate 100,000 seedlings along Brazil's large plains and low-lying coastal areas.

Far more trees are needed. For more information on how your tax-deductible contribution can help, please contact the International Pernambuco Conservation Initiative.

www.IPCI-USA.org

"MY OLD KENTUCKY HOME, GOOD NIGHT!"

by Stephen Foster

(July 4, 1826—January 13, 1864)

The sun shines bright in the old Kentucky home,
'Tis summer, the darkies are gay,
The corn top's ripe and the meadow's in the bloom
While the birds make music all the day.
The young folks roll on the little cabin floor,
All merry, all happy and bright:
By'n by Hard Times comes a knocking at the door,
Then my old Kentucky Home, good night!

(chorus)

Weep no more, my lady
Oh! weep no more today!
We will sing one song
For the old Kentucky Home,
For the old Kentucky Home, far away.

They hunt no more for the possum and the coon
On the meadow, the hill and the shore,
They sing no more by the glimmer of the moon,
On the bench by the old cabin door.
The day goes by like a shadow o'er the heart,
With sorrow where all was delight:
The time has come when the darkies have to part,
Then my old Kentucky Home, good night!

(chorus)

The head must bow and the back will have to bend,
Wherever the darkey may go:
A few more days, and the trouble all will end
In the field where the sugar canes grow.
A few more days for to tote the weary load,
No matter 'twill never be light,
A few more days till we totter on the road,
Then my old Kentucky Home, good night!

(chorus)

Note: Stephen Foster penned many other American classics, among them *Oh, Susanna!*, *Jeannie with the Light Brown Hair, Camptown Races, Beautiful Dreamer,* and *Old Folks at Home* (more commonly recognized as *Swanee River*). A century-and-a-half later, he remains one of America's most inspired songwriters. Despite the everlasting popularity of his work, Stephen Foster never experienced financial success. He died penniless in New York at the age of thirty-seven.

OTHER BOOKS
BY
TED SIMENDINGER

Tuki Banjo, Superstar*

The Rise and Fall of Piggy Church *

Jurassic Trout

Searching for Tendulkar

12 Miles to Paradise

Rich Without Money

Critters, Fish & Other Troublemakers

for more information, visit www.tukibanjo.com

*as Ocean Palmer